LOVE IN ANOTHER ROOM

CLAIRR O'CONNOR

First published in 1995 by
Marino Books
An imprint of Mercier Press
16 Hume Street Dublin 2

Trade enquiries to Mercier Press
PO Box 5, 5 French Church Street,
Cork

A Marino Original

© Clairr O'Connor 1995

ISBN 1 86023 019 9

A CIP record for this title is available from the British Library

Cover painting by Roderic O'Conor courtesy of the National Gallery Dublin
Cover design by Bluett
Set by Richard Parfrey in Caslon Regular 9.5/15
Printed in Ireland by ColourBooks, Baldoyle Industrial Estate, Dublin 13

This book is sold subject to the condition that it shall not, by way of trade or otherwise, be lent, resold, hired out or otherwise circulated without the publisher's prior consent in any form of binding or cover other than that in which it is published and without a similar condition including this condition being imposed on the subsequent purchaser.

No part of this publication may be reproduced or transmitted in any form or by any means, electronic or mechanical, including photocopying, recording or any information or retrieval system, without the prior permission of the publisher in writing.

The Publishers acknowledge the financial assistance of The Arts Council/An Chomhairle Ealaíon

LOVE IN ANOTHER ROOM

CLAIRR O'CONNOR

For Pat Osborne

CONTENTS

JUNE   11

JULY   71

AUGUST   185

SEPTEMBER   241

JUNE

Billie looks at the pictures in the Sunday colour supplement again. She sees Tony with his third wife. The children smiling at her. She puts on the light to examine the article properly. Her basement kitchen is dark even in the morning. The cluttered kitchen jumps into relief. The boiling kettle takes her attention momentarily and she puts a tablespoon of instant coffee into her outsize mug, filling it to the brim with water. She adds a spoonful of honey and leaves it in the mug to absorb the heat. She has read the article many times since the previous Sunday. Today is Saturday.

Jamie told her about the article before it was published. On the look-out to shield her from any hurt he could, yet there he is to the left of his father. She shivers and pulls on her porridge-coloured cardigan. It is June but rain lashes the barred windows of her kitchen. Last night's revellers have dumped their empty cans and take-away cartons again. She hates having to clear up their rubbish.

She unbolts the kitchen door and fills a black refuse sack with last night's debris. Wet through. She tosses the sack into an outside bin by the door.

She climbs the two floors to the bathroom. Mr Goldberg's piano hasn't started yet and the nurses on the second floor are already tucked up in bed after night duty. She thinks of them as 'the nurses'. Always two but always changing, their names never quite register with her. Her oldest tenant, Mr Goldberg, came to the house a few months after she had moved in. These rents and her part-time job at the estate agent's give her an adequate living. Nobody stays there very long. She showers. The water is too hot and then too cold. She'll have to get someone in to look at it again. She tosses her wet clothes into the linen basket, pulls on a bathrobe and descends once more to the basement.

Back at the kitchen table she examines the article once more, five pages including the photos. There's even a black-and-white picture of herself. The caption reads 'First Wife, Wilhelmina (Billie), an Irishwoman. Married in 1966'. They divorced in 1977. There are three photos of Beth. One with the twins, Toby and Josh as toddlers, the second, a mother-and-daughter portrait of Beth and Marian. The third shows Beth and Tony perched on an alpine slope on a skiing trip. The headline says: 'Elizabeth [Beth, an American], his second wife, who died tragically in a car accident in 1985'. The photo of Wendy and one-year-old Ludo takes up an entire page. Wendy looks like a schoolgirl playing mothers.

The headline says: 'His present wife, Wendy'.

Billie looks at her own black-and-white photo again. Where the hell had they dug that up from? She looks more closely at it. Youth and happiness were hers then. What was she leaning against? That giant plant stand. That new year's party that seemed centuries ago now. When they divorced, she had toyed with the idea of returning home to Ireland but Jamie didn't want to move. His friends were in London. Ireland was for long summer holidays but London was home. Baby Lottie wouldn't have known any difference either way. She had stayed. Rain in June drags one down, she thinks, as a knock on the door and a slight cough alert her to the presence of Mr Goldberg.

'Morning, Billie.' Mr Goldberg's white wavy hair makes a

ragged halo. His tall elegant frame always comforts her. The old-fashioned tweed suit has a baggy reassurance. His vigorous baritone makes everything seem important.

'Lottie rang. She's staying at her dad's until tomorrow.'

Really, she'd have to get an answering machine. It isn't fair on old Goldberg. He is eighty if he is a day. Traipsing up and down with messages for her. One pay phone on the middle landing isn't enough. She'd get her own phone connection for the living-room next week.

'Thanks Mr Goldberg,' she says automatically. 'Like some tea?' He never drinks coffee.

'No thanks.' Then he hesitates.

'Kettle's already boiling.'

'Well, maybe one cup,' he says and sits into the uncomfortable upright chair nearest the door. Mr Goldberg has been in the house almost as long as she has. Tony and she had needed help with the mortgage and Aunt Wilhelmina, whom she had been named for, brought him. 'A pianist, a quiet gentleman. He'll fit the bill.' He has been here ever since. Always the gentleman, he never invaded their privacy and after Tony's defection, he assumed the role of kindly uncle towards her. Still, she had never called him anything other than Mr Goldberg.

Her children have called him Goldie from the start. He loves them and fusses over them like a grandfather. He taught them the piano and chess and didn't lose his temper when Jamie kissed goodbye to the keyboard and filled the house with sounds of heavy metal. Jamie no longer lives at home. He has a flat and life of his own. Lottie, a purist even at fifteen, disdains pop music and still values her lessons with Goldie.

'She brought her music with her and she assures me she's practising,' Goldie says to Billie.

'Lottie knows what side her bread is buttered on,' says Billie as she hands him his cup of tea. 'Why bother with her old upright piano here when she can have a baby grand at her father's?'

'Children like variety,' Goldie says, in an attempt to neutralise her anger. 'I travelled a lot when I was young,' he adds in seeming explanation.

'I haven't had a proper holiday in years,' Billie says as she cuts into brown bread. 'By the time I've gone over and back to Ireland there's not much money left. This is the year I plan to get to the sun, if only for a week.' Hailstones batter the windows, as if to test her resolve.

'It's June.' She waves her knife at the window.

Goldie taps his toes to a tune in his head. The hailstones stop abruptly and a sudden flash of sunshine illuminates the stairwell outside the kitchen.

'This afternoon will be sunny,' Mr Goldberg says.

Tony stretches in his soft bed by his baby wife, Wendy, and their baby, Ludo. He doesn't want to start the day just yet. He wants to relish this moment of waking before the house is up and about. He touches Wendy's narrow rump and thinks of Beth. No matter how early he woke, she was always awake before him. Those green wide-open eyes would stare back at him. Disconcerting. But he never told her that. How many things had he held back from her? He wasn't the only one to feel over-protective towards Beth. Total strangers in a street would help her with parcels. Her spareness and fragility brought out the protector in everyone. Since her death, he thinks of her as smiling down on him with an omniscient serenity. Of course, by the time of her death all serenity had flown but he has suppressed this so successfully that their life together has become golden, untarnished.

The shades are down but the curtains are not closed. He can hear rain, no, hailstones. Bloody hell! Is summer ever going to come? He doesn't like running in the rain but he runs every morning, whatever the weather. He slips out from under the duvet and pulls on a tracksuit. Staying in shape is important to him. Still, he'll wait until that shower of rain has passed. He tiptoes from the bedroom and nearly falls over a pair of roller skates at the top of the stairs. Toby and Josh never seem to put anything away these days. Marian is like her mother. Beth had a place for everything. Marian refuses to pick up after her brothers. Already a feminist at thirteen! He taps his tight stomach – not an inch of spare flesh – and checks his hair in the mirror. It's a light brown and looks almost natural. His hairdresser is a marvel.

'Dad dyes his hair,' had been Marian's first hello to Wendy.

'I do too,' said Wendy.

Kids! But he loved them. Children kept you young, alert to life's possibilities. Saturday was his favourite day of the week. Even bad weather couldn't dull his spirits. As a writer, he kept office hours Monday to Friday but Saturdays and Sundays were for family.

This morning he'd have a few games of tennis with Josh and Toby. Then a family lunch at Dino's, followed by shopping with Wendy. The Hendersons were dropping in for a drink at eight. That was going to be tricky. Pam was still very upset she hadn't been cast in the TV adaptation of his book *Laughter and Tears*. They were old friends. She had been wonderful when Beth died. Kind and reassuring. You couldn't sleep with a woman and remain separate from her disappointments. But he liked a full schedule. It kept the mind tuned.

'Dad?' It's Lottie. Fifteen years old and a stunner. She has Billie's black hair and precise nose and also his generous mouth.

Genes never cease to amaze him.

'Can I run with you?'

She's dressed in shorts and a floppy top.

'Sure, kiddo – ' he affects an American drawl, 'if you can keep up with your old dad.' And he opens the door to a light drizzle.

Wendy hears the front door click and she knows Tony has gone running. She listens for his footsteps and hears two pairs instead of one. Lottie, she presumes. That's twice this week she's been up at the crack of dawn to run with him. She knows it's unreasonable to be jealous of Lottie. She's only a fifteen-year-old kid with a crush on her dad.

Marian, (his daughter with Beth) is awake but doesn't want to be. She always sleeps less when Lottie stays with them. Lottie's visits make her watchful. Marian's two years younger but somehow she feels older than her. Marian doesn't want to accept that Lottie was there before her. It's different with Jamie. He's more like an uncle than a stepbrother. Charlotte. Lottie. What a ridiculous name! Dad shortened everyone's name in the end except for hers. There was the time he had called her Mars but she wouldn't answer to it. He had accused her of dumb insolence and sent her to her room. She reassures herself yet again that dad had left Lottie's mother to marry her mother. That pleasure isn't undiluted since she inevitably remembers her mum is dead. Also, Wendy sleeps with dad in their bed now.

Jamie wakes in the new flat. Stella and he are still decorating it. He strokes her long back, delighting in its length. It was the first thing that attracted him to her. After work one night, he had dropped into the Three Ducks with Bernie for their usual pint and there she was on a high stool facing the bar, arched over the counter bantering with the barman, Ted. It was mid-December then and the bar twinkled with fairy lights and the three ducks behind the bar were flying into plastic mistletoe and a bunch of balloons. He was smitten.

She took her drinks to a corner banquette. She was with someone. A tall clean-cut type with glasses. Jamie registered his disappointment by ordering a double whiskey. Unused to spirits and not having eaten since lunch, he was tipsy by the time he drained the glass. He followed this with three singles; then he ordered coffee and sandwiches. He remembers little about that evening. Bernie talked the usual office gossip. Was 'Knockers', (Bernie's name for Stephenson's new personal assistant) 'shining the old man's balls'? Did she really live with an aunt in Surbiton? Jamie was used to Bernie's coarseness but that night it grated. His eyes kept returning to Stella. He drank Perrier for the rest of the evening. When Clean-Cut slipped into the gents, he made his move. He approached her, did a slight bow, the type Eastern dignitaries affect, and said in a very clear whisper, 'I love your back. This is my telephone number.' He bowed once more and had rejoined Bernie by the time the accountant returned.

'Smooth work!' Bernie assured him.

Amazingly, she rang him. Not that week but the next. She invited him to a Christmas party at a friend's house. They were to meet at the Three Ducks and go to the party from there. His train was delayed and he arrived breathless and bothered at the pub, convinced she'd have already left. He opened the door and was greeted by tightly packed Christmas revellers drinking with frenzied abandon. He plunged in and there she was at the bar, her backless dress revealing the delicate traces of her vertebrae. He was in love. The party was as packed as the pub but he revelled in their crushed bodies. By midnight Stella wanted to leave.

'It's a sauna in there.' She laughed as they pulled the door behind them and headed into the night.

'Can we go to your place?' she said as he helped her on with her coat, 'I live with my aunt and she doesn't care for late visitors.' Bernie's theory that nobody in the 1990s lived with an aunt was dashed.

'We can go to my mum's,' he said. 'It's quite near here, in fact. I have a room there.' He didn't want to take her back to the flat he shared with Bernie. Not on a first date anyway. Bernie's misogyny was at its worst when he was trying to be polite to women.

Billie's lights were still on when they reached her house.

'Nice place,' Stella remarked as he clicked his key into the lock.

'My parents' first home. They bought it when prices were sane, in the sixties.'

Billie was in the living-room, glass in one hand, cigarette in the other, her eyes closed. The low lamps lit her lean face and long legs. Her severe black dress accentuated her thinness. Her feet were shoeless. Goldie was playing a Beethoven sonata on the piano. He didn't stop when they came in. Music always came first in this house. Billie opened her eyes.

'Hello Jamie,' she said and she angled her head for her customary kiss. When he kissed her he knew she'd been drinking most of the evening.

'And who's your beautiful friend?'

'I'm Stella.' She shook Billie's hand.

'Good manners as well as beauty! A rare commodity these days. Most of my children's friends just nod at me. Have a drink. Mr Goldberg and I have been indulging ourselves. Celebrating the festive season, just the two of us.'

Jamie could see that Stella was charmed. And it struck him afresh how impressive his mother was. Her looks and manner held a mixture of formality and warmth that drew people to her. After Billie poured the drinks, they had remained silent in deference to Goldie's music.

'Bravo!' Jamie called out in genuine delight when he'd finished. 'This is Goldie,' he said simply, 'and it's not his fault that I didn't become a concert pianist.'

'Mikhail Goldberg!' Stella's eyes widened.

'There's only one,' Jamie confirmed.

'Delighted to make your acquaintance.'

Goldie bowed and kissed her hand. They talked to Goldie and Billie until two in the morning. Stella decided to stay the night, 'if it's all right with you and your husband.'

'Oh, my husband is happy playing in his Wendyhouse,' Billie replied with a laugh. 'He's not concerned who sleeps here any more.'

And so, in his childhood bedroom surrounded by his model airplanes and heavy metal rock posters, they had bedded down, Stella and he. They hadn't made love that first night. They slept enspooned. He nuzzled into her, delighting in his good fortune. That was December and now it is early June. A Saturday. A day when he can have Stella all to himself. He falls asleep again on a smile.

The fifteen-year-old twins, Toby and Josh, are plotting. Their bedroom is on the top floor, far enough away from the kitchen and living-room for them to be left in peace most of the time. The room spills over with games started then abandoned, tapes separated from their boxes, skateboards, schoolbooks in various states of disrepair and odd shoes destined not to meet their mates for weeks. They have revelled in this disorder since the age of nine after their mother's death. An obsessively tidy woman, she saw to it that everything was in its place. The twins have relaxed into chaos ever since. Their present dilemma is how to get a blue video for tonight. Assuming that they'll be successful, they plan to watch it when Wendy and Dad are busy entertaining the Hendersons. Marty Benson told them that *Tits and Slits* is really hot stuff.

'Do you want to go skating?'

'Maybe.' Josh looks about the room. 'There's only one set of skates here.'

'I'll look for the other pair,' Toby offers. 'Maybe Lottie's put them in a cupboard.'

Josh is annoyed. 'I told her to bring all our stuff up here.'

'Don't complain,' warns Toby. 'At least it's better than Marian tossing our stuff in the bin. I bet that's where my cricket bat is.'

'Lottie's OK,' Josh says. 'It's creepy though, the way she can spend hours at a time practising.'

'At least the baby grand gets some use when she's around. Old Goldie has her under his thumb. I'd go nuts in a house like that. Piano music morning, noon and night.'

'You accept wherever you live as normal,' Josh points out in placid maturity.

'Maybe,' Toby agrees doubtfully, 'but I'm still not over the shock of Wendy's boobs stuffed into Ludo's mouth.'

'Only one at a time,' Josh points out.

'She does it no matter who is here,' Toby protests.

'It's called "feeding on demand",' Josh informs him.

'It's called a come-on,' Toby insists. 'She gurgles just as much as Ludo when they're doing it. I nearly wet my pants last night when she bent over me with Ludo still sucking away.'

'The trouble with you is you've got sex on the brain.'

'It's hard not to,' Toby asserts, 'the way dad slobbers over her. At his age too, it's embarrassing.'

'It's his way of keeping young,' Josh soothes. 'It's a well-known fact that middle-aged men go for younger women. Maybe we'll turn out like that too,' he says hopefully.

'I prefer the way he was with mum. It wasn't all wet kisses and breasts everywhere.'

'Mum breastfed Marian. I can remember it,' Josh says.

'I can too but it was always in her room, not in front of every Tom, Dick and Harry.'

'Look on the bright side,' Josh cheers him. 'At least we get to study boobs at close quarters.'

Lottie is keeping pace with Tony. She has her mother's long legs. He preferred to run on his own. He stops, points to the new restaurant across the road. She follows him. There is no traffic.

'Like to try their breakfast special? Just the two of us?' he coaxes.

Lottie nods and they go inside.

'Just black coffee for me and a breakfast special for my daughter,' he tells the bored waiter. They sit in a plastic orange cubicle. This is the high point of Lottie's day. Her father all to herself. It's worth getting up early, she thinks, as she cuts into her bacon and eggs. Tony's stomach flips with desire as she moves the bacon to her mouth. But he's been on a 2,000-calories-a-day diet for the past five years and a man can only take so many liberties with a fifty-year-old body.

'And how's Billie doing these days?' he says as she chews.

'Just fine,' Lottie replies with her mouth full. 'The same as usual.'

'Goldie and the nurses, Abbercrombie and Wilson,' he recites in a near singsong. He doesn't know why the woman interests him after all this time, but she does.

'Oh, she gets about a bit too,' Lottie says vaguely.

'That's nice,' Tony says, hoping for a few more titbits. 'Musical events with Goldie and Babs, I suppose.'

'Not always. She had a row with Babs. She hasn't been around for the last few weeks.'

'Would you like a pancake? They're very good,' he lies, never having tasted one himself. He wants to keep her talking. The even tenor, the predictable routine of Billie's social life since he left her has always comforted him. Now he senses something askew.

'There's a lot of calories in pancakes,' Lottie says.

'Nonsense, you're as slim and beautiful as your mother. A little pancake won't hurt you.' He orders one. 'What was the row about, Schubert or Beethoven? They used to row for hours about their musical gods.' His tone is light and familiar, as if he'd only left Billie's house a day ago.

'No, not music this time,' Lottie says as she soaks up her yolk with a piece of bread. 'It was Edward.' She begins to chew.

Edward! Ed, Jamie's friend.

'Edward hasn't thrown in the piano like Jamie, has he?' he enquires.

'No,' Lottie assures him and continues eating.

'Your Prince Charming,' he laughs. 'He wouldn't be the same without a piano, would he?'

Wendy is juicing oranges in the kitchen. She starts every day with a fruit drink. Ludo is asleep in the nursery, satisfied after his morning feed. She clipped a mobile of circus animals to his cot after she put him down. She's been reading about early stimulation. Marian complains, 'No cornflakes!' as she shakes an empty box but Wendy pretends she doesn't hear.

'There was a full box yesterday,' Marian continues. ' I bet Toby and Josh finished them off last night. Filthy pigs. Can I have some juice?'

Wendy is thinking about this time last year. It had been a scorching summer. They were in Greece for a month of it. Tony and she. The apartment was small but she loved being there. After a swim in the pool they would have breakfast on their own little balcony, the day stretching ahead of them. She was seven months pregnant but felt wonderful.

'They're taking their time this morning.' The sharpness in Marian's voice punctures her reverie.

'Who?'

'Dad and Lottie. They must be practising for the Olympics. He should be more careful. A man of his age could overdo it. This juice is good. I think I'll have a refill.'

Wendy has learned it's better not to confront Marian. She drinks her juice and tries to regain Greece but it has slipped from her.

'My mum always jogged with dad. Three times around the block. But then they did most things together.' She slurps her juice thirstily.

Toby and Josh arrive for breakfast on skateboards. They whizz their way along the full length of the black and white tiled kitchen. Scuff marks outline their trail.

'I won,' Josh says as he grips the table.

'Only just,' Toby concedes as they push the boards under the large pine table.

'Pigs,' Marian says, pointing to the empty cornflakes box.

They ignore her.

'Morning, Wendy,' they chorus.

It's at times like this that Wendy feels she's a mother of millions instead of just Ludo.

Mr Goldberg is troubled. He sits in his two-roomed flat and listens to Mozart. The rooms are crowded. A piano, records, tapes, books by and about musicians fill its spaces. Photographs, from sepia to Polaroid, take up the top of his oak sideboard. Occasionally, Billie helps him to sort things out but he prefers to let things pile up on their own. He's worried about Edward, whom he loves like the son he never had. His star past pupil. The scholarship to Vienna had paid off: the two concerts in the Festival Hall had been sold out. He kept all of Edward's letters from Vienna. Their vitality and enthusiasm made him feel good. He rarely went to live concerts these days. He relived the concerts of the past through his vast music collection. But for Edward's two concerts, he had donned his mothballed evening clothes. The women – Billie, Lottie, Babs and Edward's mother, Cordelia – were beautifully attired in that restrained modern way with very little jewellery. Expensive clothes which hung well. He preferred cloaks for evening wear but he knew that was very old-fashioned these days.

The two evenings had been triumphs. Quite a number of his former pupils kept in touch with him. Gifts arrived in the post at irregular intervals from places as far away as New York and Tokyo. A special recording of this or that, a new book of memoirs by a musician of his own generation. He kept a stock of postcards from the British Museum as thank-you cards to respond to such generosity. But he always replied to Edward by letter. After the first concert, they had supper at the Connaught. The meal had been unhurried and companionable; Cordelia played the proud mother and Edward indulged her; Babs was level-headed and brisk, telling him not to get too big for his boots and to remember that she had changed his nappies; Jamie and Lottie pretended to be groupies. It was enormous fun. Expensive, too, but Edward had insisted that it was his treat.

There were only two moments of uneasiness in the evening for Mr Goldberg. Being in the Connaught brought back memories of Wilhelmina (Billie's aunt) and the early days when neither of them could afford to step across the threshold. They had often taken walks together in Mount Street Gardens just around the corner from the hotel. The second moment was when he realised that Billie wasn't enjoying herself. She was cheerful and forthcoming when she was asked a question but she was a spectator during most of the dinner. He noticed Edward looking at her from time to time and wondered if he too was upset by her restraint.

In recent weeks, since the second concert, Edward dropped in and out of Billie's house just as frequently as he had done throughout his childhood and his long-standing friendship with Jamie. But Jamie hadn't lived there since his student days. True he stayed overnight in his old room from time to time. It was Billie's company Edward sought. He put his head around Mr Goldberg's door occasionally and produced a bottle of Glenfiddich every now and then but their conversations no longer flowed freely. They seemed forced, almost performances or duties. The atmosphere wounded him in a way he couldn't define. He'd been a rigorous anti-sentimentalist all of his life; yet here he was, an old fool in his eighties, upset by a young pianist who wasn't giving him enough attention.

Billie had found the flat through Abbercrombie and Wilson. She has worked part time for the estate agents since her divorce. The flat is in Gordon Square, in a house which has retained its Victorian grace on the outside and is comfortably modernised inside. The house consists of generous one-room flats. Edward is delighted with his – just what he needs.

His piano takes pride of place by the window. The kitchen area is diminutive; a counter, three cupboards, a hob and microwave. A shower, lavatory and wash basin are tucked into a corner. The room is airy and the polished wooden floor catches the light and gives the impression of honeycoloured space. The bed, a single divan, is covered in a throw rug which matches the creamy texture of the walls. An armchair and an upright chair complete the furnishings.

When he moved in, he invited people to cheese and wine. The room held ten quite comfortably. Mr Goldberg was given the armchair, Cordelia the upright one. Billie, Lottie and Jamie sat on the bed, while Edward's musical friends sat on the floor. At the end of the evening he said, 'Now that you know where I live, you must all refrain from visiting me. This is where I will practise for six hours a day. Mum says I can invite people home as usual. That way I can entertain people at her expense. Perfect, don't you think?'

His blue eyes cast an amused glance at Cordelia. She nodded her agreement to the arrangement, saying, 'A mother's work is never done.'

Cordelia's house is on the same road as Billie's. Jamie and Edward have been friends all their lives. Same school and college. In and out of each other's houses all these years. As Billie eats her solitary lunch at her kitchen table, she rests her hot plate of spaghetti Bolognese on Wendy and Ludo's picture. Thin trails of sauce stain them as the meal progresses. She's thinking about all of the years Cordelia and she shared the caring of Jamie and

Edward. School runs and music lessons, one or both of them in attendance. Unusual for small boys, they never pushed their mothers away from them at the school gates. They kissed whoever turned up with a genuine warmth. Maybe it was because both of their fathers had left home. They wanted to hold on to what they had. Mothers who were dependable.

Jamie always attended Tony's 'family lunch' on Saturdays. Often Edward went too. Returning after such outings they would entertain Cordelia and Billie with tales of Beth and Tony. How Beth had a special little hand hoover for table crumbs. How Toby and Josh had almost drowned in the lily pond but Beth had insisted that they were hosed down with disinfectant before calling the doctor. Tony's new gym in the basement. It had a speedwalk, exercise bike, weights, rowing machine and sauna. These tales of neurosis and opulence amused Billie but they stung too.

She had been the first wife. Young, idealistic, believing in Tony, struggling through the lean times only to discover that the days of plenty were to be shared with another. Cordelia tried to stop Edward's and Jamie's excited babble about Tony's lifestyle but Billie never did. She accepted it. One had to accommodate one's soul to such things. A false denial of Tony's new life, she reasoned, would be more harmful to her. She had shared the bare floors and lentil soup years with Tony. Beth would bask in central heating and a sauna.

Her divorce from Tony had made her wary of men. She felt vulnerable and lonely. Romance was to be shut out. She knew where she was with Mr Goldberg and the nurses, and her job at Abbercrombie and Wilson. Mr Goldberg's piano comforted. His music had always filled the house. It was continuity. Mr Wilson's fussiness, when she became accustomed to it, was acceptable too. On black days, when she cursed her luck, she reminded herself that she was fortunate to have part-time work that fitted in with Jamie's school and Lottie's nursery hours. Mr Wilson communicated in imperatives or quotations. Notes arrived on the top of files on her desk, which said, 'Immediately!' 'Now' or 'Tomorrow'. When he spoke it was as if he had digested an antique book of quotations. 'As Shakespeare said, "Neither a borrower or a lender be"'; 'Nothing is more beautiful than a tree'; 'When winter comes, can spring be far behind'; 'The hungry sheep look up and are not fed.'

Toby left her formally when Lottie was six months old. Toby and Josh were born three months later. They were born on the same day that Billie started work at Abbercrombie and Wilson. On that black day, she had timidly enquired if she would also be working for Mr Abbercrombie.

'Doesn't exist, dear girl. Lends tone to have Somebody and Somebody,' was the elliptical reply she received. That was also her first day away from Lottie. She wept in the loo at Abbercrombie and Wilson and hoped Lottie was happy in the nursery.

'It's barbarous to send a child to a nursery,' Tony had protested, while remaining equally firm in his refusal to give her any more maintenance. 'The solicitors will decide,' he said. A phrase that froze her bones. Unable to deal with desertion and the law at the same time, she had settled out of court for a paltry sum, a decision she later regretted. But at that time, she couldn't face what was happening to her. Surely Tony would not do anything to injure her! She expected him to come home in a few months and say it had all been a dreadful mistake. In the meantime, she'd muddle through. The decree absolute and Tony and Beth's elaborate wedding with Josh and Toby in white velvet suits, made her position clear to her at last.

She finally wrote to her parents just before Tony's wedding pictures hit the papers. She told them about her failed marriage, Tony's desertion and the astonishing fact that three children had been born to him within a year.

'Come home to Dublin,' her mother urged. Her father was less forthcoming. 'Things will work out. At least you have work. And you have the children. Spend Christmas with us.'

Years ago now, yet sometimes it seemed like yesterday. She put down her fork. She felt bloated from the spaghetti. She had thought all anger was quenched but she was wrong. She up-ended the remains of her meal on Wendy and Ludo's wide-eyed smile, then dumped them in the kitchen bin.

They've been eating in Dino's every Saturday since time began, or so it seems to Wendy. Two years ago, she was charmed by it. The lamplit terracotta-coloured walls were warmly welcoming. Dino, the owner, always smiled and greeted his customers effusively. Does he ever take a day off, Wendy thinks, as he shepherds them to their table.

'Only the best for Signor Tony.' He winks as he says it. Their table is in fact, three tables put together and covered by an enormous cloth.

'Fresh linen every day,' Tony had pointed out to her during their first meal there. Marian had brought her friend Elvira to the family lunch. A fat girl with little eyes and thin hair that hung to her ears. Marian finds her fullness reassuring, in a way that she cannot define. Her own mother, Beth, had been too thin always. On the rare times when she had cuddled Marian she was conscious of the sharpness of bones. Tony is scrutinising the menu and he smacks his lips as he calls out items. He sits at the top of the table, orchestrating the meal.

'And for the beautiful ladies, I can recommend any of the fish dishes accompanied, of course, by one of Dino's famous sauces.'

'I'll have burger and chips,' Marian says, unconsciously thrusting her chin out as she speaks.

Elvira blushes. She does not know what to order. It's her first such meal with Marian and her family but she can tell by the way Tony is holding his head that he's not pleased with Marian's order.

'I'll try the trout with honeyed nuts,' Lottie says.

'The same for me,' Elvira says, realising too late that to order the same as Lottie is betrayal in Marian's eyes. She smiles nervously at Marian, who is seated opposite her, but Marian avoids her eyes by pretending to be deep in thought in the desserts page of the menu.

'Pasta pesto for us,' Josh and Toby say almost simultaneously.

'Don't you ever tire of it?' enquires Tony.

'No.' They are adamant.

'I will have two baby chickens, pasta and salad,' Tony announces with gusto. This is his one big meal of the week and he prefers to eat it in public. He likes to be thought of as a man of appetite. A man of many appetites. 'And Ludo will have best breast as usual,' he jokes.

Elvira blushes. Toby and Josh giggle.

'I fed him before I left,' Wendy says innocently. Tony is disappointed. Ludo at Wendy's breast is the perfection of his family table at Dino's on Saturdays. Dino doesn't mind. In fact he looks forward to it.

'This is a family restaurant,' he reassured her on her first visit with Ludo. Wendy is glad that she's paid Tony back for his long breakfast with Lottie. She had breakfast alone. The German *au pair* has Saturday off and Nellie doesn't come in until eleven. Wendy is not at ease with either of them but she needs their expertise to stay sane. Running the house and the children on her own is an overwhelming thought for her, even in the abstract. She keeps a close eye on the young *au pair*. She has put her name down at two rival agencies for a middle-aged, homely, full-time nanny but there are long waiting lists. She hasn't told Tony.

Nellie she inherited from his previous wives. An uneasy legacy. She knows Nellie doesn't like her. She can tell by the casual way she flicks her feather duster about the furniture when Wendy is in her ambit. Also by the little sniffs she emits when Wendy hands her her week's wages on Friday nights. There's the added strain in the knowledge that Nellie does Billie's house from top to bottom once a week.

When Tony left to set up house with Beth, Billie could no longer afford Nellie on a full-time basis. She felt terribly disloyal when Tony doubled her salary and Nellie couldn't resist it. That was when the once-a-week arrangement started with Billie. She had Bob and the kids to think about and good cleaning jobs weren't all that thick on the ground. Bob is the caretaker for the block of flats they live in. The wages are low but they have a flat rent-free. She had wanted Darren and Tracey to have the best and that meant she had to work long hours. Over the years she had selected the choicest bits of Tony's domestic disharmony to entertain Billie.

Wendy banishes thoughts of Nellie and smiles at Ludo in his carrycot. He's sleeping. She had put him on the wide window seat near her and she tries to persuade herself that she's really enjoying Tony's ritual.

'Hello everyone. This is Stella,' Jamie says brightly. 'Sorry we're late, train trouble,' and he sits in his customary place, to the right of his dad, having seated Stella next to Elvira. The contrast is striking. Stella is wearing a backless crushed-velvet mini-dress that moulds her spare body. Elvira appears to be stuffed into her longsleeved, frilly cotton blouse.

'Delighted to meet you at last,' Tony says. 'We've heard a lot about you.' He winks at Stella in roguish manner and introduces her to the rest of the people at the table.

'There's no back to your dress,' Toby says. Josh kicks him underneath the table.

'I read in a magazine that women should emphasise their best feature when they choose their clothes,' says Marian. 'Do you think your back is your best feature?'

'Your brother certainly does,' Stella retorts, nonplussed.

'Half-brother,' Marian insists, but she smiles at Jamie. She loves him. He's second only to Beth in her affections. 'I could buy a backless dress,' she says, flirting. 'Jamie and you could take me to a smart restaurant.'

'For your sixteenth birthday,' he promises.

'Three years to go,' chorus Toby and Josh, jangling their spoons. 'You could be fat and horrible by then,' Josh warns. 'I've read about girls' hormones.'

Elvira blushes furiously and feels oppressed by her frills.

'No fear, I take after mum,' Marian counters. 'The fatties are on dad's side of the family. Look at Uncle Lloyd.'

There's a moment of silence while the table appears to contemplate Uncle Lloyd. Dino and his waiters bring food and interrupt it.

'A glandular disorder,' Tony confesses to Stella as Dino sets his twin chickens, pasta and salad in front of him.

'I'm sorry,' Stella says automatically.

'He eats too much,' Josh says. 'He has a huge bed. It had to be made especially for him. He broke all the other ones he had before.'

'When he has chicken . . . ' Toby takes up the tale as he casts his eye over his father's meal. ' . . . he eats three or four of them and they're not baby ones either.'

'Family folklore,' Tony says lightly. 'How it expands with the telling.' He laughs but Wendy knows that Lloyd's weight oppresses Tony. When Lloyd and Tony were children they were fat boys in long short trousers. He has destroyed those early incriminating photographs but their images stay fixed in the locked safe of his mind. A salutary warning. He smiles kindly at Elvira, the only fat person at the table. She's struggling with her fish, trying to debone it. Lottie has deboned hers in one confident movement.

'Let me do that for you, Effie,' he insists in a fatherly way that she's powerless to resist.

'Thank you,' she says meekly, handing him the plate.

'Are you in love?' Marian asks Stella.

'That's not a fair question,' Jamie says quickly.

'Yes I am,' Stella says without hesitation, and Marian notices that Jamie's face is suffused in a pink pleased glow.

'Mush alert,' Toby and Josh squeal in glee and the laughter is general.

'What does it feel like?' Lottie asks, as if it's a general knowledge question.

'It hurts the first time,' Toby whispers into Lottie's ear but nobody else hears.

'Hard to say,' Stella says practically.

'Ask dad,' Marian insists. 'He's the expert in the love department.'

'Oh love!' Tony says wistfully. 'It's always different; yet it's still the same.' He looks at Wendy and she smiles.

'Three wives, all different yet all the same,' Marian says with a smile at her dad.

He is not going to allow Marian to upset the meal. 'Love is different for everyone,' he says blandly.

'I'd like to go to bed with Madonna,' Toby announces to the table.

'Who wouldn't?' Josh agrees.

'Edward's concerts were magnificent,' Jamie says in an effort to steer the conversation away from the dangerous waters of love.

'Spaghetti Bolognese for two,' Dino says with a flourish as he sets steaming plates in front of Jamie and Stella. 'Love-birds often eat the same food,' he says before he withdraws. Jamie dusts his with Parmesan cheese.

'Smells like vomit; always does – Parmesan cheese,' Toby says.

'I love it.' Stella is undaunted and she puts a liberal topping of it on her spaghetti.

Wendy is beginning to feel invisible again. It's happened to her quite a lot recently. Moments or even long periods of up to half an hour when she feels her presence doesn't matter, that she doesn't count. She moves her baby chicken around her plate. She's eating the same meal as Tony but she doesn't feel like a love-bird. She looks at Jamie and Stella twirling spaghetti to their mouths and she's jealous. She wishes she could make all of them disappear and be alone with Tony and Ludo, her family. Instinctively, she puts her hand to the carrycot. He's still sleeping. Nobody has talked to her directly. She might as well not be here.

If she weren't married to Tony, she could be – where? On a beach in Benidorm or maybe Corfu with her friend Ellen, sizing up the talent or having a siesta.

'I didn't go to them,' Stella says when Tony asks her opinion on Edward's concerts, 'I was working.'

'At night?'

'I'm an actress. Didn't Jamie say?'

'I thought you played the clarinet,' Tony says lightly.

'I do,' Stella confirms, 'but in my spare time, not professionally.'

'I play the clarinet, but I prefer the piano,' Lottie says.

'She plays the guitar and violin too,' Josh says.

'A musical prodigy,' Marian says too quickly.

Elvira has eaten three baked potatoes and wonders if anyone has noticed. She's emptied the basket nearest her and worries in case they were meant to be shared. She's looking forward to the dessert menu. Her mum doesn't allow her pudding at home. She wonders if it's possible she's suffering from a glandular condition, like Uncle Lloyd. Her fatness absorbs most of her thoughts. Bread-and-butter pudding would be lovely but it's unlikely to be on the menu in the middle of summer. It's still raining outside. Drizzle clouds the window. Maybe a selection of sorbets would be lighter.

'He's a very intense player.' Lottie is talking about Edward. 'When you watch him, you know he's inside the music.'

'I'd like to go to Vienna one day,' Marian says. 'Edward's lived there and he says it's beautiful. Will you take me, Jamie?'

'Only if you carry his luggage,' Toby says.

'Beast!' Marian bares her teeth at him. 'I think the curse of twin brothers is excruciating.'

'I bought Edward's CD,' Tony confides to Stella. 'I've known him since he was in nappies.'

'But you left by the time he and Jamie were in short pants,' Marian says succinctly.

'That's a dreadful thing to say,' Lottie protests.

'You were only in Pampers at the time so it didn't worry you,' Marian offers in false comfort.

'That's enough, Marian. Apologise or you will have to leave

the table.' Tony's voice is stern.

'I'm sorry,' Marian says, visibly shaken.

'Apologise to Lottie,' he insists crisply.

'I'm . . . ' She cannot force out the words.

'Leave the table, Marian.' His voice is coldly level and Marian does as she is told.

'Pudding?' he asks brightly in an attempt to reintroduce cheer into the proceedings.

'No thank you,' Stella says, 'I never eat pudding.'

'I'll pass too, dad,' says Jamie. 'In fact, we'll have to be going. We're meeting some people at three.' And Stella and he slip away, waving a general goodbye to the table.

'Wendy, do you want to join me in a Chocolate Supreme?' Tony smiles his full charm on her.

The first direct question to me since we sat down, thinks Wendy.

'No thank you, darling,' she says sweetly. 'I'd like the cheese board.'

'I'd like a Chocolate Supreme,' Elvira says before she can stop herself. She's ashamed of her greed in the face of Marian's banishment.

'We'll have apple pie and cream,' Josh says for Toby and himself.

'I'll have a Chocolate Supreme,' Lottie says.

'Is that wise, darling, after all those pancakes this morning?' says Tony. Lottie blushes and knows she is to be punished as well as Marian. 'Well, if you're sure . . . ' His smile is glacial.

'To preserve health is to husband our greatest capital.' Billie is sitting in the garden, drinking coffee and thinking about her father. He used to say that every Saturday of her childhood as he poured out tablespoonfuls of cod liver oil for the family.

'Nourish the body competently and keep elimination up to date and the rest will take care of itself,' he pronounced as she swallowed it down against her will. This practice took place at twelve noon. They recited the Angelus and took the cod liver oil immediately afterwards. Saturday nights and Sunday mornings were spent in 'elimination' as Billie, her two sisters and her mother stayed as close to the lavatory as possible. One sister, Constance, refused to take the cod liver oil but dad simply stood his ground and when she wailed in despair, put a spoonful down her open mouth.

'It's a habit from his boarding-school days,' her mother mentioned once, as if this explained it thoroughly. Billie couldn't understand why her father, who had been purged by priests every school Saturday of his life, had to pass on that particular barbarism to his nearest and dearest. She's never touched cod liver oil once since then, even in capsule form. The other sister, Barbara, took two capsules daily all year round and advised her patients on its benefits too. Babs, the doctor, uncomplicated and simple. She had never had an exaggerated reaction to anything in her life. Up until Edward, that is.

They had chosen their hotel for its old-fashioned appeal. Edward had stayed in it from time to time when he was rehearsing with various orchestras. They had spent the afternoon at the British Museum, nostalgically re-examining the Egyptian section, Edward's and Jamie's favourite when they were children. They teased those childhood trips back into existence, laughing once again at incidents long buried. They had planned what they would say if they ran into an acquaintance. Billie was showing him some flats in the area. They had slipped in to look at the mummies as a break from flat-hunting.

'I want to live near the place we had our first real date,' he told her when he handed her back the keys from six flats on the Abbercrombie and Wilson books. She blushed. Mr Wilson was in his office but she felt girlish and covert. He had pestered her for months since his return from Vienna. At first she had refused to listen to his chatter. Thought it an elaborate joke. As she peeled potatoes for dinner in the kitchen or listened to music in the living-room, he would suddenly appear, newly freed from his practice schedule, talking foolishly of love. His love for her. She told him Lottie expected to marry him one day but he dismissed that as puppy love.

Somewhere between Christmas and Easter, loneliness at a year's beginning or maybe the freshness of spring touched her in a way that made her want to believe in possibilities, love, new beginnings. When he folded clothes with her from the dryer or helped her put her music tapes in order, she began to feel again the warmth of sharing daily tasks. She stopped contradicting his protestations of love. Earlier she had said, 'I'm old enough to be your mother. In fact, I am almost your mother. And your mother could be Jamie's second mum.'

'I know, that's what I like about it. I would sleep with Cordelia if she was incestuously inclined,' he joked, but his eyes carried an unmistakable intensity.

It was Easter before she gave in. They made a weekend booking at a hotel. They travelled there separately. She arrived first. Her weekend case was discreetly small. She left it at the desk and headed to the bar for a drink. She was half-way through a gin and tonic when Babs came into the room. It was so unexpected that she froze. She wished she could disappear. She feigned pleasant surprise and rushed to help Babs with her bulging black bag.

'You're not dealing in drugs by any chance?' Billie enquired in an attempt at levity when Babs accepted her offer of a drink. 'I just popped in to see how Edward is doing. He's rehearsing with an orchestra here.'

'Oh, which one?'

'I'm not quite sure,' Billie had to say.

'Rather a long way to come to pop in, isn't it? I was called in to look at Roger Foyle's throat. It's seized up and he has three concerts next week. I've given him an antibiotic and an anti-bacterial spray but, between ourselves, I think it's mostly nerves.'

'I didn't realise you treated musical celebrities.'

'Oh yes, I've got six of them on my books, for my pains.'

When Edward came in it was obvious he didn't know whether to retreat or advance. Billie called to him as he hesitated, 'Over here, Edward,' and he pretended to see her for the first time.

'Hello, Billie, Babs.' He was confused.

'Babs was called in to rescue Roger Foyle's throat,' she said too quickly, 'but she thinks it's nerves.'

'Oh,' he said, quite unable to add anything else. The dark zones between mid-twenties and mid-forties suddenly seemed too enormous to cross.

'I was telling her that you're rehearsing here.'

'Which orchestra?' Babs asked him.

He was flustered. 'A little chamber orchestra . . .' His invention was ineffective.

'How unusual!' Babs said. 'I'll have to leave you both now. I have someone coming to replace my guttering.' And she left.

They laughed at their rotten luck and the million-to-one chance that Babs, of all people, should have turned up at their tryst. It made both of them uneasy in a way that neither of them would admit. Babs stood for Ms Average. At that moment they didn't want their love to be found less than perfect by anyone. They were reassured by the old-fashioned appeal of their surroundings. They resolved to continue with their weekend and not worry about Babs.

Babs and dad, both preserving health, the greatest capital, Billie ruminates wryly as she watches her overblown roses sway in a little gust of wind. She often thought of Babs as her father's child while she was the child of her mother. She had been named after Wilhelmina, her mother's German nursing friend. They had worked together in London in the 1930s before her mother returned to Ireland to marry dad. Wilhelmina became an honorary aunt and Billie's godmother.

Her father had lost interest in naming his children after Babs's birth. Billie wondered if Jamie was her child and Lottie Tony's in a similar way. Even though he was absent from the home after her first three months of life, Lottie had, almost since she could walk and talk, demanded to be with him. She herself had given him generous rights of access to both their children.

But Jamie, at eleven, knew the difference between a full-time father and a part-time one. He wasn't charmed, as Lottie was, by weekend treats and elaborate birthday gifts. There was that dreadful age between six and seven when Lottie hadn't wanted to come home to Billie at all.

'Afternoon, Billie.' It is one of the nurses, but which one? 'Just right for sunbathing, isn't it?'

She's the tall fair-haired one whose bouncy walk speaks of cheer. She's wearing a bikini and carries a Walkman, some jars of cream and a deck chair. She plants the chair next to Billie and slumps into it.

'I'm glad to be off my feet. Anne's gone down the High Street but today's not a day for shopping. I told her we should get as much sun as we can in our line of work.'

Billie likes being in the garden alone. She doesn't want to be forced into conversation. The garden's small. A little lawn, it has some rose bushes, a *philadelphus* and a dwarf morello cherry. She loves it.

'I've been terribly lazy,' she says, 'I've been daydreaming out here for quite some time.' She wants to leave immediately but doesn't want to be rude.

'How's the old man then?' The nurse nods in the direction of the house, 'I haven't seen him out and about just recently.'

'Mr Goldberg? He's fine. We had tea together this morning.'

'That's good. Only he's been a bit out of sorts lately.'

'Really!' Billie wondered if all nurses diagnosed everyone they met. A sort of professional tic. 'I haven't noticed any change in him.'

'It's just that Anne and me include him in our little walks in the park on Friday afternoons but he hasn't come the last few weeks. Seemed a bit low in himself.'

Good God! Were they pestering Mr Goldberg to go on compulsory walks? She couldn't imagine him enjoying the company of this woman.

'He gave me a tape,' she says shyly pointing to the Walkman. 'It's classical. Mozart. We never had none of that at home. Me mum and Dad were strictly Rolling Stones fans. My sister and me like all sorts of pop.'

'Didn't you do music at school?' Billie assumed it was a compulsory part of the curriculum.

'Sort of. We had a smashin' steel band but when it came to exams I had to give it up to concentrate on biology. I've always wanted to be a nurse. Mind you, the pay is ridiculous and the conditions are terrible these days.'

'I see,' Billie says, while plainly she doesn't see at all.

'Bein' in this house is just great. Mr Goldberg, well, he's so famous and all; then there's his piano practice and Lottie's too. Seems like there's always music. Before I came here I'd turn off that kind of stuff even if it came on the radio for a few minutes.'

'Is that right?'

'My boyfriend's gone off with my friend, Jenny. I didn't know a thing until I found these two tickets for Majorca. His name was on one and hers on the other. They're there now. It's been a shock but Mr Goldberg's been ever so kind. He said, Tchaikovsky is for the passions, young woman, he'll see you right. And he gave me a tape. I thought that was really sweet. Made me cry, it did.'

Billie is uncomfortable. All this drama going on around her and she's been completely unaware of it.

'It's been a bit awkward with Nellie,' the nurse continues.

Her name is Susan. Billie is pleased that she has finally remembered it.

'Why should you feel awkward with Nellie?'

'She's his mother.'

'Darren? You're Darren's girlfriend.'

'Was,' Susan says wistfully.

Is it possible, Billie muses, that Nellie has told her all this and she's forgotten it? Over the years she has perfected a method of nodding assent at regular intervals to Nellie's monologues. What's the matter with her, she wonders. Has she been living in a sealed bubble these past few months? Since the weekend at the hotel she's been living at a remove from certain things. Outwardly, her life is the same. She goes to work for two-and-a-half days at

Abbercrombie and Wilson and turns up at the Oxfam shop on Saturday mornings. Today is the first day she's missed. And that was because it was Mr Wilson's mother's day. She comes in every third Saturday, rearranges the shop to her liking, alienates the customers and talks about the 'have-nots' in that loud patronising voice of hers. This has been the outward routine of Billie's life for a long time.

There were three casual affairs in the early years after Tony left. Sex weekends really, to reassure herself that she was desirable. They had been mechanical and nothing more. Her love for Edward had changed everything. Since then, when Billie rings Babs, she's pleasant and polite. She hasn't mentioned Edward directly. But avoiding his name is significant. Babs has always taken pride in his musical career.

When Tony left, Babs was kind and motherly. She condemned him with an energy and force that warmed Billie's heart. She smiles as she remembers her execrations now: he'll get fat, he's too self-centred to love anyone but himself. Now that Babs doesn't drop by any more she's become increasingly homesick for Ireland.

They told Edward's mother, Cordelia, one night over supper. She was amazingly calm. She put down her fork very gently and deliberately on her plate and said, 'Thank you for telling me,' and smiled. Edward opened another bottle of wine. While he was struggling with the cork Billie and Cordelia eyed one another. It was a frank but also a stand-off stare, one that was taking stock, measuring safe distance. In the lamplight, Cordelia's very short hair shone, a boyish mop. Her large green eyes blinked several times but they soon regained a social serenity. Only the hands remained agitated. Several times she fiddled with knife, fork or spoon but she ate nothing after that. Billie wanted to hug her and tell her everything would be all right as she did years ago, that time Edward fell off the tree in the back garden. But she held her tongue.

Relieved that things were out in the open, Edward, in that straightforward way that only the young display, took Billie's hand after he had poured the wine. She tried not to look at their hands clasped together across the tablecloth. It seemed to her that they filled the room. She was suddenly assailed by the knowledge that her long friendship with Cordelia, one in which they had shared all of the anxieties and insecurities of bringing up children alone, was changed beyond words. She was the untrustworthy babysitter. She hadn't dangled the kid from a top-storey window but she'd kidnapped him nonetheless.

Mr Goldberg was joining them for a liqueur at ten. Billie firmly untangled her hand from Edward's and said, 'He's old and fragile, best not to upset or shock him.' Cordelia looked away and in that moment she too looked old and fragile. Her skin seemed to have loosened and her profile had a defeated look. She began to stack plates busily, her thin shoulders hunched to the task. Billie had a moment of panic. A feeling of lightheaded madness. At forty-eight, Cordelia was only a year older than Billie. And here she was, a 'young' forty-seven-year-old, carrying on with her son. The whole thing was obscene.

Since that evening her meetings with Cordelia have been quietly dignified. There are no more womanly chats about this and that. The casual dropping in has to be done by Billie to Cordelia's house. Though nothing was said directly, Cordelia has made it clear that she will not fall out with her son for anyone. They have gone to concerts, the three of them. Billie, Edward, Cordelia, the women linking him afterwards to the car, Billie insisting that Cordelia sit in the front seat next to Edward and that she's dropped off at her own house first, as always. She knows how much a nightcap with Edward means to Cordelia and she's not going to be the one to fragment that routine. Billie knows these courtesies are just attempts to paper over the cracks but they're all she has to make her feel she's a decent human being.

They make love four times a week in Edward's flat. She comes home to sleep in her own bed in Brabbington Terrace. It saddens him that she won't stay overnight. They have made progress since that first weekend. Their first coupling was overshadowed by Babs and her black bag. Nervousness and a wish for it to be wonderful made them too self-conscious. Since then, they have relaxed into genuine pleasure. What he likes best is to take her from behind after long foreplay, her buttocks supported by pillows. What she likes best is to pin him under her and to mount him roughly without preliminaries. Their world is Edward's room. She knows by heart the muted pattern of the woollen bedspread, the honeyed glow of the parquet, the way their two bulbous white china mugs sit on the counter, the chug-chug of his small freezer.

In spite of these details that have imprinted themselves on Billie, what she likes most about Edward's flat is its utter lack of domesticity. It is where he plays the piano for six hours each day. When they meet there, their intent is singular. They wish to devour each other. She lets him look after food and drink. Out of the freezer and into the microwave is his method and she doesn't interfere. They drink wine mostly; occasionally she'll have a whiskey or he'll have a gin. She won't prepare food or drink. Her reason is simple. She's been feeding Edward, Jamie and Lottie at Brabbington Terrace for years. She doesn't want to mother him here. Edward's flat is for music and love.

'Darren's always been a bit selfish,' Susan says as she applies suntan lotion to her arms and legs with an energy that rouses Billie from her reverie. The movement of the plump sausage fingers spreading the cream alerts Billie once more to her immediate surroundings.

'All men are selfish,' she says almost as a reflex. 'The world is organised for them. They don't expect difficulties and disappointments; that's why they rarely encounter them. And if they do, some woman will spend time and energy sorting them out.'

'That's a mouthful!' Susan says admiringly, 'I wish I could say things like that. I think I'm getting cynical. This experience with Jenny and Darren has put me right off. I mean only last month, I was lookin' at three-piece suites with him. I feel a right prat when I think about that now. The three of us, me, Darren and Jenny, bouncing up and down tryin' out the couches. Darren and me had our eye on one of those flats near his mum's. I expected to be movin' by the end of summer. I thought it was all planned. I've been buying electrical stuff and china for ages. Still boxed. I'll have to take some of it over to my mum's. I should have seen the signs. I must be stupid.'

'Don't be so tough on yourself. Even if something is under your nose you won't see it if you don't want to believe it,' Billie says evenly.

'I was gettin' a bit fed up with Jenny taggin' along everywhere with us. Films, meals out. Darren said she needed company because she'd broken up with Bob. I couldn't understand how Bob just walked out on her. He adored the kids. Jenny got married straight from school. Same age as me, exactly. Twenty-five and three kids. You don't expect someone like that to pinch your bloke. I'm the godmother to her eldest. I bet you, some of the time I was babysitting for her to go to bingo, she was with Darren. I could knife her!'

'I didn't know the woman my husband left me for. I don't

know if not knowing her made it any easier. I suspect not. Being abandoned brings out primitive feelings in everyone. I used to drive past their house with cans of red paint in my car.'

'What was the paint for?'

'To paint "whore" and "adulterer" on their walls. But I never did, of course. I've still got the paint. It's in the garden shed.' She points in its direction. They both laugh.

'I thought of throwing a stink-bomb in Darren's letterbox but I didn't want to take it out on Nellie, Bob and Tracey. They've never done me any harm. But I might carve up his favourite 501s. He left them in my flat.'

Does Cordelia want to paint her house with 'babysnatcher'? Billie has never told anyone about the paint until now. She put it down to shock and post-natal depression at the time. Lottie had colic for months after she was born and Jamie knew there was something wrong between her and Tony. He was seldom at home. She was getting very little sleep as Lottie slept only for brief snatches. Tony was spending his time increasingly with Beth and coming home for short vigorous bouts of fathering.

He'd lift Lottie from her cot when Billie might have just settled her down after a fractious few hours and he'd talk to her like a caricature of a devoted dad. When she would wake and squall, he'd hand her back to Billie and press Jamie into a rumbustious game of football in the back garden or snooker in the cellar. He hadn't told her Josh and Toby were on the way. She knew he was seeing someone but thought it would pass. He'd been involved with other women before. She'd simply ignored the knowledge and never confronted him. Always, he came back. She assumed this was something similar. Her mistake.

She was in the living-room when he told her. It was early evening. She'd spent the best part of the afternoon walking Lottie up and down the room to ease her colic. To no avail. Eventually, exhausted by her own crying, Lottie had fallen asleep. Too tired herself to bring her back upstairs to her cot, Billie flopped down on to the couch with Lottie asleep in the crook of her arm. Jamie was at Edward's house for tea. Billie put on the Brandenburg concertos at a very low volume on the tape deck. She dozed in her milk-stained blouse and crumpled denim skirt.

Tony woke her. He was in white Bermuda shorts and a loose white shirt. The brightness of his clothes almost hurt her eyes. She felt soiled and ugly. He looked fresh and athletic. Boyish almost. As if he'd come straight from the playing fields.

'I'm going to have two more children,' he said.

At first, she didn't understand. She smiled.

'Well, of course, we've always said we'd like four children, but right now when Lottie is so demanding, I don't really want to think about it.'

'Beth is expecting twins,' he said starkly. 'We want to get married.'

She looked at his feet. He wore white tennis shoes without a grass stain. How precisely the laces were tied! Part of her thought it was an elaborate joke. From time to time when he was going through a bad patch with a book, he'd climb up from the cellar, his writing-room, and improvise a character that he couldn't get right. The Brandenburg tape ended and the room was filled with silence. She knew this wasn't an improvisation.

'I thought we were happy,' she said plaintively before she could stop herself.

'It just happened,' he said simply. 'I love her.'

'And I bloody well love you. Where does that leave me?'

He looked genuinely puzzled, as if she'd interrupted a polite conversation with a rude question. Or maybe he felt her interest in him should cease the moment his heart was occupied with another.

'I can't live with both of you,' he reasoned.

'Why not?' she retorted. 'You seem to have managed up to this.'

'Twins,' he said as if the word was a magic talisman.

'We have two children,' Billie reminded him and she picked up Lottie who had started to whimper.

'I'm very sorry,' he said uselessly.

'Sorry isn't enough.' And a stab of pain passed over her full breasts as if the milk was aching to be released.

'What about Jamie?' Her voice trembled.

'I'll take him at weekends if that's all right with you.'

His reasonable tone upset her more than she could say.

'You'll have to tell him,' she warned. 'I won't. You're the one who wants to leave us.'

'I'll call around at his bedtime tonight.'

'I see, a bedtime story is it?' And she turned her attention to Lottie who was now fully awake and crying loudly. She placed her right nipple in Lottie's mouth and rocked both of them until a trance-like calm came upon her. She doesn't remember Tony leaving the room. Only when he'd left did she realise that she hadn't asked any questions about Beth. Who was she? Where did she live? Then, intense jealousy and rage surfaced from her fatigue. She walked the house from top to bottom, going in and out of rooms as if to check they were still there.

'Anne says jealousy is cripplin' but it's all right for her to say that with a sparkler on her finger and a date set for the weddin'.' Susan is talking again.

Billie opens her eyes and is surprised by the brightness of the sun. She's been 'dazing' as her mother calls it. Eyes closed in sunlight, letting thoughts come and go as they choose.

'I'll really have to go in.' She gathers up her cup and saucer.

'I enjoyed our chat,' Susan says.

'So did I,' Billie replies as she moves towards the back door. Inside, she rinses the cup and saucer, her mind already on the dress she'll wear this evening. She's going out to dinner with Edward.

Tony is upset. The day has conspired against him from the start. He's sweating it out in the sauna. Marian's tantrum at lunch was inexcusable. Josh and Toby let him win a few games of tennis. He urged them to put their backs into it. They pretended to, that's all. For some reason Wendy dawdled as much as possible over the shopping. She was moody. Wouldn't buy any of the dresses she'd tried on. Most of them suited her. He didn't know why she was being obstinate. Marian fought with Elvira for the rest of the afternoon. He had to drive that fat unhappy child home keeping up a stream of happy chat *en route*. Another hour and the Hendersons would be here. Too late to cancel now.

Edward delicately closes the lid of the piano. Glad to be through for another day. He clears his mind of work and gets excited at the prospect of a meal out with Billie. Why does she have to be covert about their relationship? Babs has a lot to answer for, he thinks, as he steps into the shower and gasps with delight as the cold water bounces off his body. He washes in cold water summer and winter. Variations in temperature bother him less than most people. When Billie is here, they have warm showers together, soaping and oiling each other in boisterous foreplay. Jamie took the news remarkably well. They were in Jamie's flat when he told him, a one-roomed warehouse affair that overlooked the docks. Jamie and Stella had moved there the previous month. It was the first time Edward had been in it and he found its eccentricities a little disconcerting.

The bed was on an open gallery that ran the full way around the room, reached by a removable stairs. The lower part of the room seemed almost empty. The kitchen space had a circular glass table with matching chairs, some open glass shelves and a cooker. A hammock hung by the large window and a deck chair stood in the centre of the room as if waiting for another chair to join it. Jamie was so proud of his new flat that he kept talking about its unique features. It was difficult for Edward to pick the right moment to talk about Billie. At last, Edward said, 'Has Billie seen it?'

'No, I've described it to her but that's not the same. Moving flats has absorbed most of my energy lately. That and Stella and love.'

'Speaking of love,' Edward says lightly, glad of an opening, 'I love Billie.'

'I do too,' Jamie says simply.

'What I mean is . . . ' Edward is suddenly embarrassed. He doesn't know how to continue.

' . . . in a different way?' Jamie helps him out.

'Yes, precisely.' Edward is anxious for it to be over, out in the open. His words of assent seem priggishly insincere. 'I love her madly,' he asserts in a hurried cliché.

'Yes, I know,' Jamie says. 'I guessed.'

'Really!' Edward is surprised and fascinated. 'How?'

'The night we had dinner at the Connaught, you made a point of talking to everyone except Billie.'

How simply we give ourselves away when we think we're being

so clever, Edward thinks. But he's glad Jamie knows.

'The age gap.' Edward falters and doesn't continue.

'Dad is fifty, Wendy is twenty-five,' Jamie says as if he's describing the weather. 'Mum is forty-seven, you're twenty-five. What's there to say?'

And that was all there was to it. Edward smiles at the memory of it as he towels himself. He checks his face in the bathroom mirror and decides he could pass for at least thirty. A mature thirty at that. The black hair cut close to the head would eventually turn grey. He wished he could hurry its onset. Peering closer into the mirror, he thought he detected the faint hint of lines from nose to mouth. Even if they were laugh lines, in the end they'd deepen. He was happy at the prospect.

Wendy is pretending to sleep. She doesn't want to entertain the Hendersons. They're not her friends and she's had a gruelling day. Baby Ludo snuffles in his sleep beside her. Pam Henderson fancies Tony. She's sure of that. At the Hendersons' barbecue some weeks ago, Tony and Pam grilled all of the steaks and served everyone salads as well. The team work was impressive. She'd looked on with Ludo at her breast. That sniper, Marian, caught her observing them.

'Almost look married, don't they?' she'd said in a venomously bright tone.

Wendy couldn't understand that if she was the 'baby bride' as Josh, Toby and Marian had called her behind her back, the indulged younger partner of the relationship, then why was she so miserable lately? Could it be post-natal depression? Ludo was ten months old now. And she'd been fine up to about six weeks ago. She'd read about the symptoms in various women's magazines and they all seemed to apply to her. Fatigue, bad temper, moments of panic and isolation. A year ago, with Ludo on the way and the prospect of marriage and escape from office work and her dreary flat, she felt exhilarated. Moving into a large comfortable house and helping Tony to raise the children seemed dramatic and romantic. Then she had resolved never to be the wicked stepmother. Now she dreamed of mixing a poisonous concoction that would be fatal for Marian.

The boys she could take. Noisy and dirty-minded they might be, but she had four brothers herself so she felt sure of her ground with them. Anyway, they were at home only in the holidays. There was a lot to be said for boarding schools, she decided. Marian went to a local girls' school. Privileged and over-priced in Wendy's view. She might as well be at boarding school; the fees were astronomical. When she had pointed this out to Tony, he had told her firmly that Marian had been wetting the bed most nights since Beth's death and so boarding school was out. Then there was the sleepwalking to be considered. One night Tony had found her on the window ledge of her room. It was past midnight. He grabbed her by the legs and pulled her to safety. He got locks for all of the windows the next day.

Nothing was working out the way Wendy had planned it. There were days now when she longed to be back in her little flat, far away from the demands of this new family. She wondered if she was one of those women who could love only their own children but had no interest in other people's. She loved Ludo with all her being. It terrified her sometimes. What if something were to happen to him? She listened to the daily news and kept alert to national and international disasters. A man had been knocked down some weeks ago on a street quite near High Pines. What if she had been pushing Ludo in his pram at that precise moment too? Never a voter, she decided she had better exercise her civic duty at the next election. A child needed example. Part of her confusion was to do with age. She felt very young when she considered how much Tony had packed into his life. But she felt old and weary when she was trying to steer a clear course between the hazardous rocks of family life.

Tony decides he's sweated enough. He leaves the sauna and jumps into the pool, swimming its length a dozen times. He moves with speed and grace in water. He's always enjoyed it. He hoped Wendy would be up and about by now. Nellie was putting the place in order and preparing what she called 'light refreshments', a label she applied to any food that wasn't a sit-down dinner. When Tony thought of his good fortune, which was often, he always put Nellie at the top of the list after his children. He boasted about her to his friends.

'That woman is amazing. She's seen me through three marriages. There aren't many who can claim that.'

He accepts her gruffness as a sign of deep affection. She reminds him of his mum, though Nellie is only fifty-five, five years his senior. His mother was a night cleaner all of her life. A staunch trade unionist, and an official, she fought for her colleagues' rights with determination and spirit. Once she led a three-month strike for better conditions. 'Let them stew in their own dirt for a bit,' she said into a television reporter's microphone. 'Then they'll see what fine conditions we have to work in.'

He took pride in her after her death. He loved her when she was alive but that love was tinged with fear. He had always felt she was withholding part of herself from him. When he got his place at grammar school she was delighted. Two years later, she took him aside one day and said, 'You're not cleverer than anyone in this house, just because you wear a fancy uniform. Your dad and me work hard to keep that on your back. If this house isn't good enough to bring your friends to, then it's not good enough for you to live in it either.'

He thinks about his mum as he goes underwater, momentarily holding his breath. He surfaces again. How had she known? He'd been ashamed to bring Colin, his friend from school, to his house. Colin's house had seemed so grand when he went there for tea. It had a winding driveway, two apple trees in the garden and a double garage. His house opened on to the road and only had a yard at the back for the coalshed and washing line.

When his agent sold the film rights to his fourth novel, he rang his mum with the news.

'That's great, Tony love. I'll tell your dad.'

He'd wanted to bring them out for a meal, somewhere fancy and expensive. To celebrate with Beth and himself.

'No thanks, love. We're just sitting down to my homemade steak and kidney pie, your dad's favourite. And I'm working tonight. Thanks all the same.'

'You can give all that up now,' he'd said in his excitement. 'Move out of Prescott Street too, for that matter. I can pay for a nice house for you and dad, cash down.'

'No thanks, love,' she said in exactly the same light tone in which she'd dismissed his dinner invitation. 'I enjoy my work, just like you do your writing. And as for me and dad moving out of Prescott Street, that'll be the day we go out in a pine box. Besides,' she laughed, 'we're not going anywhere now that we've got the new three-piece suite.'

She had reduced him to tears of humiliation within minutes. As soon as he put down the phone, he howled his desolation at his rag-rolled walls and his black Japanese furniture.

He swims to the end of the pool and steps out. Beth had been no help, he remembered. She said, 'She's an obstinate woman, that's all.' For a crazy moment, he wanted to drive over to Brabbington Terrace and tell Billie about it. She understood mum, had even explained her to him from time to time down through the years.

That was one of the things he missed most, having Billie to talk to about mum. Beth never forgave mum for the first time she had invited her to dinner. Dad wore his best suit and tie but mum came in one of her everyday dresses and oldest coat. She carried a plastic bag inside which were her cleaning overall and comfortable walking shoes. She was working her midnight-to-morning shift as usual after dinner.

'A bag lady!' Beth wailed when they'd gone. 'Why did she do that? Lucky we cancelled the Hendersons. How could one explain your mum's *haute couture*?'

Now that she's dead, Tony finally understands or tells himself that he finally understands his mum. He has told that story to Wendy, almost as a boast. His mum wasn't going to dress up for his fancy house or his fancy foreign wife. She was her own woman, always. He puts on a towelling robe. Nowadays, when Wendy complains about how Nellie speaks to them, he says, 'She's known me longer than you. She's not a downtrodden servant. She's a valued member of the household.' He'd have to hurry to be dressed before the Hendersons arrived.

Nellie is in Tony's kitchen cutting up fruit for a salad. He likes it served in the large Danish ceramic bowl that his translator gave him one Christmas. Nellie had her suspicions about the translator. A tall blonde. She'd seen their heads too close together on the living-room couch that summer Beth was in hospital for her nerves. In Nellie's opinion it hadn't been nerves at all, just an obsession with germs and household dust. And that hadn't started until his eyes started roving. The poor woman wore herself out. Up half the night dusting, worried in case he wouldn't be home until the small hours again. It had turned Nellie's stomach to watch it. He was always telling Beth to lie down and rest. Over and over. All that dusting and stuff was only her way of doing the opposite. The baby bride was resting still. The kids had named her well. You couldn't look sideways at her but you'd think she was going to cry. What's the point in giving a baby a name like Ludovic. That's an old man's name. But of course, they'd shortened it before the christening water was dry. Ludo, same name as a game. There wasn't one of the kids with a proper name like her Darren and Tracey. Darren was a bit of a worry right now. Off in Majorca with Jenny from number fifteen. She ought to be ashamed of herself and her with three kids of her own. Nellie felt sorry for Susan. She looked ever so professional in her nurse's uniform. Children could be a disappointment sometimes, Nellie had to admit. Still, it mightn't last with Jenny. She liked Susan, a good tidy girl with a proper job too. That was the end of the fruit. Her hands were sticky with juice. She held them under the cold tap and dried them briskly on a towel. That was everything. All they had to do now was pour the drinks. She could go home to Bob and telly at the mansions. Maybe bring him a take-away Chinese. He liked the occasional treat and what with all that bother with Darren recently, there had been rows and arguments that were hard on the nerves. Just as well Darren was in Majorca for another week. A woman needed peace and quiet in the home after a day's work. Darren was moving in with Jenny when he came back.

Wendy is pretending to sleep. She can hear Tony move about the bedroom but her eyes are closed. He moves quietly. He's dressing.

She can hear him zipping his trousers and the clank when he replaces the hangers in the wardrobe. Finally, he's bending over her. Her eyes flutter.

'Wakey, wakey,' he says. 'It's fifteen minutes to kick-off time.'

'Mmm!' she says and turns over. 'Do I have to get up?' she asks sleepily.

'Yes,' he replies and leaves the room.

She feels like a child summoned to meet the grown-ups.

Billie is feeling relaxed and well fed. Their first dinner date outside the confines of the flat, apart from that disastrous weekend. Now they're idling over brandy. Neither of them has been to this restaurant before. Edward wants to build a series of firsts into their relationship. He needs to build his own history with her, separate from his shared childhood memories: those outings that Cordelia and Billie organised for Jamie and him. Billie looks at Edward's neat hair and serious face. The dark-brown eyes are staring at her as if registering her for the first time. The lights are dim. Shaded pinks, kind to skin. Then he laughs, his face breaking into lines of humour.

'We should take a menu,' he whispers, 'as a memento, start our own collection.'

'All right,' she agrees and pushes the rather elaborate menu card into her bag. The bag is large enough to hold it. She zips it quickly. 'There, it's done.' They toast each other.

'Wendy will be down in a little while,' Tony tells Pam and Donald Henderson. 'Your usual, Don?' he asks as he clinks bottles at the bar. The bar, a genuine oak counter, is from the Old Oak. He bought it when they pulled the entire place down to make room for a block of flats.

'Yes.' Donald nods his large grey head.

'I've helped myself already,' Pam admits, as she drains the last dregs of a triple gin and tonic, 'but I could do with a refill.' She slides the glass along the counter, Western-style. She looks tired and old. Tony remembers when they romped in her marital water bed. Was that only last year? The black skirt is too short, her limbs are geriatric bony rather than girlish, and the cerise blouse does nothing for the mauve tints of her skin or for the face tucks. He pulls his stomach in, anxiety firing his gut like a burning girdle. Even Pam can't hold age at bay. The Petra Pan of her generation.

'Nellie sniffed at me as she left.' Pam is already at the self-pitying stage. She must have had a few drinks before she left home as well.

'Nellie sniffs at everyone; it's her calling card,' Tony says lightly.

'She's never liked me . . . I like kids.' Pam is now addressing the blurred space, as if focusing on the distant past. 'A shame we never had a few ourselves, Donald.' It's a shot across the bows with a renewed energy and malevolence that's palpable.

Tony knows it's going to be one of those difficult evenings. Pam's hair glints in a shaft of sunlight, its blonde smoothness suddenly wiglike. Better to open the French windows and sit in the air, he thinks. And eat something soon if she's drinking that fast. Where was Wendy when he needed her?

'I saw your ex last week,' Pam says as she dangles her sandalled feet from the stool.

'Billie?'

'The one and only,' Pam confirms. 'Something or someone is keeping her young.'

'She doesn't keep me informed,' Tony says.

'I always liked Billie,' Donald says as he sips his Scotch appreciatively. 'Damn good, this!' And he swallows another mouthful. 'She always struck me as one of life's innocents.'

'You say that about everyone except me,' Pam whines.

'I'm probably right too.' Winking at her to take the harm out of it.

'I would look innocent too if I had all my skin and fat untouched. But the acting world isn't kind to flab and deterioration.'

'You don't have to try for parts for younger women. Why put yourself through that?'

'Sometimes it works and sometimes it doesn't,' she says dismissively but defeat clouds her face. She wants Tony on her side. 'You try and explain the backbiting and hell of it all to him, Tony.'

That's the problem with old friends, Tony thinks. They assume you've an infinite capacity to listen to the same ground being covered endlessly. Tony smiles it out and passes a plate of sandwiches, wishing that bread would stop both of their mouths. But, of course, it doesn't. Donald reaches for a sandwich but Pam keeps talking.

'Tony did everything in his power to have me cast in his last mini-series but that wretch Devereux wouldn't have me. He wanted it for his wifie, the stupid cow.'

Tony doesn't say Devereux's wife is fifteen years younger than Pam and wonderful to work with. They sit in silence.

Billie is lying on Edward's single bed fully clothed. Edward is playing a Beethoven sonata. They've had two brandies since they came back to the flat. She listens to the music. The standing lamps throw off a pink glow.

'Flesh,' Billie thinks, as she opens and closes her eyes from time to time.

She enjoyed the meal. When the bill came, Edward paid it. She had to remember not to reach for her purse. Years of habit built up from when she and Cordelia took Jamie and Edward for treats. There was a momentary flash of embarrassment when he took her hand across the table and held on to it. The waiter was pouring the wine. Billie thought she caught a hint of amusement about the waiter's eyes. To hell with it! She resolved to enjoy herself. Jamie had been open and unsurprised when he told her that Edward had talked to him.

'You'll be good for each other,' he said simply, as he stood in the kitchen pouring water into a mug of instant coffee. Only the constant stirring of the mug betrayed his unease.

Billie had brought Lottie shopping the week before. Both of them had bought new summer clothes, Lottie a selection of skimpy tops and shorts, Billie two linen suits, one in cream, the other yellow. There were three skirt lengths for each suit. Very brief, two inches above the knees and one inch below. Billie reached automatically for the below-the knee-length.

'Oh mum, don't be so stuffy!' Lottie had appealed, and handed her the shorter one. She tried it on just to please Lottie and was delighted with it. She bought both suits in the shorter length. My summer of abandon, she thought to herself as they both ran for a train. When she looks at Lottie, Billie sees herself when she was her age, a fifteen-year-old beauty, except she didn't know it then. Photographs revealed it to her years later. Lottie is far more focused than Billie at that age. She knows what she wants: to be a professional musician.

At her age, all Billie wanted to do was get out of school, not because she didn't have an aptitude for the work, which she did, but because she found it overwhelmingly tedious. She had no goals beyond that. College swirled by in a haze of parties and very little study. Afterwards, she met Tony in the London office of the business magazine she had begun to work for. He was the editor. Even as she returned to Dublin, she knew she would go back to live with him. She was in love with his energy and determination. Sure of everything and his place in the scheme of things. He would become a popular writer. He was already half-way through his first novel. He wouldn't be a great writer but he wouldn't write trash either. Just a popular bestseller, he had said, without hesitation or fear of failure. And she believed him. His certainty gave shape to her life. Her doubts about herself ended as she resolved to bring about his success just as eagerly as he did himself.

In some ways, Billie reflects, she didn't really grow up until the divorce papers were in her hands, when she finally understood that she was on her own. A concept that most adults grasp by their early twenties. But she was over thirty with two children and a marriage behind her and it seemed as if someone else had lived her life up until that point. She was the mere locus of a collection of sensations that she couldn't order.

The music finishes and Edward moves from the piano and sits beside her on the bed.

'Looking for lines?' she jokes.

'No. Watching you in case you disappear. Counting our breaths. They coincide.' He brushes her cheek with a kiss.

'I'll stay tonight,' she says. 'Lottie won't be home until Monday.'

'You've never stayed before, even when she's been with Tony.'

'I know. But I'm ready now, that's all.'

'Why now?' He's excited and curious.

'No particular reason.' But she knows she's lying. The colour supplement article that featured Tony and his current household has helped her to decide. It's fifteen years since Tony told her that he was marrying Beth and that the twins were on the way. And she was still worried about staying overnight with Edward. At first, she persuaded herself that it was for Lottie's sake. Then, for her own independence, going home to sleep in her own bed was the best thing to do. But at bottom, it was the fear of appearing too willing, too eager to be with Edward that stopped her. Caution lit her reasoning, nothing else. Goodness knows, Lottie had seen her father in a variety of strange households over the years. It was time she realised her mother was entitled to live a life of her own choosing too.

Lottie is in her own room in Tony's house. It's nine o' clock. The evening started pleasantly enough. Wendy and dad had invited the Hendersons for supper. Lottie joined them briefly for pizza and salad on the terrace. Dad made it clear that it was an adult gathering, apart from Ludo who was glued to Wendy's breast. Pam Henderson was half-way through the gin bottle by the time Lottie left. She was hurling insults at producers and directors and jutting her chin up whenever she remembered to. Lottie could see she was over the hill. Pretty pathetic to be blaming everyone in sight just because she didn't get a part. You could tell she wasn't used to children the way she oohed and aahed over Ludo.

'I sacrificed my body to my career,' she was fond of saying, to explain not having children. But from what Lottie could see of her body she hadn't done a good job. Donald was a saint, as far as Lottie could see. He turned a blind eye to everything. Pam and dad had a fling after Beth died. If Lottie knew, then Donald must too.

Adults were strange. Always talking about rules and standards when it came to children but bending them when it came to themselves. That was the time Pam made them birthday cakes and bought them surprise presents. Nellie called her 'that woman' even in her presence and dad never corrected Nellie.

When Marian called her 'that woman' dad slapped her across the face. He was as surprised by his own action as Marian was. He put his arms out to cuddle her immediately but she wouldn't let him. He said he was sorry and that adults shouldn't hit children. She said she wanted her mum. But Beth was already dead. Everyone knew she wasn't coming back.

Marian can hear the music. Even in her room, it's loud. Someone keeps turning it down but another person turns it up again very quickly. Probably Pam. Drunk again, no doubt. You'd think acting in a mini-series on the box was one of the highest achievements in life. Jazz. Tinkly bits of piano, then a saxophone crosses it with mournful punctuation. Marian is busy with her large collection of photograph albums. She has a dozen in all. And she's on to number three.

She's been cutting out her dad from these pictures for the last hour. But she's getting tired. Snip, snip, her fingers go, adroitly cutting him from her infant days. She's left the hands, when he held her soon after birth. And there's his left foot on the swing as he pushed her when she was two or three. She had to leave that as otherwise she would have had to cut her mum from the picture too. It's amazing how much energy such a task can take. Living through each picture is exhausting. She'll have to leave album number four for another time but she's determined she'll complete the task. Finally cut him out of her life. Relegate him to the margins as he has done to her.

That Lottie! Soppy as a little pup. 'Goodnight Daddy,' and hanging on his neck for a goodnight kiss. Marian had hidden behind the curtains in the living-room as they ate their supper on the patio. Pam was ginned up even before she came, repeating all the twaddle about the parts she can't get. Same old record. Marian supposed dad put up with it because they had been lovers once. Adults were hypocrites.

Wendy looked half-asleep. She seems to need as much sleep as Ludo these days. Lottie kissed her goodnight too. She knows how to keep her dad happy, that one. Happy families, that's his game, but Marian won't play it. Interesting though what Pam said about Billie and Edward. Not that one could believe everything a drunk said. A jealous drunk at that. A constant weightwatcher, Pam often said ludicrous things about the very thin. And dad's first wife, Billie, had been as thin as mum. Marian has had an interest in Billie for years.

From the first, when Billie used to drop off baby Lottie in that ancient green Rover, to the most recent times when mother and daughter jog from the train. Tall and slight, there's an air of command about Billie that compels children and adults alike. After Beth died, Marian nourished the fantasy that Billie and Tony would be reconciled. Marian was seven then; her eighth birthday was the week after Beth's funeral. Tony had to lie down a lot after Beth's death. Dr Hardgood gave him tablets. Nellie and Billie organised a little party for Marian. It wasn't in her own house and dad couldn't come. He was still sleeping because of the tablets. It was in Billie's house in Brabbington Terrace. Mr Goldberg played happy tunes on the piano and there were balloons and streamers. And Nellie and Billie made a cake. A castle with a princess on top.

There were songs and games and playing in the garden. When

it came to blowing out the candles and making a wish, Marian couldn't help crying for her mummy but Billie said that was all right. Her mummy was looking down at her from heaven because mothers never forgot their children wherever they were.

Later on, Billie drove her home but dad was still sleeping. He had left a gift for her. A sailor dress with a hat, but Marian knew Pam Henderson had picked it out and anyway thoughts of the sea made her feel sick. Pam Henderson said tonight that she had seen Billie and Edward at the British Museum and they weren't just looking at artefacts either.

Mr Goldberg has been sleeping in his chair for the last two hours but he thinks he's had a short doze. He feels stiff and a little chilled. He moves his legs about while remaining seated. Saturday night. The usual mixture of pop music and voices reaches him from the nurses' flat. Susan and Anne must be entertaining again. Regular as clockwork, Saturday nights, pop music, voices. Mr Goldberg had never been gregarious. Even at the height of his fame on the solo circuit, he had dreaded the social designs some of the more ambitious hostesses had for him. They insisted on throwing lavish parties or intimate suppers for him, no matter how he tried to dissuade them. He put in appearances, whisked about the room and chatted to as many people as he could within an hour and then he made his excuses to his hostess and left. An hour was the most he could endure. It was a mystery to him how people actually enjoyed inviting crowds to their homes on a regular basis.

Lottie should ring Edward. She hadn't seen him for days. He'd been busy since his London concerts, preparing for the Salzburg and Vienna ones. Last time he'd heard her play was some weeks back. He didn't drop by as often as he used to. Cordelia didn't see as much of him either now that he had a flat of his own. It had changed her. Lottie could see that. Cordelia had always been a cheerful and calm mother. Those were the qualities that everyone admired in her. Years ago when Lottie was a child it was to Cordelia Billie always ran when things went wrong. Sickness, accidents. And she could always be relied upon to do the right thing. Now there was a strained edge to the cheer. Lottie wouldn't be like that when she had grown-up children of her own. She was sure she'd let them lead their own lives. Not that Cordelia had ever seemed to interfere in Edward's life. She was proud when he got his scholarship to Vienna. But maybe being abroad to study was different to being in London in a flat of his own. He had told everyone that his flat was for practising. Still, Lottie had to admit she did think he'd make an exception for her. After all, she was a musician.

Goldie missed him too. Before, when Edward had been studying abroad and came home for holidays, he spent time with Goldie, the two of them hammering out a few duets for fun or just talking music. This time he was different. Maybe a career did that to you. Practice, practice, practice. Solo performers had to keep chasing perfection. At least that's what Goldie had said when she asked him did he miss the duets. Lottie dialled Edward's number.

'Hello, it's Lottie.'

'Hello, Lottie. How are you?'

'All right. I'm in dad's but the Hendersons are here. They're all drinking. Marian isn't speaking to me and the twins have locked themselves into their room for the night.'

'That only leaves Ludo then.'

'Wendy took him off to bed with her. Can you come over? We

could get a milkshake. There's a new cafe. Dad took me there for breakfast this morning.'

'I'd love to but I just don't have the time right now.'

'All work and no play. It's ages since I've seen you.'

'I called in last weekend.'

'That doesn't count. Mum was there. I mean on our own. Like we used to.'

'I'll call around Monday evening when you're back home. I have to go; there's someone at the door. See you then.'

Lottie held the receiver close to her ear as if by doing so she might discover who was at Edward's door. Chemistry was what counted. She mustn't have enough of it. She threw herself on the bed, squashing her music books in the process. She pulled one from the pile. Tchaikovsky's First Piano Concerto.

The music filled the house. She didn't spare the pedals. Marian heard it as she finished snipping the last of her photos.

'Bloody show-off,' she muttered as she looked at a line of heads, Tony's heads, smiling bodiless in a row across her desk. Marian gave up the piano when she was eight years old. It was not enough to be adequate when Lottie was brilliant. She took to reading dictionaries and reference books instead. Her mind held on to what she read. The word 'parlour' came from 'parler', to speak, originally meaning the only room in a monastery in which the monks were allowed to speak. The winter of 1925 was so cold in Canada that the Niagara Falls were completely frozen. Victorian barbers offered to clean customers' teeth as part of their service. Mark Twain wrote most of his books in bed. Marian hugged such information. It was something real, beyond dispute.

Pam Henderson stopped mid-gesture, the hand extended to Tony, remained there. 'Music, heavenly music . . . ' She changed topic with gusto. ' . . . we should dance.' Tony and Donald, as if choreographed, rose in tandem and took one of her hands each, twirled her in time to the dramatic notes rising on the evening air and planted her back in her chair again, her eyes closed to everything.

'Poor bitch!' Donald said softly as he replaced her limp hand on her lap affectionately.

'Care for a swim?' Tony said.

'Well . . . I . . . ' He looked at Pam.

'We can tuck her up on a couch first.'

'OK.'

The bell in Lottie's ear deafened her momentarily. Still her hands played on automatically for a while. Marian wielded the handbell as if it too were part of an orchestra.

'The world's first juke-box was installed in San Francisco in 1889,' Marian said in a loud whisper. 'It could play only one record. It wasn't a great success.' She left the music room, tinkling her bell delicately as if performing a religious rite. She bumped into Wendy and Ludo on the stairs.

'What's going on?' Wendy said. Ludo's face was red and tear-stained.

'We were doing our orchestra practice, my beloved half-sister and I. Sorry if we woke the brat.' She tickled Ludo under the chin and he smiled his broad baby smile, extending his chubby hands to her. 'Not now, little brother. My wicked stepmother couldn't hand her darling to me. Or to anyone else, for that matter.' She threw the words over her shoulder as she made her way back to her room, happy to have hurt her two least favourite people. Lottie and Wendy, Dad's little puppets.

Wendy looked in at the music room. Lottie was cradling her head in her hands. Lottie saw the bare tanned feet approach. Her eyes followed the line of leg to the brief white skirt.

'Sorry if I woke Ludo,' she said.

'The clanging bell woke him, not the piano. He loves music.'

'Music! Play on.' The new voice was slurred and seemed to be coming from the ground. Both Lottie and Wendy turned in its direction. Pam was slung by her hands and legs between Tony and Donald, both in swimming trunks. They made for the couch with their parcel. When they dumped her on the couch, her towel fell away to reveal sagging breasts and a too-rounded stomach. Lottie thought how awful it was to become old and ugly. 'These are the best years of my life,' Pam told them.

JULY

Billie wouldn't have gone away at all except she could no longer bear to look at Lottie's face. They told her after she had finished her summer exams.

'Maybe I should have a ritual burning of the noose,' Lottie said, as she undid her school tie for the last time until autumn. 'Hello, Edward. Are you eating with us again? I must shower away the last shreds of school from my system.' She went upstairs, returning a little later with wet hair, shorts and T-shirt replacing her gymslip. They'd had a few glasses of Hungarian Chardonnay to sustain their courage.

'We've something to tell you, Lottie,' Edward said. His throat was dry but he managed.

'I don't want to hear a thing until I've eaten,' Lottie declares. 'I skipped lunch today. I went over to dad's to find out if he'd decided on Greece for the summer holiday. I'm ravenous. The train was delayed for half an hour. Another bomb scare. They haven't decided on the holiday yet. At least Wendy hasn't. I'm really looking forward to it. I'll scream if she says France.' And she dived into the hearty salad Billie had prepared. As she watches Lottie chomp and chew, she wonders if this is a crazy tale to unfold to a fifteen-year-old. Maybe she should stop it now and all three of them could eat their meal without any explanation or tension.

'This is good, Mum.' She flashes Billie a smile, her teeth evenly white on her newly tanned face.

When she has finished her ice-cream and peaches, Edward starts again. 'As I said, we've something to tell you, Lottie. Billie and I . . . well, we've been seeing each other lately.'

'That's right,' Lottie interrupts energetically. 'Sneaking off to music concerts on your own. Not even taking Cordelia or Babs a lot of the time.'

'Cordelia was at the Beethoven with us last night,' Edward protests.

'That's right, but she wasn't at any of the Chopin festival last week, was she?'

'She went to the Mahler with Babs, I believe.' Billie was surprised how distant her voice sounded.

'Anyway, I'm free from exams now and we can pack in a few concerts before this Greek odyssey. Wendy isn't going to make a snap decision.'

'It's like this,' Edward persists, 'Billie and I . . . we're lovers. We didn't want to tell you before . . . what with end-of-year exams and everything.'

Lottie starts laughing. Her laughter is spontaneous and exaggerated at the same time.

'It's a joke. I've had my first laugh of the summer hols. Thanks, mum.'

'It's true,' Billie says. Her eyes fasten on Lottie's face.

'How could you? How could you?' she spits at them. 'You're mine,' she says to Edward. 'You always said so. Ask Goldie. We're his star pupils. A pair. You said you'd marry me.'

'That was a long time ago. You were a little girl. Things change.' His voice was soft.

'Her age won't change.' She points at Billie.

'You're young, you'll meet someone else. All we've ever done is kissed at birthdays and Christmas.'

'Wasn't it enough, then?' Billie is alarmed at the leer on Lottie's face. She looks like a scorned Lolita.

'Yes of course it was.' Edward is calm. 'You're only fifteen, for heaven's sake.'

'And my mother is forty-seven. There's a bigger gap between you and her than there is between me and you.' She wipes her face on the tail-end of her T-shirt. 'I'm going to dad's. I don't want to stay here with all this going on.'

'That's right,' Billie shouts. 'You go to your dad. A man who's living with a woman half his age. He'll explain it all to you. You've always preferred him anyway, haven't you? Never mind that he ran out on you when you were a few months old. He'll take care of you like he always has.'

'At least he's not a hypocrite like you. What about Cordelia? She's your best friend and you're sleeping with her son. How would you like it if she took up with Jamie?'

When the front door bangs ten minutes later, Billie feels a wave of self-revulsion that is terrifying. Lottie has finally run out on her. She has a sense of time telescoping to the past. All those Sunday evenings in Lottie's childhood when Tony had brought her back home, Billie knew she would have preferred to be with him and Josh and Toby instead of her. The memory is suddenly acute. Edward is studying the remains of Lottie's supper as if a clue to her behaviour might be found there.

'She'll come round. You'll see,' he says. The feeble comfort makes him aware of his own helplessness. Supposing Billie rushes out the door after Lottie and says she's changed her mind about him? He knows how strong maternal ties are. Cordelia, he is fully aware, is very hurt by his relationship with Billie. They've crossed a taboo line that is akin to incest. But she has not reproached him with it. It seems to him almost as if she has trained herself to give a civilised response in spite of her feelings. He admires her for it but he won't delude himself that it costs her nothing. Mostly he puts it from his mind, but Lottie's loud concern for Cordelia still hangs in the air, makes him face the question of his debt to his mother in a way that is difficult to ignore.

Billie looks across the debris of Lottie's last supper and tries to read Edward's face. He has the serious look that in childhood he had reserved for the dissecting of frogs or scanning the skies for stars through his telescope. She wants to cry but knows she mustn't. How could Lottie run off to Tony in his Wendyhouse and accuse her of hypocrisy? Double standards, that's how. She has fallen into her own trap. She has helped Lottie accept her father for what he is by never uttering a single negative word about him. Better to relate to him in a positive way than in a bitter twisted way. Better for Lottie. For fifteen years she has kept her mouth shut. The early exhausting years she juggled with the demanding schedule of Lottie's nursery, Jamie's school, her job at Abbercrombie and Wilson and the eternal nurses on the top floor. All that time Tony and Beth lived in style and had two nannies to look after Josh and Toby, she had got on with it. Even when he built the twins a tree-house and Lottie wanted to live with him, she had kept her patience. Now, all that self-control was gone to waste. Lottie had left the house with Billie's treachery uppermost in her mind.

Cordelia and Mr Goldberg had helped her through those dangerous seas a lifetime ago. Cordelia had said, 'Be positive about Tony. At least he's going to be available for Lottie and Jamie every weekend. Take it from me, a weekend father is better than none at all.' Mr Goldberg had said, 'He'd have left some time, if not this year, next year. People like Tony do not grow old with their first wife. They grow young with their third or fourth wife.' Later, Cordelia said, 'It's pointless to get so annoyed about a tree-house. You're not really angry about the twins' tree-house; you're frightened that Lottie will choose Tony instead of you. Make it a happy time when she comes home on Sunday nights even if you have to fake it. Look at it this way; there will be years to come when she won't come home at all.'

They had protected and advised her, Cordelia and Mr Goldberg. She had let them down as well as Lottie. She had robbed Cordelia of her son and ignored Mr Goldberg for weeks. What had she been thinking of? Edward, Edward, Edward. He had wiped them all from her head. His full lips and black hair, his chin that jutted out when he concentrated, his hands that played Chopin and her notes equally well. He had made her a teenager again. Telephone calls, secret looks, forbidden trysts, all of these had energised her to reclaim a part of herself that had been stifled since Tony's defection. Why couldn't it have been a simple uncomplicated love. Why did it have to pull down the family devils on her head?

'I think we should . . . ' Billie starts to speak but is quickly interrupted by Edward.

'I think we should clear up too.' He busily stacks dishes in the dishwasher, to stop her saying what he fears most, that she'll say: 'We shouldn't see each other for a while.' Miraculously, she doesn't.

'I think we should see Mr Goldberg, explain things to him.'

Edward is relieved, light-hearted almost. 'Whatever you say; but I think he knows already. Goldie is a wise old owl. He's got a lot of empathy.'

Goldie hears them coming. He knows every creak in this house. He'd have to watch himself. After all he'd survived the war and

Uncle Joe. The knock on the door is deferential, almost timid. 'It's open,' he shouts from the depths of his chair. And Billie and Edward stand before him hand-in-hand.

'Ah, you're engaged, I see.' His tone is light, almost jovial.

'Not quite,' Billie banters, 'but we've been dancing these past few months.'

There is a moment of panic when Edward feels excluded from the grown-up after-dinner talk, but he counters it with music talk.

'The Chopin festival was magnificent, Goldie; he had it all, from Polish folk to the isolated prelude, didn't he?'

'True,' Goldie responds, 'and he got George Sand too.'

'His older woman.' Edward looks at Billie appraisingly.

'Six years between them, Edward. It seems only a hiccup when you consider our twenty-two.' But she laughs to show she's able for everything that threatens to divide them.

'A toast is appropriate,' Goldie says. He wants this to take as little time as possible. 'You know where my stock of booze is.'

Billie makes her way through the varying piles of newspapers, books, music scores to the battered china cupboard near the bay window. The top of the cupboard overflows with scores but inside there is a healthy supply of spirits. She pours three whiskeys and hands around the glasses. She notices the layer of dust on most of the furniture in the room and realises with a guilty start that she hasn't cleared up for Goldie for months.

'To you both, to whatever the future holds for you,' Goldie says in that dignified tone of his, and both of them feel the elevation of the moment. They drink silently. Edward moves towards Goldie's piano. A Chopin mazurka fills the room. The rhythmic ambiguity of the Polish folk music fills Goldie with nostalgia for Russia and he wonders if the new freedom has made any real difference to the ordinary people. In his knowing way he suspects that it hasn't. The food queues seem endless on the television news. Still, he gives himself over to the energy of the music. He knows Chopin wasn't a dangerous nationalist and that in the end Chopin's Poland was a mythical dreamland. After all he had been perfectly at home in glamorous Paris.

'I'm going to Russia,' Edward tells them when he finishes.

Goldie sees Billie's face blanche and her body stiffen. Edward turns around. 'Of course you'll come with me,' he says, as if it were the simplest thing in the world. Relief that she's included in his plans is only momentary when she remembers what a distant land it is. Obstacles mount. There's Lottie, her job, the house.

'It's only for two weeks, five concerts, Moscow and St Petersburg,' he's telling Goldie with glee, once more the star pupil who wins prizes. Glad that it's not for ever, she relaxes. 'It's the first two weeks in August, not for ages yet,' he says, having sensed some of her alarm.

'I'll manage that all right. I have my annual three weeks holiday coming and I've a backlog of holiday time that I haven't taken in years.'

The phone rings in Billie's living-room. They look up at the ceiling in its direction.

'I'll get it,' Edward offers and he sprints out of his chair.

'I'll come. It may be Lottie,' she says.

Goldie is tired. He dozes after his whiskey, relieved by their absence.

It's Tony, his voice energised by annoyance. 'She says she's not going home.'

'Well, if you can't persuade her then I'm certain I can't.' Billie's voice is tensely cool.

'But it's the school holidays. Josh and Toby are here, not to mention Ludo and Mars. It's just too much for Wendy.'

'It must be tough being a stepmother. But what can I do? At

the moment Lottie hates me. I didn't tell her to go to your house.'

'You did snatch Edward from her; she's bound to be upset. Edward's only twenty-five you know.'

'So is Wendy. I can count too.'

'That's different. Age is appealing in a man.'

'Says who?'

'Everyone.'

'Not everyone. Men say it when they run off with child-brides. I've no intention of listening to your opinions on the matter.'

'*Touché*, but Lottie thinks you're disgusting.'

'I can see you're giving her all the help she needs.'

'Would you consider an exchange?'

'Exchange of what?'

'Kids. Mars is quite willing to go to your place for a few weeks until Lottie sorts herself out.'

'Marian! But I haven't seen her in years. The whole idea is preposterous.'

'She has a few problems, granted. She's still sleepwalking and she wets the bed a few times a week. But I could pay for Nellie to do some extra hours for you. You know how loyal Nellie is. She'd do anything for me.'

'For you!'

'Well, for both of us then. I never interfered when she kept working for you when I left.'

'I hired her in the first place.'

'These petty arguments aren't going to get us anywhere. Will you take Mars?'

'No. If you don't want Lottie, you have to tell her yourself. She left here of her own free will. I'm perfectly willing to take her back but I draw the line at having Marian. Marian is your daughter. She's your responsibility.'

There is a click on the extension. Marian has been listening. It seems a long time since her birthday party in Billie's house the year her mum died. In Elizabethan times potatoes were served in a sweet caramel sauce. An albatross can fly all day without flapping its wings. In ancient Greece a Spartan man who had not married by the age of thirty lost his right to vote. At the Great Exhibition of 1851 there was an alarm bed. At a set time, it tipped up and threw the sleeper to the floor. Lottie will be here for weeks on end!

'I need a drink,' Billie says when she puts down the phone. Edward refills her glass and she gulps it thirstily. Best not to talk to Edward about it. He's heard her side of the conversation as it is. He's too young to be asking him for advice about her teenage children.

'Want to talk about it?' He's smiling.

'No,' she lies. 'I think I'll let Tony deal with Lottie this time around. After all I've been a full-time parent to her for fifteen years.' She finishes her drink. The whiskey has gone to her head and she giggles. Edward circles her in his arms, then kisses her hungrily. They collapse on the couch and do what they've been doing for months in Edward's flat.

They wake an hour later to twilight. There are two figures standing in the doorway. Billie is groggy with love, sleep and whiskey. It's Cordelia and Susan, the nurse from the upstairs flat. She grabs something to cover her nakedness and finds she has pulled Edward's empty jeans, exposing Edward's penis to view. He uses his T-shirt as a fig-leaf and they wait for Cordelia to speak.

'I'm sorry to disturb you both. There was a phone-call.'

Billie feels she must have slept for a long time, that somehow she's missed a vital link to whatever is going on. Cordelia hasn't been in her house for months. Something's wrong. Has she been waiting for this precise moment to catch them with their clothes off? Cordelia gets a throw rug from the back of an armchair and gently covers Edward and Billie.

'There was an accident. Jamie's been hurt but he'll be fine,' Cordelia says in her matter-of-fact tone. 'Susan has made some tea. He was painting the high ceiling above the musician's gallery. You know the one in his flat; it's awkward to get at. He was using an extended ladder. He lost his balance. Stella took him to the hospital. A broken leg and collarbone but he'll be fine. Babs rang me to tell you. She went to the hospital to check things out.'

The bell rings. Cordelia answers it. Edward slips into his jeans and T-shirt and then sits next to Billie, his arm around her. It's Babs, black bag in hand. Her face is blank and set.

'Cordelia's told you then,' she says. Edward removes his arm from Billie under Babs's thorough gaze. 'He'll be fine. So much for 'do-it-yourself'. Hello Susan. You're looking well. Jamie is in your ward. Sister said you're on tomorrow. That cheered him up a bit. Why are you wearing nothing but a rug, Billie?'

'I've taken a vow of poverty. Even clothes are too much of a possession. I'd better get dressed and go to the hospital.'

'No visitors after nine and they've settled him in for the night. Best wait until the morning.' Babs is brisk.

'Well, if you'll excuse me I'll put some clothes on anyway.' And she leaves the room, trailing the rug behind her.

In the bathroom where she has a hurried shower she can hear the murmur of voices. She has a whiskey headache and it's an effort to suppress anger. How the chips fall, she thinks. Fifteen years after Tony's desertion she's finally given into her own sexuality and in the space of one day, Lottie leaves home and Jamie ends up in hospital. What's day two of this new existence going to bring?

Edward is dying for a drink. He's had two cups of tea. Cordelia, Babs and Susan are revelling in hospital horror stories.

'It's the drunks are the worst. Casualty on Saturday nights is bloody hell. This man came in last week with half his ear off. The wife bit it off. She'd caught him in bed with another woman. I know how she feels though, I could've bitten off more than Darren's ear when he told me about him and Jenny. They're back from Majorca now, tanned and everything. It isn't right. Not when my flat upstairs is full of household items. It makes a girl think, I'll tell you that.'

'Anyone for a drink?' Edward is playing host.

'Tea's fine,' Cordelia says, suddenly remembering how Edward and Billie looked when she came into the room in the first place.

'One won't hurt you, mum.' It was the 'mum' that persuaded her. He hadn't called her that for years. His twenty-first birthday to be precise. He said he would feel more adult if he called her by name and she agreed. She was always afraid as a single parent either of smothering him or making too many demands.

'A gin and tonic then.'

'I'll have a whiskey. Has Billie any more Bushmills?'

'A double will do nicely. I've had a hell of a day,' Babs says. 'I had to tell a middle-aged daughter that her mother is too ill and frail to be living on her own any more. There isn't enough money for a private nursing-home and the lists are endless for the others. They'll have to live together in disharmony for the forseeable future.'

'Poor bloody cows!' Susan sympathises. 'I'd hate ever to have to live with my mum again. I'll have a G and T, Edward, since you're pouring. He's got beautiful hands, hasn't he? Must be all that piano playin'.'

'The day I can't negotiate my way around Brabbington Terrace on my own,' Cordelia says with feeling, 'that's the day I'll hang out the For-Sale sign and book myself into a small but well-run home.'

'Mum, you're forty-eight, not eighty-eight. All that is centuries away. Drink up.'

'For tomorrow we die,' Babs says with relish.

Billie senses a party mood by the time she returns to the living-room. She's three drinks behind everyone else. Mr Goldberg is at the piano playing a mazurka. Cordelia, Babs, Edward and Susan are improvising their notion of an Eastern European dance and everyone is laughing. Edward stops momentarily on her return; then extends his arms to include her. He twirls her until she's dizzy. Babs is shouting 'Bravo' at Mr Goldberg.

When Jamie wakes he puts his hand out to touch Stella but she's not there. Hospital sounds make his wakening clamorous. He's on a high rigid bed. His right arm is in a sling and his left leg is heavy with plaster of Paris. Then he remembers his accident. He had insisted on painting the very high ceiling himself. Stupid to be so stubborn. Now here he is in a hospital bed aching all over and feeling very sorry for himself. Bernie had rung the hospital late last night to sympathise with him briefly but mainly to let him know he'd send in the office messenger with the folder for the Arnold account.

'Advertising never stops, not even for the lame and the stupid,' he cracked before he rang off.

The West Indian doctor who treated him had been extremely kind even though he'd been on duty for thirteen hours. He'd tapped him in various places with little hammers before sending him for an X-ray. Then he'd kept up a stream of talk on Wimbledon while he put him together again. A trolley stops by his bed. It's breakfast. Porridge, a hardboiled egg, cold toast and tea. He drinks the tea but leaves the rest.

Billie wakes in Jamie's room in Brabbington Terrace. Her eye catches a model aeroplane and she remembers the time he made it, his eyes lit with enthusiasm, his fingers sticky with glue. She's stiff and uncomfortable. Edward's back is turned and he faces the wall, still asleep, though he stirs briefly when she gets out of bed. Her head is thumping with a hangover and she makes her way unsteadily to the bathroom. The shower is acting up again. The range of heat is from stone cold to blisteringly hot. She decides on cold.

At work, Mr Wilson is unstoppable. A sale has fallen through. 'This blasted recession will be the death of me. They were getting it for a song too. £90,000. A few years back they would have paid half as much again and felt they'd got a bargain. I don't understand it. They have the money. They liked the property. They just changed their minds. Dammit, I had lunch with the man last week. I've been chewing Rennies all morning. My stomach has been grumbling since they rang with the bad news. We're not a huge enterprise but I've always thought of us as sound. Another cancellation like this is unbelievable.'

Billie keeps her hands busy. The electric typewriter hammers her brain. She's had two Alka Selzer but her hangover is still with her. She's thinking about the ill-assorted sleeping household she left behind in Brabbington Terrace.

'Maybe we should redecorate the office. A bit of paint never hurt walls. I could get it done over the weekend. What would you think of a peaceful green or a cheerful yellow? Maybe Mrs Wilson is right. I've always been too found of beige. I've gone through the catalogues and they're my two favourites. You've a good eye for such things, Billie. What do you say? I read an article on one of the weekend supplements. It said the colours we surround ourselves with are making a statement about our image. Maybe there's something in it. Brindle, Balton and Burridge have been doing very nicely since they've opened and all their front offices are pink. The carpet is grey of course, so that tones it down somewhat. There wouldn't be a change of carpet here. Out of the question with the present cashflow, but paint, now that's a different matter. I think I'll go ahead. The green, I think. It's been useful talking it over with you.'

Nellie lets herself into 3 Brabbington Terrace. There's something different in the air this morning. In the living-room, the curtains are still pulled and the air is muggy. When she opens them her eyes take in the full ashtrays and empty bottles. Billie doesn't smoke but when her visitors do she always empties the ashtrays before Nellie arrives. The place has the look of abandon and neglect that it hasn't had for years. Like it used to have in the old days when Tony lived here.

Maybe she had a party? Nellie scowls at the sticky glasses as she takes them from the top of the piano. Old Goldie must have been here for part of the festivities. That's his Russian drinking glass, the one with the handle and swirls of a turquoise design that looks like mad sea waves. At least the old codger joined in. He's been keepin' too much to himself lately. Lipstick marks on glass and butt-ends make her curious. Billie and her friends rarely if ever wear lipstick.

She doesn't mind the extra work. Things have been dead enough around here for too long. 'Time enough for sleep when you're dead,' is what she often says to Bob. Not that there's been too much sleep at the Mansions lately. What with Darren back and installed with that woman and her kids at number fifteen. It makes her blood boil to think of it. He's taken to those kids as if they were his own. They're callin' him dad and she has him runnin' around in circles. Transformed her place, he has. Put in built-in wardrobes. And tiled the bathroom from ceiling to floor in matchin' blue and white tiles.

I suppose it must be love but she can't help thinkin' that she had her eye on him from the minute her man went off. Susan was in a bad way. She could see that. Hadn't she queued with Susan herself at any half-decent household sale for the past year? Bob said it would all be all right in the end but that was his statement on everything. Bob took things too easy.

She took the dirty glasses to the kitchen and was surprised to see Edward and Susan drinking tea at the counter.

'I'm afraid it's a bit of a mess, Mrs N. I came down to give you a hand. We had an impromptu bash last night.'

'I see,' Nellie says. Best not say more than that. Usually that gets them talkin'. At least that has been her experience with Tony at High Pines over the years. The worse the devastation the more the talk.

'In that case I'll join you in a cuppa before we start. And what are you doin' here so early, Edward?' She's known him since he was in short pants.

'I stayed over; so did Cordelia and Babs. We all had rather too much to drink, I'm afraid. Jamie had an accident. He's at the hospital, broken leg and collarbone. Fell from a ladder while he was painting the ceiling in his flat. We had a few drinks after the news and countless others after that. Hence you find us in this delicate state. Cordelia and Babs are still asleep. They're in Billie's room.'

'Jamie gets done in and you all get fallin' down drunk. Better than cryin' your eyes out anyway. Maybe Darren could finish the ceilin' for him. He's ever so handy.'

Susan looks at her coffee spoon intently then decides to speak. 'I never knew that Darren was into DIY. I couldn't get him to change a plug.'

'She's transformed him,' Nellie says with venom. 'Every time I see him now, he's got a hammer in his hand. But it can't last. It isn't fair on you.'

'I don't think I could have him back again, even if it didn't last, Nellie. I still love him. You can't get rid of love that fast but I'm workin' on it. The thing is I can't bear to look at all the stuff I bought. I think I'll try and sell it down the market. You can have your pick of what's there. My feelin's have changed, you see.'

'Men, they're never worth it. When we're young we don't know no different and Mother Nature snares us when we're innocent, that's all. Speakin' of Mother Nature, there was a woman breastfeedin' her baby bold as brass on the Victoria line this mornin'. You couldn't blame her, not really. The train was delayed for forty minutes. Another bloody bomb scare. The baby was screamin' its head off. In the end she gave it a breast. The man opposite was disgusted. He put his newspaper up to block his view.'

'I'd like children some day. Just two, though. I don't want to be the slave me mam was,' Susan says.

'Where's Lottie? She's hardly sleepin' it off like the rest of them.'

'She's at Tony's,' Edward says too quickly.

'It's only Wednesday. She don't go to her dad's till Saturday,' Nellie says with authority.

'She was upset.' Edward realises she'll get Tony's version in a manner of hours anyway and so continues, 'Billie told her about us.'

'About you?' Nellie thinks he's referring to Susan and himself. 'What about you?' She stares from one to the other.

'Not us.' Susan blushes but she's not displeased and she lights a fresh cigarette to savour the moment.

'Billie and me.' Edward's voice is unsteady but he makes himself look Nellie in the eye. He's remembering the moment Cordelia and Susan came into the living-room last night. He's always been slightly intimidated by Nellie. She's been around as long as he can remember. She gave Jamie and himself secret fistfuls of sweets during the endless Wednesdays of childhood. Cordelia and Billie allowed sweets only on Sundays.

'You don't mean . . . ' She understands immediately.

"We kept it quiet. Met at my flat mostly. It's been a bit awkward, you see.'

'Too bloody right it must be. Billie's been a nun since that rotter scarpered and now she's takin' boys into her bed.'

'I'm twenty-five, Nellie. Old enough to know what I'm doing'

'Question is, does she know what *she's* doin? It's no business of mine. I'm only the cleanin' woman. If Lottie's run off to her da, then Wendy won't be pleased. Not with the boys home for the holidays. They're a handful, those two. You know what I found in their room lately?'

Susan and Edward shake their heads.

'One of them video nasties. Me suspicions were aroused, as the detective said to the judge, after I'd cleared up the usual mess and I came across three tapes of Robin Hood. All with different covers. That's funny, I thought, but one of them had Kevin Costner on the front and I thought I'd have a peek. I'm partial to Kevvie. I popped it on and what did I see? It doesn't bear repeatin'. I'm a woman meself but I've never seen close-ups of some parts of the female body. I brought the filth home with me and left 'em a note. The upshot is they keep their room clean and tidy for the rest of the summer. They also have to pay someone for the loss of the videos. I blame the schools meself. What good is all that fancy education when they watch the same filth as any yob.'

'So Billie's got a toy-boy. I don't know what all the fuss is about,' Josh says, as he flips from channel to channel on the portable TV in his room.

'It's because she was so . . . sexless for years,' Toby points out placidly. 'After a while you take everyone's behaviour for granted, that's all.'

'It isn't as if dad's married to her any more. The way he's going on you'd think she just left him or something. It's creepy.'

'I'll tell you what's creepy. Keeping this room as tidy as a surgery. Old Nellie's got us by the short and curlies. I'm going to make bloody sure that I never leave anything incriminating lying about again. The old bat. She drives a hard bargain.'

'Lottie's going to be here most of the hols. That means fireworks between herself and Marian. Nobody is going to have time to keep tabs on us. They'll be too busy. It might work out just fine.'

'Paul is coming this afternoon. Dad says we can use the pool.'

'Wendy will be splashing about with Ludo as usual.' Toby is dismissive.

'So what. I like looking at her and Ludo is great in water. I get a real kick when I see him floating by.'

'Yeah, he's a real water baby and I'm Robin Hood,' Toby says sourly.

Marian is exhausted. She tells herself she hasn't slept a wink all last night but actually she dozed in and out of sleep most of the time. She heard their footsteps this morning, first thing. Dad and Lottie off jogging. So, it's to be every day now instead of just weekends. Bloody bitch! It served her right that Billie pinched Edward right from under her nose. It's the first time the little princess hasn't had her own way. I suppose the piano will be going night and day as well. It was awful that Billie didn't want her to stay in her house but it was reasonable too. She wasn't her kid and Tony really was a bastard trying to get rid of her like that. Pass the parcel. Pass the kid.

Still, it made you feel rotten knowing for sure that nobody wanted you. When mummy was alive she was her little helper. They kept the house in order, just the two of them. Nellie was there, of course. But they worked together always. It was mummy who taught her how to label her photos, put them in order and always keep her albums up to date, mummy who taught her a room was never quite in order unless everything in it was clean. She liked her feather duster and Nellie said if Marian cleaned the whole house instead of just her room then she'd be out of a job immediately. It was the cobweb dreams she hated the most. No matter how hard she'd try her room was full of them. Mummy would scold her, waving her feather duster like an evil wand, and then she'd wake.

It was always the same. Nothing else happened in the dream. It amazed her how her heart thumped when she woke. Often she found she'd wet the bed after the cobweb dream. It was shameful and childish, of course. She cleaned up her own messes. Had been doing it for years. Birthdays and Christmas when Tony asked her what she wanted, she wrote her list but she always added, 'and a pair of sheets'. Just in case. Queen Catherine de Medici (1519 to 1589) decreed that ladies of the French court should have a waist of only thirteen inches. Cats sweat through the pads of their feet. The swallowing of live slugs was once thought to be a cure for consumption. When Richard II was married in 1380, he had to pawn the crown jewels to pay for the wedding. One sand dune in the Sahara desert is so high it measures 1,410 feet, higher than the Empire State Building in America.

Tony sits in his de luxe cabin at the end of his walled garden and scowls at the screen. He likes to do four thousand words a day. He becomes irritable if he fails to meet his target by five. Nine to five, Monday to Friday. That has been his routine ever since he left his regular job with Bensons twenty-five years ago. He left Bensons the week Jamie was born. Mum had called him irresponsible but Billie was behind him all the way. She matched his confidence. She was sure his trilogy would be placed.

'I've written three novels and I've got an agent, Mum. It's only a matter of time. I've researched the market thoroughly. I didn't exactly walk out of Bensons' door without any preparations. I'm writing full-time now.'

'Nine to five then?' Her sharp voice queried.

'Exactly, nine to five, just like a regular worker. Satisfied?'

'It's nothing to do with me, son,' she sniffed self-righteously, doubling back on him with an energy that terrified him. 'You should worry about Billie and the baby. You left home a long time ago now.' And she stood up with alacrity and began filling her bag. That bag. Black. A cheap plastic hold-all that held her work clothes, overall, shoes, snack-box and thermos. For a brief moment he wanted to smash it against the hard kitchen tiles. The tiles smirked at him. Scenes from a nostalgic long ago. Kitchen maids and lads, churning butter, peeling vegetables, lighting fires. They peopled and crowded out her tiny kitchen just as her union work crowded him out. Her questions that always caught him on the hop. His answers that could never quite measure up. To what? He didn't know. That's what made it so exasperating. It was a no-win situation for him. Why the hell did he bother playing?

'I'm off,' she said as soon as she'd buttoned her sensible navy coat.

'I can drop you on the way. I'm going to the hospital. I want to photograph Billie and the baby.' He picked his camera up from the table.

'No need, son. The eighty-three is so handy. It stops right at the corner, now that they've finally finished the by-pass.'

'Fine,' he managed, without quite clenching his teeth. Resistance, always bloody resistance, even to the simplest thing. She'd been different with Lloyd, her favourite son, his twin. They'd been fat twins together in youth but Tony kicked his craving for sugary foods by his third year in grammar school. The taunts had taught him a lesson. Better to feel half-starved than to be laughed at. Large Lloyd, the carpenter and union man, settled in to his fat. It sat happily on him. People responded to him with cheer and ease. Lloyd took mum and dad for an hour's drive every Sunday.

Tony is weeping in his cabin. He puts his hands to his head instead of to his keyboard. What the bloody hell is going on here? It's no use going over all this nonsense with his mum. What about his four thousand words? It's all Billie's fault. This affair with Edward is making all sorts of stuff come to the surface again. What's wrong with him? His mum is six feet under. There's no bloody way he's ever going to take her for a Sunday drive. If there's an afterlife, surely she'll know by now that he did the best he could. Then a thought strikes him. What if mum and Beth are up there dissecting his flawed character? It doesn't bear thinking about.

The white walls of the cabin return his stare.

Yesterday's last paragraph beckons him on screen. There's nothing to distract him here. He chose its expensive simplicity himself. Desk, word-processor, reference books, bathroom with shower, fridge stocked with diet Coke and mineral water. The fax and the answering machine are in his study in the house. Nothing to distract him but himself. His jealousy. He's jealous of Billie. His first wife, the forty-seven-year-old mother of Tony's first-born is sleeping with her son's playmate. She ought to know better. And she has. For fifteen years since he left she did the right thing. Now suddenly she's behaving like a tart. Worse, she's sleeping with a child prodigy.

Edward was meant for Lottie. It wasn't exactly by royal edict but everyone understood it. Ever since their astounding talent had thrown them together. So what if there was a ten-year age-gap? They both won scholarships to the best music schools. They spoke the same language. If Billie messes up Lottie's music career he'll personally sharpen an axe. Lottie has given him so many proud moments already. Youth orchestra and solo work. He's been there clapping her progress. Last night she kicked the baby grand and said she hated all pianos and pianists. Marian said, 'Ah! the genius has finally rounded on her talent. Bravo!' Lottie's face was puffed from crying, ugly with the strain. His golden girl tarnished. He'd have to sort things out, no matter how unpleasant.

He hadn't slept for thinking about Billie and Edward. Billie and Ed. He was the only one who called him Ed. Cordelia took him to task about it once in that rather commanding way of hers. 'We don't give in to abbreviations in my household,' as if his predilection for such language was somehow morally suspect. Billie and Ed playing house at his expense. He still thought of Brabbington Terrace as his, though his mum had urged him to give it to Billie as part of the divorce settlement. Against the advice of his solicitor he'd complied. 'You've given her so little. You walked out of a permanent job the week Jamie was born and now you're walking into a second marriage six months after Lottie arrived,' mum said. And that was that. He moved on to a new life with Beth, the twins, High Pines and two nannies. Billie got 3 Brabbington Terrace.

Of course, there was the guilt and awkwardness at the beginning but after a few years things settled into a routine. He thought they respected each other. And now this! It's like looking at trees in the garden. You get to recognise their seasonal dress. It's restful. Then one day you look out and you get a bare tree in summer. And you know something's wrong. Women! You can't ever know what's going on in their heads. Not fully, anyway. Maybe it was a menopausal fling. He'd read about women like that. Terrified of growing older they grabbed any young skin who'd jump into bed with them. A youth tonic. He'd written about such women. They gave good mini-series value. Catered for a huge audience. And how the hell was he to placate Wendy with the prospect of his two daughters for the entire summer holidays?

Was it only last year he and Wendy were in Greece together when Ludo was only a bump! This year all of them were going for a month but Wendy keeps changing her mind about the departure date. You had to hand it to old Pam. She spotted Billie and Ed. Sharp eyes had Pam. Sharper tongue. Pity about the body, though. She gave in too much to her lazy streak. He pulled in his stomach and glared at the screen. A whole bloody morning wasted. Billie's fault. He couldn't bear the thought of Ed in bed with her. She was his. Always had been. Oh he knew about the few sordid weekends in country hotels when he ran off with Beth. She'd told him herself one Friday when he was late picking up Lottie. She spewed it at him at the door in Brabbington Terrace. But Ed was different, almost family.

Tony had been the only serious man in her life. For years it had given him a quiet satisfaction that she couldn't replace him. Almost like a respected first wife who had been cast aside in the ancient Chinese tradition, to make way for wife number two, three and whatever number was to follow. Wife number one in her own house but still under the spell and power of her husband. He had loved her. Sometimes, when he took time to reflect, he knew some of his happiest moments had been when they first moved into Brabbington Terrace. They had nothing then but their hopes and the tenants of the house to keep them afloat.

It was glorious. Every morning waking to Billie, her long limbs reaching for him, her dark spy's hair inciting him to love. Once, when they'd almost shouted in climax, she had to hold him so tightly he thought his heart was pounding for the two of them. She was sitting up but he was astride her and he looked past her to Jamie's cot. Their noise must have woken him. Jamie was staring through the bars of his cot, wide-eyed and interested, a studious look on his baby face. He had an urge to cover Billie, even though her back, that long naked back that he loved so much, was the only part of her that Jamie could see.

Hard to imagine Jamie was the same age now as he had been then. They always had breakfast together. Billie spooned food into his own mouth as well as Jamie's to encourage him in his pursuit of solids. Breast was best in Jamie's mind and as a child he was a picky eater. After breakfast, Tony would climb down the dark stairs to the cellar, his office. There among the lines of damp washing and half-used tins of paint he wrote. His desk at that time was a trestle table abandoned by the previous owners, his chair a jumble-sale bargain picked up for £3, a red leatherette swivel chair. He banged out his words on an old upright Royal typewriter.

He surveys his de luxe cabin. It looks rough and ready on the outside, almost a garden shed. But inside all is silent and harmonious. It is sound-proofed and double-glazed, the walls a simple white throughout. The Swedish firm that built it told him it would last longer than his lifetime and he's beginning to believe them. Large windows look on to trees, shrubs, lawn and the ornamental lake. The furnishings are in a light but durable pine: cupboards, desk, bathroom. The miniature kitchen is discreet. His computer barely disturbs the silence when his fingers touch it. He's come a long way from the dank cellar in Brabbington Terrace but it's there he'd like to be this morning with Billie and baby Jamie.

Tony is used to editing his life, addicted to it almost, but one thing he can't edit out is that Billie was the best. The best in bed and the best company. Theirs had been an innocent uninhibited love that held nothing back. They fitted together. There were no borderlands to the expression of that love. They shared a sense of humour. Afterwards, Beth's social sophistication could never make up for her obsession with germs and the no-go areas of their lovemaking. Later still, Wendy's childish allure and pliancy did not compensate for her lack of energy. The knowledge that Ed, whom he'd helped to make sandcastles and later on to paint toy soldiers, was now prince of Billie's body made him suffer in a way he was quite unprepared for. He cursed into his expensive silence and glared at his empty screen.

Stella visits Jamie in the afternoon. She wears a black backless dress four inches above the knee. This improves Mr White's low blood-pressure enormously. He's the octogenarian in the next bed to Jamie's. It distresses the nurse, the angelic Ms Cauldwell who had been harbouring fantasies about Jamie since she came on duty at eight and who now realises that she is out of her league. Stella amuses Jamie with tales of mayhem at her morning rehearsal. The play, a second-rate comedy of greed set in the eighties, is tough going, not least because the director spends a lot of time exploring what he calls 'motivation versus compulsion' in all the main characters. Jamie rubs her back as much as he can with his free arm.

'Nellie rang. She said Darren is free if you want him to finish the job. I said I'd ring her tonight. I think it's a good idea. We don't want to be living in chaos for too much longer. Billie rang to say Susan's on night duty this week and she'll be in to see you herself this evening. She left a message for Tony. No doubt he'll ring or call later.'

'Not until he's finished his four thousand words. Bernie sent a courier with a file for me to work on. Beecham isn't at all pleased with my indisposition. Downright carelessness is his diagnosis of the situation. I'll be out in three to four days. They've got people sleeping in corridors here and waiting lists that go on for ever.'

It is noon before Goldie can force himself up out of bed. It has been years since he's had a hangover and at first when he wakes he thinks he is coming down with something. A thumping headache makes his temples tick and a sour stomach feels like a gravel pit. He knows he will have to take things easy. He struggles out of bed, makes a pot of sweet strong tea and hugs the cup to himself as he drinks. What a night! He really enjoyed himself. He's been feeling far too sorry for himself of late. Maybe old age made you like that if you weren't careful. In spite of his hangover he feels better than he has for a long time. He had danced with Susan, the pretty nurse from upstairs. She more or less womanhandled him into it. Billie had danced with Edward, and Babs and Cordelia made up a twosome.

There had been spontaneous nights of drink and dancing like that years ago when Tony lived here, but that seemed like another age and Goldie had always left early, confining himself to his rule of socialisation: 'an hour is enough, a minute over that is too much.' Edward and he had played mazurkas, the women twirling themselves into flowing dances that were spirited and inventive. He had never seen Cordelia drunk before. It suited her. She grew girlish and energetic. And Susan had certainly been touching. She told him how his tape of Tchaikovsky's First had helped her work through her anger and misery over Darren. In fact, it had opened up her mind and ears to classical music. Posh music she called it. That had pleased him enormously. Then she kissed him full on the mouth. A shock. Women had pecked him on the cheek for years. That sleight of lips, the social kiss. Not since Irina had he been kissed like that. And he responded. Much to his surprise. He thought all of that had long since died. After Irina there could be no other for him.

She came to him still in dreams. Black hair loose on the pillow, her green eyes and full lips inviting. Always the same image. She never walks or runs. She lies still, close to him. A twenty-four-year-old beauty, one of the millions that Uncle Joe annihilated in his camps. The kiss with Susan does not feel like betrayal. It feels like life. He's been too much in on himself lately, shutting out the world more and more. Tied to the minutiae of his own habits. Maybe it was time to expend some energy. He was tired of hoarding time, energy, life itself. One splurge might be more vital in the end.

Cordelia plucks dill from her herb patch in the back garden and turns over the events of last night in her mind. She has allowed everything to become overgrown lately, including the herb patch. The mint has spread and coarsened. She decides to thin it out. Maybe dig it out entirely and confine its growth in a new pot, then sink that back into the soil. She starts to loosen the soil with a shovel, then digs. The chives look healthy, She adds them to almost everything in summer. She wears her old straw gardening hat as the sun is baking the earth. Her headache has reduced itself to a vague pain. She has drunk innumerable cups of tea since early morning. At forty-eight, this is only her second hangover. She has led a tidy and abstemious life apart from her brief marriage to Geoffrey, which was chaotic and stressful.

She had been a secretary in a prep school when she met Geoffrey. For four years she had typed letters to parents, the board of management, old boys. She helped matron when the youngest boys got ill, soothing away aches and pains with funny tales of her own invention. Life was ordered. Both her parents had died in a car crash when she was ten and Aunt Maude, her mother's sour sister, had unwillingly taken her to live with her in her neat house in Pinner. There was no question of university after grammar school. Aunt Maude persuaded her it would be a waste, indicated not too subtly that it was now her duty to get a career and a flat of her own. She was seventeen years old. She enrolled in Miss Bentwood-Smythe's Commercial Academy for young ladies.

She wore the regulation suit, hat and Cuban-heeled shoes like the rest of the inmates, and having graduated top of her class she was placed in the prep school where her loyalty and hard work were exploited to the full and she covered the work of two secretaries for less than the price of one. She rented a bedsit within ten minutes of the school and she visited Aunt Maude for Sunday tea in Pinner. Living within a stone's throw she was often put upon by the school authorities to cover this or that emergency. Pouring the lemonade at sports day, dealing with parents' complaints or queries at formal school functions.

She wasn't naturally sociable and so her pursuits were solitary: the cinema, art galleries, classical music concerts. She found live theatre too uncouth and had little interest in popular music, which seemed to absorb so many of the leisure hours of her contemporaries. She was on friendly terms with the other flat-dwellers in the house but she had no particular friendships. Her friends from grammar-school days had gone to college and were moving in different circles now. Most of her classmates from Miss Bentwood-Smythe's Academy had proceeded to finishing schools and the appropriate marriage. Their cordon-bleu cooking and secretarial skills were most useful to their new spouses who were making their way in the City or managing minor country estates. They exchanged Christmas cards only.

Then into this solitary life came Geoffrey. He came to the school to advise staff about pension schemes. Tall and dark with outsize blue eyes and a well-kept moustache, he was an instant success. Never mind that the majority of the staff were young men in their twenties struggling with a minority sexual preference and a meagre salary. He persuaded them to look ahead to when they were sixty. A ghastly thought for most of them. After his second visit, the majority of them had signed away a percentage of their salary for at least the next twenty years.

On his first visit he came to the office. Mr Hogarth the headmaster was busy. Cordelia was too. She was addressing three-hundred-and-fifty end-of-year reports. Nevertheless she wasn't distressed when he kept up a steady stream of inconsequential chatter as he waited for Mr Hogarth. Unused to any particular male attention in the work place beyond that which her clerical duties necessitated, she was flattered and flustered by Geoffrey's chat. He asked her out to dinner but she declined. On his next visit, he repeated his invitation and she accepted. Within the month, she brought him to Sunday tea in Pinner. Aunt Maude withstood his charms for ten minutes only.

Cordelia was amused as Aunt Maude recounted anodyne details from her later childhood. Geoffrey said. 'What a heroic act, to take on the role of mother and carer of an orphan, particularly an unmarried lady like yourself!'

'It was no more than my duty,' Aunt Maude said, but her thin smile showed she was pleased. 'We always kept ourselves to ourselves and Becky was my only sister. Father hadn't approved of her marriage with Reginald but that was all water under the bridge when they were both killed in a car crash.'

'How tragic!' Geoffrey observed as he helped himself to another slice of fruit cake. 'Delicious,' he pronounced as he finished it. 'Your own recipe?'

'Absolutely,' Aunt Maude said with spirit. 'That recipe was passed down from mother to me and I've told Cordelia the secret as well.'

'I'm all for tradition,' Geoffrey said with conviction. 'There's far too little respect for it in this fast and flash age. After all . . . ' Geoffrey's voice deepened with *gravitas* . ' . . . if you hadn't been filled with family loyalty poor little Cordelia might have ended up with total strangers.'

'Well not exactly,' Aunt Maude confided. 'I had agreed to become Cordelia's guardian if anything happened her parents. Becky had, I suppose one would call it a premonition about two years before her death, and she had the documents drawn up then. Of course, at the time, I signed them to humour her. She had lost a baby, a premature birth, and the trauma had unhinged her somewhat. Made her morbid. Reginald said she became overwhelmed by thoughts of death. In a way I signed to help her recovery.'

'And did it?' Geoffrey enquired.

'Absolutely. She became calm and cheerful and quite her old self again.'

During Geoffrey's tea with Aunt Maude, Cordelia found out the answers to questions she herself had wanted to ask Aunt Maude for years. This astounded her and convinced her that Geoffrey was an unusual man. Aunt Maude, to her knowledge, had never confided in anyone. On their next Sunday visit Geoffrey asked her aunt for permission to marry Cordelia. She said yes without a moment's hesitation.

Cordelia stops her digging and sits down on a deck chair near the herb patch, asking herself why she's raking over old ground after all this time. What good will it do? She hasn't thought about Geoffrey for years. Trained herself not to. And it has worked up until now. Last night's sighting of Edward and Billie, their naked limbs so relaxed in sleep after making love, has disturbed her in a way that is foreign to her. Not since Geoffrey's desertion twenty-five years ago has she felt such pain. And yet with the pain is a restless vitality that seems to offer some new insights into . . . she's not quite sure what. Of course, she feels she's made a complete ass of herself swirling about to mazurka music and talking until God know's what hour but it felt good, letting go, participating with other people in the silly things in life.

At one point, towards dawn, she had a moment of clarity which made her feel that whatever happened between Billie and Edward, it would be all right. In the half-light, their heads leaning against each other, they almost looked like siblings. Their dark thin looks assumed a similarity and symmetry that Cordelia felt the others must notice too. She was about to voice these insights to the room in general but Goldie, refilling her glass with his strong Russian vodka, interrupted the flow of her thoughts.

Geoffrey left when Cordelia was six months pregnant. She didn't worry for a few days as he travelled a lot in his work. That Wednesday morning they had breakfast together as usual. She had packed his travel suitcase for him. Shirts, socks, underwear, pyjamas. Nothing more. He said he's be back in three to four days and to take care of herself and the baby. He patted her bump affectionately before he walked out the door for ever. After a week, she rang his office and was told he hadn't worked for the company for the past three months. When she reported him missing to the police they were patient and polite.

Her dreams were full of fears. Geoffrey murdered on the M1, his body carved into pieces and later dumped in a forest miles away. Geoffrey killed by a hit-and-run driver miles from nowhere. Geoffrey, his memory lost, not knowing who he was, suffering and taking on a new identity under the supervision of a psychiatrist. Four weeks before Edward was born, the police knocked on her door to tell her the true whereabouts of Geoffrey. His real name was Philip and he was a bigamist. He'd 'married' two other women and fathered two children on both of them. He was by then being detained at Her Majesty's expense for bigamy, fraud and debt. She was coldly courteous with them and thanked them for their efforts before closing the door on them and her life with Geoffrey. It had been a year and a half of pleasure and love and now there was desertion and disgrace. She told herself at that moment that there could be no room for silliness or self-pity in the life that lay ahead of her.

She changed her name by deed poll so that the new life that

she was carrying would not be sullied by its father's deeds. A few months after Edward's birth she asked Mr Hogarth for her old job back. He had replaced her, of course, but she was shrewd enough to know that no one could do as much work as she had done. And she was right. Mr Hogarth employed her on a part-time basis with no holiday pay or other securities. He offered her a tiny flat in a converted stables on the school grounds. She had agreed with Mr Hogarth that the best story to tell the schoolboys was that she had been tragically widowed. And so her life was once more respectable if straitened.

There were no luxuries and Aunt Maude could no longer bear her to come for Sunday teas to her neat house in Pinner. She said Edward reminded her too much of Geoffrey. He had swindled her out of a thousand pounds. It had been their little secret. Cordelia had known nothing about it. At first she'd invested fifty pounds with Geoffrey and he'd doubled her money for her within a month. Then he'd invested a hundred for her and doubled that within six weeks. And so she parted with more money. She could not forgive Cordelia for choosing so unwisely.

When Aunt Maude died five years later Cordelia fully expected her to have left her worldly goods to some institution or other. But she hadn't and Cordelia was the sole beneficiary. She was able to bid adieu to the stable flat that Mr Hogarth had insisted on calling a mews and buy a house in Brabbington Terrace. The house was large but in need of considerable repair. She got it at a knock-down price and took pride in setting it to rights. How they had revelled in the space! Running and shouting into all the rooms. So much space after the dark and poky confinement of the stable. She knew they were going to be happy here. Some days after she moved in, the doorbell rang and she opened the door to a tall dark-haired Irish woman who held an apple pie in one hand and a small boy about the same age as Edward by the other.

'I'm Billie,' the woman said. 'Welcome to the terrace. Your son and mine have already made friends and my husband would like to take Edward fishing with Jamie on Saturday.' This woman became her best friend. Until this summer.

Edward is practising. His fingers race the keyboard in their own intimate drama. He's playing Mussorgsky's 'Songs and Dances of Death'. He's almost on automatic until he gets to the part where the drunk meets Death on the lonely road and the folk lamentations frighten him. He stops. He doesn't want to think about death. Life is so good to him just now. His love for Billie is out in the open and once Lottie adjusts to the idea all will be well. It's natural for a teenage girl to rebel and run off. She'd get over it in time.

He thinks about last night's mazurkas. Goldie and himself thumping them out and the women inventing their own versions of the dance. He was pleased that Cordelia enjoyed the music. The sight of Billie and himself on the couch when she came in must have been arresting. They had been so careful up to then, discreetly meeting at his place, Billie going back home on her own. The tension of Lottie's departure had lowered their guard and of course, they weren't expecting anyone to come in without ringing the doorbell first. The key at Cordelia's was only there for emergencies.

When Babs rang her with news of Jamie's accident, she had taken the emergency key as she had done maybe a dozen or so times before down through the years, to tell Billie face-to-face that Jamie was injured but not seriously. It had been instinctive. Edward knew that. Cordelia didn't pry. It wasn't in her nature. As an only child he was more than grateful that she had given him personal space and not smothered him with curiosity like other mothers. She had simply come to save Billie pain. To talk to her about Jamie instead of telephoning her. They had both used their emergency keys for acts of kindness and support throughout their long friendship.

Edward has memories, some of them embarrassing now when he thinks about them. Billie used to let herself into his house during nights of his childhood when he was fevered and ill, to give Cordelia a few hours rest. He has a vivid memory of her sponging his burning body down. He had turned his head to the wall in his embarrassment and she pretended not to notice his unease. He forces his fingers back to Mussorgsky's drunkard and Death but he knows he's only playing at concentrating. His mind won't settle. Death! Cordelia's parents were both killed in a car crash when she was ten years old. His own father was killed in a hit-and-run accident a month before he was born.

Edward is superstitious. He doesn't want to let anything spoil his happiness of the moment. He will take extra care when driving and be vigilant when he travels by tube. There have been so many bomb scares recently in London. Lewis, first violin in the orchestra, had said last Tuesday when his train was delayed for forty minutes, 'Those bloody Irish bombers. I'd love to blow them all from here to kingdom come.' Edward found himself defending the Irish, Billie's people. 'They're not all terrorists.

'Paddy-lover,' Lewis retorted.

He has often thought about Cordelia's despair when she learned of his father's death just before his birth. Every few years he asks her about it. He knows it causes her pain but he can't help himself. It's almost as if his father's life was taken to replace his. When he asks her she tells him about the two policemen coming to the door. His father had been travelling on business. He wasn't expected home until the weekend. They came on a Thursday morning and told her. She remembers thanking them as if they'd brought good news. It was only as the weeks passed and his father did not come home that she realised he was gone forever.

Ever since he can remember asking her she would say, 'You didn't know your father but he loved you. He was an exciting, energetic man full of ideas and plans. I loved him passionately. Our life together was very brief but happy. Some people go through a lifetime without meeting anyone to love. While I had him, I wanted him. There aren't many people who can say that.'

He was going to meet Billie at the hospital tonight. He wished he could think of something silly and funny to bring to Jamie. He'd always been a bad patient. That time both of them fell out of the tree in Billie's back garden, Jamie had howled all the way to the hospital in the ambulance. He had watched him, fascinated that one person could make so much noise. As it turned out it was he who had broken his leg. Jamie's was just sprained. Tony had been as fussed as Jamie. Cordelia calmed him down and prevented him from telling the entire hospital staff that they were a crowd of neanderthals. She had got him to walk her outside for fresh air on the pretext that she felt faint. Back to the music. He spreads his fingers, touches the keys and tells himself he'd better cultivate an impersonal acceptance of death, at least for the duration of the music.

Marian is sitting under an apple tree in the garden. She's pretending to read a book about China but her heart isn't in it. She looks at the pictures and lets her mind wander. She doesn't want Lottie engaging her in conversation just to prove to Tony what a pleasant person she is. The 'I can get on with my ugly half-sister' act. Things are not working out as she had planned. Now that the school holidays have arrived and she actually has time to zone in on Wendy, the house is full and she can hardly get a minute to torment her. She gave it her best effort at breakfast.

'I'm really looking forward to Greece, Wendy. There's nothing like a family holiday. Closeness, that's what counts isn't it? Those little villas are tiny. Primitive proximity that's what I like on a holiday. Could we squeeze Elvira in? Dad says that's fine with him. Poor Elvira, there's no money for a holiday either this year. Her mum says it's rotten being a single parent. You were lucky dad married you when Ludo came along but then he's a sucker for kids wherever they come from. Isn't that right, Lottie?'

'Shut up, Marian.'

'Try keeping your own mouth shut. It doesn't bloody suit me having you parked here all summer just because your mum stole Goldfinger from you.'

'Elvira can come if you sleep in the second villa with Josh and Toby. I want time on my own with Ludo and Tony. The two villas are side by side. They're two little stone houses. Villa is too grand a word. It would be good for you to have a friend along.' Wendy is weak with the effort of accommodating herself to so many changes of plan. It was so easy working in an office when one could close the files at the end of a day.

Suddenly Lottie is weeping. Big blobby tears. They roll down her cheeks and track her face, neck and nose.

'I can't understand how it happened. She's almost his mother. It's so unfair.'

'Ask Wendy. She'll explain the attractions of an old partner.'

'Sometimes you're vile,' Lottie sobbed. 'You think of nobody but yourself. That's why you're such a misery.'

'I'm not the one who's crying,' Marian says as she leaves the kitchen.

Now, sitting under her favourite tree, she wonders if there's some truth in what Lottie says. In the years since Beth's death, she has been a misery. None of her tantrums prevented Tony marrying Wendy. Ludo is a beautiful baby. There is no denying that. He doesn't seem to notice the horrible things she says about him, even to his face. He gurgles and smiles at her in a trusting forthright way. It isn't his fault that Wendy is his mum. Even Beth had her faults. Not that she liked to think about them much. When she thinks of her mum she summons up an image that is immaculate and groomed. She likes to think of family outings with mum, dad, Toby and Josh. Just the five of them, Sunday mornings in the park or sitting around the pool. A slow motion recollection that is serenely silent.

The tennis ball hits her shoulder. Toby smiles amiably as she retrieves it.

'Sorry about that. Did it hurt? Josh did it.' He's smiling, the blonde fringe in his eyes, his laces undone.

'Of course it did. Do you think I'm made of cardboard? I'll survive. Are you off to Wimbledon then?'

'Not today. Just High Pines, Wimbledon. Josh, myself, Philip and Tom. They're bringing some girls along. Do you want a game? Mixed doubles.'

'I don't think so. I'm meeting Elvira at the Pizza Hut. How about tomorrow? It's about time I got into shape. Just me and you though. No gawpers.'

'You're on,' and he picks up the ball and runs after Josh.

She prefers Toby to Josh. He's easier company. When she was little she had toddled after Toby and he let her. When Josh complained that she was making a mess or interrupting a game Toby sorted it out. Maybe she had held out her hands to Toby just as Ludo does to her? The Chinese called tea 'cha'. That's how the expression 'a cup of char' originated. Antarctica is very lonely. There are no inhabitants there. Very few plants and no trees. In 1626 Manhattan Island was bought from the local Indians for twenty-four dollars worth of trinkets. Maybe she should take Ludo for a walk.

Billie is just leaving the office and breathing a sigh of relief at having got through the day when Mr Wilson asks her to 'Run off two letters, old girl; an absolute emergency, otherwise I wouldn't ask.' Afterwards, she just makes it through the rush-hour traffic to the hospital on time. She has flowers and a few old books she's brought from home and heads towards reception. A nurse tells her the number of Jamie's ward. She nips into the ladies to fix her hair, brush her teeth and swallow an aspirin. Her hangover is still there. A mild thud. It has been a long day.

Tony and Edward are at the foot of Jamie's bed when she gets to the ward. They look like some sickly parody of Victorian distress. You know the kind of picture. The family gathers around the bed as the loved one slips into the next world. She can feel the silence as she approaches.

'Hello, Jamie.' She kisses him. 'Are they looking after you well? Hello, Edward, Tony.'

'They're doing their best, mum, but I'll be happy to leave. Hospitals are so noisy. There's no peace. Besides they wake you at the crack of dawn. I'll be out in a few days.'

'I brought you some flowers to cheer you up and a few of your old books from home.'

'Biggles, Biggles and Biggles.' Jamie examines the books and is delighted. 'Good old mum, just what I need. A regressive trip down memory lane. We can't have a chap going soft when the sky calls, can we?'

'Less of the old,' Billie says.

'Absolutely,' Tony smiles at her. 'Not when she's in the company of her young lover, isn't that right, Ed?' Tony looks from one of them to the other. He's enjoying himself. Edward is conscious that he's blushing but can't stop himself.

'Maybe I should go, meet you later?' he suggests diffidently. He's remembering all the times Tony took him fishing and turned up at sports day at school to play father to him as well as Jamie. 'Family time and all that,' he says lamely.

'There's no need,' Billie insists almost too quickly. 'We're no longer a family. Not in the traditional sense anyway. I'd like you to stay.'

'She left a message on the answering machine telling me about Jamie's accident. Can you imagine anything as callous?' Tony appeals to Edward innocently. Edward looks away, embarrassed.

'For heaven's sake, dad, I'm a grown man of twenty-five, not five years old.' Jamie defends his mother.

'I left the message on your machine because nobody answered the phone. I also faxed you. I know you don't like to be disturbed when you're writing.'

'I was disturbed enough when Lottie arrived on the doorstep with tales of your sexual bliss with Boy Wonder here. She doesn't want to go home.'

'I thought she had two homes. One with me, the other with you. As long as she's being cared for, does it really matter where she spends most of her time. After all it is the summer holidays. Or are you telling me a summer with your own daughter is a hardship? I've taken care of her for fifteen years, apart from weekends of course. Now is as good a time as any for you two to spend time together.'

'I thought you both came to visit me,' Jamie protests. 'I

was wrong, you just want to fling insults at each other.'

'Sorry, darling,' Billie says 'but your dad has such a singular view of life. It's difficult for him to be objective.'

'I can be as objective as the next man but when my wife runs off with her son's best friend, that takes some adjustment.'

They laugh spontaneously, without malice. Tony looks from one to the other and wonders what's so funny.

'Your wife?' Billie splutters. 'It's a long time since I've been that.'

How could he make such an ass of himself? It was all that wandering down memory lane this morning. Raking over the good times in Brabbington Terrace when he should have been filling his screen with words. It made it seem like yesterday really. Billie, baby Jamie, Goldie and the nurses in Brabbington Terrace. A golden age.

'Evening all. How are the hangovers?' The young nurse is smiling as she adjusts Jamie's headrest. Tony wonders if everyone has gone mad.

'Hello Susan,' Billie says. 'This is my ex-husband, Tony.' There's a hint of laughter in the introduction.

'Oh, the one who didn't get the red paint?'

'Exactly,' Billie says.

Babs is relaxing with a gin and tonic in the bath. She likes her bathroom. It's one of her favourite rooms. It's a gentleman's bathroom really. Black and white tiles on the walls and floor, an enormous claw-footed bath, a shower with brass fittings, a formidable oak medicine cabinet and a walk-in dressing room just off it. She's reflecting on her day. Her morning round at the hospital went smoothly. Mr Brogan was surprised when she diagnosed his ulcer.

'I've eaten black puddins all me life. Not to mention me rashers and onion rings. What the bleedin' hell do you mean by a special diet!'

His wife stood patiently by his bed and threw her eyes up to heaven as she smiled at Babs.

'I'll do my best, doctor,' she said earnestly, after Babs had explained the importance of his new regime.

'Bloody doctors! As soon as you go near them you get sick. I don't know why I agreed to come in here in the first place.'

Her other patients didn't argue. The ten-year-old girl who had her tonsils removed and craved a chocolate ice-cream, the battered mother of four whose ribs were healing but wouldn't consider getting a barring order against her husband. The octogenarian, Mrs Phelps, who insisted on entertaining the rest of the ward whether they wanted it or not. She sang her old tunes from a bygone era in a cracked high whine. Her bandaged nose lent pathos to the scene. She had walked into a wall and broken it.

Babs enjoys her work at the hospital. She does only two mornings a week now; the rest of her time she devotes to her private practice, specialist throat problems. Still, her work at the hospital gives her a sense that she is putting something back into the system. She had been very surprised when Jamie and Stella had turned up yesterday. Poor Jamie; even as a child he was always injuring himself one way or another. There was that time he split his lip by bumping into his empty swing. He was only three or four then. Another time, he dressed up as Batman and jumped off the garden shed. He landed on an upturned rake that Billie had carelessly left unattended. He was on crutches for three weeks. There had been a spate of such injuries when Tony had left Billie.

And now Billie has told Lottie about Edward. She had been

surprised by the tableau that had greeted her at Jamie's bed tonight. Tony was obviously cross and bad-tempered. Billie was playing her serene act, the wide-open eyes, the measured tones. Edward was attempting to hide his embarrassment by speaking slowly and carefully instead of at his usual pace. Jamie seemed to have regressed to boyhood as he hid behind a Biggles book and let them get on with it. Now and again, Billie fed him a square of his favourite chocolate, Fry's chocolate cream. Babs had never liked Tony and was surprised how much she now enjoyed his discomfiture. He was behaving like a spurned husband, as if Billie had taken up with Edward to cuckold him. It was tremendous fun to watch.

At first, she had been annoyed when she saw them at Jamie's bed. She'd wanted some time with Jamie on her own. Also, she was still in a delicate state from last night's drinking. She was cross with herself for staying the night at Billie's. She hadn't done that for years. But something about the music and Cordelia's high spirits made her stay. She knew how much it cost Cordelia to join in. She had confided her shock and disappointment to Babs over the past few months but she had also stoically accepted Billie's and Edward's relationship as something she had no right in which to interfere. That greatly impressed Babs and, watching Cordelia's happiness as Edward refilled her glass and asked her to dance, she decided to stay and be drawn into the good humour and atmosphere herself. And it had been a terrific night. Young Susan had really got Goldie on his feet and strutting his stuff.

Standing at Jamie's bed and watching Tony throw his poisoned arrows at Billie with his gags such as, 'I'll get Pam Henderson to give you the name of her plastic surgeon. She says he's wonderful. He can knock off at least ten years,' or 'You know all his childhood illnesses. Still, you should check up on what he's been up to since.

Just in case, one has to be so careful these days,' she found herself attacking Tony in a primitive defence of her sister. How ironic! Particularly when she's told Billie she's making a fool of herself.

'You can hardly talk. Wendy is half your age.'

'Bristling Babs. I see you haven't lost any of the old form. It hasn't got you a man though, has it?'

'Not that my private life is any of your business, Tony, Philip and I are quite happy with our arrangement.'

'Ah, your arrangement with Philip!' he mocked. 'I forgot about that momentarily. One can only admire his consistency.' And he bowed to her with exaggerated formality.

He really is a nasty man, Babs reflects as she sips her gin. Her arrangement with Philip suited them both perfectly. Separate flats but they spent every second weekend together. One weekend at her place, the next time at his. Neither of them cares for the domestic claustrophobia of the average marriage. They enjoy their independence and their weekends together. They have their work in common. Philip is a gynaecologist. Neither of them wanted children. It's perfect. She wasn't going to let Tony throw stones. 'Perfect,' she repeats as she steps from the bath and pulls a bathrobe around her. But there's something niggling her about her attitude to Billie's affair. Wasn't there, if she was being honest, a horrible moment of jealousy when she met them that weekend at the hotel?

She had known what they were up to immediately. Apart from the initial shock, she was amazed that Billie could attract handsome young Edward to her bed. But then she'd always known that Billie had inherited all the striking qualities of her parents. Height, dark spare looks. It was almost as if she herself was a throwback to some squat, compact forebears, cottiers and potato growers from the last century. She had always envied Billie's height and grace. She herself had become Daddy's girl through sheer effort and hard work. She was the doctor and Daddy's favourite but without her black bag would that have been so?

She decides to cheer herself up by checking out next weekend's musical events. Maybe Philip would like to go to a concert? Philip, the man she loves. Philip, the man she tells herself she loves?

She looks at herself in the steamy mirror. Her face mask has congealed to a tragi-comic hardness and she smiles, causing little cracks, breakthrough rivers on the skin. She swigs the dregs of her gin and tonic and toasts herself, wiping away some steam from the mirror with her left hand as if she'll discover something new if she looks more carefully at her image. The mask is impenetrable. Only the eyes and the mouth look familiar. She fills the sink with warm water and begins to wash her face, using cotton wool buds. Each bud turns turquoise from the face mask. She sets them afloat, festival boats on water. Philip, the man she tells herself she loves?

Maybe Tony is more than the insensitive boor she had thought him from day one. Her 'arrangement' with Philip? Had they been her words or Tony's? Arrangement sounded cold and calculating somehow. Last night there had been such an air of freedom and abandonment at Brabbington Terrace. They had all been seduced by it. Billie and Edward seemed to belong together. Their black short-haired heads inclined. The eyes following each other when they moved to different parts of the room. Billie seemed relaxed and casual in a black silk shirt and tight jeans. She was barefoot and moved with a combination of grace and abandon when she danced, her Giacometti height and slenderness dominating the room. Babs had felt like the runt of the litter, the block of wood who lacks shape and form until the sculptor puts hands on it – instead of the eldest sibling, the one who leads.

Is Tony right to sneer at her neat life with Philip? Is there something missing in them that they do not crave that cave of domesticity that most people go in for? Even when they spend weekends together they don't sleep the night through in one bed. When he comes to her place, they share the large oak bed. Generally they doze together after making love. Then he goes to the guest room. When she goes to his place, they move with the waves of his water-bed and afterwards she goes to sleep on the doctor's couch in his study. Both of them snore. Early on in their relationship they had decided not to disturb each other. Now when Babs thinks of Edward and Billie in Jamie's childhood bedroom clinging to each other in that narrow bed, a wave of jealousy engulfs her.

Philip is lying on his water-bed thinking of Babs. He's looking through a programme of a musical evening he's booked for them next weekend. It's Britten's *Te Deum* in C, Purcell's *Funeral Sentences* and Bernstein's *Chichester Psalms*. Not really his cup of tea at all but Babs will love it. He has no time for religious music. He was raised in an indifferent C of E household which left him free of any religious inclinations. Babs grew up in a Catholic household and although she has long protested she's 'free of all that', and proclaimed herself a 'non-practising Catholic,' a contradiction in terms if ever there was one, he is aware of her Catholic leanings and likes to indulge them from time to time. He smiles. Babs quite often makes the mistake that many pragmatists make, thinking that if they say something is true then it makes it so. He loves her and lets most of it pass over him. Occasionally to tease her he presses home his version of the truth. He looks at the programme again.

Adonai, Adonai   Lord, Lord
lo gravah libi   my heart is not haughty

He turns out his light and is soon asleep, snoring his way

through a dream of the Hallelujah Chorus. The choir is in a Catholic cathedral. Babs is conducting in an energetic style. Her baton rises and falls to the music. His eyes take in the gaudy Stations of the Cross, the overlit altars of saints and martyrs. He is invited to burn incense but the master of the maternity hospital intervenes and reminds him it is not in his contract.

Nellie is feeding Bob the titbits of the day's gossip at the Mansions. Bob wants to look at the replay of mixed doubles from Wimbledon in peace. He eats his take-away fish and chips from his lap.

'Not even a plate,' Nellie protests, as she pushes a plate aggressively under his bag of chips. 'I've always taken pride in my surroundings.' She looks about her at her purple-striped three-piece suite and matching curtains and sniffs with pride. Bob's eyes have not left the screen. 'I collected our holiday snaps. We look ever so snazzy in our dancin' gear.'

She places the photo on Bob's knee and blocks out the TV screen as she does so. He looks down at a blurred picture of Nellie and himself. She's wearing a full-skirted red satin strapless evening dress and he's wearing a monkey suit. They're smiling proudly into the camera. They won third prize in the foxtrot competition at Butlins last month. The same night he'd had a dicky tummy but Nellie wouldn't let him get out of it. They'd celebrated their victory with the Pennycooks from Edinburgh, a young couple with three small children. Nellie went on the gin for the night but he'd stuck to ale.

'Very nice, love,' he says as he hands it back to her.

'What a day I've had, Bob! You can't imagine. Bloody hold-ups to and from Victoria. Startin' and finishin' the day with bomb scares and delays is no kind of life. And when I get to Brabbington

Terrace there's a queer lot of mixed doubles goin' on. First I see Darren's Susan perched up on a kitchen stool with Edward. You know Edward?' She waits for a reply.

'That's Funnyfingers, the prodigy i'n' it?'

'Yea, him. There he was with Darren's Susan havin' breakfast.'

'She's not Darren's no more, now that he's done a runner with 'er in number fifteen.' Bob figures if he talks for a bit, he can get back to the game. Nellie is a stickler for what she calls communication in their relationship. Relationship, he didn't know that's what they had. He blames the soaps himself. Nellie sets the timer to video them when she's at work and gorges herself on the week's soaps at the weekends.

'That's immaterial,' Nellie says with tone. Immaterial, it's her word for this week. She learns a new word each week, writes it down in her vocabulary notebook and uses it every chance she gets. Life was easier before Nellie took that literacy course.

'As I said, it's immaterial,' Nellie repeats herself with satisfaction. 'There was Susan and Edward perched on stools at the breakfast counter and I suspected the worst straight away. They were lookin' like cats that shared the cream. 'But I was totally wrong. Do you know who he had been doin' it with?'

Bob's eyes swivel from the screen and he tries to come up with a likely floosie for Funnyfingers. Nellie taps her toes. He gobbles a few chips to concentrate.

'One of them prima donnas. An opera singer, like they have on Channel Four.'

'It could have been,' Nellie says reflectively. 'Good thinkin', Bob,' she says as if she's awarding points. 'But it wasn't. It was . . .' and she pauses dramatically, ' . . . it was Billie.'

'Are you sure?' Bob likes Billie.

'Course I'm sure. Edward told me bold as brass. And

that's not all. Young Lottie's run off to her da's. She feels her mum snatched Edward from her right under her nose.'

'Her da has done more than his share of babysnatchin'. Still, it's different for a man. An older man is distinguished. A young woman can look up to 'im. He can teach her things.'

'Like what?'

Nellie's belligerence alarms him. 'Like how the world works, how to get on,' he says lamely.

'Like how to service an old randy goat, you mean.'

'It won't last,' Bob warns.

'Nothin' lasts,' Nellie says sourly. 'Look at Darren and Susan. I'm left with my mother-of-the-groom outfit and nowhere to wear it to.'

Wendy can't sleep. It's not just that Ludo's suckling woke her. Before having Ludo she had no idea of the enormous pleasure she would get from feeding him. A sexual pleasure almost. Sometimes she wonders if other women feel the same but none of her friends have children so she has no one to talk to about it. She hopes there's nothing wrong with such feelings. Tony has been odd and difficult since Lottie arrived the other night. And tonight when he got home from the hospital after visiting Jamie he went straight to the fridge and made a double-decker sandwich, piling everything on to it, cheese, ham, gherkins, tomatoes, cucumber. She was astounded. He never ate after seven o'clock in the evenings. Something was up.

He brushed her enquiries aside, told her Jamie would be fine but that it was his mother, Billie, who was in need of hospitalisation.

'They stood there on either side of Jamie's bed,' he said with feeling, as he spread low-cal mayonnaise on his high-rise sandwich.

'She had a skirt that went almost up to her armpits. He had a nervous smile on his face as if everyone should be happy for them. Can you believe that?'

Wendy didn't know what to say. She was confused by his anger and his obvious upset. Why should it bother him what Billie did? She was the old first wife, the one he had discarded years before. Then it hit her. The year Tony left Billie, she herself had been ten years old, almost the same age as Jamie was then. Why the hell should he get annoyed that Billie was having a fling with Edward? Was it because he was the same age as Jamie and herself? Up to this it had been Beth's ghost that she feared. From time to time when the house gets out of hand even with Nellie's ministrations, Tony will sigh and say, 'Beth would die if she saw this pigsty.' She never points out the fact that Beth is dead and it is her house now. Mostly because she doesn't feel it is hers.

It's Tony's house and the children's and Nellie's but somehow it eludes her. There seems hardly any time between Ludo's feeds to get a life going for herself. Now, on top of all of this he's upset with Billie. It's exhausting. Why couldn't life be more clear-cut? Relationships that are long since past their sell-by date shouldn't spill into the present. She has a house full of other women's children. When she met Tony first she was attracted to the fullness of his life. He was a man of experience. An older man who could guide her through calm seas and stormy ones too. It would be an adventure. With her youth and his age and experience they would make a good team. Since then she's learned that Tony is a one-man band. Now, he's peeved that someone whom he'd already thrown out of the orchestra is tuning up her violin with the solo pianist.

Nellie knew all the details of the recent goings-on. Wendy realised it the minute Nellie appeared during lunchtime today.

She and Lottie were at each end of the long kitchen table. Ludo was crawling about banging saucepans. Wendy had made a spinach quiche with salad and apart from Ludo's childish clangings there was peace as they ate. Both girls loved spinach.

'Afternoon all,' Nellie greeted them as she plonked her bag on the draining-board. 'I was held up on the Victoria line again this morning, more bloody bombs. I was a half an hour late when I got to the terrace, so I've been chasin' my tail all morning. I'll have a cuppa before I start.'

'I'll make it, Nellie,' Marian says brightly and she's on her feet with a smile and waiting on the old crone as if she's Lady Muck. Marian hustles by Karin, the *au pair*, who is liquidising carrots for Ludo, and pulls out the plug of the liquidiser.

'You must use the other power point,' Karin admonishes Marian in that accented didactic tone in which she speaks English.

'It will only take a moment,' Marian says. 'I'll plug it back in for you then.'

'I have cleaned the bedrooms, Nellie. I woke up this morning with too much energy. Josh and Toby did their own room. I think they are a little infatuated with me. That is good if it makes them tidy.' Karin smiles at Nellie as she speaks.

'You're an angel,' Nellie assures her. 'Like a cuppa?'

Wendy concentrates on her food and tries not to mind too much. Sometimes she feels she is the odd one out in Tony's team. She looks at the potted mallow on the patio with its delicate but abundant colour. Light pink to mauve, one of her favourite shades.

'Would you like some quiche?' she asks Nellie, determined to be pleasant and in spite of herself relieved by the sudden quietness.

'What's in it?' Nellie asks suspiciously.

'Spinach and it's delicious,' Lottie says.

'In that case, I'll stick to a slice of bread and butter. Can't stand spinach. Too strong a flavour for me but you enjoy it, Lottie; you'll need your strength.'

And Wendy knew that she'd already got the full story of Lottie's flight at Brabbington Terrace. Why was she stuck with this nosy bitch? Marian pours tea for Nellie and Karin refills Wendy's cup.

'Can I take Ludo for a walk, Wendy?' Marian says.

Wendy is alarmed. Marian has never given Ludo much attention up to this. She swallows her tea slowly and panic rises. An image of Marian running headlong down a hill with Ludo in his pram looms.

'Where to?'

'Just around the gardens in his pram.'

'Let her take him,' Nellie urges. 'You can help me clear out the pantry. I'd be ever so grateful.' Nellie flashes her full set of false teeth.

Wendy feels she is invisible.

Billie wakes in Edward's bed. Her nose is almost to the wall. He is curled in tightly behind her, his hand cradling her belly. She moves her legs, forcing him to move his. She turns and looks at his half-closed eyes. Knee to knee, belly to belly, he pulls her towards him and stops her mouth with a kiss before she can speak. His intensity pleases her. Their wet mouths swallow and suck. She can still taste him on her mouth from last night when she sucked him to climax before they both fell into an exhausted sleep. Their tastes and smells are mingling now in the intimate tent of the bed. She guides his hand from breast to vulva and arches her body to pleasure. Her cry is loud and clear. A good job the flat is sound-proofed, she thinks, as she climbs over him on the way to the loo. He's still not fully awake. She runs a brisk hot shower and is dressed with a cup of black coffee in her hand by the time Edward wakes fully.

'I've got to run to beat the traffic,' she says.

She pecks him on the mouth and runs off before she can be sucked back into that tunnel of pleasure again.

'A woman has to put bread on the table,' she says as she goes.

Traffic isn't too bad. She should make it to the office on time. 'Punctuality is one of the first laws of business,' is one of Mr Wilson's favourite maxims. For months now her office life has been functioning on automatic. Mr Wilson's dire warnings about recession and competition have hardly touched her. She's been aware of them only as one is aware of background music. You note it's there but after that you don't listen. She's tackled her work with energy and speed, newly alive to the energy that she wants to expend elsewhere with Edward. She switches on a tape and is astounded when Tony's voice fills the car. Her attention is distracted momentarily and she almost runs into the car ahead of her when it stops suddenly. Before she can register what he's saying she tries to figure out how the tape got there in the first place.

They had met twice at the hospital when visiting Jamie but that was all. It was the most direct contact they had had in years, certainly since Lottie had grown. She was sure she'd listened to a James Galway tape on her way to Edward's last night. She had been careful to lock the car. It had been put there after that. She shivered at the realisation of what that implied. Anger coupled with a sense of invasion took hold. How dare he? What the bloody hell was he up to? After fifteen years of her getting on with her own life, how dare he intrude now? She listened to the tape. She'd missed the beginning of it. ' . . . You will always have a special place in my heart, Billie. I know when you get over this silly fling with Edward you will ask yourself, why didn't anyone warn me?

I'm speaking as a friend, someone who cares about you deeply. If you only knew how much you've hurt Lottie, I'm sure you'd change your mind. We've all been through infatuations. It's part of the human condition. But Jamie's childhood playmate . . . If you thought about it deeply you'd realise you're Edward's aunt. Not by blood strictly speaking. Aunts don't sleep with their nephews except in incestuous classical plays. Stop now before you're in too deep.'

The words took hold of her, filling the car, her head. She stopped the tape before she could hear any more. What was he? Her guardian angel. The fifteen-year-old can of red paint in the garden shed, the one she hadn't used, came to mind. Maybe if she had used it, he wouldn't be preaching to her now. 'Do as I say, not as I do,' was obviously his attitude to her. Arrogant bastard.

Billie decides as she slips the tape on to the passenger car seat that she doesn't need anyone to purge her of Edward, least of all Tony! She recalls the bliss of the chocolate cake and the taste of Edward in her mouth last night. She wonders if the pot of red paint has solidified in the tin. She decides to post the tape to Wendy at High Pines. Let Tony talk his way out of that one. She edges her Mini into her usual space outside the office and only then notices the painters and decorators talking to Mr Wilson on the pavement. He's waving his hands about and giving instructions. She goes to her office and plugs in the coffee-maker. She needs a mug of strong black coffee.

'Ah, there you are,' Mr Wilson observes a few minutes later, as if he'd been looking for her for a long time. 'They've arrived. I've changed my mind about the colour for the outside windows and door. Signal red. A powerful colour, full of strength, a colour with drive. I've got the same firm of decorators as Pargeter, Phelps and Dodds, and as you know they're a firm without blemish. I'm aiming for tone and drive and I'm jolly well going to see that I get it.'

Signal red. That's the colour of the ancient tin of paint in her shed.

Mr Goldberg is having tea with Susan at Cream Delight, a local coffee shop. They've had a leisurely walk around the park with Anne, Susan's flatmate. She hasn't joined them for tea. She's meeting her future mother-in-law in Richmond and she's gone back to the flat to put on her best dress and face before the encounter. She's nervous. She's marrying a man who was raised in a town house, and who went to a summer house in Cornwall or to Europe throughout his childhood. She grew up in a high-rise flat in Brixton and went to the local school, where she had to put up a fight to hold on to her dinner money. Nursing has been the pinnacle of her ambition. Besides, her skin is black. No matter how often Jeremy has assured her that Mummy is amazingly liberal she can't quell her nerves. Goldie and Susan spent the walk reassuring her of her talents and grace but she remains unconvinced.

'Tea?' Susan asks as she mothers Goldie. She's already buttered his scone. He's wearing the spotted bow tie she bought him last week. He knows it clashes with his striped waistcoat and suit but he doesn't mind. He's having a good time. His daily walks with Susan and sometimes Anne have become the highlight of his days and he doesn't want to question this simple happiness.

'Yes, my dear, thank you.' He moves his cup towards her.

'Anne is doin' herself no favours puttin' herself down like that. She's a real stunner, i'n't she? Jeremy's a lucky man. He's a bit stuffy but maybe all solicitors are like that. I never met one before him. He's ever so nice to Anne. I'll miss her when she's gone. We've been great mates but maybe her marriage will change all o' that. It won't be the same when she's livin' in Richmond.'

'You'll still see her at the hospital,' Goldie reassures her.

'She wants me to go to the weddin' but I'm a bit nervous. I'm sure Jeremy's people are very fancy. I might wear the wrong thing. I know I'm common as muck.'

'Now, now!' Goldie shakes his head at her, 'Weren't you scolding Anne for putting herself down just now! You mustn't make the same mistake yourself. I'm sure anything you choose would be charming.'

'Me mum says my taste is so loud it could be heard in Honolulu and since Darren's run off with Jenny I've gone right off weddins. Besides, I've no one to bring. The invitation said Susan Armstrong and friend.'

'I'm sure you've got lots of friends to choose from,' Goldie says smoothly.

'Not really,' Susan laughs infectiously. 'In Brixton, where Anne and me come from, the only man you'd ask to a weddin' would be a fiancé or your husband. We didn't go in for those . . . what do you call them? . . . pla . . . something relationships.'

'Platonic,' Goldie rescues her. 'If you're absolutely stuck, my dear, and you could bear the company of an old fogey like me I would be only too delighted to accompany you to Anne's wedding, as your platonic friend, of course.' And he fills his mouth by biting into his scone. He can't believe his heart is racing like a lovesick schoolboy but he knows it is.

Susan is genuinely surprised. Imagine going to Anne's fancy wedding with the famous Mikhail Goldberg on her arm. Of course he is ancient but then you can't have everything. Mind you, the old dear has smartened himself up a lot lately. He's putting himself about more. Afternoon walks, trips to the library, concerts with Cordelia and Babs. She smiles at her spotted bow tie at his neck. These past few weeks she has enjoyed going out for an afternoon walk with him. She's grown to like his company and besides she's been so lonely since Darren left. He doesn't mind her talking about her troubles and it's not everyone who can take that.

'That's bloody great, Goldie.' She's been calling him by his nickname for a few weeks now. 'We'll knock 'em dead.'

Philip is waiting for Babs in the Festival Hall. He's eating a salad sandwich and drinking his second cup of coffee. He loves to arrive early for a concert. The buzz of the crowds in the foyer and the pre-concert music pleases him. Tonight, two very young musicians, a flautist and violinist, entertain the public. One girl is wholesome, the other, the violinist, still encased in puppy fat. The music drifts across the foyer, loud enough to be listened to but it doesn't dominate.

It's a warm evening. The women are in colourful summer dresses or various combinations of shorts and T-shirts, the men in light suits or jeans. Philip has had a busy day. He delivered triplets in the afternoon, the fruit of the *in vitro* method. All healthy babies, three-and-a-half pounds to five-and-a-half. The mother, a woman with no English, babbled a poem, a prayer, or simply nonsense throughout the labour pains. She never uttered a cry or scream, just got on with her recitation. He found it strangely compelling and appealing. And the utter joy when one by one the babies came. The husband, a short dark man with tattooed arms, paced the waiting room. Philip handed each child to her as they came. The nurse washed and weighed them. The mother cried with happiness. A large-boned woman in incongruous pigtails, a woman-child herself, welcomed her two daughters and son to the world. She asked the nurse to wash her face and free her pigtails. She brushed her thick blonde hair vigorously and had a cup of tea herself before introducing her man to his new family. He came into the room timidly like an intruder does but when he saw his children he exhibited an odd mixture of shyness and arrogance that Philip found touching. Then he kissed his wife on the forehead, not the lips, and inclined his head in a half-bow to Philip. Philip congratulated him.

Babs waves to him across the foyer before she makes her way to the self-service counter. He loves the very bones of this woman. Her compactness and strength. She still has the strong calves of the hockey player she was in her youth. She joins him with her tray of orange juice, salad and a scone. She fiddles with her handbag and produces her container of cod liver oil capsules, offers him one, then downs her own with juice. He swallows his, an obedient child. He never touches the stuff except when he's with Babs.

'I've had a hell of a day,' she mumbles through a mouthful of scone, 'I've had it up to here with throats. Maybe I should have specialised in something else or gone into another line of work entirely.'

'I had a wonderful day. Mrs Polanski delivered three bouncing babies, no complications.'

Her smile is warm and inclusive. 'That's fantastic, Dr Babygood.' It's her pet name for him. 'A three-in-one, well done!' All her irritation with her own day is wiped out by his good news. It's one of the things he loves about her: she's easily moved to good humour.

Jamie is dozing in the hammock in his flat. Propped up with cushions to his back he swings gently from side to side, occasionally opening his eyes to catch a detail of his newly painted flat. His dockland home now has a distinct maritime flavour. The walls from floor to the very high ceiling are rag-rolled in a mixture of uneven blues. A fishing net hangs on one corner of the ceiling, while a stuffed whale encased behind sturdy glass is screwed to the facing wall as you enter the room. A present from Babs, his godmother and favourite aunt. He moves his right leg impatiently; the plaster of Paris is heavily autographed. He looks at it as if it is an object separate from him. He regrets afresh his silly accident last month and chews away at his main worry, which is that Stella may tire of him.

She's working tonight. She has quite a decent part in a new play called *Submerged By Waves*. A woman wrote it but he can't remember her name. He'll meet her at the party at the end of the run. Bernie was very crude about her. Claimed a mate of his had a fling with her way back when she was a copywriter. But that was Bernie all over. Stella was very impressed by the script. She was weary of playing variations of vamp or young upwardly mobile wife, her stock-in-trade. Her character is that of an ambitious engineer whose brother inherits her father's company. The brother hasn't an ounce of business acumen and he takes the advice of sycophantic hangers-on. Disaster follows and the company is in real difficulty. Finally, the brother turns to the sister to bale him out. She makes a deal, a seventy thirty per cent share of the company in her favour. His back is to the wall and the bailiffs are ready to move in. He signs the papers. She sets about rescuing the company. It's an uphill climb strewn with obstacles but she emerges victorious and in control.

He's happy for Stella, of course. He's even helped her with her lines, reading the part of Stephen, the demon brother. She's such a good actress that when she turned her scorn on him in the reading he found he was genuinely disturbed and upset.

Darren is doing a wonderful job, he must admit. Quite surprised him really. The hours he spent sanding the layers of engrained old paint on the musicians' gallery, getting it just right. He had been fiercely jealous of Darren when they were kids. Occasionally on Saturdays Nellie would arrive with Bob, Darren and Tracey in tow. Billie would have invited them to tea. Bob always looked uncomfortable until he had freed himself from his suit jacket and enquired if there were any odd jobs that needed attention. And of course there always were. He'd be his own man again with a hammer or saw in his hand. At tea, Nellie sat at the top of the table in what she called 'one of my outfits', often leaving her flowery hats on her head throughout the proceedings. She said Conservative jumble sales were the best place to find such glories.

After tea, Jamie and Darren, depending on season, were sent into the garden or up to the unoccupied attic to play. On their own they proceeded to beat each other to a pulp until one of them gave in, usually Jamie. After that they could settle down to some real play, soldiers, board games or whatever. But there had to be the ritual slaughter first. Once, Jamie had timidly enquired if they could skip the fisticuffs and just get on with playing but Darren had given him a bloody nose for his pains.

He half-expected Darren to urge him into a boxing round or two the day he arrived to decorate the flat. He lay on the hammock working on the Arnold account while Darren worked. Darren whistled along to a very loud Capital Radio but the memory of his pugilistic powers prevented Jamie from asking him to lower the volume. Every few hours Darren would take a break and hand him a mug of tea or coffee. Then he'd talk about 'woman trouble' and tell Jamie such intimate sexual details about Susan the nurse and Jenny the separated mother of three, his current love, that Jamie was nervous Stella might come home and be horrified at such male chauvinist smut. The next time he went to Brabbington Terrace and saw Susan on the stairs he could hardly meet her eyes. He felt he knew every inch of her body. From his reading of Darren's situation he thought any troubles he had were largely of his own making. Not that he said that, of course.

He hopes Stella will stay with him for ever. He forces himself to wipe away the last vestiges of self-doubt about her. A part is only a part. Just because she asks him to read the part of the weak-minded brother doesn't mean she's typecasting him. She's a working actress, after all. She needs him only as a sounding board. Someone to read the brother's lines so that she can concentrate on her own.

Tony is swimming. It's two o' clock in the afternoon. He should be in his writing cabin getting on with his novel. He's had a difficult, stop-start morning, cranking his way from one sentence to the next but never getting to the stage where the words flowed. Wendy is surprised by the break in his routine. She watches from the patio. Karin is paddling with Ludo at one end of the pool. The agency rang this morning with good news. They have a capable middle-aged nanny who could take care of Ludo and help with light housekeeping. Karin, the beautiful Fraülein, is no longer needed. But how to tell her? Worse still, how to persuade Tony to accept it? He likes having Karin about the place. He tells Wendy she's great company for Lottie and Marian. It's true that Karin and Lottie run together in the mornings now and Marian has picked up a few phrases in German and uses them, whether appropriate or not, in her new-found attentions to Ludo. Things have settled down to some extent since Lottie's arrival into the household some weeks past. Josh and Toby are spending a fortnight at a residential summer camp in Scotland. It's the one favoured by their school and so they'll be among friends. She misses their boisterous cheer. They could always be relied upon to speak to her without being snide.

She has to admit though, since Lottie's arrival, apart from the odd flare-up between the two girls, Marian has appeared more settled and isn't wetting the bed as frequently. She's also giving Ludo a lot of attention, unusual for her. She had dreaded leaving her alone with him on that first walk but since that day things are easier between them. She's beginning to think that the holiday in Greece will be quite manageable and pleasant.

If only Karin could be gone by then! She watches Tony, a vigorous confident swimmer, swim the length of the pool again and again. How many times? She's not sure. She should be counting.

Tony is remembering the first time he went to the public swimming baths with his mother. Lloyd was with them too, of course. Twins, they went everywhere together until Tony got a place at the grammar school and Lloyd went to the secondary modern. They were no more than three or four at the time. Chubby little lookalikes in swimming togs. Lloyd had dived in when mum had turned her back and they both registered horror as Lloyd floated from them, sailing from the shallow end towards deep water. He can't remember if mum really screamed. He definitely saw her mouth open and close but he knows he cried with shock and fear. Lloyd was smiling and floating, floating and smiling until the instructor jumped in and hauled him out. The instructor and mum talked very slowly then to Lloyd. They told him he would be a very good swimmer because he was confident in the water but he was going to teach him how to do it properly. Tony was still howling. Mum told him not to make such a fuss.

He remembers the countless times Lloyd dived to glory at junior school while he stood shivering on the sidelines dreading the moment his name would be called out. Since the names were called alphabetically he was always after Lloyd. Now as he strikes water with ease he can still taste that early fear. He always expected Lloyd to go under and was surprised when he didn't. Billie turned him into a strong swimmer. That first summer when they visited her parents in Dublin they swam every day. Not in a local swimming pool, either, as there didn't seem to be one. In Billie's house it was the most natural thing in the world to swim in the sea. Mostly they went to Bray. He packed the old green Rover with her parents, baby Jamie and her young sister Connie. And they sang their way to the seaside after the initial Our Father to get them there safely. The da, as they called him, said the prayer but they all joined in to please him. He didn't know any of the songs but he liked to be at the wheel while they sang with gusto.

Her da always started with a song he had sung to them in childhood. Now he sang it for Jamie, who joined in with some of the words and clapped his hands to the rhythm.

> Up in an air balloon, boys,
> up in an air balloon,
> all around the little stars
> sailing round the moon.
> I'll take you back to heaven
> by jingo very soon,
> just you and me and
> baby Jamie, up in an air balloon.

There were endless verses but that seemed to be the chorus. Every time da repeated the chorus he put in another person's name until everyone in the car had been up in an air balloon. It made Tony feel good leading his jolly troupe to the sea. At home he'd failed to get mum, dad and Lloyd to drive off anywhere with him. Lloyd was the one who took mum and dad for a drive on Sundays and that was that.

That first day when they reached the beach, da and mammy were just as eager to dive into the sea as the rest of them. Tony was surprised and delighted. Mammy with her brown hair held in a bun had that severity mitigated by a frilled one-piece suit. Da slipped his togs on under a towel. Within moments they were rushing to the sea, this spare tall tribe of Billie's. He brought up the rear with Jamie. They swam out, racing each other with delight, parents pitted against children. He bounced Jamie in the shallow waves, anxious that Jamie's first introduction to water would be free from fear. As they swam back towards him after some time, da's glasses misted (he never took them off, not even in bed according to Billie). Mammy's bun, unravelled, transformed her into a sea maenad.

Billie's and Connie's short bobbed hair twinned them momentarily into boys. He was filled with a sadness that his mum, dad, Lloyd and himself had never shared a moment like that, not even once.

When they had gone for day trips to Blackpool as children, mum and dad had sat on a rug on the beach eating sandwiches and drinking endless cups of sweet milky tea from mum's outsize beige flask. Lloyd left him way behind as he strove to fight his fear of drowning. That early image of Lloyd as a toddler smiling as he floated towards the deep end never left him. It was during that summer in Ireland that he finally relaxed in water.

It was the second-last day of the holiday and they were in Bray again, this time with squat Babs sitting on da's lap on the back seat with ma, Connie and Jamie. He remembers thinking how could Babs be the favourite with her da when she was a dwarf among giants but then he thought of fat Lloyd, his own mum's favourite, and he realised that these preferences were irrational. He hoped he could be fair-minded when Jamie had a sibling. Now, swimming the full length of his own pool he thinks of his clever Marian, her beauty soured every time she takes up cudgels against the world. He recognises for the first time that it's not only Beth's early death that has marked her. He must own up to his own part in the business too.

If he hadn't fooled around with every two-bit actress or got involved in that intense affair with his Swedish translator in the first place, would Beth have given into her neuroses so quickly or deeply? No wonder Marian was obsessively tidy. Beth wielded a duster with the grace of a ballet dancer. It is Marian's only way of keeping in touch with her mother. How stupid he must be not to have seen that sooner? The bed-wetting and sleepwalking started only after Beth's death. He remembers vividly her acute distress and shame that first morning when she woke to find herself in the coldness of her own stale urine. She had run to Nellie to cover it up for her. Not to him. He had been too immersed in his own guilty grief to have given her much notice at the time. He had ignored his own daughter when she needed him most. For the first time in his life he has to face the fact that he might not be the benign patriarch that he thinks he is.

That day in Bray, the second last one of the holiday when Billie and he had left baby Jamie with his grandparents and walked off on their own for an hour or two, comes to him now as if it happened only last week. It had been achingly hot, their joined hands dribbling rivers of sweat as they held on to each other on that walk. They left the noise and heat of the crowded beach and after some time came to a secluded empty stretch of sea. There was nobody else in sight. Billie pulled off her clothes and raced into the waves; he ran after her dropping his clothes at intervals. He was swimming eagerly, determined to catch up with her before he realised he hadn't hung back first, that twisted sensation of the gut warning him that you can drown in water, baby Lloyd smiling and floating from him towards the deep end of the pool of their shared childhood.

Some of his poorer writer friends, the ones who write literature as opposed to his good reads, tease him unmercifully about his swimming pool. They tell him it's crass and vulgar. He agrees with them but he knows he wants his own stretch of water. He can command and master it at any time he chooses. The Roman bathhouse, Beth called it because of its columns and four Roman busts. His indoor pool was a victory badge. Now as he finally steps out of the water and flops on to one of the high benches that line the large glass windows of the swim house, he catches a glimpse of Wendy as she looks in his direction from the patio. These days she always seems to be watching him or somebody else, or else sleeping. Where has all her energy gone?

She was putting on weight too. Not enough exercise. With her height it didn't show too much yet but if she kept moving at a snail's pace in a year or two she'd turn into a pudding. A tall pudding but nevertheless a pudding. She's no excuse, not with a pool and gym at her disposal. He'd have to talk to her about it.

Wendy's eyes follow Tony as his white-robed figure makes its way back to the writing cabin. She's never intruded on his sacred nine-to-five routine but she's wondering if today should be an exception. After all, he's already broken his routine with a long swim. Marian and Karin swing Ludo by the arms on to the patio. He's gurgling with good humour. The two girls have walked the legs off him at the local park and he's just about ready for his afternoon nap. She can tell by the way his eyelids are beginning to droop in spite of his laughter.

'He said "Mar",' Marian says. 'We were pushing him on the swing. I stood in front and Karin was behind him. We were careful, just gentle pushes. He held on tight and loved it. When we stopped the swing, he said "Mar". He put his hands out to me to lift him down and he said "Mar". Karin heard it too.' Marian's eyes are shining.

Wendy thinks, his first word and I wasn't there to hear it. His first word and he calls Marian not her. Wendy lifts Ludo and is reassured by his familiar weight. 'What a clever boy!' she says, 'but it's time for your nap now.'

Lottie is dreaming. It's early afternoon but she's fast asleep in her pretty pink third-floor room. Her dark hair looks darker against the floral pillowcase. It's almost shoulder length now. Since leaving Billie's house, she's tried to change the superficial things that made them resemble each other but of course, bone structure cannot be changed, at least not without the surgeon's skill, and she remains her mother's daughter. Nights are the worst for her. She dreads saying the final goodnight and going to her room. Even if she showers or baths to relax the moment she lies down the image that torments her is that of Billie and Edward 'doing it'.

They crowd out her mind even on the verge of sleep. She sees them, a tangle of limbs criss-crossing each other in an ecstacy of love. She fights what she sees in that inner eye, is jolted to wakefulness several times a night and wakes up each morning quite exhausted. Nevertheless, she sets her alarm clock for seven to go running with Karin. It was a dreadful disappointment to her when

Tony told her that he preferred running alone, at least during the weekdays. That's when he got his creative juices going. It set him up for the day. He knew she'd understand. Weekends were different, he assured her, he didn't write Saturday and Sunday so he'd be delighted to have her along then. She said of course she understood but she felt he was pushing her back to her childhood timetable, the weekend child, the one who was entertained on Saturdays and Sundays but must be gone by Monday.

The day he said it to her, she had been at High Pines for a week and her first instinct was to turn from him and run 'home' to Billie's. But she couldn't do that. She had banged the door at Brabbington Terrace but not before she had called her mother an ancient seductress. How could she go to Billie with a silly story about running with her dad? So she told Tony she understood and asked Karin to be her running mate instead. Since then Karin and Lottie leave the house at precisely ten past seven, returning at ten to eight. They have breakfast together, orange juice and cereal, and then Karin starts her day with Ludo. Lottie returns to her pink room and if she's lucky to a dreamless sleep for a few hours.

But today is different. Even with the exertion of the run behind her, when she lies down her inner eye summons a vision of Billie's and Edward's bodies so out of scale that the distortion terrifies her. Billie's mouth opens to swallow Edward's entire head. His penis grows so large it ruptures Billie when he enters her. She wakes time and time again, her longer hair matted to her head with sweat.

Eventually, she has a shower and lies down with her Walkman clamped to her head. Maybe music will keep them away from her. And now Lottie is finally sleeping. She dreams of Billie as she first remembers her. Billie, her hair tied in a playful ponytail, is baking in the kitchen in Brabbington Terrace. She sings as she bakes, her floury hands in motion with the tune. Lottie is watching her. She lolls in the rocking chair near the gas fire. She moves forwards and backwards to Billie's singing but she doesn't join in. She doesn't know the words. Billie stops singing briefly as she flattens the mixture on the baking-board. She reaches to the shelf for a pastry cutter. She begins to cut out shapes, her head bent to the task as well as her hands, all singing stopped. Lottie approaches the table, almost silently. Billie is unaware of her presence. Lottie sees the line of gingerbread men. They all look alike. Then something catches her eye and she looks closer. One of the gingerbread men is growing on the table. It's Edward. Billie is pleased. 'Look: it's Edward,' she says as if it's the most natural thing in the world. There's a knock on the kitchen door. It's Goldie with Will (the window cleaner). 'I'm here to clean your windows or alternatively to sing,' Will announces importantly.

'Can you sing as you clean?' Billie enquires, without taking her eyes from Edward the gingerbread man.

'He's the best; of course he can,' Goldie assures her in his solemn Russian way, 'Lottie can accompany him on the piano. Let us begin,' he says with a formal bow and smile in Lottie's direction.

Lottie wakes. Piano scales fill her ear. Up and down so many octaves. She's confused. She thinks, how silly I am to play scales for Will to sing to, how could anyone clean windows to such music? Then she realises she's been dreaming. The tape on her Walkman is silent. The music is coming from the music room. How odd. Still groggy, she gets on her feet to investigate. Apart from the music, the house is strangely silent, that stillness that hot summer afternoons imposes when the inhabitants are in the garden asleep in deckchairs. She bumps into Nellie, who's wheeling a bedlinen cart on the second floor landing.

'Afternoon, ducks. You've been sleepin' lights out. I left clean sheets outside your door. I didn't want to wake you. At your age, you need your rest. Hormones, that's the cause of it. I hope someone talked to you about it. Remind them if they haven't. Knowledge is never a burden.' And she wheels her cart noisily into Wendy and Tony's room after a perfunctory knock.

Lottie continues to the music room. Marian is labouring up and down octaves while Ludo crawls about at her feet. The music stops when she sees Lottie. Marian blushes and is suddenly shy. She reaches for Ludo and she moves his hands, plonkety, plonk over the keys.

'Ludo is learning to play,' she says without looking at Lottie. 'Bella rang. She's coming over at four. Said she wanted to talk to you. She seemed very excited but Nellie said to let you sleep. You do look tired.'

'I can't sleep,' Lottie says before she realises she's confiding in Marian, 'I mean I can't seem to get a good night's sleep.'

'I expect it's all that business with Billie and Edward,' Marian says and she bangs Ludo's fingers on to notes. 'When my mum died I started sleepwalking. Still do from time to time. I read in a book that the body and mind are connected. It was real spooky. Like if bad things can get into your mind something happens to upset your body too. It scared me. Made me feel I was possessed or something because of the sleepwalking. I thought maybe my mum's soul was restless, so, I was sleepwalking. I can't explain it properly.' Marian's fingers crash down on the piano, startling Ludo who whimpers.

'See, this is all I did. You can make that sound too.' She clunks his fingers on to the keyboard and he's reassured once again.

'It must have been horrible for you when Beth died. I can't imagine a life without Billie. Of course I hate her right now and

I don't know if I can love her ever again but I wouldn't want her to die. I wanted her to die when it happened, something instant like a car crash, but now I miss her sometimes. Not so much at the weekends. I feel such a fool.'

'I feel foolish a lot of the time but it's mostly to do with Tony. He forgot my mum very quickly. Sometimes I think if I left home he'd forget all about me after a few days too.'

'But you're only thirteen!' Lottie says uselessly. 'Where would you go? I saw a documentary about young people sleeping rough near the Embankment and Charring Cross Station. They were sleeping in cardboard boxes and after a while their feet rotted because they left their shoes and socks on all the time and it was difficult trying to wash in public toilets.'

'A few times I thought I might run away to Billie's. It's silly I know but I think she's kind.'

'Not to me. She's a cradle-snatcher and . . .'

'So is Tony. Wendy's only half his age. They say it's different for men. I don't believe them. Men want a good time, that's all.'

'Did I hear someone say that men want a good time?'

It's Bella, Lottie's friend. Her blonde curls bob around the door frame before she comes into the room. She never just walks into a room in the normal way. She has to check it out first. Her white skimpy shorts and T-shirt show off her skinny bronzed body with maximum provocation. Lately Lottie has even found her energy provocative now that she's getting so little sleep herself.

'Marian, I'm surprised at you.' says Bella, the mature fifteen-year-old. 'At your age I was still playing with dolls.'

'I've got Ludo,' Marian says as she yanks him to his feet, then on to the music stool, her doll-rabbit from the hat. Ludo smiles at Bella as if on cue.

'Oh, he's got three teeth,' Bella observes, 'and of course he's got what it takes between the legs. I bet you'll break some hearts when you grow up, Ludo.' She tickles him under the chin. He escapes and crawls away to freedom. 'I'm beginning to think that Will doesn't love me any more,' Bella begins in her usual breathless manner.

'I told you he was common as muck,' Lottie says in that superior tone that she reserves for universal observations. 'I'm not in the least surprised; you could tell by his tattoos.'

'You're just a snob,' Bella says airily. 'You couldn't look at a boy unless he was a careful dresser and attached to a musical instrument. I like a bit of rough trade and the only instrument I'm interested in is his musical rod. If he can make me howl, I'm happy.'

'I think you read all that kind of stuff in dirty books.' Lottie is trying to be aloof. 'You haven't done it ever. You like talking dirty, that's all.'

Marian is feeling a little out of her depth here. She's not quite followed everything that Bella said. Not that she'd admit it for a moment. There must be quite a difference between thirteen and fifteen. It's a pity Bella has changed things. For a while there Lottie and herself seemed to be getting on quite well. She hoped she wouldn't be asked to take sides. She liked Bella's company. She was always up to some adventure or other. Not like Elvira who could sit doing nothing for hours on end until she had to shout at her in exasperation and then she felt guilty because Elvira had no dad and her mother was a temp, always changing offices and worrying if there would be another job when the present one finished. She decides to take Lottie's side against Bella if it comes to an argument. It was good talking to Lottie as if they were real sisters. During the Middle Ages, meat often rotted. The meats of the rich were often perfumed to hide the smell. Musk, violets, primroses. In medieval England, dentists were called 'tooth-drawers'. They wore pointed caps and necklaces of the teeth they had extracted. Pontius Pilate is looked upon as a saint in the Ethiopian culture.

Billie can't wait to get to Russia. It's not a place that she knows very much about or that she's ever had a particular desire to see but it will be getting away, even running away for a time. And it's far, far away. How many miles she's not sure. But it's a long enough distance to get away from Lottie's face. Not that she's seen very much of her lately. Since the night she told Lottie about Edward, she has retained the image of Lottie's face streaked to ugliness with tears. Then the triumph in her voice when she reminded Edward of her mother's age. These days when Lottie comes to Brabbington Terrace it is for her music lessons with Goldie or maybe to collect some clothes or tapes from her room. If their paths cross in the hallway or on the stairs, Lottie gives her the briefest of nods and says 'Hello' but that's as far as it goes.

Goldie assures her that Lottie is surviving and it's best to let her re-open the lines of communication again in her own good time. She does not know if she has taken his advice because it's good or simply that she's too cowardly to force Lottie to communicate with her. She misses her from the house, particularly during weekdays. They have eaten an evening meal together for years. It's hard not to miss such routines. Then, of course, if she's honest there are days when Lottie does not cross her consciousness at all. Those are the days when her work at Abbercrombie and Wilson proceeds in a slightly comic fast-forward, as if other people's buying and selling of property is as insignificant as Monopoly. Only yesterday Mr Wilson had invited herself and Olive, the current temporary secretary, for a snifter at the Horse and Hare. He was astonished when she had downed her whiskey in two to three gulps and said she had to dash as she had forgotten Bob was coming to paint her bedroom. A lie. She hadn't wanted to offend. Mr Wilson's offers to partake of strong drink at his expense were as rare as Christmas but he was celebrating the completion of the outside painting of the 'firm' as he liked to call it. She knew he expected some conversation in exchange but when she sat down between his toupeed pin-striped figure and Olive's spreading hips in one of the miniature alcoves in the Horse and Hare she knew she'd have to leave promptly.

A recollection, like a home movie, of the irregular occasions she had sat in such an alcove with Mr Wilson celebrating one of his deals, came to her. The year Tony had walked out on her, those occasions had been a highlight. At least she knew she was doing the work properly, enough to be invited for a drink by the boss. Her self-esteem must have really been in her boots then. She's glad she sent the tape to Wendy. Her anger with Tony is so intense it seems to manifest itself in a physical restlessness that won't allow for ordinary social intercourse so she makes her excuses and leaves. In the car, she sees her white knuckles as they grip the steering wheel. She drives to Gordon Square with the impatience of one escaping the devil. Her key sticks in the front door lock and she thinks she will kick the door down if she can't manipulate it properly. Finally, she takes the stairs two at a time and she surprises Edward who is still practising. Normally she wouldn't call around before eight. He is playing something, she thinks by Mozart, maybe the little G Mminor Symphony.

Its melancholy and drama do not stop her from interrupting

him. She is propelled by a violent desire to have their very bones locked together at this minute, not ten minutes hence. He is surprised by her arrival. She has slipped out of her panties and pulled down his underpants and they're both tumbling to the floor with that awkward manoeuvring that coupling while still dressed entails. She feels his penis stiffen to an instant bone of pleasure and she comes almost instantly. Strangely, she's not thinking about him at all. She's remembering a summer in Bray when Tony and herself slipped off for a swim on their own, leaving baby Jamie with da and mammy. Afterwards they fell upon each other, their wet sandy bodies squelching to climax and she had thought at that moment that she would never know such pleasure again.

Lottie and Bella are watching Will clean Mrs Kirby's windows. It's his first day back from Butlins and Bella can't help herself. Mrs Kirby's house is in a crescent with a well-kept green in front of it. Mostly retired people live here. The green is planted with mature cherry trees or laburnums. In April and May when the golden yellow and light pink bloom, the vivid laburnum following the faded cherry, the old people walk here in ones and twos, their first airing after winter. Now, nothing is in bloom in the green, just Bella's cravings. It's a sticky July afternoon, the heat hanging clammily in the air. According to the weather forecast rainstorms are on the way. Lottie and Bella pretend to play tennis on the green; at least they hit the ball backwards and forwards to each other, Bella's eyes follow Will as he whistles his way through his work. Lottie is wearing immaculate tennis whites, her little pleated skirt twirling as she runs. Bella is wearing a jagged cutaway cerise T-shirt that just about covers her little sprouting breasts and matching mini-shorts that are cut high on the thighs. Lottie is disturbed by Bella's voyeurism but she's excited by it too. Maybe she'll pick up some tips on how to handle an older man since she's plainly failed with Edward.

From time to time, Mrs Kirby's white-bunned head emerges from her front door as she checks on her worker. The house, a generous-sized 1920s villa with peaked roof and an acre of garden, is in pristine condition. The front lawn looks as if no one has ever trodden on it. It's bordered by fussy little flowers in red, white and blue that Lottie can't name. Mrs Kirby is a royalist and has lost sleep lately over the Princess of Wales's marriage difficulties. She has her name down on the library waiting list for the new book on the princess. She wouldn't buy it, that would be disloyal, but she wants to check it out nonetheless. So far, her information has been confined to the extracts in the newspapers which she's read avidly and then complained about in her quavery voice to her neighbour and friend, Mrs Maughan. She loves her house and garden with a passion and has refused to move to a small flat for the convenience of her two greedy sons. She has a daily woman and George, her gardener and handyman, to look after the house and grounds. But it's the gardener's annual holiday now. She's at the mercy of Will, a man recommended to her by Mrs Maughan, who uses him occasionally. She's nervous of men with tattoos. His anchors and mermaids have made her watchful.

Bella wishes Mrs Kirby would get into her creepy old car that looks like a coffin and drive away. Will says she goes shopping every day. Leaves the house, usually at two, and returns by half past three. He says the car is a vintage Austin Seven and is in great condition. It's five past two now and the old biddy hasn't still emerged with her shopping bag. She's popped in and out to check that he's not slacking but that's all.

Marian is on the Northern line. She's nervous. She doesn't normally travel by tube. She walks to school during the academic year and Karin accompanies her on the underground in the summer. Mostly Wendy drives her about and, of course, Tony fills the Jag up with everyone for the usual Saturday lunch at Dino's. For weeks now she's had this overwhelming desire to visit Billie at Brabbington Terrace. She'd been quite excited when she thought she might have exchanged summer schedules with Lottie and spent her time with Billie instead of at High Pines. Billie's dismissal of the idea, the phone-call she'd overheard, had only heightened this excitement. If she could get inside Billie's house her life might change for the better. She'd been so moody lately. Even Toby, her favourite, got a tongue-lashing from her from time to time. On the day Josh and himself were leaving for the summer camp in Edinburgh, he had bent to kiss her cheek in a fond farewell. She withdrew at the last minute and told him not to be soppy. He shook hands with her instead in a formal adult way, pressing an envelope into her hand. Afterwards when she had waved them off with, 'Goodbye toads, at least the place will be germ-free for a while,' she had walked back to the house with a deliberately cheerful stride, a 'see-if-I-miss-you' walk. When she got indoors, she opened the envelope. It was a £20 note with a Snoopy card in which Toby had written, 'For my favourite sister. Get yourself a new giant book of fantastic facts. Toby.' Her reading, apart from prescribed school texts, consisted of historical tomes, biographies and those bumper books of fantastic facts. Good old Toby. He'd given £20 to the cause and she'd called him a toad.

Now, as her watchful eye checks each station, London Bridge, Monument Tower, Moorgate, Barbican, Angel, King's Cross, as she travels northwards to Billie and Brabbington Terrace, she suffers last-minute doubts about her mission. She's meant to be at

Elvira's house. She's given Elvira strict instructions to lie on her behalf if Wendy or Tony rings. She's threatened her with the Greek holiday. Elvira desperately wants to go with her. She's never been abroad before. She's even stopped scoffing sweets and puddings on the sly to look good in her swimsuit. So far, she's lost eight pounds. Elvira sits in her mother's tiny flat, with the roar of traffic outside on the busy main road. It's a stifling afternoon but she's afraid to go outside even for a breath of fresh air in case the phone rings and it's Tony or Wendy. She's in a double bind. If she lies to them about Marian's whereabouts they might not want to bring her to Greece. On the other hand, if she doesn't cover for Marian, she won't want her along on the trip.

Euston, Camden Town, Kentish Town, Tufnell Park. It's the next stop. She checks and rechecks the map on the inside of the train. The serene Indian woman in the saffron sari sitting next to her wonders why she is so restless. The tall black boy in his pumped up runners and U2 T-shirt is unaware of her tension as he stretches his long limbs to comfort. He hems her in. When the train stops at Archway she has to jump over his outstretched legs. She makes her way to the nearest exit and she's facing a pub with a rampant lion on a frieze above the doorway. The pub is on a corner and she's taken aback at the amount and volume of traffic that thunders by. She has no idea how much further Brabbington Terrace is but she knows this is the stop. She gets out. It can't be too far.

She crosses the road to where the pub is and stops a few people outside it to ask directions. A Muslim woman can't help her. She has no English. She moves off like a floating black bird, her long clothes revealing only ankles.

'Sorry, luv,' a middleaged woman says, 'the only place I know 'ere is the bleedin' shirt factory. I've worked there the last ten years but I don't look around me until I get 'ome to Tufnell Park.'

'Brabbington Terrace, is that where you want?' A voice intrudes as the woman heads off to make more shirts. The man has that red-haired, red-faced Irish look about him. He's in the traditional summer builder's gear. Cut-off jeans, with tiny spatters of cement and a string vest. He's sunburned with massive clusters of freckles on the shoulders. Marian is wary of him.

'Thank you, but I think I remember where it is now.' Her voice is childishly dismissive.

'No need to be frightened, young one. I'm goin' that way myself. I'm repairin' a roof on one of the houses in the terrace. Number thirty.'

'That's Cordelia's house,' Marian says. Lottie has been talking a lot of nonsense about numerology lately. She told Marian since Edward's house was number thirty and hers was number three, they were bound to end up together. It stood to reason. Marian had pointed out that reason had nothing to do with it and even if it had, she countered, Edward's flat was a number nine. Lottie wasn't in the least defeated. She pointed out that nine was really a combination of three by three. In fact, she said, it confirmed their ultimate destiny together since the number of Tony's house was sixty three, another combination of threes and her present abode. Marian isn't still convinced that the red-haired man isn't a secret murderer of teenage girls but since they're on a busy street full of traffic and people, she decides to walk along with him.

'Ah, you know Mrs Dexter then. A bit uppity until you get to know her but very generous with the teapot and sandwiches, I'll say that for her.'

'She's a friend of my . . . aunt.' Marian decides on 'aunt' to describe Billie. What does one call one's father's first wife? 'My aunt lives in number three.'

'You're a niece of Billie's then.'

Marian is taken aback. Does he know everyone in the neighbourhood?

'I had a dance with her in the Fiddler's Elbow last week. She does a great "Walls of Limerick". The young fellow she's knockin' around with would want to loosen up a bit though. A few classes with Willie Kennedy would set him right. But sure he tried his best. It's hard for the English to fit in,' he ends, mysteriously.

Marian has only a vague notion what he means but the main thing is that he knows Billie and Cordelia, so he mustn't be a secret axe-murderer after all. She lets herself relax. They turn at a greengrocer's and walk along a street of second-hand shops which sell furniture, clothes, electrical equipment. There's a cobbler's and a café. They turn right again at the café and along a street of semi-detached brick houses, the majority of them set in flats. On the doors, she notices numerous bells with different names. There are a lot of people on the street. Two West Indian boys are repairing a very old Mercedes. Their ghetto-blaster fills the street with sounds of Jennifer Warne's 'Ain't No Cure For Love'. A group of lively children chase each other with a water hose. The water drenches their light summer dresses, sculpting them to their exuberant bodies. An old man snores on a deck chair under his sun hat on the sweltering crazy paving that used to be a little garden. Here and there over-full dustbins impede their progress.

'I married one of the nurses from number three. A Galway girl, Maeve Keogh. She had a flat in Billie's house for three years. Some great nights we had there. The singin' and dancin', not to mention the drinkin'. Her old man was still there then. Maeve and myself couldn't understand it. Runnin' out on a handsome woman like Billie. That's years ago now. My eldest is fourteen.'

Marian lets the talk flow over her. She's getting uneasier about the welcome she might receive the nearer they're getting to

Brabbington Terrace. After all, she's Beth's daughter, the woman Tony left Billie for. Maybe she should just turn back, get on the tube and go to Elvira's.

'You have a look of her about the eyes,' the man says as he stops and surveys her for a minute. They're standing at a set of traffic lights. When the green man comes on they cross the road and turn left into Brabbington Terrace. She can see extended ladders leaning against Cordelia's house. Cordelia is in the front garden, a battered sunhat on her head. She's wearing a man's shirt and very old jeans and she's drinking tea from a china mug. A big black-haired man is sitting on the windowsill and drinking from a large bottle of Lucozade. Marian is aware of the two sets of eyes watching her progress as she walks towards them.

Tony is listening to a programme on Radio Four. It's about a man called Alberto Gallini who lives in Milan. He helps people to 'disappear' by supplying them with a new passport, a new country to live in and sometimes even a new job and wife to go with the new name. There are interviews with women whose husbands have disappeared and never come home. Their relatives talk of the anxiety and the lack of peace. They can't forget them. Sometimes they try to persuade themselves that their husbands are dead. They plead with the interviewer. They say they only want to know if their husbands are alive. They needn't come back. Just clear things up, that's all. The interviewer talks to some of the 'disappeared'. The majority of those say they had to 'disappear'. They were unhappy. They needed a new life. Quite a few were escaping from mothers. They knew mama wouldn't understand they had to get away from her as well as everyone else. So Alberto arranged a 'suicide' or a 'disappearance'. They were happy now. It was better. A new name, a new wife, a new life and no mama.

Tony toys with the idea of contacting Alberto but he knows it's only a fantasy. Wendy deserves that he 'disappear' after the fuss she made about the tape. Billie sent it to her through the post. Billie was heartless sometimes. He had tried to be a friend and she had thrown that offer of friendship back in his face. He had not realised that Wendy could express such anger. The names she had called him. Viper. Dirty old man. Lecher. Lusting after his first wife while living with his third. It had energised her in a way that was transformational. Since the tape arrived last week, he felt he was living with a different woman.

After she had abused him soundly for his his lecherous intent, she said she was going out to clear her head. It was half past five. She drove off, leaving instructions for Karin, and she didn't come back until midnight. She checked Ludo in the nursery, then flopped into bed beside him without a word. He pretended he was asleep and concentrated on breathing evenly. The following morning, she was up before his seven o'clock alarm. He went ahead with his usual two-mile morning run. She wasn't at home when he got back. Karin was feeding Ludo in the kitchen while Marian spoke a few German phrases at him. He did his work-out in the gym for a half an hour and ate his breakfast of orange juice, a slice of toast and coffee before making his way to his writing cabin for his usual start at nine. She was nowhere to be seen as he left the house.

A few times during that morning he was tempted to walk to the house just to check if she was there but he forced himself to stay put. It would be ridiculous to let her know that she had disturbed his routine. Billie's new lifestyle and its effects on his household were beginning to tell on his work. For the first time in years he was behind with work. He prided himself in being a professional writer, the one ahead with his manuscript rather than behind. Only last week he had taunted his friend, William, who had written successful novels (a trilogy on life in the 1920s on a Welsh farm), that maybe his next book would never see the light of day, because he couldn't make some basic decisions about the structure. William, a kind and sensitive man, agreed that it sometimes appeared like that to him too. He was also stuck on the ending. He'd written up to six endings already. He'd discarded all of them. He knew everyone was losing patience with him, his wife, kids, agent, publisher, but he couldn't seem to come to a decision. Tony had been abrasive in his advice. 'Simply decide, mate, that's all you need to do.' And he poured William another whiskey and patted him on the shoulder. He couldn't admit he was having concentration problems himself and was falling behind with his own manuscript. He wrote popular novels. He was expected to do a job of work and hand the stuff in on time. This was the first time that *Angst* came to his keyboard and he didn't like it. It was Billie's fault and now Wendy was adding to it. He was usually two novels ahead of publication.

He has protected his ego as much as he can, describing in comic terms Billie's new love to those who knew them both. He displays concern and support by saying he suggested that Lottie come and live with him while the storm lasted. He says everyone needs a fling and it's a good thing that Billie is finally letting go. He was the only man in her life before the Boy Wonder. After all, variety is the spice of life and she might as well sample some of it. It's a good job her father, the old puritan, is dead or he'd have sent her to Lough Derg as a punishment. Her mother, he feels, will be quite taken with the idea. A tall woman with fine bones and without a grey hair in her head to this day, she married her next-door neighbour, a decade younger than herself, within two years of the father's death. They still live in their own houses but they sleep alternate weeks in each other's beds. That reminds him, a weird strain probably runs in the family. Her sister, Babs, the throat specialist, has a similar arrangement with a gynaecologist, her lover. Except they haven't married. Still, you had to admire the spirited Irish.

His own mother had always admired Billie and she was a woman of discernment. And his father to this day sent a card to Billie at Christmas and for her birthday, which was more than he sent to him. It didn't do to get bitter. He never gave into bitterness himself. Life was short and he hoped Billie would enjoy her little romp. After all, she had done a terrific job raising Jamie and Lottie in spite of his defection. A man had to admit his faults or face a stranger in the mirror every morning. She was entitled to a bit of fun if anyone was. He had assured her of his support and friendship if ever she needed it. And he was a man of his word. Everyone knew that.

He was drinking more and writing less and soon other people would notice. It wouldn't show in the work for a while but it was only a matter of time if this slow period continued. Max, his agent, was one of the best in the business. Tony and he shared jokes about those writers on his list who gave into the 'artistic temperament'. That's the way he wanted to keep it. Max appreciated his Monday-to-Friday, nine-to-five routine. It had made them both considerably richer over the years.

The fridge in the writing cabin that usually held mineral water was now filled with beer. These past weeks when he came to a dead end in the novel he reached for a beer. The action was becoming reflexive. He was afraid to bring spirits to the cabin. Childhood memories of his Uncle Alfie prevented him. Uncle Alfie, his father's brother, the one who was away at sea most of the year, arrived home on holidays at various odd times of the year. Never Christmas or Easter, festive times for ordinary mortals but maybe the first week of September, the start of the new school year or February when there was still no hint of spring in the air. Tony would have to share with Lloyd for the duration of Alfie's visit, which ranged in length from two weeks to two months. Uncle Alfie spent his days and nights in the company of a whiskey bottle. Mum was amazingly tolerant. Once, when he told her that he missed not having his own room and enquired about Uncle Alfie's date of departure, she'd said, 'Your Uncle Alfie gave your dad and me the deposit for this house. Without his help we couldn't have bought it. He'll be going when his ship is ready and not before that.' And that was the end of it. Amazingly, a few days before his departure he'd sober up and apparently he wouldn't touch a drink again until his next visit home.

Tony, as his fingers fumble their way over the keyboard, every now and again checking his word count on the monitor anxiously, wonders if the genetic strain in Uncle Alfie, the one that drove him to consort only with a whiskey bottle on his leave, has finally broken out in him now that he's reached a crisis. The word crisis frightens him. Something is happening to him – but is it a crisis? And who can he turn to? When he thinks about it in any depth, he realises he wouldn't feel comfortable confessing his present foolishness to anyone. These feelings started when he learned of Billie and Edward's liaison. He's already had to suffer the indignity of a tongue-lashing from Wendy because of the tape and she's operating from another orbit as far as he can make out since then. Increasingly, she's leaving Ludo in Karin's and Marian's care. A woman who was literally glued to her baby until that tape came in the door. It's the insecurity of not knowing what all of this means that disturbs him. He sent the tape to Billie in the spirit of friendship and maybe a little of the high spirits with which he'd try out new plots or storylines on her when he was stuck in a novel in the early years. They had lots of fun and sometimes sex after such play-acting.

He'd arrive up from his writing cellar in Brabbington Terrace, sometimes with nothing but shorts on in the summer. In the hot summers, the cellar was stifling and it had only one tiny window. Billie could be reading *National Geographic*, one of her favourites, or chopping vegetables in the kitchen. They were semi-vegetarian, not through conviction but out of economic necessity. Without preliminaries he would say, 'I begged you not to make Wilks a partner. Have you seen these accounts?' and she would respond, sometimes without even raising her head from her task. He improvised chunks of tricky dialogue like that. It was one of the things he missed when he moved onwards and upwards with Beth. Spontaneity and improvisation filled her with anxiety. Deviations from her normal schedule made her feel insecure. The first time he tried a dialogue improvisation on her was during the honeymoon.

They went to Venice. In spite of the heat and her ballooning belly, her height and fine bones made her look majestic on a gondola. They were sailing down an overcrowded canal pretending they were the only ones there, persuading themselves that the trip had been worth it, that it was a romantic thing to do, when he fell to his knees and said the following, 'I can't go on. I think we've made a terrible mistake. Why not cut our losses while we can?' She fainted. Back at their hotel suite, when she had been revived and put to bed, he explained about his improvisation techniques. What he didn't say was that he had momentarily forgotten he was with her. He had launched into a routine as if Billie was with him. He takes a large mouthful of beer from the can as he remembers that Venetian heat. The hotel doctor said she needed bed-rest and no excitement. After she fell asleep he roamed the streets alone. He went from bar to bar, café to café. After some hours, he went to the room of a very young street prostitute. He remembers her childish breasts and her skinny knees, little else. She helped him into a taxi and told the driver what hotel to take him to. Beth pretended to be asleep when he fumbled his way to the bed. Next morning they were solicitous of each other but they knew the honeymoon was over.

He'll get fat if he keeps drinking beer secretly like this. Large Lloyd, his cheerful twin, smiles into his consciousness. Lloyd, the singing carpenter. A happy man in his two-up, two-down. A union man, who provides for Mabel and his kids, Molly and Dave, who takes his dad for a short drive every Sunday afternoon, not to break the routine after mum died. Tony realises something new. Up to now, he's always assumed there is something bogus about Lloyd's cheer. A kind of improvisation of happiness and goodwill. A way of making up for his lack of material progress. But supposing Lloyd is really happy. Supposing what you see is what he is? Then what?

After the traumatic improvisation on the gondola in Venice he felt a distance open between Beth and himself that was unbridgeable. Most of the qualities that had drawn him towards her in the first place; her preppy clothes, the well-ordered mind, the sense of a life-plan, her fair skin and blonde hair, so different from Billie's brown skin and very black hair, began to irritate him. He began to feel they were precious and contrived. Only the thoughts of the twins kept him going. Their birth excited him. He felt magnificent. Three children in one year. Lottie and now twins. He didn't dwell on the manner in which he had broken the news to Billie. Months before Lottie was born, he knew he was going to leave. Once he had decided, even though he didn't communicate this to Billie, he felt she would come to realise it herself. Of course she hadn't, and he had been genuinely shocked by that, but you couldn't nurse other people's delusions and hurts for them. It only made them weak.

After Venice, Florence. Beth was excited by the works of art. Her training had been in the fine arts. He forced himself to be attentive to her for a few days as they trailed around endless galleries and mouldy old churches. He had a crick in his neck from looking up at ceilings as she pointed out 'exquisite features'. Everything was dilapidated and gone to seed to his eyes. He was genuinely surprised that people paid good money to see such things and regarded it as one of the trips of a lifetime. He was getting the honeymoon written off against tax as a research trip for his next novel set in Italy and England. By late afternoon Beth was exhausted from the art forays and Tony was tired from boredom but also from the muggy heat. They both lay down for an hour or two before dinner. Beth did her best to appear vivacious and refreshed after the rest and shower, and each night she dressed well, wearing evening gowns that were startling in their magnificence. Mostly they were held up by narrow little straps or none at all. They showed off her blooming white breasts in a creamy, enticing manner. Empire line, they fell in a plentiful sweep from under the breasts to her ankles. The fullness of such folds both hid and accentuated her pregnancy. The play of the dining-room lights on the many different satins of the gowns, pink, red, deep blue, vivid purple drew attention and approval to her.

The head waiter, once he knew of her condition, told the rest of the hotel, and there was a glow of other people's goodwill and concern in which she basked and which she accepted graciously. After dinner and a small liqueur, they lingered on the terrace and chatted about the day's events. Mostly Beth talked. She went over the artistic highlights of the day, recounting in minute detail the very brushstrokes of a particular picture that he had found quite monotonous and in need of a clean-up. There was a murkiness, a hint of musty brownness that clung to almost everything they looked at. Of course, he communicated none of this to Beth. He let her prattle on. It was her honeymoon, after all. He had ceased to think of it as his after the gondola incident. He made love to her after that but with exaggerated care for her safety, as if by such contact they might endanger the safe progress of the pregnancy. She had assured him she was feeling well and strong again. He could see the hungry need in her eyes and he held himself back from it. He escorted her to their bedroom from the terrace and tucked her into bed like an invalid child before he hit the night clubs.

He told her he needed to discover the real Italy, to walk from one little neighbourhood bar to another. To make contact with real people: fisherman, dock workers and the like. In reality he took a taxi from one overpriced nightclub to the next, only stopping long enough to prise the most beautiful woman from her partner to dance with him, then making a quick getaway as the local man had rounded up a few of his buddies to claim 'his' woman back. One night, after too many drinks and feeling dizzy from trying to keep up with an energetic disco number, he wasn't quick enough. They caught up with him at the exit. There wasn't a taxi in sight. Two of them in leather jackets which bulged with muscles held him against the rough outside wall of the club. He remembers registering how uneven it felt against his back. They held him with arms of steel as their friend the 'wronged man' punched him in the groin. He needed to double up in pain but the leather twins would not allow him even to bend at the knees.

'You stay away from my woman.' The man literally spat in his face and almost as an afterthought he produced a knife and cut a casual line across Tony's upper arm. For a ghastly moment as the knife glinted in the night air, Tony thought he was going to castrate him. He fainted. When he came to, it took supreme effort to call a taxi and wait for it. He was terrified they would come out again but he was too weak to walk anywhere. His left sleeve was seeping blood, as if the entire arm might separate at any moment. When he got to the hotel, the hotel doctor attended to him. He knew the doctor did not believe his story about going to a rough pub near the docks and interfering in a knife fight between two of the regulars. But hotels like to preserve decorum at all costs and after he had cleaned Tony's wound, given him an ungentle injection to prevent ulceration of the wound from setting in, he insisted on escorting him to his room to explain Tony's heroic adventure to the signora. On the way to the room he reminded Tony that he was booked in for another week and that he would have plenty of time to recover before his journey to Rome. Tony got the vivid impression that if he left the hotel before his due date the doctor would not only blow his story but personally unstitch his wound to cause him maximum pain.

The light was on when they went in. Beth was in bed reading an outsize book on art in Florence. The doctor played his part well, reassured her of the superficial nature of the cut, upbraided Tony for frequenting tough bars and hoped that the sordid incident would not spoil their last week in Florence. He left them with a solemn bow and solicitous smile that cut through Tony like a knife. As soon as the doctor closed the door, Beth was on her feet fussing over him and cursing his need for authentic research for his novels when it took him to dives and hell-holes. All he wanted was sleep but her agitation made her walk the floor. She rang room service for two hot chocolates. To calm their nerves she said. He felt so flattened after his adventure he doubted if there was a single nerve in his body.

She related a similar incident that had happened to her father. The shy professor and his colleagues one night strayed from their usual bars within walking distance of Harvard Yard. One of them suggested they should sample a real working man's pub and they headed to a spit-and-sawdust bar in Boston. They returned with bloody noses and aches and bruises for their pains. Her father, a natural pacifist, had interfered in a fight between two regulars, attempting to explain to them the senselessness of their actions. More at home with Homer or Socrates, he was unprepared for the violent reaction this provoked. The two erstwhile enemies forgot about their mutual hostility and rounded on daddy and his friends. Her mom blamed the Irish. It had been an Irish pub but her father had insisted that they were Italians. Tony was prepared to side with dad. He had taken a positive dislike to mom at the wedding. A tall faded blonde who was naturally bossy. She asked a lot of questions and expected answers, particularly of him. She had enquired in detail as to his material obligations to his first wife, as she called Billie. Beth's and her father's personality seemed to diminish in her presence.

'Good old dad,' he says as he raises his cooling cup of chocolate to his mouth, 'I'm convinced they were Italians too.' He felt remarkably sober. Maybe shock did that to you.

'Promise me you won't go out to places like that again,' she pleaded with him. And he promised.

He went to sleep almost instantly. He dreamed he was driving through the Burren in Ireland with Billie. That amazing landscape in the west. Endless miles of rock interspersed with the shocking brightness of wild flowers that are so rare that they only grow in one or two other places on the planet. From time to time they get out of the car and examine the burial house of an ancient saint. Peeking through holes on the roof they imagine they see the holy man's bones. Billie crosses herself and says a prayer. He's embarrassed but he forces himself not to look away. Suddenly, as so often happens with the illogic of dreams, he's standing on a cliff edge. He sees a massive mountain of grey clouds gather behind him. He's thinking there's thunder in the air. He looks down at the rocky escarpment below him. Beth and not Billie is standing beside him. This makes him very angry. She's serenely unaware of his feelings. She gazes over the stones in wonderment. She's wearing a red satin evening gown. He grabs her, pushes her towards the edge until he's holding her by her feet. He's dipping her in clouds. All but the feet vanish into their woolly density. Then he remembers she's carrying twins. Boys. He pulls her to safety gently. She seems unaffected by the experience. A car horn honks. It's an Italian taxi. The driver seems impatient to get going. Just as they approach the taxi, two men in leather jackets jump out from behind a furze bush. They dance in tandem to the music from the car radio. They brandish flick-knives playfully. Tony wakes in a sweat of fear. He's jolted into the present by a brisk knock on the cabin door.

'Who's there?' he says as a delaying tactic. Nobody ever disturbs him when they know he's writing. He dismisses the fact that he's been falling behind in his writing schedule for weeks and nothing is being disturbed except his preoccupation with his past. Nevertheless, he doesn't want to be discovered with empty beer cans or the smell of alcohol on his breath. In a deft stroke, he plonks an old manuscript on top of the large wastepaper basket, disguising its true contents, empty beer cans. He rushes to the lavatory and rinses his mouth with mouthwash. He flushes the loo. Shouting above the sounds of plumbing, he says, 'Just coming,' and makes his way towards the door. He crunches up a few blank pages and tosses them in the direction of his desk as if they are discarded ideas, signs of a hardworking writer. He opens the door to Wendy. Because he's spent most of the morning recapturing his ill-fated honeymoon with Beth, when he looks at Wendy, he's struck by her similarity in looks if not temperament to Beth.

'Billie rang,' Wendy says without preamble as she comes into the room. 'Marian is with her at Brabbington Terrace.' Wendy is wearing a white linen mini-suit with short sleeves. Her tanned body moves with energy. The shoulder-length, blonde-fringed hair is newly highlighted. She is crisp and looks cool.

'Oh!' is all he can manage. He's not quite sure what this news means.

'Billie thinks it might be a good idea if she stayed overnight. She'll bring her home tomorrow night after work. I agree with her. Marian is a sensitive child. Her tongue is just a defensive weapon.'

'Only a month ago you were convinced she was a witch.' Tony is taken aback at Billie's and Wendy's agreement on anything at all, least of all Marian, his most difficult child.

'I've had to revise my opinion of her, that's all. She's been wonderful with Ludo these past few weeks. I must say Billie isn't at all what I imagined her to be.'

'Have you been to Brabbington Terrace?' He's mildly outraged. He had never thought of the two women making contact, particularly after the tape.

'No, we spoke on the phone, but you can tell by someone's telephone voice if they are sincere or not and I knew her main concern was doing the right thing for Marian. Toby and Josh are home. I picked them up from the eleven o'clock train. They look wonderful. Very fit, almost like real mountain men. Toby has a slight Scottish lilt. He made friends with a local boy, Hamish. He wants to know if we can squeeze him in on the trip to Greece. I said that was fine. After all, Marian is bringing Elvira.'

'The world and its mother seems to be travelling to Greece with us.'

'I thought you enjoyed playing the old pater. You certainly enjoy it on Saturdays at Dino's. Billie said she sent me the tape as she didn't want you doing things behind my back. Karin has given me a week's notice. She's going back to Munich. She misses her boyfriend Klaus too much.'

'That's pretty selfish of her, I must say. After all we've done for her. A week's notice!'

'It's all under control.' Wendy pats his hand in that sexless way that home helps adopt with pensioners. 'I've managed to get a woman through the agency. She can start as soon as Karin leaves. She'll be quite used to us before the trip to Greece. You mustn't fret.'

Tony senses a shift in his power base. He is the one who usually reassures Wendy. He does not like to be at the receiving end of such assurance. He feels diminished in some inexplicable way. Silly really! Domestic arrangements were a woman's business after all. There was nothing to be upset about. Nothing of any substance anyway.

Marian is sitting in Billie's basement kitchen eating a pasta pesto. The light is on even though it's early evening in July. She's eating with appetite.

'Toby and Josh eat pasta pesto nearly every Saturday at Dino's. I'm sure this is much better, though.' Her mouth is stained with the sauce.

After Billie had rung Wendy with the news that Marian was staying overnight, Marian rang Elvira. Poor Elvira! She had stayed indoors from three in the afternoon until the phone rang at half past seven. Her trip to Greece was secure. She hadn't needed to lie to anyone. When her mother came in at ten o'clock, tiddly after several drinks, she was surprised to find their two-roomed flat immaculately clean and tidy. Elvira needed to work off the nervous energy that had built up in her during the day.

'A bit more house-cleaning like that, my girl, and you'd soon knock off those pounds. Mind you, you seem to have lost a bit since the warm weather came. Things are lookin' up for both of us, it seems. What with you off to Greece in a few weeks time and now it seems this job of mine may not be as temporary as I was led to believe. Old Wilson took me to the Horse and Hare for a few drinks again. Make us a cup of tea, there's a love,' Olive finishes as she collapses into her favourite armchair.

Billie watches this nervous blonde child eat at her table and talk almost non-stop and wonders is it only a few weeks ago that she sat at that very table trailing spaghetti sauce across the colour supplement photos of Tony his wives and their children. She feels she's a very different person now. In the hour or so she's spent with Marian she understands how much she misses Beth, how angry she is with Tony for replacing her mother with Wendy. Also that she loves baby Ludo, favours Toby over Josh, thinks Nellie runs High Pines and she's going to miss Karin, the *au pair* who's leaving. When Cordelia appeared at her door with Marian shortly after six, almost as soon as she got in from work, she was surprised and wary. She recognised Marian immediately and assumed that Tony had sent her, like a parcel exchange despite her protests on the phone some weeks ago. Her relief at finding it wasn't so fired her with an enthusiastic welcome for Marian, almost as if she had been expecting her. Marian responded with a waterfall of words that was still in full flow.

'Lottie still loves you, although she hates you,' the sage thirteen-year-old is telling her. 'She misses you too, mostly during the week.

We've been talking a bit lately, you see. I'm still jealous of her. She's so well . . . herself, if you see what I mean. Always has been. Not like me. But I've tried to like her better and it has made a difference. She was easier to like when her heart was broken. It made me realise she couldn't have everything. She doesn't wish you were dead or anything. She just needs to keep out of your way for a bit.'

'I see,' Billie says and wonders if she does really. But she's happy Lottie misses her and she wonders what kind of a mother she can be to steal Edward from her daughter. Then she remembers his naked body beside her, above her and below her, so many vivid moments of lust. That naked sexual urge that she'd somehow killed off in herself for years. Once she'd rediscovered it, she could no longer allow herself to see Lottie as an obstacle. There was no denying such cravings. Marian finishes her food and looks at Billie expectantly. What to do with her for the evening?

'Could we visit Goldie?' Marian says. 'I'd like to see him again. He played at my birthday party. The one you had for me when mum died.'

'He may not be in,' Billie says quickly, to avoid disappointment. Lately Mr Goldberg has really been stepping it out. Concerts with Babs and Cordelia, walks and God-knows-what outings with Susan, visits to the library and to his tailor. Of late, he'd got several new suits and somehow grown younger. Susan and he have become great chums. Billie would have been jealous except that her mind and body are occupied with Edward. But those pleasant evenings when Goldie and she used to sit in the living-room listening to the lugubrious opening chords of Rachmaninov's Second Piano Concerto as it built in intensity to the magisterial drama of Richter's version seem to be a thing of the past. One Christmas she had given him a present of a video of *Brief Encounter*, his favourite film, with the musical score of his favourite piece of music. He had been so touched that he cried. The only time she ever saw him weep. He said in a suddenly Russian formal way, 'You must excuse my tears. They are for my Irina. I am not unhappy with the gift. It is just that you have chosen too well.'

A knock on Goldie's door finds him at home. He ushers Billie and Marian into his rooms with a graciousness that is reserved for expected guests. He doesn't, as some adults do in the presence of children, point out their rate of growth or enquire about school subjects. He entertains them by playing them a disc of Argentinian tango music. While they listen he hands Billie a glass of Bushmills and Marian a glass of ginger ale.

Marian thinks the music is very strange. Not what she expected from Mikhail Goldberg, the famous pianist. It hardly seems like tango music at all. At least not the kind of tango music they dance to on the telly. Its wonderfully mournful and whimsical chords fill the room. Marian is suddenly sad. Very sad. She misses her mum and for the first time in her life, she realises that Beth is not coming back. Not ever. She can't stop crying. The room fills with her sobs. Billie and Mr Goldberg exchange looks but remain seated. The whimsical squeeze boxes are at one with Marian's sobbing. Finally, the disc ends. Marian's face looks raw. She dabs at it with a damp tissue.

'I don't know what you must think of me. I've never cried like that before. It was the music . . . '

'Only those whose hearts are dead fear the power of music,' Goldie says. 'You are a beautiful young girl. You will laugh and dance to music again. Listen. Your mother took you to ballet classes. I'm sure you remember a little.'

He puts on Bernstein conducting a Stravinsky ballet. At first as the music plays Marian looks at the crumpled tissue in her hand, then tears it into tiny pieces and puts it into her pocket. As the music gathers momentum, her face seems to clear itself and the primitive feeling of the music enters her body until her feet want to dance. She stands up awkwardly, aware of her body. It feels heavy and in a curious way unused. She went to her last ballet class the day before Beth's accident. Her mum dropped her off and picked her up. It had been their last real outing together. She thinks of Beth and how she moved like a dancer through the house, dusting her way to intensity. She would dance an improvised funeral dance for her now.

And she did, shyly at first, unsure of her feet and too aware of her surroundings, but gradually letting the music move her feet and body until she felt herself float upwards with it. She spun herself to a finale and gave a little bow. Mr Goldberg and Billie applauded in a stately fashion. Marian blushed with pleasure and self-awareness as she sat down once again.

'You dance well. Remember most emotion in music is memory and you will always find your feet,' Goldie said and he turned off the music.

There was a knock on the door and then it opened. It was Susan from upstairs. She was wearing her nurse's uniform, already dressed for night duty.

'Evening everyone. Goldie, it looks like I can't turn my back but you get a party goin'. I'll have to watch you like a hawk at the weddin' or you'll be charmin' all the ladies . . . ' Then she noticed Marian's tear-stained face. ' . . . and you're far too pretty to be left on your own with him. I'm glad Billie is chaperoning you.'

'This is Marian, Tony's daughter,' Billie says, but she can't concentrate on the introductions. Wedding? Whose wedding?

'I'm off to the hospital now. I'll pop down for our usual walk tomorrow, Goldie.'

'I think it's very sensible for an older man to marry a nurse,' Marian says and they all laugh.

'Now there's one for the books,' Susan says. 'He's bringin' me to a friend's weddin', a posh do next week, love, but if he proposed this minute I'd probably say yes. He's peculiar but I've gotten used to him.'

Goldie feels the room fill with the thumping of his heart. He is highly conscious of Billie's and Marian's presence but he has not risked love for such a long time; he isn't going to make the same mistake twice. If she laughs in his face then he'll lick his wounds bravely in public.

'In that case, my dear, I would be highly honoured if you consented to be my bride.' He gave a low sweeping bow in Susan's direction.

Afterwards when Billie thought of the sheer melodrama of the proposal and its acceptance, she began to think that the wedding might not go ahead. That the misunderstanding of a thirteen-year-old girl could propel into marriage two adults with an age gap of at least two generations between them seemed farcical. But she knew at least part of her reaction was a selfish one. Goldie had always been in the house with her. She was frightened of the day when he wouldn't be there, when his music and wit were no longer a part of her home.

When Nellie shares the news of Goldie's and Susan's forthcoming nuptials with Bob as they drink tea at a Bring-and-Buy sale, he's shocked.

'Seems like they've all gone off their rockers at the terrace. People should respect generation gaps and not meddle. And what's Darren goin' to say?'

'It's none of his business now. It might teach him a lesson.'

'About what?' Bob is suspicious.

'About life.' Nellie is airy. 'There's no need for you to be lugubrious.' It's her word for this week. Her literacy tutor, Rodney, has told her that her thirst for new words is remarkable.

'I'm not lugu . . . whatever the word is. Where's it all goin' to end? Billie is sleepin' with the Boy Wonder and now Susan's goin' to marry her grandfather. I'd have my suspicions about a man who's in his eighties and has never married no one up to this.'

Nellie puts her cup back in its saucer daintily and waves to a neighbour she spots at the cake stall.

'He lived with a woman called Irina in Russia years ago. The two of them were put in one of those horrible camps. She didn't survive. He did. He told Susan all about it. By the way Billie's off to Russia next week for a fortnight. Edward is doing some kind of a musical concert tour. And the High Pines contingent will be in Greece for the first three weeks in August. I'll be on my light duty roster. We'll have more time together. Won't that be nice?'

'Lovely,' Bob agrees lugubriously.

'We can have an *al fresco* lunch one day. I've saved up enough coupons for that picnic equipment. I'm expecting it any day now in the post. We'll treat ourselves to an extra night of bingo. I just thought, I have my outfit for Goldie's wedding, the one I had made for Darren's and Susan. Nothin's wasted really,' Nellie concludes with satisfaction.

Both Tony and Wendy answer the door when Billie returns Marian to High Pines. There's a moment of awkwardness when Tony asks rather crossly why Marian went to Brabbington Terrace in the first place.

'Because I wanted to see the house you lived in before you married mum and the time I went there for my party I was too young to notice anything much.'

'I enjoyed her company. Maybe she'll visit with Lottie some time.'

Billie pauses briefly on the step as they invite her indoors. She decides to go in and have one drink, then leave. Tchaikovsky's Piano Concerto No 1 fills the house. Lottie must be keeping up her practice schedule. The interior of the house isn't at all what she expected. Not that she had been in it before but she had always expected it to be vulgar over-the-top décor associated with the tasteless *nouveau riche*. Festooned curtains, plump upholstered furniture, ghastly over-familiar art prints in ridiculous gold frames. It couldn't have been further from that impression. The floors were of stripped pine with good but well-worn rugs. The rooms that she could see were furnished with a spareness that appealed to her. Solid pieces but just the right amount. There was a feeling of air and space about the place. Original art decorated the walls, a mixture of old and modern. Beth's choices, presumably. Through the terrace doors she could see a row of very tall pine trees at the end of the garden. Josh and presumably Toby are sparring with two boys in the garden. They wear red boxing gloves. The sun glances off their redness, making them appear quite lethal.

'Toby,' Marian squeals and runs into the garden at full speed. Billie sees her tackle him and bring him to the ground. Josh looks disgruntled at the interruption to the game but Toby hugs her.

Wendy looks quite pleased to see Billie, which she finds curious. Wendy is dressed in a playful T-shirt and shorts with tropical island scenes depicted on them. Her face is relaxed and open. Her blonde-fringed hairstyle and face bear a remarkable similarity to Marian's. She could pass easily for her older sister. In spite of the playclothes she impresses Billie as being something more than the young doll-wife. She is mixing Martinis for Billie and herself. Tony is drinking beer from a can. He seems nervous and on edge.

He is dressed in tennis whites. He's probably had a game with one of the twins before she came. He sits on the couch opposite Billie with that exaggerated sprawl that some people adopt to proclaim they're at leisure.

'Marian is a very sensitive girl,' Billie says to fill the silence. 'I like her. It's hard on a daughter to lose a mother so young.'

'Particularly when the father remarries,' Wendy says, as she hands Billie her Martini and sits beside her. 'I think I didn't understand that until quite recently. I knew she didn't like me and that prevented me from understanding. Then as wife number three one is very insecure anyway.'

Billie is taken aback by such frankness. She scans Tony's face and knows he is making a remarkable effort at pretending he's unconcerned. He lifts the can of low-calorie beer to his lips in a lazy, slow motion way. It seems remarkable to her now that he caused her such misery. He looks so ordinary. The brown hair, still thick if recessive, looks tinted close up, the brown eyes rather doglike and unlively, and the body, for all his efforts at keeping in shape, already shows signs of effort unrewarded. The waist has thickened considerably. She feels certain she could pinch more than an inch. There will come a day when he looks in the mirror and his brother Lloyd will look back at him, his worst fear. She feels no desire to lie down with his body. An image of Edward's and her naked bodies, coiling their lengthy thinness to pleasure comes unbidden to her mind. She knows she's blushing.

'You mustn't feel ill at ease by my third-wife status,' Wendy says, misinterpreting Billie's blushes, 'I've been far too touchy and quite stupid about so many things. It's like as if I've been in some kind of trance, at a distance from reality for a long time.'

Tony can't understand what's going on. When did Wendy become like this? Assertive and airing her fears in public. Is this really only the second time she's spoken to Billie? Or have they been planning this for weeks? They seem incredibly at ease for two people who hardly know each other.

'That can happen easily enough,' Billie agrees. 'You're not the first and you won't be the last woman who has felt insulated from reality until one day it hits her straight between the eyes. Still, it's better to have a rude awakening than none at all.'

'I must be invisible,' Tony says. His lips are smiling but the smile doesn't reach his eyes. 'Maybe I should spar with the boys and leave you girls to chat?'

'There's no need,' Billie says, as she drains the last of her Martini and stands up. 'I've got an appointment at eight.'

And suddenly Billie is gone. They watch from the doorway as she fits her tall body into the ridiculous green Mini and drives off.

'I suppose you think you're very clever,' Tony rounds on Wendy as she close the door. 'Why did you humiliate me like that in front of Billie? What do you want from me? I've given you everything, a beautiful home, a baby . . . '

'You've given me! That's just the point, isn't it? You think you've given me everything. But what about what I gave you? My youth, Ludo. I try my best with all your other kids. I live in the house your second wife designed. This house revolves around you, your writing schedule, your weekend leisure activities, not to mention the sacred feast of the Saturday lunches at Dino's and the socialisation with your friends whether I feel like it or not. I've adapted to your routines, your lifestyle, but you haven't even made one concession to me. But all that will have to change. I'm not putting up with it any longer.' And she leaves him standing open-mouthed at the end of the stairs as she climbs up to the nursery to check on Ludo without even a backward glance at him.

He makes his way to the drinks table. He needs something stronger than a beer. No wife of his has ever spoken to him like that. He opens a whiskey bottle. Uncle Alfie crawls to consciousness somewhere at the back of his head but he dismisses him and pours a double whiskey. Beth had never challenged him openly about anything. She was civilised and believed in the institution of marriage and the traditions that were built into the system. She kept her suspicions to herself. As long as he came home she was willing to pretend all was well. He had realised that quite early on in the marriage and had used it to his full advantage. Even when she was in the hospital being treated for depression, she blamed herself for her condition. She said she had everything to live for, a good husband, wonderful children, a beautiful home. She didn't know what was the matter with her. She knew the treatment was costing him a fortune. She would do her best to get over her anxieties and obsessions. It was shameful, she said, a woman of her education and intelligence to be addicted to housework. It was unfair on him but also the children. She knew she shouldn't expect young children to tidy away every single toy immediately after using it. It would make them anxious and nervous and unable to deal with the disorder that is a large part of the world. She would do her best to overcome her difficulties and be a good wife and mother. That last day, when he found her on her hands and knees scouring the wooden seat of the toilet bowl until she had scored and scarred the wood, they both knew she would never get better. At least while she lived with him.

He had come straight from an assignation with Inga, his Swedish translator. It was a Saturday and he came home on time to take the family to lunch. At that time they patronised a French restaurant called Le Gourmet. Beth simply said, 'Excuse me,' and immediately got the children ready for lunch. After lunch she drove Marian to her ballet class. He took the twins to a Batman film. That night the Hendersons were over for drinks. Pam was on a high. She had just got news that she was to be cast in the American mini-series *Valley of Nightmares*. She would play an upper-class English woman who is running away from her past and who settles in a peaceful valley in midwest America. And yes, you've guessed it, she ends up in a valley of nightmares. Pam did most of the talking that night. Beth, the perfect hostess, listened politely and made sure that everyone had enough to eat and drink. Pam grew raucous with drink and at one point in the evening when the four of them were sitting by the pool after a playful swim, she said, 'What I really need is a massage, a Swedish massage for total relaxation,' and she winked at Tony.

Tony was aware of Beth's watchful eyes, the ones that, no matter how early he woke in the mornings, were always looking at him. Next morning – it was Sunday – she said she was going to church as usual, got into her Volvo and drove off. By midnight that night he was at a hospital claiming her body. She had driven down the motorway at a hundred-and-ten miles an hour. When a police car followed her, its siren blaring, she drove headlong into a motorway café. When they gave him her belongings in a plastic bag, he searched them for a note, an explanation. There was none. Inside her handbag, there was a crumpled hand-out which read,

> Don't give up.
>
> Visit Mr Burroughs today.
>
> HE can change your life.

Come and see.

He reveals to you all of the hidden secrets, evil eyes and lurking dangers that may harm you. If you really want something done about the matter, here is the man who will do it for you in a hurry. Don't tell him, let him tell you.

Underneath there was a Third Avenue address in New York. When Tony told the twins and Marian that Beth had gone to heaven, Marian said, 'She's too young to go there. Anyway, you don't believe in heaven. I heard you argue with mummy about it.' She ran to her room and locked herself in. Only Nellie with the promise of a birthday party in Billie's the following week managed to coax her out again.

He drains his whiskey and pours another. Over five years have passed since then. After her death, he slept a lot. The doctor gave him tablets. He took his consolations where he could. Pam Henderson and a string of actresses whose names now mostly escape him. Afterwards, in bed with Inga, he was surprised to find he was impotent. When he looked at her, he saw Beth's eyes looking back at him. He thought he was cracking up. His work saved him. The weekday nine-to-five routine at his desk, that solid constant at the centre of his life, was the only thing that he felt sure about. Work hard during the week, play hard at the weekends – that had been his routine until he met Wendy.

How could she accuse him of not making any concessions? He hadn't slept with another woman since he met her. What did she want? Blood? By the time he met Wendy he was ready to become a family man again. He had kept the tradition of the Saturday lunches going through thick and thin. Even when his current sleeping partner had lured him with the promise of a dirty weekend in the country, he had said it would have to be after the family lunch on Saturday. Saturday mornings he played with the kids. All of them. He was not a man to turn his back on his responsibilities. He had told Wendy from the start about his large family. It wasn't as if he'd lured her through false pretences. She seemed perfectly happy and accepting of everything until Billie sent her that bloody tape. He was prepared to see with hindsight that it was a mistake for him to make the tape in the first place. But he had been concerned for Billie. He didn't want her to get hurt. To make a fool of herself with a man half her age. He was too soft. That was his problem.

'You're settlin' in to the hard liquor early in the day, aren't you?'

It's Nellie. He hadn't heard her come into the room. She's wearing her usual multi-coloured housecoat and she's got a yellow duster in her hand. She starts dusting the sideboard and its heavy load of family photographs.

'I sometimes think it's like a shrine,' she says, her back to him as she dusts each photograph in its silver frame. 'Best to lay off the whiskey. It will only make you feel lugubrious. Face up to what's botherin' you. Don't sink your troubles in a bottle; you'll drown.'

'It's Billie,' he says like a child confessing to a parent. 'I think I love her.'

'You think you do. That's all.' Nellie continues with her dusting. 'It's her sleepin' with young Edward that's brought them feelin's on. You're angry with her and you've no right to be. You walked out on her years ago, when Lottie was still at the breast. When you left Brabbington Terrace you lost any claims you had to interfere in her life. Fix up whatever mess you're makin' here and be quick about it. Young women today won't take a lot of the rubbish that my generation put up with from men. And good luck to them is what I say.'

Billie is in the Oxfam shop sorting out the latest donation of clothing into bundles of different sizes. It's been a quiet morning so far. It looks as if most of the regulars might be away on a holiday, wherever they've scraped up the money. Or else they're saving their few pounds to buy some of the winter stock which will be put out in the middle of August. She's on her own and glad of it. Mrs Wilson is in the Canaries. She's a nosy old bat. Over the past few Saturdays she's been fishing for news with such titbits like, 'My dear, you're looking so well. Positively youthful. What's the secret? I could do with a resurrection myself.' Billie has held her at bay with platitudes such as, 'I always find the summer rejuvenating, don't you?' or 'I use the Body Shop range of creams and find them marvellous. You should try them.' But she was not to be fooled.

'I think you're in love,' she said boldly over the coffee and chocolate biscuits last Saturday. She knew she wouldn't see Billie for a few weeks.

'I am, with myself,' Billie said, and they both laughed. But Billie could tell the old biddy knew she was holding out on her.

'Love is a two-edged sword,' Mrs Wilson says as she wipes some crumbs from the corner of her mouth with a handkerchief. 'I suspect Reginald has become a little soft on the latest temp in the office.'

'Olive?' Billie has been so preoccupied with her own life she's hardly noticed either of them for weeks except in the mechanical functioning of office life.

'Yes,' Mrs Wilson says sourly. 'They've been having drinks after work lately and he took her out for a Chinese meal last week. It's all very worrying. We both know Reginald isn't the marrying type. I hope he's not harbouring foolish notions. You know how I adore our annual holiday in the Canaries. Just the two of us. Well, he broached the subject of a third party joining us this year. That woman. I doubt if she has two pennies to jangle. A divorced woman whose husband is God knows where. At least my understanding is that he doesn't even keep in touch with the child. And they live in a poky flat on Milton Road. Only the truly impecunious live there.'

'So the three of you are going to the Canaries?' Billie asked.

'Absolutely not,' Mrs Wilson almost spits at her, 'I nipped it in the bud very quickly. I told him our annual holiday was sacrosanct and that he could take whomsoever he liked wherever he liked at another time. I'm hoping the holiday will clear his head.'

Billie has not divulged her plans for Russia to Mrs Wilson. She has said vaguely that she'll probably go home to Dublin for most of the holiday and maybe spend a few days in Cornwall on the way back. She likes that part of the country. In truth, she feels she's running away to Russia with Edward. In spite of Marian's reassuring news that Lottie misses her and doesn't wish her dead, she still feels ill-at-ease on those occasions when they bump into each other at Brabbington Terrace. Goldie tells her that Lottie is keeping up a very strenuous rehearsal schedule, expanding her repertoire and keeping her usual one in good shape. She's using her heartache to make strides with her music. Billie can hear that improvement for herself when Lottie's music fills the house. Lottie usually has supper with Mr Goldberg after the lesson and Tony picks her up after that. He doesn't want her travelling by tube late at night. A few times lately when Lottie wasn't ready when he called, she offered him coffee while he waited. The first time, she thought she might be upset seeing him in the kitchen that they'd once shared but she felt she could hardly leave him on the doorstep when Wendy and he had been so hospitable to her.

She was surprised she didn't feel any discomfort. They had coffee and chatted about this and that. She felt completely at ease in his company. She knew then she no longer resented him or his new life. She was over the hurt at last. She also knew he was the one not at ease. He was trying too hard to be amusing and entertaining. When Lottie came in with her usual 'Hello, mum. Are you ready, dad?' holding herself rigidly at the kitchen door with that closed face that locked Billie out, she knew it was Lottie's face she was running away from. She has been asking Mr Goldberg about Russia but he isn't too forthcoming.

'My Russia is tinged with the savagery of the dark times. It's best not to inflict that on you. You must make of it what you will. There are so many Russias. The land of onion domes and palaces, the land of shortages and queues, the land of music and ballet. You will find your own Russia and, when you bring it back to me, I will tell you about my Russia – but not before.'

She finds his response quite frustrating but he's immovable. The jealous part of her nature has begun to dwell on life without Goldie at Brabbington Terrace. Susan, after Goldie's celebrity reception at the Hamilton-Green wedding party, has begun to appreciate what she's got in Goldie. He melted Mrs Hamilton-Green's heart in moments and when he consented to play a Mozart piece, she was overcome. She said she never realised her new daughter-in-law had such interesting friends. Jeremy, Anne's groom, had the performance videoed on the grounds that it will be archival material when Goldie eventually kicks the bucket. He imagines selling the tape to *The Late Show* in years to come. And at the end of the evening Goldie insisted on accompanying Anne's three brothers as they played a rap number. Everyone danced, from the stiff upper lips on the Hamilton-Green side to the laid back, take-it-easy man, on Anne's side. Susan realised that Goldie was still a celebrity, that his reclusive years only increased his cachet. As she said to Anne affectionately, 'The old bugger is the real thing. They're lining up for his autograph. Isn't it bloody marvellous!'

These days Billie has to tear Edward away from the piano. He's doing nine hours of practice instead of six. As the Russian trip approaches, he grows more intense. Cordelia watches from her careful distance and feeds him well when he comes home. She asks no questions beyond his preferences for food. She wants his Russian tour to be successful. She wishes Billie weren't going with him in case she jeopardises his success but she is wise enough to keep these fears to herself. From time to time when she goes out with Babs to a film or concert, Babs says, 'For the life of me, I can't understand it. You're a great woman to be so accepting,' but she only smiles in response. Cordelia knows about acceptance and life's cruel twists. She survived her primitive living conditions in the converted stables at the school and made it a jolly adventure for Edward. She survived her bigamous marriage to Edward's father by deciding on a decent if fictitious end for him to protect her son. She could wait. She was good at that.

Edward tells Billie he can handle the Mozart, Chopin, Beethoven and the Mahler end of things. It's the Russian part of his programme that terrifies him. He thinks he must be mad to have agreed to play Tchaikovsky, Glinka, Balakirev and Mussorgsky in the land of their birth. It's suicidal. He'll disgrace himself. Admittedly, the Tchaikovsky piano concerto is the only full Russian work on his programme. He's playing a *pot pourri*, a sort of jolly *glasnost* of the rest. The bits of Glinka seem almost like folk-songs or ancient airs to Billie. The same notes repeat themselves in different guises. They call on a kind of universal remembrance. Edward says, 'Glinka said that for Russians it is a matter of either frantic merriment or bitter tears . . . love is always linked with sadness.' They're lying on the floor just holding each other. They haven't eaten or made love since she came in. She can feel such tension in his body that she doubts she has the power to release it. She knows he longs to touch his keyboard, not her. When she suggested that she should go back to Brabbington Terrace and that he should sleep or simply do some extra practice, he burst into tears.

He wants her to stay. Of course he does. He's just nervy. He's had a bad day with Balakirev. The B Minor Overture on Russian Themes is confusing him. Only yesterday he thought he had finally cracked it. Today he found no matter how he tried, the wholeness escaped him. He needs to relax, he tells her. He would be miserable if she went home. And so she stays. They make their own attempt at wholeness towards the end of the evening. It's the first time since they have become lovers that she does not feel transported by his young body.

Babs is angry. Philip can tell by the way she's chopping the cucumber. He's chopping an onion and weeping copiously. They're in his flat making a Saturday lunch. He likes it best when it's her turn to visit him. They've had a relaxing morning. They spent a few hours lazily perusing the stalls at Camden market. He bought some coins to add to his collection, a boyhood habit that he's never allowed to lapse. Babs bought some secondhand biographies and a very old archaeological tome. They had coffee and enjoyed watching the crowds pass by and now they're home and she's murdering a cucumber for no reason that's apparent.

Stravinsky's *Persephone* is on in the background. An opera he's not over-fond of but it's one of her favourites. He's not a man given to crying so he enjoys the eye-wash that the onions afford. Babs is dry-eyed. Onions never affect her. He's a patient man. That's what makes him a good gynaecologist. When Babs and he first met as interns at the same hospital and he told her he wanted to become a gynaecologist, she said, 'A male gynaecologist is almost a contradiction in terms,' and he knew exactly what she meant. He didn't take offence. Philip is one of those rare men who values women and doesn't see them as fearsome irrational creatures as the majority of his male colleagues do. He gives his pregnant patients time to express themselves, unlike most of the conveyor belt system of ante-natal care.

Babs will say what's on her mind when she's ready. In the meantime he enjoys his lachrymose onion cutting and he can cry for Persephone, the reluctant bride of Hades, cut off in the Underworld. He knows by the end of the disc her mother, Demeter will have come to her aid and Persephone will see light again, at least for a third of the year.

'It's Connie,' Babs says cryptically. He waits. Babs the eldest, Billie the middle sister and Connie the youngest.

'She's coming . . . ' Chop, chop, chop. She's hacking carrots now. Philip wipes his eyes, tosses the onions into the wok and stirs.

' . . . tomorrow.' Chop, chop, chop. She stops, tips the contents of the chopping board in on top of the onions.

'Billie is going to Moscow tomorrow and Connie is flying in. Sometimes I feel . . . oh, I don't know . . . Let's open the wine before lunch. I need a drink.'

He keeps stirring. He can hear the cork popping above the sizzling contents of the pan. She hands him a glass of wine and tosses back a large mouthful of wine herself. She moves about the kitchen, filling the dishwasher and returning things to their cupboards, all the time drinking quickly from her glass. He turns down the heat under the wok, ladles out two bowls of soup and puts them on the table. It's not good to drink on an empty stomach. She drains her glass and picks up her soupspoon. He passes her a brown roll. They eat in silence for a moment or two.

'Sometimes I feel like a blob or a block. I mean Billie and Connie got the height and the looks when they were handed out. Billie is off with her young man to the other side of the world and Connie is flying in for a shopping spree. You know how I hate shopping for clothes. She can't wait to get away from Robert and the kids for a week and spend her days in Oxford Street. They're always telling me I've got the best of both worlds, a good career and you. I do love my work. I know that. But supposing you met someone else who agreed to spend every second weekend with you, would I be replaceable?'

The one glass of wine has gone to her head. He can see that. Babs has never had a head for drinks but she obviously needed to have a drink taken before she could ask him that question. He puts down his soupspoon carefully as if testing gravity and looks at her. Her lower lip is drawn in, a mannerism he has noticed she adopts when she's concentrating or worried. He stands up abruptly, the chair scraping the tiles, moves towards her and lifts her like a bride, runs with her over the threshold of the bedroom door and lays her gently on the water bed.

'I love you. Nobody will ever replace you. I'll never share my waves with anyone but you.' He moves on the bed, making waves as he speaks. 'You are my Helen of Troy, the most gifted and beautiful of the sisters.'

AUGUST

A large contingent has come to the airport to see Edward and Billie off. They are surprised but happy. It has broken the atmosphere of Edward's growing nervousness over the past week as the departure date approached. Edward is checking in the luggage. Billie has suggested that Cordelia go with him to give them a little time together before joining the others and herself in the bar. Cordelia is wearing her best silk dress and jacket. It's a gentle baby pink and accentuates her blondeness and her tanned healthy appearance. There's a two-hour delay before boarding. Just as well there's a crowd, Billie reflects. Less time for Edward to get nervous even with a two-hour delay. There's a festive air, almost a carnival feeling to it all. Goldie and Susan are wearing matching bow ties and cream linen summer suits. The generous cut of the pants and the long jacket minimises Susan's extra pounds. Goldie is keeping his tailor as busy as he did in his younger dandified days. He sports an ebony walking stick with a solid silver handle. Heads turn to look at them. Billie can see that Susan is enjoying it all. He insists on ordering champagne for everyone.

'You are going to my homeland. Be my guest. We will drink to your enjoyment and Edward's success,' he says, as he raises a glass to her.

Anne and Jeremy are the biggest surprise of all. Billie hadn't expected them but apparently, since their wedding, Susan and

Goldie make up an occasional foursome with them. Anne is sporting a scarlet velvet dress with a matching miniature hat and very high red shoes. Jeremy looks, as he always does, sober barrister style. They make a dramatic couple. He holds her hand like a teenager. Babs and Philip have come too. Philip is in jeans and a sports-jacket, his usual weekend clothes, but Babs looks lively in a lime-green summer suit. It picks up the green glints in her eyes. Philip appears to be nuzzling her ear a lot as if he's just discovered a new erogenous zone.

Connie, the youngest sister, newly arrived from Ireland, is dressed like a child at the seaside. She's wearing multicoloured luminous shorts and T-shirt with matching runners and aquamarine visor. Around her neck she has a plastic necklace that has a miniature bucket and spade hanging from it.

'It's all I brought,' she explains to Billie. She's taken aback at the glamour of the farewell group. 'I told Robert I need an entirely new wardrobe and I intend to get one. What's he like in bed?' She cocks her head in Edward's direction.

'Dynamite,' Billie says.

'It's not only the hands that are talented then, you lucky thing. Robert's gone right off it since his vasectomy. I know I said six kids was my upper limit. I did my bit and I felt he should do something to prevent a seventh but it's gone bloody ridiculous. The way he goes on you'd think they cut it right off. Bad timing, you off to Russia and me in London. I'll have to make do with old Babs then.'

Nellie, in voluminous flowered dress, topped by one of her Conservative-jumble-sale hats, is vetting Stella as Jamie stands anxiously at her side. Stella wears a dazzlingly white, very short backless dress, white pumps and extraordinary white gloves that start at the knuckles and end at the elbows. Jamie's sling is as white as her dress but the plaster of Paris on his leg looks grey in comparison. Bob is standing on the edge of Goldie's group looking uncomfortable in an unfamiliar suit. Nellie beckons him to join her. Edward and Cordelia rejoin Billie. Goldie is refilling everybody's glass again. Cordelia sips her champagne. A rosy flush suffuses her face and Billie can't tell whether it's anxiety or just the champagne. The two women compliment each other's outfits.

'Edward bought it for me last year,' Cordelia says. 'Quite an extravagance but I love it.'

Billie is wearing a short black dress with black sandals. She pinned her silver bird brooch, a present from Tony after Jamie was born, to its neck. She's excited about the trip. The largest country in the world. She's going to enjoy every minute of it. She looks at her watch and is surprised to see it's almost boarding time. She moves about her group saying individual goodbyes. Goldie kisses her, Russian-fashion, on both cheeks and assures Edward that he's a genius and his concerts will be successful.

'Just trust your fingers, my boy,' he tells him.

Jamie tells Billie he'll miss her but she's to have a damned good time and he presses £50 spending money into her hand as he says, 'The Arnold account worked out brilliantly. They've asked me to do another product for them. I got a big bonus.'

It's a bit of a bore going through the passenger check but at last after a quick look around the duty-free they're aboard. She takes the window seat as Edward is a nervous flyer. The plane is filling up fairly rapidly. Billie is thinking about the time she went to India with Maureen, a college friend, after they finished their finals. That's the last time she travelled a very long distance. The excitement of planning the journey kept them going throughout that final year. The trip itself was a bit of a disaster as Maureen turned out to be quite a fussy traveller and resented Billie making trips on foot or by bus to out-of-the-way places. Maureen never deviated from her schedule. Billie did her best not to let it interfere with her enjoyment but inevitably it did. The photograph of the two of them in front of the Taj Mahal shows them scowling into the sun. India finished their friendship. After that Billie went to London and met Tony and Maureen became a geography teacher and married an ex-priest.

The air hostess is demonstrating safety methods in case of an accident. Edward smiles at Billie as she shows them how to blow up a life jacket, but his knuckles are white with tension. Another hostess makes her way up the aisle to Billie's seat. She has to lean over Edward to hear what she is saying. Billie is surprised to hear that a man, 'her husband', is looking for her. She follows the hostess off the plane with a backward reassuring smile at Edward. Just inside the boarding area she sees Tony. The air hostess reminds her that she has ten minutes only.

'Has something happened Lottie?' Alarm spreads through her body and she is conscious that her hands are perspiring.

Tony seems not to take the question in. He's wearing a light beige summer suit with an open-necked matching shirt. She wonders if he's ever going to answer her. What's the matter with him?

'We're leaving for Greece. We board in half an hour. Lottie's fine.' He sounds robotic. Defeated almost. Billie can't figure it out. 'I wanted to say goodbye to you. I spotted you in the bar earlier with the others. Nellie was there too. I didn't want to intrude.'

'That's right. Susan is giving her a lift home,' Billie says.

'She came to the airport to say goodbye to you, then.'

His voice seems distant and pained. 'I never said goodbye to you properly. When I left you. For Beth, I mean. It's been on my mind lately. I need to know that you forgive me.'

'It's all water under the bridge, Tony. We're both different people now. I've got to go. Have a good holiday.' She walks quickly, almost runs, back to the plane. She couldn't bring herself to say, 'I forgive you.' Why the bloody hell should she? It had taken him fifteen years to understand the cowardice of his going and now he wants forgiveness. No way!

Edward is white with anxiety by the time she retakes her seat. She makes light of Tony's calling her from the flight.

'He had half an hour before the flight to Greece and just wanted to kill time. You know how restless and selfish he's always been. People don't change as they get older. They just become more themselves. We'll order champagne once we've taken off.' She kisses him full on the mouth. The man on the aisle seat next to Edward coughs his disapproval. He heard the air hostess distinctly say the woman's husband wanted her urgently. Kissing him full on the mouth too. A mere boy. Women today! He reflects with satisfaction on the wisdom of his bachelorhood.

Billie slips an effervescent sedative into Edward's champagne. They toast each other and drink quickly. After three glasses Edward says he's feeling quite relaxed but a bit tired and would she mind awfully if he had a snooze. Edward sleeps through the film, dinner, time zones, tea, until finally, an hour from Moscow, he wakes. Billie is reading Tony's latest blockbuster *Furtive Footsteps* and enjoying it. It's a good read, perfect aeroplane reading. Edward can't understand how he's slept so long.

'Exhaustion,' Billie says simply.

He's hungry but they're not serving any more meals. The air hostess gives him a miniature packet of biscuits, a Toblerone bar and a coffee. He scoffs the lot and curiously feels even hungrier.

As they're coming in to land at Moscow airport, Billie tells him to suck on the hard-boiled sweet the air hostess has given them and she holds his hand tightly. His face is ghastly pale. So pale his black hair looks artificial. They land without incident. It takes quite some time as they queue to have passport and landing papers verified and then on to baggage reclamation but finally they're through. The arrivals area is very crowded. They push their way forward as best they can. They're heading for an exit to get a taxi to the university but before they get there, an elderly grey-haired man with stooped shoulders approaches them. He's carrying a placard with Edward's name on it. Beside his name there is a drawing of a piano.

'Please, excuse me,' he says timidly and points to the placard, 'I am Professor Demenov from Moscow University.'

Edward introduces Billie and the man kisses her hand. It's very hot. Billie feels her dress is sticking to her.

'I have little English,' the man explains. 'I bring you to university.' He smiles continuously as if to make up for his poor English. They drive there in his Lada. It's stiflingly stuffy in the car. Billie's first impression of Moscow is of a large ugly city in need of repair. There seem to be innumerable high-rise utilitarian blocks everywhere. There are very few cars on the road, an oddity, since this is meant to be the capital. Trolley buses rattle by at regular intervals. The people on the streets seem poorly dressed; their shoes are particularly poor, she notices. On their way the professor points out a few buildings and monuments of interest: the Central Lenin Museum; the Trade Union House, a green building with white columns; a monument to Pushkin built by the Moscow people. Finally, they are in the university area. There is a large number of yellow buildings with lots of trees. There are twenty-eight buildings in all, the professor tells them, forty thousand students, sixteen departments and seven thousand professors. He recites the statistics with a familiar pride. He stops in front of one of the buildings and announces, 'You are here.' He parks the car and they follow him indoors. They enter an enormous circular hall with statues inset on ledges at regular intervals.

The professor leaves them for a moment and goes to one of the many rooms that lead off the hall. He returns almost immediately, leading a group of men with him. What strikes Billie about them is their enormous range of heights. One man appears almost a giant while another is surely a dwarf. The other three are of average height. They are all professors at the university and they welcome them very formally to their college. The giant, Dr Lazlo, is in charge of Edward's programme. He has a young face under a thick head of white hair as if suddenly at a specific moment in time trauma had transformed him. His face is tanned and his blue eyes are alert with intelligence. The dwarf, a Dr Roskolnokov, is Professor of English and speaks the tongue flawlessly with an Oxbridge accent. His brown hair is jelled severely from the forehead in the manner that some pop stars favour. He is dressed in tweeds, with a waistcoat in spite of the very hot weather. His shoes are brogues and are polished to a high gloss.

Billie is so transfixed by the contrasting appearances of Dr Lazlo and Dr Roskolnokov that she's unable to concentrate on the introductions to the three grey medium men. Except to pick up on the fact that they're in the music department and Dr Lazlo is their head of department. Dr Lazlo leads his guests to a room off the hall. It is a high-ceilinged circular room painted a buttercup yellow, almost a miniature of the entrance hall. At regular intervals on white stone ledges on the walls there are busts of Mozart, Chopin, Tchaikovsky, Mahler, Haydn, Brahms, Beethoven and many others, presumably Russians whom she can't recognise. In the centre of the room there is a table covered in a salmon-coloured damask cloth and laden with food. It appears to be a buffet. As she gets closer to it she sees roast chicken, caviare, crab, devilled eggs, salads and pickles. She asks for a lavatory before eating. She needs to wash that stale aeroplane feeling from her hands and face. Dr Roskolnokov leads her off through a maze of corridors of echoing marble to her destination. As they walk, he talks to her. She marvels at the exact perfection of his English accent. He could be on BBC 2.

'You mustn't let my lack of height distress you unduly. I don't. One must adjust to one's inadequacies sooner rather than later in this life, don't you think? Otherwise one could be severely unhappy.'

'Yes, I'm sure you're right. I'm sorry if I stared at you.'

'Better to stare than look away,' he says philosophically. 'You are not pure English bred. Your accent?'

Billie laughs. 'I'm not English at all. I'm Irish. It's the island west of England.'

'Ah, the one at the edge of the world. The IRA I have heard a little about – the Irish hatred of the English. But you love an Englishman. You have gone against your people in this?'

'Not precisely.' Billie feels cornered. 'You ask too many questions.'

'You have a face that invites questions.' They walk in silence until he points out the tiny green door that is the ladies loo. Inside there is only one toilet bowl and a minuscule sink. She wonders if the women who work in this building have to walk as far as she did to relieve themselves. On their journey back to the buffet room, he tells her about his lifelong ambition to visit London. When they return they find the others have drinks in their hands.

'Thank goodness you're back,' Edward says. 'Now we can eat. They wouldn't start without you.'

Dr Lazlo clears his throat and there is silence while he welcomes Edward, the protégé of his old friend Mikhail Goldberg, on this, his first visit to Russia. He hopes it will be the first of many. Also, he says he would like to convey his department's good wishes and felicitations to Wilhelmina, his charming companion. They raise their champagne glasses to Billie and Edward on this their first evening in Moscow.

Afterwards in their hotel, one of those youth hotels that had been built for the Olympics, Billie asks Edward how come she was Wilhelmina all of a sudden. Lazlo didn't understand about 'Billie' he told her. Thought it was a boy's name. Then he had explained that her real name was Wilhelmina. That's all. She was feeling grumpy and tired by then. After all she hadn't slept on the plane. Roskolnokov had driven them to their hotel after the reception. His car had been adapted for his height, she noticed. He explained to them the intricacies of the Russian hotel system as he queued with them to book in at reception. It took over half an hour as several coaches of tourists had arrived just ahead of them. He handed over their passports and gave them their keys, travelled up to their seventh floor room with them and introduced them to the *dezhurnaya*, the floor manageress, a massive woman with coiled hair, to whom, he explained, they would have to hand their keys when they went out. They were lucky, he told them, to be on the seventh and not the twenty-fifth floor as the lift often broke down and seven floors was not too taxing to negotiate. He warned them to shower early in the morning as the plumbing was not reliable after eight. Too many demands on it. The hotel catered for four and a half thousand guests! He advised them to try the *kasha*, a kind of buckwheat porridge and *kefir*, a thin yoghurt, for breakfast. He gave them a map of the metro system which baffled

Billie since all the names of the stations were written in the Cyrillic alphabet. He had, however, pointed out the nearest metro to them which was just across the road from the hotel and he had written the name of the station in the Cyrillic alphabet with an English phonetic pronunciation next to it. He gave them some kopecks and small denomination roubles with which to purchase the metro disc.

Groggy with fatigue and drink, Billie makes for the shower. No water, not a dribble. She tries the small handbasin. There's a thin stream. She thinks she'll conserve it by plugging it but there's no plug. She looks in the bath for one but there's none there either. Exasperated, she spreads her face cloth and one of the thin towels that hangs on the towel rack to catch the last of the water. Roskolnokov had said the *dezhurnaya* would sell them mineral water or tea or arrange to have their laundry done but Billie doesn't feel up to facing the coiled Medusa just yet. She undresses and brings the wet towels with her back to the bed. She lies on the bed as Edward sponges her body, the front, then the back. He is gentle but she can feel the rough fabric of the towel chafing her skin. It's arousing in a strange primitive way. She kisses him when he's finished, one of those deep intimate kisses and he knows she wants him. He pulls off his clothes quickly and begins to sponge his own body with the towel, so vigorously she can see red friction marks on his skin. They don't dry each other. They come together in a noisy moistness, their wet skin making little plopping noises that make them laugh.

Next morning, the early sun streams through the flimsy curtains. It's only half past five but Billie gets up anyway and has a delicious shower. She watches the shower gel make sudsy rivers on her body. She washes her hair. It dries quickly, her short black bob. She puts on and takes off a face mask and after that she feels ready for her first day in Moscow. Edward is still asleep. She dresses and leaves the room to make her first deal with the *dezhurnaya*. She is parched with thirst as there is no air-conditioning and they'd drunk so much the night before. The gorgon is at her desk, counting packets of something. They look like tights to Billie from a distance but when she sees her approach she puts them away quickly.

'Water?' Billie asks. Roskolnokov has advised her to confine her English to one or two words when talking to hotel staff. The woman produces a large bottle of water from under her desk.

'Two dollars,' she says, her face impassive. Billie gives her the money and says thank you. The woman inclines her head slightly but does not speak. Edward is awake when she gets back to the room. They drink the water from toothmugs, then Edward showers and dresses. It is still only seven o'clock and breakfast isn't served until eight. They decide to have a look around the neighbourhood. The height of the hotel surprises them by daylight. The street is already busy with trolley buses. People going to work presumably. They cross the road to check out the metro. Inside, hundreds of people are on the march. Muscovites slip the metro disc in place and rush towards escalators. They queue for some discs now rather than later. Billie uses her phonetic phrase book and secures the discs from an elderly woman with very loose skin. She sits inside a tiny glass-fronted kiosk.

Outside once more, they stroll a few blocks. The buildings are without distinction. The upper parts seem to be flats and the lower parts are shops of various kinds. There is very little advertising of a western nature. You have to go up close to a window to discover the nature of business conducted within. They see an electrical shop that sells old-fashioned looking washing machines and rather clumsy fat cookers. A bakery carries only two types of bread and one type of cake and very little of it at that. They come to a little park with trees and seats and a statue to some hero or other where they sit down for a while and watch the Muscovites pass on their way to work. Then they head back to the hotel for breakfast. They ignore Roskolnokov's advice and have eggs with caviare, tea and a roll, followed by a coarse type of sausage. They discover there is a separate dining-room for every two floors of the hotel. Theirs is enormous, with enough space to feed three hundred at a time. Billie finds it somewhat dehumanising to think of herself and Edward as part of the great tourist rabble eating at the trough. The tables are set in monotonous horizontal lines, reminiscent of boarding schools and other institutions. Lingering isn't encouraged unless you are doing a black-market currency exchange with one of the waiters. Billie says she doesn't feel up to such bartering yet and besides they need to change money officially to get their currency slip marked for going home. They do so at the official *bureau de change* in the hotel. The roubles look and feel unreal. So many of them. Thick bundles. Toy money.

They go back to the metro and insert their disc like everyone else. They take the down escalator and are surprised by its dizzy descent. It's mountainously impressive. Their caviared eggs swill in their stomachs.

'The Underworld,' Billie shouts above the noise of people.

When the escalator stops they are both unprepared for the magnificence that surrounds them. Chandeliers light marbled floors and walls. There is no dirt or graffiti as in the London Underground.

'I could live here,' Edward says.

The train stops at many equally beautiful stations on their route. From the windows they see tiled or copper murals to the heroes of the revolution. They manage to get out at the correct station and walk the rest of the distance to the university. Lazlo is there with an affable 'good morning' and immediately starts a detailed discussion about rehearsal hours and performances with Edward. Billie is waiting for one of the grey men. She can't remember which one. He's going to show her some of the sights of Moscow while Edward rehearses with the orchestra. He comes within five minutes of her arrival and executes a low bow combined with 'good morning'; then he says, 'Kaganovitch will be honoured to show you Moscow.' Kaganovitch apologises that he does not as yet have a car. Such a luxury might be his, he implies, next year.

Billie assures him she's very impressed with the metro and so they start on their day. He's a good if a rather colourless guide. He doesn't talk continuously but points out what he thinks might most interest her. They start at Lenin's tomb in Red Square. Billie is dismayed when she sees the length of the queues but Kaganovitch flashes Billie's passport at a guard and they are moved on to the tourist queue. This queue lasts twenty minutes instead of the four-hour one for Russians. Lenin himself is a disappointment. He seems quite small and yellow. She doesn't know what she'd expected.

The size of the Kremlin almost overwhelms her. She's used to seeing mock-ups of Trinity Tower in the centre of the Kremlin's west wall in films. That doesn't prepare her for the size of everything. There's so much of it. Cathedral Square with its bell-tower and the massive two-hundred-ton broken bell is extra-ordinary. She can't hold the names of the individual cathedrals in her head for long. They go into the one that is the private church for the tsars. Kaganovitch tells her that Ivan the Terrible was excommunicated from the church after his fourth marriage. When he wasn't allowed to participate in full church ceremonies he built a staircase and porch which allowed him to eavesdrop on the main event.

She is touched by the story. A man who did foul deeds but who still wanted to be included in devotions. She looks at the cannons around the Kremlin walls. Napoleon had to leave them behind when he left Russia in a hurry in 1812. The museum collection is impressive, Fabergé eggs from the tsar's family, the fascinating English collection of silver that Elizabeth I had sent to Ivan the Terrible when there was talk of a possible marriage between them. A diamond throne that looked unreal and endless royal dresses and armoury.

Kaganovitch's commentary is helpful yet restful. She does not feel rushed or besieged with information. He looks at exhibits that interest him while she follows her own tastes but even so, by one o'clock she's exhausted. She needs to sit down. There are very few seats for the public to sit on as they view Russia's splendid past. Her legs ache. Billie says she would like to treat Kaganovitch to lunch, something special. He has been an excellent companion. Where would he suggest? Her question embarrasses him but she does not know why. He looks beyond her as if he hasn't quite heard her. Then, he refocuses on her as if he's taken a firm decision.

'I would like to dine at McDonald's,' he says.

They queue outside McDonald's for half an hour. Billie tries not to concentrate on her feet. Kaganovitch entertains her with stories about the music department. Lazlo is an impressive man but a dictator nonetheless. There are cutbacks in all departments. Kaganovitch, who used to share a secretary with four other members of staff, now shares one with eight. Nothing can be done. There are more students but less money. Everywhere it is the same. His wife, a medical doctor, could tell a tale or two. A TV crew from the West came to her hospital. They were making a programme on serious topics, the after-effects of Chernobyl, the full extent of AIDS in Russia. They asked about disposable syringes. They could not believe the hospital had none. Moments later, inside the plastic brightness of McDonald's, Kaganovitch eats his Big Mac, milkshake and double fries with the relish of a teenager.

They travel together to her metro stop for the hotel. Kaganovitch kisses her on both cheeks like an old friend and gives her a guide to Moscow in English. At the hotel, coaches have just disgorged another hundred or so tourists. They are queuing grumpily for registration as their tour guide placates them as best she can. Billie takes the lift to the seventh floor. The Medusa is not at her desk. She must work nights only. Even she must need sleep. At her place is a smallish woman with a tidy bun of grey hair. Billie shows her the room card and is given her key. The woman smiles. Billie says '*Spasiba* – thank you', a phrase she's picked up from Kaganovitch during the day.

Edward is still at the university. She tries the shower. No water. She washes herself with the few dribbles of water in the tap and falls on the bed, grateful finally to be off her feet. She is aware of the rumble of traffic outside and the bright sun penetrates the thin and flimsy curtains but the pull to sleep is irresistible.

Wendy is happy. In spite of everything or because of it. She doesn't know and it doesn't seem to matter. Tony's down mood is having no effect on her. He knows it and resents it. The plane trip to Athens has been bearable. Ludo is a marvel. He is interested in everything and doesn't cry or show any signs of fear when the plane leaves Heathrow. The new middle-aged nanny, Miss Hogarth, allows Marian and Lottie to take turns looking after him. Josh, Toby and Hamish play computer games and listen to their Walkmans. Elvira gets sick but is organised enough to do it into her sick bag. It's her first time flying. She's ashamed that her stomach has let her down. Marian doesn't mock her but suggests gently that maybe she should drink mineral water only until they reached terra firma. Elvira, who has been looking forward to her first plane food, nods her agreement.

At Athens, they have an hour's delay before their short flight to Iraklion. It is stiflingly hot in the airport. The noise and bustle of airport personnel and people in transit adds to the feelings of discomfort but they are soon on their flight for Crete. After take-off the children are excited at being over water. Tony keeps himself apart from such infectious enthusiasm and buries his head in a newspaper. They have no sooner finished the light snack than the plane lands at Iraklion. They are put on a bus and brought to Arrivals. Soon, they are in the confusion of young boys wanting to carry their luggage or taxis shouting for custom. It's hot, very hot but the sea breeze blows a freshness too. Their destination is to the west of Iraklion.

They bundle themselves into two taxis and are on their way. Off the main road, the track narrows. They pass a few donkeys laden with goods, followed by slow walking owners. At the bend of a road they almost run over a goat, an obstinate goat who, in spite of the drivers honking their horns takes his time about moving. Marian notices the strangeness of painted tree trunks. Lottie plays plaintive Irish tunes on the tin whistle. Toby, Josh and Hamish look out for local talent and Ludo sleeps on nanny's lap, finally worn out by his first long journey. Elvira has recovered enough to be able to look forward to her first Greek meal. Wendy is enjoying this moment of arrival. Tony keeps up a sporadic conversation with the driver. Finally, they arrive.

The two villas are being rented to them by a farmer. They pick up the keys. The farmer, Ari, a handsome man crowned with coal-black curls, shakes Tony's hand solemnly and fills him a glass of cloudy ouzo. He waits while Tony tosses it back in two or three gulps. His wife, Helen, a fat woman, kerchiefed and dressed in a dowdy summer dress, gives Wendy a round cloth that holds a goat's cheese. The cheese smell invades the car on the last hundred yards to the villas. Then they have arrived. The two villas are side by side and within sight of the sea. The children scream with the delight of release and mobility once again. Ludo wakes up and seems surprised by his new surroundings. Lottie and Marian swing him between their arms and run with him towards the sea. Elvira holds back, uncertain which way to go.

'This is home for the next few weeks,' Wendy says kindly. Elvira, grateful for such a welcome, helps nanny and her unload the luggage. The boys are getting out of sticky jeans and flinging them to the ground. Tony has opened both houses and is already inside.

'I was born to shop,' Connie says as she flops amid her assorted bags from Harrods and Liberty on to Babs's couch. 'I wonder how Billie is getting on with her toy-boy. To tell you the truth, I never thought she had it in her, did you?'

'It depends on what you mean,' Babs says lightly. Connie is already irritating her and it's only been forty-eight hours. How will she survive the rest of the week? Babs looks at the gangly thirty-nine-year old mother of six. She's wearing a turquoise halter top that barely covers her breasts and a skirt that is little more than a belt. She blows smoke rings as she waits for Babs's reply.

'Billie is beautiful in a . . . in a Spartan fashion,' Babs says simply. 'Beautiful people get more chances than . . . than the rest of us.'

'Do I detect a teeny weeny bit of jealousy? I hope I do. I was stunned with it, jealousy I mean. When I found out I couldn't sleep for nights. I kept waking Robert, begging him to lick my breasts or at least sleep with his arms around me or something. In the end I opted for an anti-wrinkle cream and a good flirt with the young men who collect the carts from supermarket car-parks.'

'You don't use your energy properly; you never have,' Babs says with the placid certainty of the eldest sibling. 'If you were doing something worthwhile you wouldn't be dwelling on Billie's life. You'd be too busy living your own.'

'I'm not exactly lady of the manor, you know. I'm on my feet morning to night with the six of them. If it isn't the school run, I'm ferrying them to ballet, basketball, tennis, friends' houses. It's never bloody ending and sometimes I think Robert is the biggest child of all. Do you know he still can't use the microwave?'

'Learned helplessness,' Babs says. 'He makes a mess of it each time; you pooh-pooh him and do it for him. That's all. It's the same with the kids. The three eldest are old enough to discover the public transport system.'

'You're right. But then you're always right. I should make more time for myself. But what would I do with the time if I got it?'

'It really doesn't matter. Get out of the house. Go for long walks. Sit in a café and read a newspaper. Just recognise that you are an individual. You don't have to have your kids about you day and night. In the long run it won't be good for them. They'll become too dependent on you. Then the real world will be difficult for them to handle on their own.'

'I need a drink. Pour me a gin and tonic. All I need right now is to hear I'm a bad mother as well as everything else.'

'Everything else?' Babs enquires as she pours the drink and hands it to Connie.

'I told Billie about Robert's vasectomy. He didn't seem much interested in sex after it. I thought it was one of those male macho reactions. Affecting him, if you see what I mean. But a few weeks ago, I was clearing out one of his jacket pockets to take it to the cleaners and I found a receipt. A credit card receipt for two. Hotel accommodation and dinner. He said it was for Tom and himself. That weekend they'd attended a conference in Waterford. Tom forgot his credit card and he'd run out of cheques. But I didn't believe him. Tom is the most organised person I know.'

'Did you ask Tom about it?'

'Yeah. He backed him up all right but . . . You're right. I've never used my energies properly. You've got your career, Billie at least got her degree before marrying Tony but I just got the hots for Robert and married him straight after school. What the hell do I do now if he leaves me with six kids?'

'You could be wrong. There's a strong possibility you are.'

'No,' Connie says quietly. 'I followed them one night after work. She's a partner in the firm. Petite but fiercely motivated. You know the type. Power suits and sweet smiles that can wither. They took her car. They went to that French restaurant that Robert's always telling me we can't afford. They had a window seat. I could see their heads together over the menu.'

'Maybe it was business.' Babs realises that Connie has let this thing eat away at her, possibly for months.

'Oh, it was business all right. Love business. The bastard!' she adds with ferocity as she puts her glass out for a refill.

'It's the most natural thing in the world to look at a menu together if you're having a meal with someone. I'm sure you're getting upset about nothing at all. It was a business dinner, nothing more.'

'Oh, he told me that he'd had dinner out with her ladyship when he came home. Even told me what they ate.'

'Well, then, it was all above board.'

'It was a double bluff?'

Connie's eyes are earnest. As she looks at her, Babs is beginning to wonder if the downside of Connie's hyperactivity, the days every so often when she can't motivate herself to get out of the bed, is just a symptom of something more serious. Robert has always doted on her. She can't imagine him having an affair.

'Billie is having it off with baby Edward. I'm sure Cordelia couldn't have imagined such a thing this time last year. You see, everything is possible in this scurrilous world of ours, my dear sister. She told me he was dynamite in bed. Told me at the airport. Rubbed my nose in it, so to speak. Robert could be having it off with tiny Tina.' Babs realises that Connie is drunk. It will be another five minutes before dinner is ready. She opens a packet of peanuts and empties them into a bowl. She chews on a few to encourage Connie to eat something but Connie is in full flight and pushes the bowl away impatiently.

'The only thing I could think to do in retaliation was to come to London and buy a complete new wardrobe. Hurt him in the pocket since I can't reach his heart.' She fumbles in the miscellaneous bags and pulls out various receipts. She looks at them with a certain amount of satisfaction, then she shreds them like confetti and throws them in the air. They land on her short black hair. An adorned shopping bride, she slumps back into Babs's deep leather chair and says, 'I hope you're having a good time in Russia, Billie. Give him one for me.'

Billie is dreaming. She is walking in Red Square in a transparent ankle-length gown. She is leading a procession into St George's

Hall. Its white and gold walls glow. Mikhail Gorbachev and Mr Goldberg are leading Lazlo, Roskolnokov, Kaganovitch and a large crowd in her direction. Gorbachev stops and raises his right hand. He's pointing to a list on the wall. A list of the honoured. A calligrapher steps forward with pot and pen. In gold leaf he writes Edward's name in the Cyrillic alphabet. There is tumultuous applause. A dwarf steps forward and says, 'We have melted down some of the silver of Queen Elizabeth I to make this for you.' It's a silver piano on a plush purple cushion. Edward says, 'There will be some problems with tuning.' Billie wakes.

Edward is asleep beside her, his lips slightly parted as if in surprise or delight. His eyes move underneath his lids. He must be dreaming. She can't remember his coming in. There's a lot of noise in the corridor. Footsteps moving up and down, doors closing and opening. She can hear the rumble of trolley buses from the street too. Maybe the noise woke her. She fumbles for her watch by the bedside table. It's almost midnight. She reaches for the mineral water bottle and dribbles thirstily from it. She doesn't know whether she's hungry or not or if Edward's had dinner. How could she have slept so much? Maybe there's water. She'd love a shower. Miraculously, there is. Tepid but it's better than nothing. Edward is still asleep but she's too restless to go back to bed.

She dresses and decides to see what's available in the hotel. She wouldn't mind a light supper. She closes the door behind her and goes into the corridor. It's narrow and quite sinister. The Medusa is at her desk at the very end. As she walks towards her she's conscious of all of the comings and goings in the rooms around her. Several dark-skinned men in leather jackets seem to be going to different rooms on some kind of business. Russian girls with dyed blonde hair and cripplingly high heels are knocking on doors and going in. A few of the men approach the Medusa and give or are given something by her. Their actions are so quick, Billie wonders if she's imagined it. Maybe they are simply passing her their keys as she herself is about to do. 'Is there a restaurant open in the hotel?' she asks her with the help of her phonetic phrase book. The woman shakes her head. Billie decides to see for herself.

When she gets to the lift, she waits beside one of the men in the leather jackets. They get on together. There is another leather-jacketed man in the lift when it arrives. She presses the button for the ground floor and tries to tell herself there is no need to be frightened.

'You want change money,' one of them says as the lift descends.

'No thank you.'

'You have tights to sell? Cosmetics? I buy.' The second man says.

'No,' she says automatically.

'Maybe tomorrow,' the first man smiles. 'I here in hotel always.'

'Maybe,' she says. She wishes the lift moved faster. It stops at the second floor and a middle-aged couple get on. Finally, she's at the ground floor. There are coachloads of tourists queuing with their passports at reception. They are placidly weary and listen with dazed expressions to their guide. She could do with a cup of coffee or even a drink. The guide is speaking in English to her weary troops. 'The restaurant is closed but when you check in you will be given a package of food. Some bread, a chocolate bar and an apple.' Billie wishes someone would give her a package of food. She's suddenly ravenously hungry.

She follows the sound of noisy music. It's coming from the ground floor bar. It's muzak, presumably in Russian. The bar is crowded. Groups of people sit at tables or by the walls on high stools. The atmosphere is somehow hectic. Billie is trying to figure out why this is so. She moves towards the counter and says 'Beer, please.' A bottle and glass appear quickly. 'Two dollars,' the barman says and she pays and sits on the edge of a noisy group of singing Germans who have ignored the muzak and are lustily recalling their fatherland in song.

Edward wakes and reaches for Billie and finds she is not there. He checks the luminous dial of his watch and discovers it's two o'clock in the morning. Sleepily he gets out of bed to see if she's in the bathroom. He's alarmed when she's not. He pulls on his clothes quickly and heads for the door only to discover it's locked from the outside. He mutters in frustration and walks up and down the room. Finally, he sits on the bed fully dressed and curses. A few minutes later, he hears the key in the door and Billie comes in. She's carrying two bottles of champagne, a tin of caviar, a lump of cheese and a little packet of crackers. She looks pleased to find him awake. She's slightly merry after three beers.

'I brought us a midnight feast,' she says expansively as she lowers her booty to the bed and kisses his forehead.

'I was frightfully worried,' Edward says pettishly. 'I had no idea where you were and the door was locked when I tried to get out.'

'Never mind; I'm back now. I only went as far as the ground-floor bar. I had to lock the door to hand the key into the Medusa. She could cast an evil spell on us.' She nibbles the side of his mouth. 'How did your rehearsal go today? I had a wonderful day with one of the grey men. Kaganovitch. He's not really grey when you get to know him. But I was so tired after it all. I slept.'

'I didn't wake you. I was exhausted myself. It was nine by the time Lazlo dropped me off. We went to a Russian restaurant for dinner.'

Billie is annoyed that he had dinner out without her but she doesn't want to say it. Instead she invites him to her feast by popping the cork of one of the bottles and filling two glasses. She nibbles the lump of cheese and bites into a cracker alternately. The beer has made her hungry. He drinks from his glass in a half-hearted fashion. 'I have to be at the university by nine tomorrow,' he says, as if reminding himself of the fact.

'You mustn't stay up eating and drinking with me if you're tired,' she says, 'but I intend to finish the bottle and the cheese and crackers.' She speaks with the deliberation of a woman with a mission.

He tosses his glassful back, the bubbles wetting his nose, and puts his glass out again. They drink the bottle with an impressive speed, Billie pausing for her crackers and cheese between gulps. In that oozy alcoholic state, crumbs of crackers down the front of her blouse, he strips her. And she strips him. Just enough clothes to get at the parts they want. They struggle on the unmade bed, the room whirling about them until they've reached home.

They both have a slight hangover in the morning. Over a breakfast of orange juice, weak coffee, eggs and slightly stale bread rolls, they comfort each other with hugs. Billie swallows two Panadol and gives half the remaining packet to Edward in case he needs them for the rest of the day. She's meeting Kaganovitch at the nearest metro station at ten o'clock. Edward has to leave immediately after breakfast. He won't see her until ten that night but he has booked a table for dinner through Lazlo at a cooperative restaurant. Lazlo, Roskolnokov, Kaganovitch and his wife are coming too. So, it will be quite a party. Tomorrow there are no rehearsals, just a three-hour practice on his own. He can let his hair down, enjoy being with her instead of clock-watching.

Kaganovitch is waiting for her outside the metro when she

arrives. Today, he isn't wearing his grey suit. He has on a pair of very old jeans and a faded T-shirt with 'I love New York' stamped on it. His grey hair is newly washed and she smells a rather unpleasant aftershave.

'Good morning, Wilhelmina,' he says, 'I am in western clothes today. I do not have to go to the university in the afternoon. Dr Lazlo has instructed me to occupy your day.'

She tries not to laugh and thanks him, then asks if they can go to Arbat Street. She has been reading about it in the guide book he had given her.

The children are up early and go down to the beach soon after dawn, even though they have been awake most of the night in the excitement of finding themselves in a house on their own. All except Ludo, of course, who, along with nanny, slept with Wendy and Tony in their house. Lottie, Marian and Elvira have one room. There is a double bed and single in it.

'I'll have to have the single, I'm afraid, just in case I . . . '

'That's all right, Mars,' Lottie had said in such a warm way that Marian didn't mind the abbreviation of her name. 'Elvira and I will have to fight it out then. I bags the window side of the bed.'

And Elvira agreed instantly. There are two sets of bunk beds in the other bedroom, so Josh, Toby and Hamish have a bed each with one to spare. Josh and Toby claimed the upper bunks. They left both bedroom doors open during the night and they told noisy and scary ghost stories. At one point at about one o'clock in the morning, Tony wanted to go next door to tell them shut up and get some sleep but Wendy stopped him.

'It's their first night. They'll exhaust themselves tonight and they'll settle down tomorrow night. Don't spoil the magic for them.'

'You're getting very tolerant of late,' he says, burrowing into the bedclothes as if it were the depths of winter and not a very warm summer's night.

Their bedroom is quite large. It has a big double bed, a double wardrobe and dresser. The second one, Ludo's nursery for the duration, is smaller. It holds a single bed for nanny, his travelling cot, a suitcase of his favourite toys and a little cupboard that Wendy has made into a nappy-changing area. Downstairs, the kitchen runs the length of the little house. It has the small traditional windows that don't allow too much light but since the door will nearly always be open it can't get gloomy. Off the kitchen is a cool store and pantry. Outside, in the back, there is a crude wooden shed that's a store for paints and a few gardening tools. Tony plans to work in there. Wendy thinks that the heat in such a confined space will get to him but she doesn't say it. Christina, a middle-aged grandmother from the village, is going to look after them. Her black clothes and solemn air make her seem almost immortal, a character left over from a classical tragedy.

Wendy resolves not to be intimidated by her as she has been by Nellie. She loves the sun and the sea. Everything is going to be wonderful. The nanny is very good with Ludo. He responds to her air of command with good nature and ease. Wendy is picking up invaluable hints on how to cope with Ludo's liveliness and high spirits. She knows Tony doesn't like Miss Hogarth because she's plain. Her black hair is streaked with grey and she wears it cropped to above the ears. A bulky woman, her grey nanny's uniform does nothing to soften her features. But Wendy trusts her. That intangible fear that has surrounded her during the past year or so has lifted. She feels she is a woman in charge not only of Ludo but of all the other children as well. And it doesn't drag her down. She can see what a timid child Elvira is, how pathetically grateful she is to be on her first foreign holiday with a real family.

She can help her towards self-confidence.

That first morning when Tony wakes to the children's squeals soon after dawn, he turns towards Wendy and takes her in his arms. She's still heavily asleep. He puts his hand on her naked left breast and kneads her nipple until it's stiff and alert. He puts his other hand on her vulva and finds it's warm and open. She groans in her sleep and moves towards him. He enters her without preliminaries and she's fully awake when he comes. He does not heed her needs or rhythm. He satisfies himself, turns away from her without a word and sleeps until eight. She lies awake staring at the whitewashed walls and the wooden slatted ceiling, telling herself it will be all right eventually. He's angry with her for getting on so well with Billie, for her cheer and her recent ability in managing the needs of all of the children. Marian no longer frightens her. Her verbal arrows don't bring Wendy down. Everyone is more or less in an *ad hoc* harmony by now. Everyone except Tony. And she's damned if he's going to spoil her holiday. She gets out of bed at seven, picks Ludo up from his cot before nanny wakes and runs with him to have an early morning swim on the beach with the others.

Tony hires a rickety old van from Ari for the duration of his stay and heads off on his own to Iraklion soon after ten. When he comes home in the late afternoon, he talks about a museum of antiquities where he's spent most of the afternoon. He complains about the inedible little sweet cakes he's had in a café and asks if there is anything decent to eat for dinner. Wendy says they've all had a wonderful dinner of fresh fish and a mixture of vegetables. Christina cooked it in the middle of the day because they'd been ravenous having been up so early. He can have some bread and fish but all the vegetables are gone. He spends the rest of the day until nightfall in his shed. His fingers tap lethargically at his laptop.

He knows it's not the real thing. He patterns the rest of his days on the first. After a few days the children grow tired of asking if they can go with him on his jaunts in the van. They accept his absence and gravitate towards Wendy. She enters into all their games with the same gusto and intent as their own. One day they bury each other to the waist in sand and pretend to be statues. Another day, they go fishing with some of the local men and get photographed with the catch of the day. This fires them with enthusiasm to try their hand at fishing from the pier. Wendy organises a donkey expedition to Iraklion to buy the tackle. Ari overcharges her for the hire of the donkeys but she doesn't mind. She leads the expedition, leaving Ludo back at the house with nanny. The boys follow close by, followed by Marian and Lottie, who are deep in conversation. Elvira trails in last place but Wendy shouts to her, 'I'm relying on you as second in command to protect our rear,' and she's rewarded with a magnificent smile.

She books an aeroplane tour of the island another day, leaving it open for Tony to join them or not. He doesn't come. Josh and Toby resolve to be pilots after their experience. They're bubbling over with it for days after that. Elvira manages to hold on to her stomach and even holds the wheel with the pilot when they fly over their two little houses. Christina grows less solemn as Wendy gets to know her better and she shares her recipes and her views on men with her. Both are simple and experienced. The swimming is best of all. Wendy can't get enough of it. She practically lives in the water with Ludo, who is becoming quite a waterbaby.

Josh knocks out part of Toby's front tooth one day when they are sparring with boxing gloves. Hamish runs to the beach to tell Wendy. She's making intricate sandcastles with Ludo while nanny does some mending. Hamish's doleful Scots accent somehow makes it seem more tragic than it is. When Wendy gets to the children's house Toby is bearing up, grinning in a ghastly manner saying through a mouthful of blood that Josh hadn't meant to hurt him. Josh is white-faced as he studies the results of his handiwork. Marian kicks him intermittently in the shins. Wendy ignores the kicks as Josh really does bully Toby quite a lot of the time. She tells Hamish to run ahead to the farmhouse to Ari, to say she is coming. They will need the Land-Rover to get Toby to a dentist or doctor in Iraklion; she isn't quite sure which. She leaves Ludo sitting comfortably on nanny's lap, puts Toby on Homer, a placid old donkey, and walks to the farm with him. There she transfers him to the Land-Rover. Marian sits with him in the back. Wendy finds herself singing silly songs at the wheel, one of the ones Tony sometimes sings to Ludo and must have sung to Marian too because she joins in the chorus.

> Up in an air balloon, boys,
> Up in an air balloon.
> All around the little stars,
> sailing around the moon.
> I'll take you up to heaven
> by jingo very soon
> just you and me
> and Toby and Marian
> up in an air balloon.

The local doctor is out on a house call so it has to be a dentist. He seems to double as a vet, which causes Wendy a moment or two of doubt as they wait with an assorted menagerie, from a pet goat to a Siamese cat. He cleans Toby's mouth out and examines the damage. The tooth will have to be capped. It looks worse simply because of the blood. Toby's Bart Simpson T-shirt is a decided red rather than yellow at this stage. He can fix the tooth in a few days if she wants. He can take an impression of it now. Or they can wait until they get back to London. She agrees to an appointment later in the week.

The dentist, a middle-aged grey-haired man, gives Toby one of his son's T-shirts. He says he can return it on his next visit. Toby is quite himself again now that his mouth is cleared up and he is no longer bloodstained. Wendy suggests a treat before their journey back. They cross the road to a taverna. They sit at a table on the street. She orders grape and fig juice with sweet cakes for the children and a small ouzo for herself. She feels in need of a restorative after the tooth escapade. She leaves the money on the table for the drinks and goes to the back of the taverna to the ladies' loo. That's when she sees Tony. He's at a table of men, hard drinkers by the look of them, and he's entertaining them with some story or other about Nellie. At that moment, the barman brings another tray of drinks. Tony pays for them.

Nellie and Bob are out on their balcony at the Mansions having a picnic. They had been all set for a day-trip but the blasted pipes had flooded in the Smith's flat first thing this morning. Bob had spent most of the day in number thirty-five in wellies and wearing his plumbing hat. Nellie was determined they wouldn't lose out; she told him so when he returned to their flat exhausted and in need of a beer and a bit of sport on the telly. She had 'transformed' their balcony into a little Riviera. She was all set for the picnic now. The coloured umbrella was up, the plastic chairs were out. The new picnic gear, a striking red-and-white, looked smashing. She'd even hung a basket of busy lizzies to tone in with the colour scheme.

Life was what you made it, she told him. Today was marked

down for their picnic day and they were damned well going to have it, she said, as she opened plastic boxes of salad and poured from a flask of tea. She was wearing one of her 'dressy informals', a turquoise dress with jacket. She was hatless but she had a sun hat nearby just in case. It was a bit windy on the balcony, it being an end balcony with no protection, but then you couldn't have everything. Bob had to agree. Some days he felt he couldn't have anything at all. He brightened considerably when he'd struggled through his chicken with plastic cutlery and Nellie opened the cooler box which held a six-pack of beer.

'I bet we're having just as good a time as the lot of them. Who needs Russia or Greece to have a good time? Give me my old London town any day of the week,' she says as she pops a bottle of Babycham for herself.

Goldie is thinking of Paris, or maybe Vienna, for his autumn honeymoon. Susan hasn't travelled anywhere outside England except to Boulogne for a day trip, so she's leaving the decision to him. Sometimes, he is amused that he is contemplating matrimony now at his age. He wonders what Irina would make of Susan. Chalk and cheese, he thinks. Useless to speculate. There's no doubt about it, the whole business has perked him up no end. Made a new man of him, in fact. Of course, he's intelligent enough to know what people will think of their union. He doesn't mind her musical ignorance. There's something extremely touching about opening up the world of classical music to her. She has a natural ear. Too impatient or maybe unwilling to learn to read music, she's already mastered simple tunes on the piano, which delights him as much as herself.

Now that he's decided for Susan's sake to put himself about again he's eagerly sought after by the most ambitious hostesses.

He accepts only if Susan accompanies him. He can see how it exasperates those formidable matrons that his presence depends on an outspoken Cockney, a slip of a girl in her twenties but it gives a cutting edge to their social life that makes it interesting for him. Now he wonders why he's spent the last decade almost as a semi-recluse in Brabbington Terrace. That's another thing: Susan is busy looking at houses. She thinks she's found the one she likes. He wants her to choose it as she will be living in it long after he's gone. All he stipulates is that it will have two generous rooms downstairs that he can use as a self-contained flat. He'll set that up in the arrangement he's always been used to at Brabbington Terrace. She can do whatever she likes in the line of furniture and decoration in the rest of the house. She wondered about their bedroom. He says they can have one together of course. They needn't share it all the time. He's an old man. He'll be honoured to share it with her from time to time.

Billie knows a very good interior designer that Abbercrombie and Wilson uses. Susan has contacted her, a young woman in her twenties, and they are busy with plans. It's wonderful to see her shine with happiness at the thought of becoming a woman of property. And not having to slave to pay a mortgage, she says. That's the beauty of it. Imagine buying a house cash down. He says it will make up for the other things she won't have in the marriage. He can't turn his old body into that of a youthful lover but he can give her a home of her own.

'I've had it up to here with young men like Darren. What I need is a nice dependable father figure and that's what I've got.'

Billie thinks they are on their fourth bottle of champagne but she can't be sure. The restaurant is very large but smoky. At every table someone is smoking. The floor is a warm pink marble. Two large fireplaces, also marble, dominate each end of the room. Finally, there is a row of columns up the centre of it. The tables, covered with pink damask cloths, have privacy as each one is flanked by its own columns. Waiters in black trousers and green jackets with gold braid look like advancing cavalry as they bear their silver serving-dishes aloft in the wide central area between the two sets of tables. It seems like hours ago since they had hors d'oeuvres, blinis (buckwheat pancakes with caviar) and cucumber salad. Service is equally slow at the other tables but nobody minds. Roskolnokov ordered two cushions as soon as he arrived. The waiter didn't smile. He seemed to know him quite well. He is now sitting, apparently comfortable, though his legs dangle on air.

Lazlo's face has that red glow of false heartiness that drink gives. He's holding forth, rather arrogantly, Billie thinks, on that composer, this conductor. From time to time his fingers drum in time to the music. Four musicians in traditional costumes are playing folk tunes on a podium underneath a stained-glass window which depicts cheese, wine and bread.

Billie is talking to Kaganovitch's wife, Anna, a startlingly beautiful woman with the body of a dancer. She's got articulate tapered fingers that map the air to emphasise a point. Her black hair is tied back in a severe dancer's knot but severity melts when she speaks. Her full lips and intense grey eyes give her a film-star quality. Anna is a doctor and by western standards earns a pittance, but Billie can tell by listening to her talk about her work that she is very dedicated. She is open and frank and has very good English. She tells Billie that Kaganovitch and she have a two-roomed flat. They are lucky. She had only a one-roomed flat with her first husband, a violinist.

'I left him for Igor.' She smiles fondly across the table at the grey man. 'Too much stress living with a musician. Igor lectures on music and writes on it too. It is a much saner life. Always I was hemmed in by Ivan's practice. Day and night, the violin bow cut through my life like a . . . ' The hands talk in the air. ' . . . like a saw.'

'You did not love him any more,' Billie says, not understanding.

'Love!' The heavy Russian accent draws the word out to an indecent length. ' I still love him but I could not live with him. I still go to the Conservatoire to hear him play. He has beautiful hands. I fell in love with his hands.'

Billie is confused or maybe just drunk. She needs more food. She reaches for a bread roll from the basket on the table.

'Dohnanyi, some people say he is restrained but competent. I say . . . ' Lazlo bangs the table for emphasis and the bottles clink. 'I say he harnesses the energy of the orchestra. He is a quiet genius, a man of integrity not a cheap showman.'

'He certainly has pushed Solti's Chicago Symphony Orchestra into second place,' Edward says, as he refills his glass.

'Dohnanyi and Cleveland on the Decca label! So many records. Something to be reckoned with!' Roskolnokov agrees.

Kaganovitch says nothing. He is looking at his wife's hands. Billie wonders has he been listening to her conversation with Anna. Hardly. Maybe he loves her hands just as she loved Ivan's the violinist's hands. Billie laughs. It's too much drink and too little food and now the absurd surreal image of all the hands in the world, separated from their bodies but playing instruments, that's suddenly popped into her head. Roskolnokov thinks she is laughing at him. She can see the pained watchful eyes below the gelled hair staring at her.

'I must bring you to the circus. Introduce you to my brother,' he says in his ringing Oxbridge tones. 'It is my turn to amuse you tomorrow evening, I believe.'

Lazlo is not amused by his rudeness. 'We are all honoured to entertain you on your stay in Moscow, Wilhelmina. Edward's sponsored visit to our country not only brings honour to our university but also money to our department. Edward will be coming back to Moscow in December for one of the December Evenings at the Pushkin Museum. It is all arranged. I hope you will travel with him.'

'We'll see,' Billie says, 'It's a long time away yet.'

'A musician's diary is filled for years ahead if he is lucky,' Lazlo says, and two waiters finally approach the table with food.

They take a taxi back to the hotel. Billie has eaten her way to sobriety but Edward is quite drunk. It has been a long day. The trunk of the taxi is full of her miscellaneous purchases from Arbat Street. Mostly art work. It was absurdly cheap and generally of a high standard. She had bought oil paintings, lithographs, charcoal drawings, even had one of those self indulgent portraits done by a street-artist as Kaganovitch stood patiently by.

'This is a good likeness,' he told her as they both examined the work. 'You must not think me rude but you are very much like my wife Anna. She too is very beautiful. You will see her tonight at dinner. She is a beauty and she married a beast.' He laughed at his own joke as he picked up the numerous bags of her purchases and they made their way to a café. They sat at a pavement table and drank hot chocolate as crowds of tourists made their way through the stalls of Russian dolls, hand-painted jewellery and chess sets. From inside the café the mournful tones of a saxophone cut the heavy summer air.

Tony is hunched over his laptop in the shed behind his whitewashed summer house. Every morning, no matter how much ouzo he's drunk the night before, he forces himself out of bed and down to the sea. He walks here. He doesn't jog as he does in London. It's hilly terrain and he doesn't want to end up with a sprained ankle or worse. He thinks of Pheidippides running twenty-three miles to Athens, giving the world its first marathon. But it doesn't rouse his competitive spirit. After he contemplates the horizon from his island, he makes his way to the shed until Christina shouts that breakfast is ready at nine. He taps, taps, taps. After breakfast, he returns to the shed for more. He's pushing the words out, fearful if he doesn't. He doesn't know what precisely he fears. All he knows is that this is what he's done for years. Done it with discipline and without too much anxiety.

Two books ahead always. The present one is set in Greece. Some of the holiday will be tax deductible. Background research. Authenticity. He'd taken a trip to Iraklion to walk around Knossos. He'd bought dozens of postcards of fractured gods and goddesses disporting themselves on columns or lying down awaiting a moment of love. But none of it helped. It was all a heap of old stones. The novel is set in Athens and Crete among expatriate English people who leave behind London and its grey weather to find sun, sex and happiness in the land of the ancient gods and goddesses. He's twinning some of his modern characters with the traditional ancients. He has a wise and hard-working Athena type who falls hopelessly in love with a Dionysus, a rich, handsome, randy alcoholic who gets involved with a fleet of modern maenads. Months ago in London it had seemed funny and engaging but here, on 'set' so to speak, it hasn't so much slipped away from him as never come alive. He feels he's lugging dead stone statues about with him.

But still he persists. He works till one, has a siesta and heads for Iraklion and the taverna most afternoons. He's persuaded himself it's research. The local drinking men have accepted him as a friend. He calls them by name: Alexander, Niko, Socrates and Paul. He has learned a lot from them. They tolerate the tourists but do not respect them. He, of course, is an exception. A writer, a man of culture. The Greek men look on women tourists as fair game. Their own wives are at home on the farm with the children or at work in the factory or office. What harm does it do to anyone if they pleasure a foreign woman or two during the season? Greek men strut and promenade their stuff or they sit in the taverna, their manicured hands moving over their worry beads, ready to put their hands to better use if they're lucky.

Hands. Billie's dreams are full of hands, both attached and detached from bodies. She goes into a Russian shop. She knows it is a Russian shop because everything is labelled in the Cyrillic script. Everything is in boxes. Nothing is on show but yet she knows that the boxes are full of hands. Some attached to torsos, others not. She approaches the counter and only then notices the dwarf who is barely level with it. The dwarf resembles Roskolnokov but it is not him. He wears a fringe. A distant cousin, she thinks. He fills the counter with boxes. She opens them with great care and pays solemn attention to each hand as she examines it. Each hand has a speciality. The first hand when she releases it rushes off to an old dusty typewriter and types furiously.

The second hand scurries about until it finds a large bottle of cod liver oil capsules. It pops them merrily into lines of disconnected mouths. The third hand wields a hammer and nails and happily does odd jobs about the shop. The fourth one plays a violin. The fifth a piano. She grows alarmed. All the hands are busy about her. She opens the next box. The hand reaches for a brush and paint and there before her eyes is a detailed picture of the Kremlin. The hand moves to another canvas and after another quick brushstroke she's looking at a picture of the British Museum.

She opens the other boxes but they are all empty. She turns towards the dwarf to ask for an explanation but he's vanished. She'll have to make her choice on her own. She studies each hand carefully, paying particular attention to the thumbs and the length of the life line. Eventually, she chooses the painting hand. She puts it back in its box and leaves the shop with it under her arm. Out in the street, she's not in Russia at all. She's in Brabbington Terrace, standing on the pavement watching a removal van fill up with stuff from her house. Susan in her nurse's uniform is supervising the removal men. They are carrying Mr Goldberg's piano. She wakes.

Edward is being sick in the bathroom. She can hear him vomiting. There are tears on her cheeks. Ever since she's arrived she's been dreaming. At home she can't hold on to a dream long enough to remember any of it. Edward was downing vodka like a true Russian by the end of last evening. There were a lot of silly toasts, to what or to whom she can't remember. She kept to champagne and very small sips of it at that. She has a slight headache, not strong enough to merit a headache tablet. She reaches for a glass and pours herself some mineral water and decides to let Edward get on with it on his own. She checks her watch; it's only half five. She puts on her Walkman and listens to some Bach. She sleeps. They both sleep until noon. Edward's groans finally wake her. She pushes him until he wakes.

'Don't touch me,' he begs, 'the room is floating. I feel so ill.'

'You drank too much,' Billie says as she gets out of bed.

'You should have stopped me,' he says plaintively.

'I'm not your keeper. You're a big boy now, well able to think for yourself.' She heads for the bathroom.

No bloody water, just enough to wash face, hands and teeth. This is our first real day with time to spend together since we came, she's thinking, and he's on the flat of his back. She pulls on jeans and a T-shirt and arranges for a tray of tea and rolls with the *dehurnaya*. It's the benign woman. The Medusa has long since left. She feeds Edward sips of tea from a spoon and a few pieces of a roll.

'I'm going out. I'd like to go back to Arbat Street, explore a bit on my own.' And she leaves him.

On Arbat Street she looks at the delicious length of its pedestrian thoroughfare and she's determined to have a good time, to haggle over prices now that she knows the difference between a rouble price and a dollar one. She heads for a stall of hand-painted brooches and picks out a half a dozen ones that she likes. She asks the price in roubles, argues with the fat man who shakes his head vigorously but finally reaches a compromise price and the brooches are hers. She picks up, on her long journey from one end of the street to the other, a hand-painted chess set, two silver bracelets, an icon and a consignment of Russian badges and medals that Jamie might like.

It's Jamie's twenty-sixth birthday and Stella has organised a party for him. It's in their flat, now fully, if sparsely, furnished. Bernie, Jamie's copywriter pal, is well into his fourth drink and has already been turned down by a remote Modigliani actress. He hasn't given up hope yet as the entire cast of *The Girls of Essex*, Stella's current play, are here. Philip, Babs's Philip is sitting on a window seat, reassuring a very pregnant woman that her obstetrician is the best, after himself, of course. Babs and Nellie are handing around plates of food. Some people are sitting on the floor. Two are swinging on the twin hammocks at each end of the room.

Jamie is walking about, his leg still encased in plaster, but he manages to give the impression that it's a fancy dress leg, all part of the celebrations. Tony sent him a generous cheque for £2,600 to help with the mortgage on the flat. The letter from Crete was strange. He said they were all having a good time in their own way but he wasn't specific except to say that Ludo was walking. He'd see him for the usual family lunch the Saturday after they got back. Billie had left a case of his favourite wine with Stella and a beautiful model of an early Curtiss seaplane to add to his collection. It is the best party of his life. Stella organised it. The theme is the fifties. She's wearing a black satin ballgown to two inches below the knees, with frothy stiff underskirts. It's backless, of course. Her black suede high heels are beaded with little pearls. All the men are in formal evening wear and the women's dresses seem to fill the room.

'This is an original,' Nellie says to Babs as she points to her dress, a royal blue nylon with a bouquet of roses at the waist. 'I took it down from the attic, washed it by hand myself. You can't smell mothballs, can you?' She sniffs anxiously at her underslip in spite of Babs's reassurance. 'Poor Bob, he's missin' all the fun. Rodney says I'm an avid socialiser. Avid.' She bites into the word with satisfaction.

Roskolnokov and Edward are waiting in the hotel lobby when Billie returns. She had forgotten this is the night for the circus. Edward is pale and looks very tired in spite of his day in bed. Roskolnokov greets her with a hint of a bow. 'Lazlo said I must apologise for my discourtesy last night,' he says, as he hands her a delicate posy of miniature roses.

'Thank you. The flowers are wonderful. There is no need for an apology.'

'Oh, but there is, my good lady. I tell people to ignore my lack of height but sometimes I cannot help myself being bitter about it.'

'I was called Lanky Legs at school myself. I understand. Please, think no more of it. I must leave these bags in my room and have a quick wash. Will you have a drink while you wait.' Edward blanches at the mention of a drink. She kisses him quickly and heads for the lifts.

The circus is in a permanent building. It is a large company with an amazing variety and quality of acts. Billie wishes she could be munching popcorn or candyfloss to relive the circuses of her childhood. Edward holds her hand, squeezing it tightly from time to time. Roskolnokov sits back in his seat, taking everything in his stride: strong men who can lift forty-five kilograms, dancers who perform with trained doves to the strains of the 'Blue Danube', maidens on camels who do the dance of the seven veils, troops of people cartwheeling completely covered in a sack, performing bears skipping on multi-coloured balls. Billie is enthralled. It's wonderful, much better than she had expected.

One act, involving three clowns with a cake, fills her with poignant feelings she can't quite define. One clown comes into the ring to tumultuous applause. Another clown stands to the side and plays the most heartrending music on an accordion. The other two open up a box they've brought with them. Inside, there's a cake. The first clown looks at the cake with anticipatory pleasure. He motions to the third clown to bring the cake to him. The third clown bends down, lifts the cake tenderly from its box. It is decorated with lighted candles. He holds it in his hands somewhat unsteadily. The music trills and shakes as the clown makes his way across the ring. It's painful and nervewracking. Several times he almost drops it but doesn't. Billie gasps with the audience.

Now, he's only a foot from the table. He goes into a spasm. The music becomes loud and hectic. He arrives at the table shaking from head to foot. The first clown sitting at the table turns around casually and knocks the cake from his hands. The accordion music is reduced to a plaintive asthmatic wheeze. The clown, now cakeless, looks at the puddle at his feet that was once a cake. The lights dim. He throws up his hands in despair. There is thunderous applause. Billie is weeping. Roskolnokov passes her his diminutive handkerchief.

Afterwards, Roskolnokov takes Edward and Billie backstage. The clown with the cake is a big cheerful man with a firm handshake. He says, 'Please to thank you,' when she tells him he was wonderful. That's the extent of his English vocabulary. The strong man is shy and sits in a corner by himself. The desert maidens are as captivating off stage as on. They ask her has she any tights to spare. They are hard to get in Russia and essential for their type of work. She promises to give tights to Roskolnokov for them. The principal dancer kisses her on both cheeks and tells her she is a true friend of struggling artists. Then a dwarf remarkably similar to the one in her hands dream comes in. He is Roskolnokov's brother. His hair falls forward boyishly in a fringe. He is wearing jeans and a shirt with the Tower of London on it. Roskolnokov introduces Billie and Edward. He speaks in the same perfect tones as his brother. He is at his ease and pleased to meet people who live in London. He has performed there twice. He points to his T-shirt. There will not be too much travelling in the future he tells them dolefully, now that the state is removing subsidies from the circus. So much for the 'new freedom.' These days they are lucky to be able to feed the animals.

'You are very alike and yet different,' Billie says to Roskolnokov about his brother in the car on the way back to the hotel.

'Twins,' he says simply.

There is silence after that. He drops them at the hotel. In the bathroom they are amazed and gratified that there is water for a shower. They splash eagerly with the glee of children. Edward's hangover is finally gone. His eyes are bright and clear once more. They kiss each other hungrily. The water is suddenly freezing cold, then it shudders to a halt. They squeal in pretend terror and Billie chases Edward around the room, whacking him with a towel. He pretends to cower and falls on the bed as if dead. She jumps on top of him, administering the kiss of life with a quiet intensity. The telephone by their bed rings. They are both alarmed. It is nearly one o'clock in the morning. Edward answers it. They both listen as a voice in a heavy Russian accent says, 'You want sex, a party? I can arrange.' Billie makes a grab for her dressing gown and puts it on. Then she checks the door. It's locked. Edward says in his most polite tone, 'No thank you, my wife is with me.'

They are suddenly and coldly alert to that side of life where sex is for sale and available in hotels. Billie gets into bed in her dressing gown and pulls the sheet up to her chin. Edward feels his erection is somehow embarrassingly inappropriate. He slips on an underpants before getting under the sheet. He puts out his arms to Billie and cradles her head and shoulders with that alert care a mother gives her new born infant. They do not sleep for a long time.

Babs is relieved that Connie has returned to Dublin. It's good to have the flat to herself again. Not for the first time in her life, she reflects that she's a woman who needs peace and space to herself. Connie had disgraced herself at Jamie's party, making up to anyone in a pants under thirty. Jamie had introduced her to his friends as his 'young aunt'. 'Almost brother and sister,' Connie had insisted.

She danced with anyone she could persuade on to the floor. She made an exhibition of herself when they played 'Blue Suede Shoes'. Still, she'd gone home happier than when she'd arrived. If only she could develop herself independently of Robert and the kids.

Cordelia is pleased with Edward's brief letter. Hardly more than a note but it contains all she needs to know.

> *Dear Mum*
> *So far I haven't disgraced myself. The two concerts in Moscow pleased Lazlo. I'm invited back for next December. Billie is seeing more of the country than myself as my schedule is fairly gruelling. We take the trans-Siberian express to Petersburg tonight. Lazlo is sending this letter through a contact at a fast post. Just wanted you to know I was thinking of you. I tried ringing you but the phones are impossible.*
> *Edward*

Billie is in the Hermitage in St Petersburg. She's taking one of the organised tours. The guide, a young man in his twenties with an American accent, is taking them through the place at an incredible speed. She can see the place is absolutely enormous but what's the point if they can't pause and ponder? So far, they've twirled through rooms with chandeliers of rock crystal and Italian mosaic tables, gazed at the splendour of the Hall of 1812, walked through the Corridor of the Generals, nodded in the direction of some rooms with Titians, Raphaels and Leonardos.

Now they're approaching a piece of sculpture by Michelangelo called 'The Crouching Boy.' The guide says, 'We have only one piece by Michelangelo in our country. The sculpture is called "The

Crouching Boy". It was made by him for the famous Medici chapel in Florence but later it was eliminated from the project and that is why the sculpture is not polished. So it is very interesting for specialists. They can study his manner of working. You should look at it from underneath because it was meant to be up on a height.' Billie approaches the piece. The boy is crouching, wary, but there's an alertness there too. He looks as if he's ready to spring forward into his future. He is eager, nearly ready. He just happens to be waiting for the pistol shot. She's suddenly overwhelmingly tired. She needs to sit down. The guide is busily corralling his group for the next room.

She hides behind the sculpture until he's gone, then she reaches the nearest chair just as she feels her legs might have given way. She knows she's very tired. But her fatigue is more than physical tiredness. The overnight train journey from Moscow to St Petersburg was quite exhausting. Lazlo saw them off at the teeming station. It looked as if the world was leaving from it. People thronged and milled in the steamy summer night. Billie doubts if they would have managed to get on the right train without his shepherding. He assured them a Dr Yalnakov would meet them at St Petersburg when the train pulled in the following morning at half past seven. And the good doctor was there, a timid man who spoke in staccato bursts of antique English and greeted them with, 'You are welcome to our splendid St Petersburg, city of Peter but now also of future dreams.' They stood shivering on the platform in spite of the early morning sun, listening with careful gratitude to the small bald man who would take them to their hotel. This time, their hotel is palatial and baroque in the grand old style, almost a museum piece.

The lobby is high-ceilinged with enormous copper chandeliers which fail to dominate. There aren't huge queues waiting for registration as they have seen every day in their Moscow hotel. Yalnakov simply steps forward with their passports and magically they are registered. Three porters help with their luggage in spite of there being so little of it. They dole out the two suitcases and Billie's various shopping bags from her Arbat Street shopping spree amongst them with the serious concern reserved for philosophical matters. They are dressed in red uniforms with gold braid. They look like living replicas of a military past, statues almost, as they stand in the lobby until they move forward on some silent cue to take the luggage.

There is no lift. They walk to their third-floor room, Yalnakov leading. The pink marble staircase leads them upwards to a corridor so wide that entire families could live on it with room to spare. The floor is covered in an elegant if faded rug of green and gold. Their room is half-way down the corridor. Inside, the room is streaming with light, lit by four enormous windows. The central light is a chandelier. It looks as if it is genuine rock crystal. The bedside lamps seem to be miniatures of the same design. The bed is huge and high in a dark wood, possibly oak. Yalnakov shows them the bathroom: a very deep bath, no shower and a washbasin that seems curiously tall as it rests on a carved wooden podium.

He leaves them to rest, assuring them he has left instructions for a wake-up call for Edward for eleven. He's meeting the orchestra at noon. After he leaves they rejoice in their new luxury, admiring the space and the grandeur. They are too exhausted to bathe. The train was so crowded and noisy they had hardly slept on the entire overnight journey. The sleeping compartments were very small and all around them there seemed to be drinking parties in progress. They dozed in their separate bunks, waking every now and again to the rhythm of the train and a drunken cheer.

Now they collapse with relief in their tsarist room, enormously grateful that the big bed is so comfortable. They hold hands and sleep until the wake-up call. It consists of a persistent knocking on their door until they answer. There are no telephones here.

And now as Billie views Michelangelo's unfinished 'Crouching Boy', she admires its rough unpolished marble but senses something else apart from the literal figure. From her seat she looks at the distant shadow until the boy's features become Edward's. Edward is alert too, ready for his take-off on the international circuit. He has years of practice in his young life behind him. He's wary but every muscle in his body is ready for this. She closes her eyes to blank out Edward's features. When she opens them, Michelangelo's boy is a young girl. It's Lottie. Also, ready for the off. Lottie, too, if Mr Goldberg is to be believed, will have a solo career. She has the talent and drive. She will travel to foreign cities to be met by people who will give her rehearsal and performance schedules.

Billie knows that she doesn't want to spend the next decade or so as Edward's travelling companion. The one who has to be kept amused or entertained while he gets on with the real business of music. When she met Tony all those years ago the time they both worked on the business magazine, he was ready and alert too. Alert to his own possibilities. He knew he would make himself into a writer. She knew he would too. With her help and support. Their entire marriage had been based on the accepted fact that he was the one with talent, the one who had to be cosseted and looked after, the one whose routines and schedules dominated the house. Until he chose to leave the house. And she was the one left holding the babies, juggling with part-time work, too proud to really fight for proper maintenance, relieved that at least he'd take the children at weekends. And now, fifteen years later, she's fitting into Edward's schedule.

Why? Because her body craves his. Because her body aches when it's apart from him. At the Conservatoire in Moscow when he played Tchaikovsky's First to a hushed audience she heard the music through her body, his fingers playing her, twinning them in that intense drama of the notes. Fingers, notes, bodies. How our bodies let us down. And hers would. Sooner than his. Ten years on maybe, after a decade of such international caravanning following Edward's star, she would wake one morning to find the realisation of her mortality and decay in his eyes. Did she want that? Ten years of physical bliss but what then? Could she find that rapture again with someone else or would it be too late? Would Edward leave with the apparent indifference of Tony or would his be a guilt-ridden exit, more in the manner of an offspring letting down a parent at the last moment? This time there would be no baby in her arms. No battle for maintenance. Would he pension her off?

She doesn't want any of this to happen. Yesterday, before they left Moscow, they went to see an exhibition of photography. Most of the photographs had never been seen by western eyes before. Vintage Russian prints from the period 1840-1940. Some of the photographs had been taken by Dmitri Ermakov, a military photographer who travelled extensively in the Russian empire. Edward and she had been greatly amused by the picture entitled 'Spinal Massage'. It was a sepia print of one man sitting upright on a military bed while a second man stood on his shoulder, his hands balancing his body by holding on to the other man's upper arms. He was giving him a spinal massage, presumably relieving the tensions of a long campaign. They both wore brief towels around their midriff. You could see the muscles of their bodies clearly. After the picture was taken had the man felt better? Or was it posed specifically for the camera, the man not gaining any relief at all? Or had Ermakov merely taken what he saw as it happened? Hard to know. Would Edward's young body relieve her when she needed a spinal massage?

She won't stay to find out. This is her summer, their summer of abandon. She won't journey towards autumn with Edward. Her tiredness lifts. She focuses on Michelangelo's 'Crouching Boy' again. He is merely a marble boy once more, an unpolished piece of sculpture for the world to marvel at once again. She will have to become alert to her own future, her own possibilities.

Lottie plays the tin whistle on the beach after her swim. She's missing her piano more and more. It's as if her hands have been cut off or simply put to other uses that don't make any sense. She's looking forward to going home. Home to her piano. Which home? Which piano? Brabbington Terrace or High Pines? Both, she supposes, as she'll have to stay with mum once school starts once more. Marian and Elvira are chasing Ludo. He's able to run more steadily now. Lottie notices for the first time that Elvira has lost weight. It must be the heat and running about on the beach. She really looks quite attractive. She's laughing as she catches Ludo before Marian. He's thrilled to have the two girls competing for his attention.

Tony listens to their noisy play from his shed. The door is wide open to let in what little air there is. He fingers his new beard with one hand as he taps his laptop with the other. His novel has somehow found a shape of its own during the last week. He's been in the shed almost continuously since it's kicked in. He's moving with it, going with the flow, so to speak, glad that his hands are doing real work again. He knows the first third of it will need massive reworking but he daren't go back in case he loses the run of himself. He'll even make Max's deadline, if this keeps up. Max, his agent, the man who made High Pines and all that's in it possible. He thinks fondly of his swimming pool and longs for its known length, almost like a lover.

Wendy and Christina are cooking. They peel fruit while the pots bubble. They speak on and off as one of them checks on the food. The silences are companionable. Wendy is going to miss Christina. She wishes she could take her back to High Pines with her and give Nellie the boot. Nanny bustles about preparing food for Ludo. He's said goodbye to Wendy's breast. Weaned on Crete with the help of sun, sand and nanny. Wendy feels lucky. Nanny pretends to be bossy but she's not really. These past few weeks she's been marvellous. Ludo responds to her authority and he's become quite the little boy under her guidance. But nanny isn't over-possessive either. She shares Ludo with Marian, Elvira and Christina. Lottie seems to have cut herself off from Ludo since they came. She prefers to go for walks on her own or to play boisterous games with the boys. And Tony has been in such good form for the last week. He hasn't been inside a taverna. He barely pauses for food and fruit juice. His presence is once more benign, not something that oppresses. His new beard suits him.

'I told him I'd have everything in apple-pie order for his return,' Nellie tells Bob for the third time. 'I can't understand it. Ringin' all the way from Greece.'

'It's called keepin' in touch,' Bob assures her.

'You don't think he was checkin' up on me then?'

''Course not. You've worked for 'im for donkey's years. He knows he gets his shillin's worth.'

'Speakin' of donkeys. He's bringin' me one from Greece. Asked what I'd like in the way of a souvenir, so I said one of those sweet little donkeys with baskets. It'll look ever so nice on my telephone table. I didn't tell him about Mr Goldberg's proposition. Thought it would upset him. Imagine me doin' for Susan and Mr Goldberg. Expansion. That's what Rodney called it when I told him. He suggested I should branch out. Start a little business. Take on one or two more women. It's a lovely house. I am pleased for Susan. She deserves all she gets after what our Darren done to her. I could call the business 'Nellie's Girls'. Has a ring to it, doesn't it?'

'Don't do nothin' rash till you know how you're fixed,' Bob says into his beer. 'We've managed well enough on what we have up to this. Better be careful than sorry.'

Marian is drawing family portraits on the sand with a stick. She joins everyone together by their hands. There's dad with his mum and dad. Granny is dead now but she was good fun, sneaking them sweets behind Tony's back or singing to them in that quavery voice of hers. Then there's Tony's first wife, Billie, with Jamie and Lottie. Her mum, Beth, gone to wherever people go when they die. It was commonly believed in the Middle Ages that bees hummed the Hundredth Psalm in their hives at midnight on Christmas Eve and that cattle turned to the east and bowed. Josh, Toby and herself. Now there's Wendy and Ludo. They take up quite a bit of beach. Goodness, she's forgotten her American grandparents, Beth's mum and dad. She draws them in quickly. Granny Liz is tall and bossy but she knows she loves her. She cried the last time Marian went to Heathrow airport to see them off. That's two years ago now.

Grandad William hadn't cried at all but he held her hand very tightly until he had to let it go at the boarding gate. He gave her all his remaining sterling, £300. It was to get a beautiful winter coat. Just like the ones Beth used to buy her every second year. They told her they would love her to visit them in Cambridge,

Massachusetts. She had been afraid to say she'd go because she knew she'd let them down by wetting their bed like a baby. She knew their house must be ever so neat and tidy because that's where her mum had grown up and she had been a stickler for hygiene and tidiness. A thought just strikes her. She hasn't wet the bed once since she's been in Crete. Maybe the bedwetting is behind her now. If it is she could visit her American grandparents. American Indians used to award a feather to anyone who killed an enemy.

Now that Billie knows she is going to leave Edward, every minute has to be savoured. She won't tell him until they get back to London. He needs to be at his best for his recital on Friday night. She thinks about Cordelia and decides to send her a postcard. They will be home before the card arrives. She will tell Cordelia about her leaving Edward before she tells him. Billie knows Cordelia will be relieved, grateful even, and maybe it will help mend things between them. She's not foolish enough to think that Cordelia will forgive and forget her affair with Edward but it will be a gesture in the right direction. She knows she cannot undo the hurt she has caused Cordelia. She falls on Edward on the 'tsar's bed' – that's what they've christened it – and gobbles him up with her eyes, hands, mouth.

He is full of energy and love. Everything is going so well. There has been no friction with the orchestra. Bookings are heavy for the recital. He has Billie to himself in their Russia-of-the-tsars room, far away from Brabbington Terrace and all the people they know. Mostly they stay in bed in between rehearsals. There is no such thing as room service but they have learned how to shop locally and bring champagne, bread and cheese to their room, eating downstairs in the rather intimidating baroque dining room only in the evenings. They are booked for *Swan Lake* but have declined all of the other kind invitations, musical and social, that have come their way. This is their time.

Waking and in her dreams, Billie worries that she may not have the strength of character to leave him when it comes to it. At such moments, she pulls him closer to her or grabs him crudely for her own satisfaction. She cannot have enough of him. She is consumed by him. When they do venture outdoors, she sees his face on every tall young man on the street. Waiters walk like him. Street musicians have his hands. Hands. She remembers her hands dream and realises now that she must find something for her own hands to do. When he has gone. When she will have told him to go, when her entire body will be wracked with its loss, she will have to fill her hands with something. Not only to keep busy, to forget him, but to recall herself. To have purpose and drive in her own right. Not the purpose and drive that have kept her going through years of hard work at Abbercrombie and Wilson. Something intrinsic to herself. Years ago ma had a little prayer on the kitchen wall at home. It said:

> If a child lives with ridicule,
> he learns to be shy.
> If a child lives with shame,
> he learns to feel guilty.
> If a child lives with praise,
> he learns to appreciate.

Somehow, she'd never really learned to appreciate herself. She'd lived through other people for most of her life up to this. She'd drifted through college with no real purpose. She'd met Tony at work in her first job in the business magazine. He fired her with his ambitions and she'd made them hers too. You can't live your life through other people's successes. You have to make your own. She wouldn't repeat the same mistake with Edward. This summer had put a lot of things in perspective for her. She needed to change. For herself.

She needed to kick over the traces. Take risks. Try new things. She needn't stay on at Abbercrombie and Wilson. She didn't have to live in Brabbington Terrace. In fact, now that Goldie would be moving out, it seemed the end of an era. Maybe it was a good time to move. Get a smaller place. A two-bedroom flat. Just enough space for herself and for Lottie. In three years' time Lottie would be out of school anyway and she had plenty of space at her father's house.

Selling the house would give her money and freedom. A chance to start again or, in her case, a chance to start for the first time. But what could she do? She was bored with the business world as viewed from Abbercrombie and Wilson. What else was she good at? Art. She had loved art in school but when it came to a career, da had insisted that she get an Economics degree and, he hoped, a remunerative position in the business world after that. He had made it clear that he knew she wasn't as smart as Babs who had been clever enough to do medicine. Is that why she had never put her heart into it in college? Maybe why she ran off to London after that summer trekking through India with Maureen? She had taken the first job that had come her way that August. She had run to London and found Tony.

Hands. She would take a chance with art. Go to art school, concentrate on getting through for herself. She listens to her Ute Lemper tape on her Walkman. Edward is rehearsing. She walks through the crowds on Nevsky Prospekt. What the hell! If art college doesn't work out she can always try something else. She's not going to be content for Abbercrombie and Wilson be the sum total of her working life. She'll put the house up for sale as soon as she gets home. It's time she did some living just for herself.

As Tony's plane lands at Heathrow, he feels vigorous and alive, ready for anything. It's been a splendid holiday really, all things considered. He'd put himself through a lot of silly grief at the beginning of the holiday. He'd learned it was pointless hankering after Billie and the past. That part of his life was over for good. He couldn't think what had gotten into him. Nellie was right. That woman was amazing. Didn't she say that he thought he was in love with Billie? And she had been proved right. He had a lot going for him and he shouldn't forget it. He wasn't like his twin Lloyd, content just to get through in life. He would be swimming in his own pool within the hour.

The kids look marvellous. Brown and healthy. Even Toby's capped tooth looks natural enough. He'll keep the new beard for a while. He feels good. It's comforting to know that Nellie will have everything in order for them when they get home. He's even got used to the battle-axe of a nanny. Ugly as sin but she seems useful enough. He thinks wistfully of Karin and wonders if she's happy in Munich. And what about that business with Billie? It could only be a flash in the pan. Young Edward will need fresher flesh soon. Then we'll see how she'll be fixed. She always had a haughty streak. He looks at Wendy's young blonde head asleep on his shoulder and smiles with satisfaction. He knew how to look after himself. No doubt about it.

SEPTEMBER

Lottie has returned to Billie's house to be near school during the week. She spends the weekends at Tony's. She's civil to Billie, in that way adults are who don't know each other very well. She keeps to her room mostly. She's converted it into a bedsitter. Even bought a Baby Belling cooker so she can eat up there if she chooses. Which she does. A lot.

Mr Goldberg is in the process of moving out. Susan has been packing his portable goods into boxes for weeks now. His furniture, heavy oak and rosewood, has never looked better. She polishes it every week. The For Sale sign is up outside Billie's house. Lottie won't discuss the proposed move with her. Billie is hoping to sell most of her furniture with the house. A fresh start. A clean break. She has boxed clothes and books for Oxfam. Jamie has moved all his things to his new flat. His room is now empty except for a bed, a wardrobe and a chest of drawers.

The firm decision she took about Edward at the end of her holiday in Russia has been pushed to the back of her mind. She keeps postponing it. When Cordelia met them at the airport on their return, Billie almost confided in her. It had seemed so simple then. The end of August, the end of summer, the end of the affair. Nowadays, every time they make love in Edward's flat she tells herself it's for the last time. Away from him, her body tells her another story. And so it goes on.

As soon as Billie decides to sell the house, it no longer seems hers. Domestic tasks she did as a matter of routine now remain undone. As a consequence things pile up and await Nellie's care once a week. Susan's and Goldie's boxes crowd the hall. These days Billie feels in transit when at home.

Tony has handed his first draft of the book to Max. 'Rough hewn but draft two will sort out the dead wood,' he assures him. Life at High Pines has resumed its more sedate routine since the start of the school year. The twins write their first letter home. 'Roll on mid-term.' Marian is Ludo's guardian angel. She even shows Tony her Tudor House project and listens to his suggestions for some of the miniature furniture. All is well until Nellie announces that Billie's house is up for sale.

'It's a blow. Unexpected like. I know I shouldn't get attached to places but I do. Bob says I'm too emotional for my own good. Billie seems to have lost all interest in the place. Normally I go in there on Wednesdays and give it the once-over but since she's come back from Russia all she does is the washing and the dishes. Once a week isn't enough to keep a place in order. And another thing: she has the place littered with toy stages. Somethin' to do with this design course she's signing on for. I'm all for education myself but it's hard to see the point in what she's doing. I shouldn't be rattlin' on but it upsets me to see a place go downhill. She only told me the day before the For Sale sign went up. That's what really got me.'

'It's understandable, Nellie. I've a soft spot for the place myself.'

Tony is pacing the terrace. He's mixed Nellie a cocktail. Vodka, sherry, Bailey's Irish Cream, pineapple juice and crushed ice.

'Drink up, it will do you good. It's no stronger than a punch,' he lies.

'I've never let a drop past my lips on a job before.' She finishes her long drink and Tony gives her a refill.

'You're finished for the day. I'll drop you home and we can bring the rest of the Bailey's to Bob.'

'He'll be expecting me at seven. You know how he likes his dinner on the dot. I've spoiled him. At least on the food front. But there's no changing things now. He was that upset about Billie selling the place that he clammed up on me for the rest of the evening.'

'Tell you what: we'll bring him a take-away. What do you fancy? My treat. All work and no play makes Jack a dull boy, and Jill too.'

Nellie giggles.

Edward is playing Mr Goldberg's piano. There's nothing left in the room except the piano and two chairs. The rest of the furniture has been moved to Goldie's and Susan's new house. Goldie sits next to him on the large piano stool. They're playing a duet. Their own joint composition. Composed when Edward was only ten years old. Susan and Billie are sitting on the chairs. They sip champagne from half-pint glasses. There are six bottles on the floor, three empty. Billie and Susan have been drinking for some time. Edward and Goldie have been playing almost non-stop for the last two hours.

'It's amazing the way they both know when to stop and start,' Susan says.

'Mmm! Starting and stopping is an art some of us have never mastered.' Billie is thoughtful. Reflection that follows on alcohol.

'Do you play duets too?'

'Only in an amateurish way. When Jamie was young we had great fun with duets. Lottie always scorned my clumsy fingers.'

She's looking at Edward's neck. There's a strength yet delicacy in it that's enhanced as he bends over the piano. A small curl straggles at the nape. She'd like to reach out and touch it but she stops herself. It's three weeks since they've returned from Russia but she's no nearer to telling him that they should part. How the flesh ensnares us! Why not coast along until the future comes? Her father had a saying, 'The future is now,' when any of his daughters postponed a chore.

'You'll miss Goldie's music,' Susan says.

'Yes, hugely.'

'They're taking the piano tomorrow.'

'Are you both moving then?'

'No. Goldie says we have to do things properly. I'll stay here until the wedding. It's only two weeks. I'll visit him in the meantime, of course. Mum says he's a real gentleman. She loves the house. I'm really looking forward to being a woman of property.'

Susan's happiness is palpable. Billie wishes she could be as lighthearted about her own future.

The beat of the hangover tattoos Billie's head with stern needles. She wakes on the couch in her kitchen. Raindrops. The din of them on the barred windows waken her. She's in a strange robe and cocooned in a duvet. Too hot. She falls to the floor in an attempt to free herself. The room swims darkly about her. The last thing she remembers is drinking a bottle of champagne from the neck. How lovely it felt as it spilled on to her chest and hands. So refreshing! It's an effort to fill the kettle and plug it in. There's an indignant note from Lottie on the table.

> *You puked all over your bed last night. Edward and I*
> *had to clean you up.*
> *L.*

After two cups of black coffee, she gets under the duvet and sleeps soundly. When she wakes she swallows two Panadol and has a tepid shower. It's warm for mid-September. She decides to sit out in the garden and let the day pass as it will.

'Afternoon, Billie. Tony wants to see you. He's in the kitchen.'

It's Nellie in her nylon apron, topped by a floppy black hat. Its black feathers add to the funereal effect.

'I'd rather he came out here.' She has a crick in her neck from dozing. She adjusts the cushions to support her back and neck. She wishes she were asleep in her own bed.

He's in tennis whites and is smiling.

'Those chairs are holding up well.' He taps the rattan chair as he sits into it. 'Jumble sale 1969. £3 for two. Remember? Cordelia got that gate-leg table for a fiver. We had a barbecue to celebrate. Those were the days!'

'What do you want? Tripping down memory lane is a waste of time.'

'You're wrong. It's useful and healthy to look at the past.'

'Which past? Your memory has always been more selective than most.'

'Maybe it has. I don't regret the things I've done as much as those I haven't.'

'Why are you here?'

'Lottie's upset that you've put the house up for sale.'

'She hasn't said anything to me.'

'Well, she wouldn't, at the moment. It's difficult for her. She idolises Edward.'

'I suppose so, but I think you're enjoying all the rumpus. It gives you a chance to stand on the high moral ground for a change. She should talk to me but whatever she says I won't change my mind about the house. I've spent enough time here. It's time for me to move on. This house is too full of memories. Things I didn't handle properly. It's had too much attention from me. I need to live somewhere else. A place that doesn't bind me.'

'I'm not here to ask you to change your mind.'

'As if you could. I make my own decisions.'

'Good for you.'

'Don't patronise me. I think I'll go in and continue packing. I'm filling a few boxes each day. I'll have to sell the bigger pieces of furniture. They would look ridiculously out of place in the new flat.'

'You've found a place already?'

'Yes. It's near Jamie's. I've paid my deposit. It's a converted warehouse. I need lots of space. I've signed on for a part-time MA course in stage design. The flat is perfect for large stage models.'

'You're leaving work?'

'No. I'll do flexi-hours to suit the course. Mr Wilson knows it would take him a long time to train someone to be as efficient as me. We struck a bargain. He's a man who understands value. I'd better go in. I'm expecting a couple to view the house in ten minutes time.'

'A hundred-and-ten thousand. That's the highest offer you've got.'

'Has Mr Wilson been talking to you about my business?'

'I'm Mr and Mrs Smythe. Appointment to view at 6.30. I rang Mr Wilson with my offer. A hundred and twelve thousand.'

'Why?'

'Why what?' Tony's smile is strained.

'Why do you want this house? I don't think I could sell it to you.'

'It's not for me, exactly. Well, not all of it anyway. I'd like the cellar and the basement. Nellie and Bob would live in the rest of it. And, of course, Lottie would hold on to her own room. No need for her to move at all.'

'I see. It's all planned. What would you do with the basement and cellar?'

'Use it as an office to write.'

'But you have your cabin at High Pines?'

'Yes. But lately all that expensive simplicity has begun to weigh on me. I'd like to get back to a bit of gritty realism. I wrote the trilogy in that cellar.'

'You want to get back to chilblains in the winter and boiling heat in the summer?'

'Exactly.'

'But Nellie and Bob have a flat of their own.'

'Not if Bob gives up his caretaking job. It goes with the job. If they were living here, Bob could go back to being a plumber for a living. Nellie would keep on her cleaning jobs. It would give them more comfort and security. A place of their own, at least for their lifetimes. After they died, the house would go to Jamie and Lottie. I can't say fairer.'

'Can't you? You're an extraordinary man. You want to look after Nellie and Bob until death but you walked out on me and the two kids without even a backward glance. I was so shocked I agreed to that tiny allowance. That was your meanest stroke. I can sell my house to anyone I like. And right now, I don't like you.'

'But I'm the highest bidder?'

'So! How much does this house mean to you?'

'A lot. I wouldn't want to buy it if it didn't.'

'Be specific. How much?'

'I've topped your highest offer.'

'It's not high enough. I've maintained this house since we moved into it. I had to take a low-paying part-time job to be able to look after my kids and keep the house. You walked out the moment you tasted material success. Your second wife shared that. If you really want this house, it will cost you two hundred and fifty thousand.'

'That's a lot of money. Looks like Billie isn't one of life's innocents after all, my love.' Pam kisses Don's nose playfully as she gives him a drink.

'Wrong. It's because she's an innocent that she's demanding such an astronomical sum. She's not just plain greedy, right Tony? She'll sell at a hundred-and-ten to any buyer but for you, my pal, it's a special price. What a woman!'

'I don't know what to think.' Tony is pacing their living-room. It's an odd room. Triangular in shape with two massive windows at the base of the triangle.

'You were so right to come to my pyramid room after such an encounter.' Pam's hand arcs the room as if to underscore its charms. Grey rag-rolled walls with Egyptian murals top and bottom. A Pharaoh couch and two outsize Pharaoh chairs. Rush matting, the colour of sand. Nothing else. There's a vast solidity about it.

'You could handpick a buyer to offer her a hundred-and-fifteen. An actor for instance. Greg would be perfect. His voice carries such authority. Even when he says, "Pass the salt," I'm impressed.'

'She'll need money soon for the new flat,' Don says matter-of-factly.

'I've a week to think about it.' Tony perches on an arm of one of the massive pharoah chairs. 'It's a ludicrous amount of money to ask for a house in Brabbington Terrace. We bought it for £25,000 and we thought it a fortune in 1966. We lived on lentils and bruised fruit from the market for the first two years. It took years to get gas-fires in all of the rooms. We had to heat the tenants' rooms first. We always had soups.'

'Jesus wept. He thinks he's Charles Dickens all of a sudden. The truth is you couldn't wait to run away from the lentils to the central heating of High Pines. What's done is done. Think about the money.' Pam inhales deeply then lets out slow deliberate smoke circles.

'Why do you want it so badly?' Don asks.

'I don't know exactly. I got such a shock when Nellie told me it was up for sale. She's been cleaning that house for years.'

'So! She can clean the warehouse that Billie's buying.'

'It wouldn't be the same.'

'And you laugh at me for being in therapy!' Pam's voice is cold. 'This is sick stuff. You don't want your first wife to sell her house because the cleaning lady would miss the kitchen floor.'

'Put like that it sounds ludicrous.'

'It is. Turn your back on the place and get on with your life. It's dangerous to meddle in some things.'

'I'm not meddling. Lottie doesn't want to move house. As a father I'm concerned for her. That can't be called meddling.'

'She's so spoiled. When I was her age, I was touring the country with a new play to learn every week. Our digs were dismal. Paraffin heaters or nothing at all. She'll get over the move. She has so much else going for her. Children are survivors. Well, some of them are anyway. I nearly had a kid at Lottie's age but I had an abortion instead. It was primitive in those days. A botched job. No chance of having a kid after that. They took too much out or something. Still, when I get pissed I go for Don about the kid business. Not his fault, of course. Never tells me to shut up. That's love, I suppose.'

Tony has been in the cabin now for days. Day and night. He's unshaven. The beard that looks out at him from the mirror has lots of grey. He hasn't been sleeping well since his meeting with Billie. Wendy says if he needs a few days on his own, then that's what he should do. Nanny and Marian are in the house with her. No need to worry. Sturdy, flat-footed nanny. Ever since she came things have been changing. Now, the Greek gorgon Christina is going to live with them as well. Wendy must have planned it while she was in Greece. The perfect housekeeper. Not just a daily like Nellie. Nellie wouldn't be needed any longer. Wendy had spoken in a low reasonable tone as if things should proceed in an orderly sequence. He knew that he wouldn't be able to tell Nellie that she wasn't needed. He needed her. A small pension, Wendy suggested, if he felt badly about it, but she couldn't have a woman working for her who didn't even like her. She'd had enough of Nellie's moods and that was that. A month's notice starting from next week. Either that or she would take Ludo to her mum's until things were sorted.

'What things?'

'A separation or something. If I'm living here, I have to be in charge of the household. I'll never be in charge as long as Nellie is here.'

But Nellie had been the one constant in his life. He didn't want to lose her. He didn't want to lose Wendy either. The first flush of passion was gone but he needed her. She might take Ludo away. His son, born in his fiftieth year, his favourite. The only one whose nappies he'd changed. Wendy, who had been so compliant in courtship, was turning into a formidable tactician.

The For Sale sign at Brabbington Terrace was an omen, a way of holding on to Nellie. The nightmares about mum had come back. Ones he hadn't had for years. A black winter's night. So dark it is difficult to see. No street lights. Mum, Lloyd and he walking through long narrow streets. Mum ahead. She's telling them they'll soon be home. He loses a shoe and can't keep up with them. He's hobbling. The shoeless foot is sore and wet. He's crying but mum can't hear. Their voices grow fainter and fainter. They're gone and he's lost. The other nightmare. The one in the swimming pool. Lloyd floating down the deep end, smiling. He shouting Lloyd's name until everyone around the pool is alerted. Mum slapping his face.

He taps out his options on his laptop. Get Greg the actor to buy Billie's house for him. Buy a different house for Nellie and Bob. Bring Lottie to High Pines permanently. His days are spent imagining the outcomes of his various choices. On the fourth day in his cabin, there's a brisk knock on the door. It's Cordelia. She's neatly got up in a grey suit. He's conscious of his unshaven appearance.

'Has Billie sent you?'

'No. I've come to offer you my house instead of Billie's.'

'How extraordinary!'

'I heard of your predicament. If it's Billie's house you want and no other, then I'll leave now. But if it's a similar one then I hope that you'll consider mine. A small house with a large garden would be more suited to my needs.'

'Have some coffee.'

'Thanks. I'll probably sell anyway, even if you don't buy my house. I need some movement in my life. A change.'

'This thing with Billie and Edward.'

'I'd prefer not to discuss that. They're both adults. I won't interfere. It's a strain but I've adjusted. That's all I want to say about that.'

'My mum approved of Billie in a way that she never did of me.'

'We shouldn't expect approval from our parents. At least not after we've become adults. We should grow beyond that.'

'Sold the house! Why? When?'

Edward has just finished one of Cordelia's homemade steak and kidney pies. It's Tuesday night, his evening to come to dinner.

'Because it's too big for me. I'm buying a small house with a large garden.'

'Close by?'

'Not really. Provence.'

'France! But you never said anything to me about it.'

'I didn't think I'd need your approval. I'm leaving the furniture. You can have what you like. I'll sell what's left.'

'But I've no space for any more furniture.'

'The house in France has simple rustic furniture. I'll leave it as it is. I don't want to spoil its character.'

'You've seen it then?'

'Yes. It's the one I rented last year. I asked the owner to let me know if she ever put it on the market. Her letter arrived last Wednesday. As soon as I knew it was available, I knew I wanted to leave here. I'm so lucky to have sold my house so quickly. And a private sale too. No middleman to take a slice of the profits.'

'Who bought it?'

'Tony. He wanted Billie's house but you know that story already.'

'But . . .'

In Cordelia's house, Lottie chooses Edward's old room for herself. She's familiar with it and doesn't wish to change it. It's a double room. There's plenty of space even after the baby grand is moved in. She moves some of her furniture from Billie's house and her little cooker. A proper flat of her own. Tony has the cellar and basement. He plans to work here in the mornings and in his cabin in the afternoons. Nellie and Bob are already installed.

'Your very own tool shed in our garden, Bob. A momentous occasion.'

Billie sells her house and feels lucky. She's glad Tony is in Cordelia's house and not hers. Now that Cordelia got a house in France out of the deal, she feels less guilty about Edward. Her new warehouse flat is almost empty. She sold her furniture with the house. She's pleased to be rid of the clutter. She bought a high bed and a low couch. Her drawing board, props and stage models are all she needs besides. She's happy. She hasn't seen Edward for over a week now. Too busy drawing and making models. There's a dishy man in her props class. They've had drinks in the pub near the drama school. She's already way ahead in her assignments on the course. She has never felt so alive since . . . since the day she played the role of foundress in the convent pageant in junior school.

Edward is crying. He howls into his pillows. He's alone in his flat. Things are moving too fast for his liking. Cordelia in Provence and Billie in her bloody warehouse flat, all within the last two weeks. Lottie lives in his house. The house that he always thought would be his eventually. He feels abandoned, betrayed. By Cordelia and Billie. Cordelia gave him all the family photograph albums before she left. 'I'm travelling light,' she'd said in a skittish girly way. 'I have your photo in my locket. That's all I need. Come when you need a holiday.' Not at all like a mother.

Marian is helping Tony build a Lego castle for Ludo. They're concentrating too much to talk. Almost finished. Marian sucks in her lower lip in that way Beth used to do when she was satisfied with a job well done. Tony reaches for the last little knight. Marian grasps it at the same time. They place it carefully on look-out duty.

'I think I'd like to go to America this Christmas. Spend some time with granny and grandad. What do you think, dad?'

It's the first time she's called him dad since Beth died.

Lottie plays a duet with Edward at Goldie's and Susan's wedding. They steal the show and glow in the admiration. Billie slips off early to finish her drawings for a production of *Antigone*. She's a deadline to meet. Edward takes Lottie home and sleeps the night on Nellie's couch in Brabbington Terrace.

NEST-EGG FO

"Don't move!"
Mannering stood very still, then began to raise his hands.
The automatic pistol pointed steadily at his stomach. He could just see the glitter of the man's eyes.
"I want those eggs, Mannering, and I want them quick." He thrust the gun forward. "Where are they? Don't stall, talk!"
Lorna was writhing on the bed, her eyes pleading. "Don't do it," she begged, "don't make him angry."
"How do you know I've got them?"
Mannering saw the trigger move, and stood motionless. Behind the man he saw Lorna flinch. The shot snapped out, just a loud crack . . .

Also by the same author

The Baron and the Chinese Puzzle
The Baron Goes Fast
Bad for the Baron
The Baron on Board
Help from the Baron
Affair for the Baron
The Baron in France
Salute for the Baron
Danger for the Baron

and available in Hodder Paperbacks

Nest-egg for the Baron

Anthony Morton

HODDER PAPERBACKS

Copyright © 1954 by John Creasey
First published 1954
Hodder Paperback Edition 1961
Second impression 1971

The characters in this book are entirely imaginary and
bear no relation to any living person

This book is sold subject to the condition that it shall
not, by way of trade or otherwise, be lent, re-sold,
hired out or otherwise circulated without the publisher's
prior consent in any form of binding or cover other than
that in which this is published and without a similar
condition including this condition being imposed on
the subsequent purchaser

Printed in Great Britain
for Hodder Paperbacks Ltd.,
St Paul's House, Warwick Lane, London, E.C.4,
by Richard Clay (The Chaucer Press), Ltd.,
Bungay, Suffolk

ISBN 0 340 15113 7

CONTENTS

Chapter		Page
1.	Beauty and The Beast	7
2.	The Golden Eggs	14
3.	The Missing Mr. Smith	23
4.	Lorna Goes Home	30
5.	Fenn	39
6.	Sharp Shooting	45
7.	William Brash	53
8.	Police Work	60
9.	News from Wainwright	71
10.	Dragon's End	77
11.	The "Museum" by Night	84
12.	Search	92
13.	Clash with Brash	100
14.	Missing Man	107
15.	Second Murder	113
16.	Why Murder Mannering?	122
17.	Flood	129
18.	A Cause of Fear	136
19.	At Crummy Day's	147
20.	Discovery	153
21.	Remand	160
22.	Dragon's End Again	167
23.	The Real Dibben	178
24.	Hornet's Nest	185

1

BEAUTY AND THE BEAST

THE girl was so young and pretty, and the man so old and plain. "Plain", in fact, was the word which only the kind of heart would have applied. He was ugly. He had a big, veiny, bulbous nose, and thick, coarse lips; little eyes which seemed buried in their sockets; and he was painfully thin. Nature, warmly generous with gifts to the girl's face and figure, had savaged the old man wickedly, for he had a humped back and short legs; pity stirred easily for him, once revulsion was past.

The girl walked with him, slowly. His back was bent, hers beautifully straight; he limped, she had the grace of the very young. Her forearm, rounded and golden brown, was without a blemish; his hand, grasping it, was like a claw made out of rotting leather. He clasped her tightly, as if without her help he would not be able to move along.

Most who saw them, stared.

Even Mannering did.

He was coming from the other direction. Their backs were towards Bond Street, with its swift ebb and flow of traffic, scurrying people, and fashions. It was still a shopping place for the very rich, although no longer exclusively for them.

Mannering faced the old man and the young woman. Half-way between him and the strange couple was his shop, Quinns, with its narrow window and oiled dark-oak fascia board with the legend Quinns in old English lettering, and gold paint. The shop was famous and, for different reasons, so was Mannering. Yet strangers would have been intrigued as he drew nearer the couple, for he was in sharp contrast to the old man. Tall, tanned, handsome—and all these enough to be striking.

The few people in Hart Row, a narrow street where several exclusive shops attracted the knowing as well as the wealthy, saw the couple become a trio just outside Quinns. In the window a jewelled crown was displayed upon black velvet. The jewels caught the light and showed a hundred colours; gold glittered, and in the centre of the crown was a single diamond which might have been first cousin to the Koh-i-noor. It was worth a fortune, although the dynasty for which it had been wrought and set by craftsmen of an Oriental kingdom had long since perished.

Until that moment no single person had passed Quinns without looking at the crown. Most had lingered. A surprising number had remarked that it couldn't be real—no one would take a risk with a genuine jewelled crown in a shop window. All these comments had been heard inside by Mannering's assistants, for an elaborate loud-speaker system had been installed to enable a man at the back of the shop to hear what was said outside; that was one of Mannering's many precautions against burglary.

Everyone near by, then, had paused to look at the crown; three women, two of them Americans, were at the window now. The old man and the girl passed the window. The old man glanced at the crown, then looked away, and said:

"This is the place, Miranda."

The girl did not speak.

"I hope, I only hope, that we can trust them."

The girl said nothing.

She glanced at Mannering, but had no more interest in him than the man had in the crown of such splendour. Her eyes were blue, so clear and bright that Mannering was reminded of the sea in Naples Bay on a summer day when Vesuvius brooded and Capri crowned the Mediterranean loveliness. Her hair was fair, a pale-gold colour, brushed straight back from her forehead and hanging below her shoulders. It was like a golden cloak, and glistened just as beautifully as the crown.

She wore a simply cut linen dress of apple-green, with a wide yellow belt and yellow shoes, and she carried a small pigskin dress-case.

"The man I want to see," said the old man, "is Mannering himself, John Mannering. We must insist, Miranda."

Miranda did not speak.

The old man's voice was quite remarkable, especially because it was so unexpected. A harsh, croaking sound would have seemed natural; in fact, he had a soft, smooth, cultured tone, and spoke as if he were aware that his voice was his great asset, and must be used with caution and with skill.

Mannering drew back.

Sylvester, a grey-haired man with the manners of a courtier, was on the other side of the door. He opened it. The girl freed her arm, took the old man's elbow, and thrust him gently inside. Sylvester bowed. The old man shot a swift, suspicious look at him from those dark, buried eyes. He was breathing heavily, and a beading of sweat fringed his lined forehead.

"Good afternoon, sir," welcomed Sylvester. "Will you please sit down? It's very warm—a tiring day."

He pushed a chair forward.

The girl glanced at him gratefully, and helped the old and ugly man to sit down.

"Thank you, thank you," said the man. The girl did not speak. "I wish to see Mr. Mannering. Is he in, please?"

Mannering was still outside the door.

"He isn't at the moment, but I expect him back soon," Sylvester said.

"Then we will wait."

"You're very welcome, sir." Sylvester bowed, and moved a little to one side. "If you care to look round, you will be equally welcome."

"I haven't come to buy," said the little old man testily; "I've come to sell."

"We would have great difficulty in selling if we didn't sometimes buy," said Sylvester, with the same practised courtesy. He glanced at the girl's pigskin case, as if wondering what was inside. "I will tell you the moment Mr. Mannering arrives."

The old man nodded.

The girl still didn't speak.

Although both looked round, neither of the callers paid particular attention to the shop or its contents. Theirs was the quick, casual gaze of someone who was not really interested, who knew that nothing here was likely to hold their attention. Some beautiful antiques, the oldest dating back to the thirteenth century, some cabinets with a golden sheen almost as beautiful as the girl's hair, a suit of mail armour once worn by a jousting knight—and on the walls, paintings by masters, all old and of divers sizes, would have fascinated connoisseurs and anyone with even a little knowledge of the past; and of beauty.

The lovely girl and the ugly old man looked from one to another with impatient, fleeting interest. They treated a Rubens and a Constable with equal indifference. Glass showcases held rare jewels and jewelled *objets d'art*, one filled with pieces matching the crown and coming from the same forgotten Court. But none of this interested the couple.

Mannering observed all this, from the street.

Sylvester disappeared.

A young man sat at the back of the shop, listening to the comments of the people outside. Then Mannering came in, nodded briskly at the couple, and went to his office, to the right at the end of the long, narrow shop.

Sylvester was waiting.

"They asked to see you personally, sir."

"Did they say why?" Mannering rounded a bow-fronted Queen Anne desk, and sat down as he spoke.

Sylvester stood near the door, venerable with age, courtly of voice as well as manner; a little too English to be true.

"The old man says they've come to sell," he said. "I didn't ask for details; I had a feeling that the man would probably resent it. He appears to be nervous, and when outside said that he hoped that we could be trusted!"

Mannering grinned.

"What did the girl say?"

"She hasn't uttered a word," Sylvester told Mannering. "If you'd like me to find out why——"

"I'll see them at once, I think," decided Mannering, and gave a crooked smile. "She's really something out of the top drawer."

"Very lovely indeed, sir." Sylvester hesitated. "It's strange that she hasn't yet uttered a syllable."

"Shy, too!"

"Have you noticed," asked Sylvester reflectively, "that she has a strange kind of calmness?"

"Strange?"

"It impresses me that way."

"Bring them along," said Mannering, "and I'll tell you later if I agree."

He pushed his chair back a little and glanced up at an oil-painting on the wall opposite. His own face looked down at him—above the dress, almost the regalia, of a Regency buck. There he was, with many colourful frills and furbelows and a sword in its scabbard, a gleam in his eye, and an amused twist at his lips. His wife had painted it.

"As you ought to be and often wish you were," she had said when he'd first seen it.

The door opened.

"Mr. Smith, sir," said Sylvester, with faint emphasis, "and Miss Miranda Smith."

Mannering rose to greet them.

The girl's pale hand was on the old man's crooked elbow, as if she were urging him forward and giving him the courage to move. Once they were inside, the door closed on Sylvester. By Mannering's foot was a switch; when it was down, Sylvester could hear every word and every sound in the office; another of the many precautions which Mannering's nimble wits and insurance-company stipulations conspired to create.

But this was obviously just a harmless couple.

Mannering pressed the switch down; Sylvester heard a rustle of movement, a few words of greeting, and then:

"Miranda," said the old man, "let me have that case."

He took it from her, and put it on the desk. His breathing was a little harsh. The deep-set eyes held a strange, excited glint. None of this appeared to affect the girl at all. She sat erect and unmoving, on an upright chair; long ago, she had been taught to carry herself well, and now the poise came naturally. She had a nice figure, too, not heavy, perhaps not fully developed; the figure of a girl of nineteen or twenty who would soon come to womanhood.

She did not speak.

Glancing at her, Mannering saw what Sylvester meant. Hers was a strange calmness; almost unnatural. Yet everything else about her was so natural and lovely that the word "strange" seemed wrongly applied.

"Mr. Mannering," said the old man, "I've come to you because I'm told you are an honest man."

"I hope you haven't been misinformed," said Mannering, promptly and with proper gravity.

"So do I. Soon find out," said the old man. His voice was a little forced now, but was still remarkable for its clear tone. "My name's Smith."

"So I understand."

"Pendexter Smith."

"Really," said Mannering, as if the first name conveyed a lot to him and he now fully understood the identity of his visitor. He didn't. Sylvester had thrown doubt on the "Smith" with the faint emphasis; it was easy to forget that there were a great number of people really named Smith but few who had been christened Pendexter. "How can I help you, Mr. Smith?"

"I have something to sell," Pendexter Smith announced.

He set the small case on his knees, then took a ring of keys from his side pocket. It was a big bunch, clinking and winking. He selected a key swiftly. His fingers had that look of rotting leather, there were ridged, blue veins and livery-brown spots on his hands; yet the fingers were nimble as he thrust the key into the lock of the case and turned it.

The lock clicked.

He didn't open the case, but took the key out, thrust the bunch back into his pocket, and then peered at Mannering. His ugliness became more apparent; even to Mannering, who was now getting used to him, he was almost repellent. The deep-set eyes glittered like something reflecting the light a long way off. His thick, flat lips were turned back. He was almost hideous as he leaned forward, narrow, pointed chin stabbing, narrow shoulders hunched; he reminded Mannering of a vulture.

"In this case I've got something worth a hundred thousand pounds," he said, gustily. "I wish to sell it quickly, for as much as I can get. Will you find a buyer?"

The girl looked at Mannering, her blue eyes darker in the room, unsmiling, calm, serene.

2

THE GOLDEN EGGS

"I'll try to find a buyer," Mannering said quietly. "but if it's worth that money, it may take a little while."

For the first time, he wondered if the old man were quite right in the head. The girl's manner was beginning to disturb him, too; Sylvester was right, her pose wasn't natural; it was too child-like. Yet he recalled the way in which she had taken the old man's elbow and guided him into the shop; and, later, into the office. She had known what she was doing then.

"May I see what it is?" asked Mannering, mildly.

The old man placed his two hands on the top of the little brown case. The swollen joints made the hands and fingers look more bony and much thinner even than they were. He pressed against the case possessively, giving the impression that for a moment he was afraid.

"I'll show you," he promised. "I'll show you, but you don't believe what I say, do you?"

"About what?"

"That what I have here is worth a hundred thousand pounds."

"Until I've seen it——"

"All the same," said the old man, with a kind of bitter fierceness. "All dealers are the same, they deny the value, beat you down, cheat, and swindle, they'd cheat their own kith and kin!"

As nearly as they could, his buried eyes glared, as if he expected an angry response, Mannering on his dignity.

Mannering smiled amiably, and said, "Dreadful lot, aren't we?"

"In my experience——" began Pendexter Smith, but

broke off abruptly. "All right, all right, I'll show you what I have. But mind you"—he raised one hand, to point a waggling finger—"I don't trust you."

"I don't blame you!"

Throughout all this, the lovely girl sat erect and still, her hands clasped lightly in her lap. They were nice hands, and the long, thin fingers were tipped with filbert-shaped nails which had neither coloured nor natural varnish to make them glisten. She wore just a touch of lipstick and a little powder; no rouge at all. The serenity of her blue eyes had not changed. She looked now at the old man, now at Mannering, half questioning—as if she were interested in what was passing between them, but had no desire to speak.

Was she—dumb?

"If I leave them in your charge I'll want every possible kind of assurance that they'll be looked after," Pendexter Smith went on. "Don't think I'll let you get away with anything."

"I hope you won't." Mannering was amiably emphatic.

The old man looked as if he didn't quite understand this attitude; he remained suspicious and wary, and it was a long time before he lifted the lid of the case. Then he did so slowly. His manner created a sharper interest in Mannering; it was as if he were going to reveal something which was breathlessly beautiful and really worth a fortune. The odds were all against that; much more likely he was a bit touched, and had a trifle which he had invested with a fabulous value. Yet his manner made Mannering lean forward with quickening interest, and even made his heart beat faster.

The girl leaned forward, too, her eyes glistening with sudden excitement.

The old man threw back the lid.

"There!" he cried.

Inside the case was a nest, a bird's nest—made of spun gold. Inside the nest were five jewelled eggs, and if one could judge from the look of them, diamonds, rubies, emeralds, and sapphires were set in eggs of solid gold. Each the size of small hen's eggs, they lay in the golden nest as if a fabulous bird which could lay jewelled eggs had left them there, and flown away.

. . . . .

"You see?" Pendexter Smith's voice became almost shrill. His eyes glittered, his hands hovered about the eggs as if he suspected that Mannering would snatch them, and he meant to protect them with his life. "Five jewelled eggs in a golden nest, worth a hundred thousand pounds at least. The only one like it in the world, Mr. Mannering! Why, the gold itself must be worth ten thousand pounds."

He watched Mannering, as if expecting a denial.

"Yes," said Mannering slowly, "I can well believe it."

"You *agree*?"

"It's so obviously true."

In the pause that followed, the old man looked at the girl, who was staring at him, not Mannering. Mannering judged her expression to be one of expectancy, but couldn't really be sure. She didn't look so very different from what she had all the time.

"Miranda," said Pendexter Smith, "it's beginning to look as if we've found an honest dealer." His eyes snapped at Mannering. "How much do you think they are worth to a collector, Mr. Mannering?"

"I'm not going to guess."

"You can estimate, surely."

"A collector who wanted them badly enough would pay your price."

"You see, you see?" cried Smith, exultingly, "I was right! A hundred thousand pounds for the jewelled eggs." He lifted the case, dropped it heavily on the desk in front of Mannering, and rubbed his hands together briskly, obviously beside himself with delight. "I knew I wasn't far wrong, Miranda."

THE GOLDEN EGGS 17

Mannering then saw the strangest sight.

The old man jumped up and put an arm about the girl's shoulders, hugged her, and kissed her. That should have seemed obscene, but it did not. She turned to look at him, and now all the calmness had gone, her eyes glowed, her hands were raised and clenched. Mannering thought, "I believe it's given her hope," and certainly hope seemed to blaze in her eyes, giving her a new, fierce radiance.

"We'll have you right," cried Pendexter Smith, "don't worry about it, we'll have you right!" He squeezed her again, then turned to face Mannering, quivering with excitement. Standing, he was only as tall as Mannering was when sitting. "How soon can you sell them? Tell me, please, quickly."

"I can't even begin——" began Mannering.

"But it's vital, I must sell them quickly! How soon?"

Mannering found it hard to say, "A week, a month, or a year. I simply don't know. We'll have to find a collector if we want the full price, and collectors with fortunes aren't growing on every tree. There's no way of telling you how soon you could get your hundred thousand. I'd certainly advise waiting for a month or more in the hope of getting several offers. I think I know of two or three men in London who might be interested, others in Paris and Rome, more farther afield. You must be patient."

Pendexter Smith thumped the desk, made a silver inkstand jump and the pen rattle, but did not make the case move an inch.

"But I can't wait! I just can't wait."

"If you sell at once, you'll get the value of the gold and the jewels plus ten per cent or so," Mannering told him. "No more. If you wait——"

"But I *can't* wait!" The old man began to froth at the corners of the mouth. "Don't you understand? Can't you get it into your thick skull? I just can't wait. How soon?"

Mannering said, "You don't need all the money at once, do you?"

"No, but——"

"You can borrow on the value, and——"

"So there you go," breathed Pendexter Smith, "usury upon usury. You'll lend me twenty thousand pounds at a ruinous rate of interest. Any fool would if he had the money, but I'm not doing business that way. I want a buyer quickly, can't you find one in a week?"

"No." Mannering was brusque.

With anyone else, he would have been annoyed by now. Perhaps he was annoyed with Pendexter Smith, but the girl calmed him. She no longer looked excited, but there was something different in her manner; a serenity touched with a happiness which hadn't been there before. The word "hope" was in Mannering's mind when he looked at her.

As she stared at the old man, there was deep affection in her expression; what won the affection of this young and lovely creature for so grotesque a man?

It was not a thing Mannering could begin to try to understand.

The old man was leaning forward.

"Listen, Mr. Mannering, I'll sell for seventy-five thousand pounds. A quick buyer and I'll take seventy-five, five per cent commission for yourself. Isn't that worth the effort? Eh?"

His hands were clenched, there was no doubt about his desperate eagerness.

The girl was so lovely, too.

"I'll lend you ten thousand pounds, free of interest, for three months," Mannering said abruptly, "with the eggs as security, of course. If we haven't found a buyer at your price we'll have them valued and I'll buy at valuation, which won't be less than fifty thousand. Will that do?"

The old man didn't answer at first.

The girl now watched Mannering, as if she knew that he had become a vital factor.

The old man said abruptly, suspiciously, "Why should you make such an offer? Come on, tell me—why should you lend money without interest? You just want to get your hands on the nest of eggs, that's all, it's a trick to——"

The girl moved, her hand rested on his shoulder for a moment. It seemed to startle him. They looked into each other's eyes, and it seemed to Mannering that she was trying to convey a message which she could not express in words. She was truly dumb, of course, he no longer doubted that. Allied to such beauty, it was hurtful beyond words. And dumbness wasn't all; there was no sign language between them.

Mannering said, "If I find a buyer, Mr. Smith, I'll get a big commission. That would be well worth my investment. But please yourself what you do."

Pendexter Smith turned away from the girl.

"Ten thousand pounds," he said, as if to himself. "Free of interest."

"Yes."

"Today?"

"As soon as you've shown me your legal right to the nest of eggs," Mannering said, "and if you can do that within half an hour, you can have the money today. It's twenty minutes past two," he added, "and the banks close at three."

There was a long pause.

"Legal right," echoed Pendexter Smith, in his attractive voice. All his tension was gone; it was as if he knew that what he wanted was within his grasp, and he could not think beyond it. "What kind of proof do you want, Mr. Mannering?"

"Where did you get this from?"

"Oh, it isn't mine," said Pendexter Smith, "it's Miranda's. I'm simply helping her. Legal proof, now." He was speaking almost in a whisper. "I can quite understand that you need some evidence of good faith. Yes, but——"

He broke off.

His eyes lit up, and he clapped his hands together.

"Oh, I can do it, I know the way. I can't satisfy you in half an hour, but I can during this afternoon, if——" He hesitated, looked sharply at Miranda and then at the nest of eggs, and added more briskly, "If I may leave Miranda and this in your care while I go."

"Is there anyone we can telephone? Or any way in which I can help?"

"No," said Pendexter Smith, almost sharply. "No, I can manage quite well, thank you. I don't want Miranda to come with me, though. If you'll call a taxi for me, I'll be back in an hour. Two, at most. Will she be in the way?"

"No, but——"

"A taxi, please, a taxi!"

Mannering pressed a bell by the side of the desk, and Sylvester promptly opened the door.

"Sylvester," said Mannering, "ask young Trevor to go and get a taxi, will you?"

"At once, sir."

"Thanks."

"Is it for a long journey?" asked Sylvester.

"Eh?" said Pendexter Smith. "Oh, no, City, that's all. Not far. Hurry, please." He was moving from one foot to the other, like an agitated bird. The door closed on Sylvester. "Mr. Mannering, you'll give me a provisional receipt, won't you? Forgive me, but——"

"Yes, of course." Mannering drew paper, pen, and ink forward, and under the old man's intense scrutiny, wrote out a receipt that he felt sure the man would like.

> "This acknowledges receipt for temporary custody one spun gold nest and five jewelled eggs, of an approxi-

mate gold weight of 50 ounces, all being the property of Miss Miranda Smith and left in my custody by Mr. Pendexter Smith."

The old man read it slowly.

"Excellent," he pronounced, "most comprehensive!" He watched Mannering sign the note, then folded it across and across and placed it carefully in a worn, black leather wallet. He stuffed this back into the inside pocket of his long-waisted coat, then turned to the girl. "I won't be long, Miranda, you needn't worry."

He smiled at her.

She smiled back, mechanicallly; Mannering was sure that she hadn't fully understood. There seemed to be a kind of telepathy between her and Pendexter Smith, who patted her slim hand, then turned and bowed to Mannering; his little eyes almost invisible.

"I shall soon be back," he promised. "An hour, at most."

He went out of Quinns walking with some difficulty, as if he were at a loss without the girl's support. Sylvester actually helped him into the taxi.

"Go to the Bank of England, first," he said, "the Bank, please." He pulled the door to, and it slammed. The taxi, already facing Bond Street, moved off and turned left into a stream of traffic.

Mannering did not see any of that.

Mannering was alone with a very lovely girl, who looked at him with those limpid eyes, which were almost blank; the expression "dumb blonde" crossed his mind and brought with it a twisting spasm of pain.

There was a small room on the first floor, with pictures round the walls, all old and valuable, a few *objets d'art*, a Chippendale table, and several comfortable winged-back chairs; this served both as waiting-room and show-room.

The girl would be better off there, and he would not be so conscious of her presence.

"I'd like you to wait in another room," he said.

She looked at him, questioningly. Then she looked at his lips, and he thought he understood what she meant. He spoke very clearly and slowly, believing that she would be able to lip-read. After the first attempt, she shook her head, but stared at his lips until he tried again.

The next time, she nodded and stood up.

He took her upstairs, showed her magazines, some books filled with colour plates of jewellery, offered her cigarettes, and, when she had refused, left her on her own. She was quite calm.

Sylvester or his assistant went up to the room every ten or fifteen minutes. Mannering received several reports. Miranda was glancing at the books—she was interested mostly in the pictures—and finally, she was sitting and staring straight ahead of her, without expression.

An hour passed.

Two hours passed.

By then, Mannering was feeling edgy and ill-at-ease. Sylvester had taken the girl tea, and come down to report that she hadn't stirred.

Mannering hurried up the narrow, twisting staircase, ducking by force of habit to save banging his head. He reached the room, but didn't go in.

The girl was sitting where he had last seen her. The tray of tea, with two tiny cream cakes and some wafer-thin sandwiches, was on a table by her side, untouched. She was looking at the wall; and where before there had been eagerness in those lovely eyes, now there was fear that no one could possibly mistake.

"Miranda," began Mannering, and went in.

She didn't hear him; of course she didn't. He took a step nearer, and she must have seen him, for she jumped wildly and then cowered back, holding her hands up in front of her face, palms outwards.

3

THE MISSING MR. SMITH

"It's all right," Mannering said, very slowly. "It's all right."

The girl stared at his eyes, not at his lips. Her expression set his own heart thumping heavily, painfully. Slowly, he pointed at his lips; and she saw the movement.

"It—is—all—right."

She let her hands fall, and they stayed like that. The fear did not leave her eyes. She looked round, from corner to corner, and then back at Mannering, as if hoping that he understood what she meant. He thought he did: she was asking for Pendexter Smith. He shook his head, mouthed, "He will be back soon," then moved towards the table and poured out a cup of tea.

"Drink this, please."

She looked at it, then took the cup and sipped; but her gaze was in a corner or on Mannering, as if she were still searching.

"He—will—soon—be—back," Mannering tried to reassure her.

She looked blank.

"He—will—soon—be—back."

The girl closed her eyes for a moment, and when she opened them again, they were misted as if with tears. She stood up, put the cup down slowly, and went towards the door. Mannering followed her.

At the foot of the stairs, Sylvester stood tensely.

He backed away. The girl went down, taking each step

very carefully. At the entrance to the shop she hesitated, and then looked round with great deliberation. She glanced into the office, then walked straight to the front door.

Sylvester's assistant, a youth in the early twenties, named Trevor, opened the door for her, watching her intently as he did so. Everyone who saw her seemed fascinated; hypnotised. That was partly because of her strained expression, with its look of fear and longing.

Mannering was close behind her.

The girl stepped into the street, and looked up and down, then turned; and her eyes were misty with tears, her lips weren't so steady as they had been. She glanced at her watch, then at Mannering; and suddenly she turned and walked towards Bond Street. She seemed to glide along, at quite a remarkable pace. In Bond Street the crowds were thickening with the evening rush, everyone seemed to be in a hurry. Taxis, private cars, bicycle boys, all sped past; or came, sharply, noisily, to a standstill as a policeman's arm raised. The windows of the exclusive shops drew little attention. Everyone was in a hurry, except the policemen standing on traffic duty at the cross-roads near by.

Yet everyone paused in their haste, to look at the girl.

A dozen men, as many women, caught sight of her, checked their headlong walk, and then, after staring at her, went past more slowly. Most of them turned back to look. A policeman took a moment or two off his pressing duty to look at Miranda. He knew the owner of Quinns well, saw Mannering, and seemed to be trying to ask a question.

The girl looked up and down, as if searching for the little old man. She saw no one remotely like him, no one to give her hope.

More and more people watched her. One lad, in his twenties, might have been gaping at a goddess.

Miranda glanced at her watch again. It was twenty minutes past five; and the old man had been gone for nearly three hours. She closed her eyes, and a tear squeezed its way through her lashes and fell upon her cheek. Two middle-aged women stopped, as if they could not bear to pass without offering help.

"Are you all right, my dear?"

The girl didn't open her eyes.

"She's quite all right," Mannering assured them. "She's had a nasty shock, but she's with friends. Miranda, we'd better get back."

He took her arm firmly. He wouldn't have been surprised had she shaken his hand off, but she let it stay. Two women dressing the window of a shop opposite stared. A notice in the window read: *Stocktaking Sale Tomorrow.*

Miranda Smith allowed herself to be led towards the shop, inside, and to the office. There, still in the case, stood the golden nest and the five jewelled eggs. The girl stood looking down at these, and tears came more freely, running down her smooth cheeks and making tiny lines in them.

"What are we going to do?" asked Sylvester, helplessly. "How can we help her?"

. . . . .

Lorna Mannering, in her studio above the Mannerings' flat in Green Street, Chelsea, was looking out of the huge north light, over the roofs of London. She was in a calm and reflective mood. John would soon be back. They were both having a good period, her work was going well, he was busy without being overworked. The portrait on her easel was at the stage where she wanted to keep going back to examine it closely, seeking blemishes, ready with the simple stroke with brush or palette knife which would remove the blemish.

The light was still good.

She wore a green smock, so daubed with paint that it was almost a coat of many colours, but her dark, wavy hair fell loosely to her shoulders. She had a slightly sallow complexion, and in repose she could look sullen; almost aloof.

She didn't, now. Her well-marked eyebrows were almost level, she gave no hint of strain. She was contented.

It was half-past five.

She moved away from the big window in the roof towards the long, narrow window overlooking the Thames and the distant houses, the Battersea Power Station, the bridges. River traffic flowed, Embankment traffic hummed. Sometimes John came home this way, and it amused her to see whether she could pick out their Rolls-Bentley from the steady stream. It was surprising how many expensive cars passed; money wasn't as tight as some people liked to make out.

The telephone bell rang. She could just hear it, downstairs in the living-quarters. She went to the instrument on a table up here, but it wasn't switched through. She lifted the receiver and could hear without being heard if she spoke.

"Mr. Mannering's residence," said Ethel, their maid.

"Hallo, Ethel, is Mrs. Mannering there?"

"Well, sir, she's in the studio, but——"

"Ask her to come to the telephone, will you?"

"Yes, sir, half a mo'."

Lorna went to the hatch through which she had to climb down into the flat itself. There was a sturdy step-ladder always in position. She heard Ethel's footsteps, saw Ethel's tousled, pale-brown hair.

"All right," she called promptly, "just switch me through."

"Oh, you heard him," Ethel said. "Okay, mum."

She was willing; she would never be really good . . .

Lorna waited, her expression different now. In the past few seconds something had changed her mood completely. There were two reasons. First, the fact that she had heard John's voice; it could still affect her; she could get almost mushy, especially in some moments. She hadn't, then; she'd felt the warm glow which was so much a part of life. Then

THE MISSING MR. SMITH 27

he'd spoken again, wanting her on the telephone, although it was an unwritten law that when she was working she wouldn't be disturbed unless the telephone were switched through. Only an emergency would make him break the rule, he was more considerate than anyone else.

What was so urgent?

It did not necessarily mean trouble; it might do, but it probably didn't. Her heart began to beat faster as she reasoned with herself. She seldom felt like this, and hardly ever without justification; as if she could tell that John had come face to face with trouble, that the serenity of the past few weeks had been broken abruptly.

"Hallo, darling," Lorna greeted.

"Hallo, sweet," said Mannering, and Lorna knew in a moment that it wasn't too serious, she'd been silly. "Sorry to interrupt, but I've a problem."

"I've finished work for the day."

"Oh, fine! You can put on a hat and come to the shop?"

"Well, yes, but——"

"I know I'm crazy," Mannering said, and there was a hint of laughter in his voice—but it was rueful laughter, he wasn't really amused. He was more puzzled than worried, Lorna thought, and that puzzled her in turn. "Take a deep breath, will you?"

"Taken."

"The craziest thing happened this afternoon. I'll tell you all about it later, with all details. The immediate thing is that I'm landed with a blonde, a——"

"Oh, darling," Lorna said, and she became suddenly light-hearted; it wasn't trouble at all, there was no shadow of menace upon them. "I thought you were after a murderer or half Quinns' stock has been stolen! Is she a dumb blonde?"

He didn't answer.

"John, are you there?"

"Sorry," said Mannering, slowly. "Yes, she is. She is exactly that—literally dumb. She came here with an old man and a fortune, the old man went off and didn't come back. I don't know a thing about her, where she comes from, where she lives, who she is. I'm going to see Bristow, but I can't leave her here. Be a pet and come and get her."

"You mean, she's to stay with *us*?" Lorna didn't exactly protest; just didn't receive the news with any enthusiasm.

"Oh, she won't be with us for long! But she's scared out of her wits, and you're more likely to help her than anyone else."

It was Lorna's turn not to answer.

The shadow, which had lifted, came back. For some inexplicable reason, it was darker than it had been. She knew that logically she had no reason for feeling the cold hand of fear, but all the same it touched her. With any other man, this would have meant that an afflicted girl had been left on her own, and was frightened because she was lost. With John Mannering, it meant—it might mean—almost anything. Already he was talking of going to Scotland Yard, and that brought sharp, hurtful memories of criminal cases he had investigated, of dangers faced, of fear and menace.

It was the side of his life that she hated, but it was part of him to take risks, to champion the cause of the helpless and frightened, to——

Nonsense!

"All right, darling," Lorna made herself say brightly, "I'll come at once."

"Fine!" said Mannering. "Bless you."

He rang off.

Lorna put down the receiver slowly. As slowly, she went to the hatch, and down the step-ladder, climbing backwards.

Ethel was coming out of the bathroom.

"I'm going out for an hour, Ethel, and I think we shall have a guest for dinner."

"Oh, that's all right, mum."

"I shouldn't make any fuss," Lorna said, smiled, and went into her bedroom.

She tidied her hair, dabbed powder, looked at herself critically, and knew that she wouldn't go out with a patched up make-up if it weren't for the note of bewilderment and uncertainty in John's voice.

She couldn't throw off those shadows.

She wished that she could fight the mood off, but knew that only events would do that. Being married to the most renowned judge of precious stones, *objets d'art*, and certain periods of art in Great Britain was one thing. Being married to a man whom the thoughtless dubbed "an amateur tec" or those under American influence called a "private eye" was a vastly different matter. John seemed to act as a magnet to criminal cases which turned on precious stones. He had a history that was strangely chequered, but the simple facts now were that he worked with the police as often as he worked against them, and that he was as familiar with his name in newspaper headlines as he was with Scotland Yard and the business at Quinns.

Now he had a dumb blonde on his hands—with her "fortune".

Lorna recalled his moment of painful silence on the telephone. There was no doubt at all that he meant dumb literally; the girl who had been landed on him at Quinns could not talk.

It wasn't going to be easy. Abruptly, Lorna decided against more make-up, and hurried out, calling to Ethel as she closed the front door.

Five minutes later, she was in a taxi heading for the West End and Quinns.

. . . . . .

Lorna had not seen the man standing in a doorway on the other side of Green Street, some distance along, staring at her. She was round the corner when he crossed the road, entered the Green Street house, and walked up the stairs.

He hesitated on the landing of the Mannerings' flat, then took a gun from his pocket, weighed it in his hand, put it back in his pocket but kept a hold on it; then rang the bell.

Ethel answered.

When she saw him, she opened her mouth in a scream which wouldn't come.

4

LORNA GOES HOME

LORNA MANNERING paid the taxi off at the end of Hart Row, and walked to the shop. She looked right for Bond Street; her suit was by Dior, her shoes had come from Milan, she had an air about her which made women as well as men glance at her quickly and then look again. She was frowning as she hurried; still worried, but telling herself she was getting in a flap without any need.

Sylvester was at the shop door when she drew up. He opened it quickly, bowed, and smiled. She saw in a glance that he was troubled, too.

"Good evening, Mrs. Mannering."

"Hallo, Sylvester." She had time to smile; she always had time to be pleasant with those whom she liked. "I understand that we've a visitor."

"We have indeed," said Sylvester, "and I confess that I'm worried about it, Mrs. Mannering."

Her heart missed a beat.

"Why?"

"I think you'll understand when you see her," the old man said.

Lorna nodded, and led the way to the rear of the shop. Mannering heard her coming, and moved out of the office. She judged from his expression that he was as worried as Sylvester. She hadn't liked this before, and she liked it much less now.

He squeezed her arm.

"Thanks for hurrying, sweet. And sorry about wishing this on to you, but——"

"She isn't ill, is she?" Lorna asked. "I mean—mental?" She raised her hands, helplessly.

"She's physically dumb, she may be deaf," Mannering said, "and she's certainly scared stiff. I wish I knew why. It can't all be because the old man hasn't come back. If she could say a word if would help, but——"

"I'd better see her," Lorna said. They moved towards the narrow stairs. "What old man?"

Mannering told her, briefly; she knew the outlines of the story by the time they reached the waiting-cum-showroom. Another assistant, a young man in the late twenties, was dusting over some canvases which Mannering knew had been dusted four times in the last hour.

"All right, Wainwright, you can get off," he said.

"Thank you, sir. Good night. Good night, Mrs. Mannering."

Wainwright, an earnest young man anxious to learn the business, was the son of an old friend and client of Mannering. He reached the door, gave a rather taut smile, looked back at the girl, and then went out. His expression made Lorna's heart quicken; she hadn't yet seen the girl, but Sylvester, John and Wainwright were all equally affected.

"I didn't think we ought to leave her alone," Mannering said, half-apologetically.

They went in.

The girl was in the winged armchair in a corner behind the door. She stared at the window, the roofs, the blue sky, and the wisps of cloud. Her lips were set tightly, her body and her face was obviously at tension; but the harrowing thing was her eyes. They held all the fear that a child could hold. On a small table was a note-book and pencil, and Lorna saw Mannering's writing; Sylvester's, too—as if they'd tried to communicate with the girl that way.

There was no sign of her handwriting.

A floorboard creaked.

Mannering spoke.

The girl did not turn her head; obviously she had not heard them and did not know that they were there. Her hands were clasped in her lap. She sat upright, not leaning against the back of the chair—as if she dared not relax.

"Miranda," Mannering called, loudly.

She didn't glance towards him.

He went forward, across her line of vision, and when she saw him she started violently; a strange, gasping sound came from her lips, her gaze was transferred from the scene outside, to him. The sharpness of her fear faded when she recognised him; but as she watched, her breathing came in short, sharp gasps—the shock had really frightened her.

She looked at his lips.

"This—is—my—wife," Mannering said, very clearly. "She—will—look—after—you."

The girl shook her head, not comprehending. Mannering tried again, as Lorna stepped to his side. She looked at the girl with a compassion which had been born the moment she had set eyes on her.

The girl appeared to understand, this time, and looked at Lorna. She didn't try to speak.

"All right, John," Lorna said, "I'll look after her. She can't stay here any longer. I'll get her home. I think we ought to ask Roy Richardson to come and see her."

"Good idea," Mannering agreed. The girl's eyes still fascinated him. Her sleek, gold-coloured hair still had that lovely sheen, her complexion had no blemish, she had the freshness of a young girl—and fear which no girl should even begin to know. "Telephone Roy as soon as you get back, will you? He's in Town, I saw him at the club a couple of days ago. If he can't come himself, ask him to send someone who might know about—well, this. Although whether this is a doctor's job——" He broke off. "Worth trying, anyhow." He faced the girl again, and she stared at his lips, expectantly. "I—want—you—to—go—with—my—wife." He pointed at her, then at Lorna.

This time, Miranda understood the dumb-show. She nodded, and stood up slowly. As she moved towards Lorna, something in her manner suggested that she was ready to trust herself to this woman who she had only just met. As faith, it was pathetic.

"Did you keep your cab?" Mannering asked Lorna.

"No."

"You take the car, then. Is Ethel in?"

"Yes, darling!"

"Of course, she answered the telephone." Mannering hardly knew what he was saying, he was so preoccupied. "You carry on."

"When will you be home?"

"Oh, not late," Mannering said. "Not late at all."

He accompanied them downstairs and along to the car park, on a bombed site not far from Hart Row. The girl walked without looking right or left; as if she were sleep-walking. People stared at her. Mannering opened the door of his black Rolls-Bentley and helped the girl in one side, while Lorna switched on the ignition and pushed the self-starter.

"I won't be long," Mannering promised again.

"Try not to be." Lorna smiled, mechanically, and started off.

Mannering stood and watched. Young Wainwright, in a

taxi which was waiting outside a hat-shop near Quinns, looked out of the window, waved, and nodded.

Mannering had told him to follow them, but had said nothing to Lorna; he didn't want to worry Lorna, there might not be any need to.

He watched the car turn the corner, with the taxi in its wake, then returned to Quinns.

Sylvester said, "The strong-room is locked up, sir."

"Good. That man coming from the insurance company?"

"Yes, sir."

"If he thinks the nest-egg should be taken to a safe deposit or a bank for the night, let him have his way. Don't take it from here by yourself, though, ask for police guard. All clear?"

"Perfectly clear, sir."

"Good."

"As Larraby is away and no one is at the shop all night, perhaps you would like me to stay," said Sylvester.

"No," said Mannering. There was a limit to what one could ask of an old man. "If the insurance people are satisfied about leaving the nest-egg in the strong-room, I'll have someone on guard in the street during the night. Perhaps you'd better stay here until I call you."

"Very good, sir. Good night."

"Good night."

The traffic in Bond Street was much thinner. A few dawdlers were looking at shop windows, mostly with the obvious look of sightseers up from the country. Mannering walked briskly, looking round for a taxi, but it was five minutes before one came along with its sign up.

"Scotland Yard, please."

"Right, sir."

London slid by. The driver drove through stately streets, where, for a few brief hours, there was parking room; past tall, stately houses; across Piccadilly, towards Clarence

LORNA GOES HOME

House and the atmosphere of centuries, the guards in scarlet tunics and bearskins; into the Mall, then St. James's Park, thronged with women in light cotton dresses, men in their shirt-sleeves, children, eager to see the lake and the wild duck disporting themselves on or near it. Soon the taxi turned into Parliament Square, with the massive buildings on two sides, the Abbey and the Houses of Parliament on the others. The square was crammed with sightseers, there was much more traffic here. They were forced to stop. A couple standing on the pavement, the man with a camera at his face, caught Mannering's attention. The girl was so like Ethel, their maid, that he had to look twice.

It wasn't Ethel.

Lorna and the girl should be home by now. They would be in five or ten minutes, anyhow.

He paid the cabby off outside the Embankment entrance to the big new C.I.D. building of Scotland Yard, and walked towards the steps leading to the main doors. A sergeant on duty in the hall recognised him.

"Evening, Mr. Mannering, haven't had the pleasure of seeing you for a long time."

"My loss, Tom," said Mannering, and shook a man who had not expected to be remembered at all. "Is Mr. Bristow in?"

"Mr. Bristow, sir? Haven't you heard?"

"Heard what?"

"Oh, he's had a bit of luck, Bill Bristow has," said the sergeant. "Gone to South Africa on a job, gold-smuggling racket, it was in the papers a week or so ago. He isn't likely to be back for another two or three weeks. Tell you who is in his office—Mr. Fenn."

"H'm," said Mannering, dubiously. "Ask him if he'll spare me ten minutes, will you?"

"Right away, sir!"

Mannering waited, smoked.

He wasn't sure whether to be pleased or sorry that Superintendent Bristow, whom he knew extremely well, wasn't here. He would have gone straight up to see Bristow, being sure that Bristow would take him seriously and exert himself to help; but there would have been a drawback, too. Bristow belonged to a shadowy era in Mannering's chequered career. Bristow knew that the now respected and highly reputable dealer in antiques, jewels, and *objets d'art* had once been a jewel-thief who had set London by the ears. Bristow was ninety-nine per cent certain that Mannering had forsaken that life of crime; but to Bristow, Mannering would always be the Baron, cracksman extraordinary.

Fenn was a younger man, to whom Mannering was the respected owner of Quinns who liked to play detective and sometimes did so with exasperating success.

Mannering knew him slightly. A tall, thin man, slightly convex about the midriff, with a long face, lantern jaw, dark eyes; a brooding kind. He had advantages which few Yard men had; was well-read, well-bred, educated at a lesser Public School and Cambridge. There were those who said that he was likely to have a brilliant career.

The sergeant came from the telephone.

"He'll be glad to see you, sir. You don't need anyone to show you the way up, do you?"

Mannering grinned and winked, as the sergeant expected. Mannering hurried to the lift, which was empty, open, and on the ground floor, took himself up to the second floor, and then walked towards Fenn's—really Bristow's—office. He tapped, and went in on a deep "come in".

Fenn was on the telephone. He stood up, slowly, rather awkwardly because of the instrument, and waved to a chair. Mannering sat down. Fenn did more listening than talking. Now and again he grunted or made a monosyllabic comment, to show that he was alive. He had big, dark, bold brown eyes; intelligent eyes. Mannering had a feeling that he was glad of the chance to assess his visitor; that he was deliberately letting the telephone conversation drag on, so that he could size the caller up.

That didn't matter.

Outside, the traffic hummed along the Embankment, the quiet wind rustled the branches and the leaves of the plane-trees. A few miles along on the Embankment, Lorna would be at the flat, where several of the windows also overlooked the Thames. She would be there with the girl, Miranda, and probably she had already called Roy Richardson, she wouldn't lose any time.

"I'm awfully sorry," Fenn said, holding the telephone mouthpiece against his chest. "Won't be long."

"It's all right," said Mannering.

He waited.

. . . . .

Lorna hadn't noticed the taxi which followed her, hadn't noticed Wainwright, she was preoccupied only with the girl at her side. It was nerve-racking simply having her there, sitting so still, staring ahead with those lovely eyes. She could understand why John had been put off his stroke; why Sylvester had been so troubled. The worst thing was that she couldn't see any way of helping.

She left the car outside the house, one of a small terrace of three-storey houses which had been badly damaged by bombing; only half of the terrace remained. The Mannerings were in the middle of these. Lorna glanced up at the window, noticed nothing unusual, and led the way into the house. Wainwright's taxi passed the end of the street. The girl just followed obediently; too docile by far. Lorna put a hand on her arm; the girl didn't resist. They went up, the girl moving so smoothly and gracefully. They reached the top landing, and Lorna took out her key, then rang the bell to let Ethel know she was coming in.

She opened the door, and led the girl inside.

Ethel didn't come hurrying from the kitchen. No one but these two women moved.

"We'll go to my bedroom," Lorna said, "I think you'll be better resting."

That didn't convey anything to Miranda.

Lorna led the way, and they went into the bedroom, which overlooked narrow back gardens, the backs of houses, and, if one looked right, the Embankment and the rippling Thames. Chelsea was quiet. The evening air was very warm, and Lorna went across and opened a window wide. She was puzzled because she couldn't hear Ethel.

She pointed to the bed.

Miranda Smith shook her head, and went to a chair; she couldn't have made it clearer that she did not want to lie down. Lorna looked into the girl's face and said with very careful enunciation:

"Wait—here. I—will—soon—be—back."

The girl looked blank.

Lorna pointed to the door, then went to it. As she reached the hall, a man appeared from the study, carrying a gun.

. . . . .

The man's face was hidden by a scarf, which covered his nose, mouth, and chin. Only his eyes showed, small, glinting. He had come so suddenly that he brought terror with the speed of lightning. Lorna's heart jumped wildly; then she screamed: "Miranda!"

She hadn't a chance to move before the man thrust the gun at her breast. Above her own fear there was a realisation touched with horror.

Miranda could not hear that cry of warning.

5

FENN

Chief Inspector Fenn put down the receiver at last, moved round his desk, and offered his hand. He had an unusually broad hand with a quick, powerful grip.

"Sorry to keep you so long, Mr. Mannering, but you know how it is." His dark eyes held a suggestion of a twinkle. "Sorry Bill Bristow's not here—and I expect you are, too."

Mannering found it easy to grin.

"All I need is help, from Bill or from the up-and-coming stars doesn't much matter."

Fenn chuckled. Mannering thought, "We'll get along." He had a feeling that Fenn thought much the same thing, too.

"Don't say you're changing roles," Fenn said, "usually you hand help out, don't ask for it."

"Someone's been misleading you! Seriously——" Mannering leaned back in his chair, Fenn sat on the corner of his desk, swinging one long leg. "I've an odd story and a missing man." He spent five minutes on the story and didn't think that he'd missed out many pertinent points. With some men, he would have doubted whether all the points had been taken in; it didn't occur to him to doubt Fenn's quick grasp.

". . . I know what you and the Press will say," Mannering finished, "the old man wished the girl and the nest-egg on to me, leaving me holding the baby. All right, I was fooled. But——"

"A man would have to trust you a long way before he'd leave a fortune in your lap," Fenn said dryly. "You had plenty or reason to believe that he was coming back."

"Thanks."

"Delighted! I'll see if anything's known about this chap,"

Fenn said. He leaned forward for the telephone. Everything he did was smooth and leisurely; he had an air of confidence and competence. "Hallo, give me Grimble—Hallo, Grimble? Anything odd turned up today? . . . H'm, no, that wouldn't be it. I'm interested in an old man, very ugly, hunched back, almost a dwarf. . . . Just check, will you?" He put the receiver down and said to Mannering, "And the only clue is that he asked the taxi-driver to take him to the Bank."

"Yes."

"We can pick up that cab, anyhow," said Fenn.

He pressed a bell. He wasn't going to let any grass grow under his feet, yet didn't give an impression of haste.

The door opened on a tap, and a large and comfortable-looking man came in, a Sergeant Day.

"Oh, sergeant, you know Mr. Mannering, don't you? . . . A black taxi, fairly modern, picked up a passenger in Hart Row this afternoon, at about half-past two, and was asked to take him to the Bank of England. The passenger was old, very ugly, almost a dwarf. Check on the cabbies, will you, and step on it."

"Right, sir."

"Thanks."

The door closed on Day.

"Good of you to get moving so quickly," said Mannering.

"Wouldn't expect you to come here with a fairy story," said Fenn, "and the quicker we move now, the better later on. Where's the girl now?"

"At my flat."

"With your wife?"

"Oh, yes."

"Not worried?"

Mannering said, "I sent one of my assistants after them."

He didn't go on. He hadn't said much about being worried, but he had drawn a picture of the girl's fear; and Fenn had picked that up quickly. If the girl who could not talk were so frightened, it might be because she was fearful of an attack; and if she were with Mannering's wife, then both of them might be in danger. That was good reasoning.

"Tried sign language?" asked Fenn. "I can lend you a chap who knows the deaf-and-dumb alphabet backwards."

"She doesn't seem to know it. We've tried everything. She doesn't seem to understand the simplest phrases, even when written down for her."

"Hmm," grunted Fenn.

"Psychiatrist's job, but Richardson will know."

"Yes. I don't know how long it will be before we've some news," Fenn added. "I'll be in the office for a couple of hours yet. Shall I ring you at Chelsea?"

"I'll be grateful. And will you———?"

"Put a couple of men in Hart Row? Yes!"

The telephone bell cut across Fenn's words and Mannering's grin. Mannering was feeling more at ease than he had for some time. Fenn had that kind of effect.

Mannering stood up.

"Oh, yes," said Fenn. "He's here." He held the telephone out. "It's your man Sylvester."

"Thanks," said Mannering.

He put the receiver to his ear, and waited, nameless fears crowding back. That was the strangest and the worst part of this; the way fears built up out of nothing. It was because of the girl, of course, and that infectious fear which was so deep in her that it soon caught others.

"Hallo, Sylvester."

"Hallo, sir," said Sylvester, primly. "The insurance assessor has been, and says that provided proper precautions are taken he will be quite happy to leave the—ah—nest-egg in our strong-room. He would like the police to watch, in view of the obvious possibility of trouble."

"That's been arranged."

"Then I don't think there's anything else to worry about, sir. Unless you——"

"What made you call me here?" interrupted Mannering.

"There wasn't any reply from your flat," Sylvester told him.

Mannering didn't respond to that at once; didn't move. He saw Fenn get up, as if the Yard man were affected by the sudden change in his visitor's manner. Fenn moved round, so as to see Mannering better in the light from the window.

"Are you there, sir?" Sylvester sounded alarmed.

"Yes," said Mannering, very softly. "How often did you ring the flat?"

"Three times, sir, the last just before I called Scotland Yard."

"Has Wainwright telephoned a message?"

"No, sir. Surely——" Sylvester caught his breath.

"You forget it," Mannering said. "Go home. Good-bye." He put down the receiver, and found himself looking into Fenn's eyes. A moment of silence seemed to last for an age, before he said, "The maid was at the flat. My wife and Miranda Smith should have been there half an hour ago or more. I don't like it."

"Got your car here?" Fenn asked.

"No."

"I'll send you round in a Squad car," said Fenn, "and have a patrol car alerted." His finger was stabbing the bell-push. "Unless you'd rather go by taxi and have a Squad car and a patrol standing by, one at each end of the street, say."

A bleak smile tightened Mannering's lips.

"You're good, and very good," he said. "Thanks. Yes. I'll keep the Squad car in sight until I get to Green Street." He was already moving towards the door. "It may be a false alarm, but I don't understand it."

"Take it easy," Fenn urged.

. . . .

Mannering's heart was pounding.

He paid the taxi off at the end of Green Street, nodded to the driver of a Squad car to whom he had spoken at Scotland Yard, then turned into the street. This was fairly wide, and most of the tall, narrow houses on both sides had been bomb-damaged. At the far end, which ran into the Embankment, there was a large, empty site. A policeman stood near the end house, and Mannering knew that a patrol car was round the corner, probably parked on the empty site; the men would be ready at any alarm.

Mannering reached his house.

The front door was open. Would Lorna leave it like that? She might, if she were preoccupied, and a new tenant of the ground-floor flat had an absent mind and a scoffing attitude towards all who locked their doors. "I've never locked my front door, and I've never had anything stolen." Mannering thought of her fleetingly as he went up the stairs. He walked quickly, making no attempt to hide himself. He knew that the stairs might be watched, a stealthy approach would give its own warning.

He reached his landing.

The door was closed; the fanlight over it was open a few inches. That was unusual. He thought that he heard a movement on the other side of the fanlight. He hesitated, then took his keys out of his pocket. He began to whistle. He could hear no sound now—but that was normal enough, the only thing that worried him was the sound he'd heard. Then he saw a shadow thrown towards him—the kind of shadow there would be if someone were standing on a chair to look into the landing and on to the staircase.

Mannering put his key in the lock, and turned it, taking his time. His heart pounded more violently as he pushed the door back. He looked along the wall, where an assailant would be likely to lurk, but no one was there. A man might be behind the door; if he flung the door back, it would probably catch the man out. He didn't. He went forward, leaving the door ajar, his manner as natural and casual as he could make it.

"Hallo, darling!" he called.

There was no answer.

He still felt very close to panic.

Lorna would have come straight here; Mannering was convinced beyond all doubt now that she had run into serious trouble. He looked about the square hall, trying to appear natural. The kitchen door and the bedroom door were ajar, the others were closed.

"Lorna!" he called more sharply.

There was no answer; no sound; no movement.

"Where the blazes has she gone?" he said, *sotto voce,* and went straight for the bedroom door. He looked right and left, but still saw no one, no lurking figure, no shadow. It was possible that a man had been waiting here, attacked Ethel, attacked Lorna, attacked Miranda Smith.

He thrust the bedroom door wider.

Lorna lay on the bed, trussed hand and foot and gagged; but conscious. Her eyes seemed to glare. He took a long stride forward, warning himself that whoever had done this might still be here, lying in wait.

Then he saw Miranda, trussed like Lorna, sitting on a chair.

Mannering caught his breath.

Suddenly he heard a movement at the door. Lorna's eyes told him that she was trying to flash a message; she could not guess that he had deliberately walked into this trap. He pretended not to hear the sound or to notice Lorna's signal; it wasn't until the man spoke that he spun round.

"Don't move." The voice was muffled, unhurried.

"What——" began Mannering, and was round in a flash.

A man, wearing a brown-linen scarf to hide most of his face, covered him with an automatic pistol held in a small, pale hand, which was quite steady. A peaked cloth cap was pulled low over his eyes, it was impossible even to guess what his face was like.

"Don't move," he repeated more sharply.

Mannering stood very still, then began to raise his hands.

The Squad-car sergeant would be coming up the stairs by now, but he would take his time. Lorna wasn't badly hurt, the girl's eyes were open, Mannering could concentrate on trying to find out what it was all about.

He knew something else.

The automatic pistol pointed steadily at his stomach. He could just see the glitter of the man's eyes. He had a feeling that it wouldn't take this man long to shoot; and he could empty the gun into him, Mannering, before the police could open the door.

The man said, "I want those eggs, Mannering, and I want them quick." He thrust the gun forward. "Where are they? Don't stall, talk."

6

SHARP SHOOTING

LORNA could not move. The dumb girl could only stare at the two men, with fear mirrored in her eyes. The man, shorter than Mannering by half a head, stood two yards away with the gun thrust forward and his muffled voice carrying its own message; he spoke with the voice of desperation.

Mannering moistened his lips.

"What—what good are you going——?"

"I said don't stall. I mean business. I don't care who gets

hurt. I want old Smith's nest-egg, and I'm going to get it. Make up your mind whether I'm going to get it without a lot of trouble, or whether I have to shoot you up first, take your keys, and go and break into Quinns. *I* don't care."

There was a sneer in the voice; there was also that edge of desperation. The man couldn't stop his hand from trembling a little, and that was ominous in itself.

Mannering said, "How do you know I've got it?"

He saw the trigger finger move, and stood motionless. Behind the man, he saw Lorna flinch; the terror in her eyes was as great as the girl's. The shot snapped out, just a loud crack. The bullet went a yard wide and smacked into the wall.

"Talk, Mannering, or next time I'll put it in your guts."

He was still trying to quieten his own nerves. Mannering saw that, and made a swift decision.

"Get to hell out of here!" he roared. "What makes you think I'm scared by a little runt like you?"

He didn't move.

He was telling the Squad man not to move yet, either.

Lorna was writhing on the bed, her eyes pleading, he could read the message: 'Don't do it,' she begged, 'don't make him angry, he'll shoot you next time.' Mannering couldn't even try to reassure her.

The man with the gun said more tautly, "You keep quiet. Where are those eggs? Don't—don't make any mistake. I mean business. Do you want to stay married, or would you rather be a widower? Because I can shoot your wife as easily as I can shoot you. Where's that gold?"

He was still two yards away.

His hand was still unsteady, and if his nerve broke he might do what he threatened.

There was a slight smell of cordite in the air; and behind Mannering powdery chippings from the wall dusted the fitted carpet.

"I mean business," the man repeated. "If you don't think I do——"

"All right," Mannering growled, "all right." He saw Lorna's body go limp with relief, but the man with the gun didn't relax, just kept his distance and kept Mannering covered. "It's all at Quinns."

"You're telling me! Strong-room?"

"Yes."

"Okay," said the man with the gun, "we're going to the shop. You're going to let us in, you're going to open the strong-room, and you're going to help me get away with the eggs. Understand that, and don't make any mistake. If you try any tricks, I'll shoot you. And I'll tell you something else that won't make you jump for joy."

Mannering said thinly, "Listen, my wife——"

"Never mind your wife and never mind Miranda Smith. I was going to tell you something. I'm on the wanted list, for murder. If the police catch up with me, I'll be strung up. You know the old saying—might as well be hanged for a sheep as a lamb. See what I'm driving at?"

The muffled voice made the words, the implied threat, and the menace sound very great. And the man had beaten his attack of nerves.

Mannering said, "No, I——"

"Well, sharpen your wits." That was a sneer. "Someone told me you were good. I'm beginning to doubt it. I'll tell you what I'm driving at. I can't be any worse off, even if I kill you. And I'll shoot to kill if you don't do exactly what I tell you."

Mannering shifted his position.

"I—I'll take you to Quinns."

"Just to make you want to do the job properly, get this into your head. If I have to shoot you, I'll come back here and finish the job. I've a pal outside, and this is how it will work. You'll go downstairs just in front of me, and I'll have the gun in my pocket. You do just what I tell you until my pal shows up. Clear?"

Mannering muttered, "All right."

It wasn't as good as it had been, by a long way. The man's finger was loose on the trigger, his words betrayed his edginess. It wouldn't take much to make him shoot. Mannering was being forced out of the flat, but the Yard men outside wouldn't dare to let this crook get away with it. Probably be allowed to start going down the stairs.

His gun would be close to Mannering's back all the time.

Mannering felt the sickness of fear.

"What's the matter, tired?" the man sneered.

Mannering turned slowly round. He looked at Lorna, tried to convince her that he wasn't worried, actually fluttered an eyelid in a wink. She wouldn't take any notice, she would guess how he really felt. But she didn't know about those waiting police.

Mannering crossed the hall. There was no sound outside, except from a long way off: the wail of a car's horn. The man with the gun was a yard behind him. A back-heel, a sudden lunge to one side, might see him through; but the risk was too great.

He opened the door wider.

"Listen," he said, "keep that gun out of my ribs." At least the Squad men would know what was happening.

"Just keep moving," the man ordered.

Mannering opened the door wide. He stepped into the hall, without glancing right or left. He didn't see the Squad man, but caught sight of something disappearing down the second flight of stairs. The gunman came behind him, still a yard away. He slammed the door.

Lorna was back there, with her fears and her awful helplessness.

Mannering started down the stairs.

"Don't make any mistake," the gunman said, "and re-

SHARP SHOOTING 49

member I can only be strung up once." He gave a little, muffled laugh, then jabbed Mannering in the back. The jab hurt. "Faster."

"You can't get away with——" began Mannering.

"You try and stop me!"

Mannering went on. He didn't see anyone on the next landing, on the stairs, anywhere. The Squad men must be lying in wait; but where? They knew the risk, obviously they were trying to minimise it. But the gun was very close, and pulling the trigger would be almost a reflex action.

Mannering felt cold sweat on his forehead. His nerves were steady enough, but he was icy cold. He reached the landing, one above the empty hall. The street door was ajar. He passed the front door of the flat beneath his; it was closed. He went past and reached the head of the next flight of steps.

"Stop there," the man ordered.

Mannering stopped.

He looked round, heart still thumping.

The man in the mask was looking at the closed door of the flat. He backed towards it. That flat was the most likely place for the police to be hiding; perhaps he had heard a sound or noticed a movement. Although he moved towards the door, he kept Mannering covered. The only place for Mannering to run was up or down the stairs, either way he would be a clear target. If he had to take his life in his hands, he could wait for it.

The stranger pressed against the door. It didn't move. He seemed satisfied, drew nearer Mannering, and ordered:

"Get moving."

Mannering went down the stairs one at a time, slowly and deliberately. It was tense enough for him; what was it for the man with the gun? He could hear soft, sibilant breathing, as if the man were frightened of making any sound. They neared the next landing—the hall. Here there were two locked doors. The man seemed to hesitate, as if he were going through the same precautions again. Instead, he growled:

"Hurry!"

Mannering stretched out a hand to open the front door wider. He heard nothing, until the man behind him gasped. He spun round. The man was staggering, his gun waving. He squeezed the trigger, a bullet spat out and smashed into the floor. He pirouetted round, the gun dropped, and he fell against the wall and then slithered down.

Chief Inspector Fenn in person came rushing down the stairs. A round glass ball, a paper-weight, rolled to the side of the hall, and lay still.

"Only thing I could do was to throw that at him," Fenn said, "I was afraid he'd shoot you in the back. Feeling all right?"

"Just—mildly terrified," Mannering confessed.

Fenn wiped his forehead and his neck, and loosened his collar.

"If this is the kind of job you get yourself mixed up in, I can understand why Bristow used to tremble at the sound of your name! Sure you're——?"

"I'm fine," said Mannering; and then moved.

He saw other men coming down the stairs, knew that more were hurrying from the street. One was actually on his knees beside the prisoner, taking off the scarf. People from the other flats were coming out, nervously. Mannering waited for nothing, but raced up the stairs, pushed past two Yard men, and flung himself at his own door. He remembered that the fanlight was open, and shouted:

"It's all over, darling, all over! He's caught, I'm fine, fine! It's all over."

He put the key in the lock and thrust the door open.

Then he remembered Ethel.

He hadn't seen the maid, and she might not be alive. He went swiftly to the kitchen, calling to Lorna, flung the door back, and saw Ethel sitting in an upright chair, trussed like the other two, and with her eyes wide open. All of them were safe, all could be free in a few minutes.

He waved weakly to Ethel, said, "Won't be two jiffs," and went swiftly to see Lorna. At the bedroom doorway he staggered; that was reaction from fierce nervous tension.

"Easy there." Fenn was coming in briskly.

"I'm all right," Mannering said, and straightened up with an effort. "Er—come in and meet my wife." He gulped, went forward, saw Lorna lying there helplessly, imagined again the fear which must have tormented her.

Then he turned towards the corner.

Miranda sat, eyes wide open, staring at the window, victim of dreadful fears. And to add a touch of horror was a fact which Mannering had only just noticed. Lorna was gagged. Ethel was gagged. But the man had not troubled to gag Miranda.

. . . . .

Not far away, in the garden of an empty house, the police found Wainwright, with a lump on the back of his head and bloodshot eyes, but not badly hurt.

All he remembered, he said, was walking past Mannering's house, after paying off his cab; and being hit on the back of the head as he passed the corner by the empty site.

. . . . .

"What *had* we better do with her?" Lorna asked, helplessly.

Mannering said, "She probably needs hospital treatment or a nursing home, or——"

"That might scare her even more," reasoned Fenn. He was proving very human as well as capable. "Why not let her stay here for a day or two? I'll make sure that your flat's watched back and front. You say you'll ask Richardson to come, and he's as good as any for a start. Let her stay for the night, anyhow."

Mannering looked at Lorna.

"Up to you," he said.

"I think it would be better to have her here," Lorna agreed.

She spoke slowly, and her lips were red and puffy where the gag had been. When she walked it was awkwardly, because the circulation hadn't come back to her legs properly. But she was in much better shape than Ethel, who was on a couch, lying down, shivering violently and very close to tears.

Miranda, freed now, had walked slowly and with difficulty, just staring about her with her secret fears.

Fenn had brought a sergeant who flicked his fingers at her in the deaf-and-dumb alphabet, but she hadn't responded. He hadn't done more, wouldn't until a doctor saw her.

"I'm very grateful, Mrs. Mannering," Fenn said. "I must get back to the Yard. The prisoner will be there by now, and there might be news of Smith. You say you hadn't seen him before, Mannering?"

Mannering recalled the face of the man whose mask had been stripped off; a thin face with deep-set eyes and a broad nose; the face of an ugly man whom he hadn't seen before.

"No."

"Care to come with me, and see if we can't find out more about him? You'll spare him, Mrs. Mannering, won't you?" Fenn was almost too amiable; was this an iron hand in a kid glove?

Lorna looked searchingly at the Yard man, then gave a quick smile. Fenn didn't know it, but that smile was a rare one; and it meant that she accepted him. And his own smile was disarming, he had a natural, likable manner.

"Not for too long," Lorna said, "I need a lot of consolation."

"We won't be long," Fenn assured her. "I think——"

He stopped abruptly, for a man outside raised his voice,

in exasperation if not in anger. There was a little scuffle in the hall, and then a young man came striding in, a stranger to the Mannerings, and apparently a stranger to the police.

He said, "Which of you is Mr. John Mannering?"

"I am," Mannering began. "What——?"

"Do you know where Miranda is?" the young man demanded roughly; and it was obvious to all who watched that he was restraining himself with a great effort, that he was almost quivering with anxiety.

And rage?

7

WILLIAM BRASH

THE young man was wholesome-looking, probably in the middle-twenties, nice-featured in a homely way, dressed in a Harris-tweed jacket and flannel trousers, with bright-brown shoes. Having made sure who Mannering was, he ignored Fenn and a police-sergeant; he wasn't far from glaring.

Mannering didn't answer.

The young man took a step forward, and demanded, "Do you know where she is?"

"If I do," said Mannering, mildly, "can you give me one good reason why I should tell you?"

That put a spark to the fire, as was meant. The caller's eyes flashed furiously, his hands clenched, his cheeks turned bright red.

"I mean to know where she is, understand? Come on, tell me, or——"

Then he made his great mistake; he shot out a hand and gripped Mannering's forearm. He was two inches shorter than Mannering, but broader across the shoulders, and he looked powerful and fit. None of that availed him. Mannering twisted his own forearm, gripped the young man's, twisted again and pushed—and the visitor went staggering back, out of the doorway and towards the head of the stairs. He couldn't stop himself, and the sergeant grabbed him.

Rescued from a headlong flight down the stairs, the newcomer looked both badly shaken and bewildered. His face was now a bright red, the red that a coy young maiden might turn if she were deeply embarrassed, but the rage had died from his bright-blue eyes; bewilderment replaced it. He rubbed his right wrist, as if wondering if it had really happened, or whether this were part of a dream.

Mannering beamed at him.

"Good evening," he said. "Can I help you?"

Fenn made a smothered noise behind his hand; the sergeant, who knew Mannering far better than did Fenn, hid a grin. The young man noticed neither of these things, just looked uncertainly at Mannering. He moistened his lips. His colour began to recede; even when the flush had gone, he had a fair, pink-cheeked face.

"Because I will gladly help," went on Mannering, "if I can. You were inquiring about——" He paused, invitingly.

The young man gulped.

"Miranda. Miranda—Smith. Is she—is she here?"

"May I know who wants to know?" asked Mannering, with the most genial of smiles.

"Er——" began the young man, and then seemed to shake his head. "Er—my name is Brash. William Brash. Er—Bill Brash," he added emphatically, as if that would convey a great deal. "I—er—I'm a friend of Miranda Smith. It's very important that I should know where she is."

"Why?" Mannering's voice was honey-sweet.

"Well——"

"Supposing you come in," said Mannering, "and tell us all about it there."

He stood aside. The young man who called himself Bill Brash followed, and Fenn brought up the rear. The sergeant looked regretful because the show was over too quickly.

Mannering closed the hall door and led the way to his study. Bill Brash was still bewildered and a little out of his depth, but Fenn seemed fascinated. A different Mannering had come upon the scene, a man in a guise he had heard about but hadn't seen before. He could imagine any man who crossed Mannering being scared of him. He could begin to understand the reputation which he had built up, even at Scotland Yard; and the awe in which some policemen seemed to stand of him.

Yet Mannering looked the same——

The change was in his smile, just a quirk of his well-shaped lips; in a kind of courtliness; the lift of his head; a manner that was almost impudent—a step farther, and it would have become arrogance. He not only looked different and spoke in a softer yet clear-cut voice, but he also moved differently. He was on the attack. It wasn't a very strong attack, and the opposition wasn't likely to be powerful, but that was the big difference; he had taken the initiative completely. Fenn felt oddly sorry for Bill Brash.

The study was a small room with one large window overlooking distant houses, the Embankment, and the Thames; a familiar scene and welcome on that warm evening. The furniture was obviously antique; Fenn recognised two William and Mary slung leather chairs and a carved-oak settle which must be at least four hundred years old. Yet it didn't strike one as being old-fashioned. It had an atmosphere which was peculiarly its own; and Fenn, his mind very alert, decided that it suited Mannering.

"Sit down, Mr. Brash," invited Mannering, and pulled up a chair. "And you, Mr. Fenn." Not Chief Inspector. "I don't see why we shouldn't have a drink. Whisky? Gin? Sherry——?"

"Er—no, thanks," said Brash, blankly.

"Lemonade?"

With the nuance in a word Mannering could drip sarcasm.

"Well, yes, please," said Bill Brash.

Mannering was startled, and Fenn gulped. There was a short pause. Mannering, knowing full well that Fenn was summing him up and not missing a trick, began to wonder what Bill Brash was really up to. Was he deeper than he seemed?

"And you?" Mannering asked Fenn, gravely.

"Whisky-and-soda, if I may."

"Gladly," said Mannering, and poured out. He had a whisky-and-soda himself. "Mr. Brash," he said, as he thrust the lemonade into the young man's hand, "Miss Miranda Smith and Pendexter Smith were at my shop this afternoon, but——"

Brash flashed, "Isn't she here?"

"I want to know why you think she might be?"

"She went off with your wife," Brash declared. "I know, a girl at a shop opposite Quinns told me. I came here just as soon as I could, because I must see Miranda. Look, Mr. Mannering——" He got up and moved forward, his voice and his expression alike appealing. "*Is* she all right?"

"Yes," said Mannering.

Relief sprang into the young man's eyes. It was impossible to guess the real cause of it, but it affected him swiftly, almost physically. He backed to his chair, and dropped into it. Lemonade, still effervescing, spilled over the side of his glass, and he looked at it quickly but without real comprehension.

"Thank God for that," he breathed.

"What did you think might have happened to her?"

"Anything! She was with her Uncle, he's hardly responsible for his actions, you can never tell what he's going to do next. I'd heard him say he was going to see you, that's why I went to Quinns. Lucky thing that girl was at the shop across the road." Brash sipped his lemonade, then put it on a small table, next took out a silk handkerchief and dabbed his forehead and his neck. "Is he here, too?"

"No."

"May I see Miranda?"

He hadn't been told positively that Miranda was here. It was possible that he was trying a trick question, but he looked far too naïve for any such cunning; in fact, he looked almost too simple and straightforward to be true. But there seemed no point in further evasion; he was as likely to talk after seeing Miranda as he was now—more likely, perhaps.

"No," said Mannering. "Pendexter Smith went off on his own. Miranda's here, but not too well."

Brash flashed, "Why not? Is she hurt?"

"Why——?"

"For the love of Mike tell me the truth, don't stand there vaccillating!" roared Brash, and his face turned as red as a turkey cock. "Where is she?"

He jumped up and strode to the door, pulled it open, and rushed into the hall. Fenn, startled, was a yard behind Mannering as Mannering followed. Brash made for the kitchen door, not knowing what it was, thrust the door open and strode in.

Ethel, now sitting and fanning herself out of her fears, was by the window. Young Wainwright was standing near her, with a pewter tankard of beer in his right hand. Wainwright looked startled. It was an odd moment for Mannering to realise that he hadn't really seen Wainwright before, except as a mild-mannered, competent, and hard-working young man with a sound knowledge of antiques and *objets d'art*. He was learning fast about precious stones, too. Now, still in his black coat and striped grey trousers, he looked different;

the tankard caused that. It made him more human, less a stuffed dummy.

Brash swung round.

"Where is she? Come on, it's time——"

"You like trouble, don't you?" asked Mannering, very softly. "But I'll forgive you, this time. I'll find out if Miranda wants to see you. Chief Inspector——"

"I'll stay here," offered Fenn.

"You're very good."

"Of course she'll want to see me," Brash cried. "There isn't any need——"

Mannering looked at him from narrowed eyes. He stopped. It was another example of the way Mannering could change. Fenn could even understand what had made Brash break off and gulp.

Wainwright came from the kitchen.

Mannering went into the bedroom. Lorna was at the dressing-table, doing nothing except looking at the girl. Miranda was sitting in exactly the same position, hands in lap, blue eyes wide open, seeing things which weren't there, because nothing in sight need frighten her. The impression of fresh, lovely youth was very strong—and when he contrasted that with her affliction, Mannering felt a sharp twinge of almost physical pain.

All he wanted to do was see them both when Brash came in. He didn't say a word to Miranda, but crossed her line of vision, and so made her look up. He smiled, and pointed to the door, then called:

"All right."

Did she know what he meant?

Fenn came in first, obviously intent on seeing what happened when these two met. Mannering had the best position, standing by Lorna's side, hand on her shoulder, able to see first Miranda and then the youth.

Bill Brash stopped short; he looked as if he hadn't really

believed that he would see Miranda. He was overjoyed. His lips parted, he held his breath. Gradually, the delight spread from his eyes over his face, he went forward again swiftly, and dropped to his knees in front of her.

It was oddly touching. The days of ardent, kneeling swains had gone, yet Brash knelt before this girl swiftly, unthinkingly, naturally. He took her hands and looked up into her eyes; and he gave Mannering the impression of pleading with her.

The gleam of recognition in her eyes was unmistakable. She wasn't as glad to see him as he was to see her, but she showed no signs of dismay or dislike. She looked at him, making no attempt to free her hands from his clasp.

"Are you—all right?" Brash asked.

The words hardly carried to Mannering and Fenn; and that didn't matter. He formed them carefully, so that the girl could lip-read. And she did, for she nodded. Brash stayed where he was, as if he could hardly believe that she was not hurt, could still hardly convince himself that she was really there.

Wainwright appeared in the doorway.

He had left the tankard behind, but brought his new manner with him; a confidence, perhaps a kind of selfassertiveness, which he never revealed at Quinns. He watched Bill Brash steadily, then looked at the girl. It was evident that he liked looking at her; and that was hardly surprising, for she was really something to see.

"Excuse me, sir," Wainwright said to Mannering, "is there anything more you want me for tonight?"

Mannering answered promptly, "No, you carry on. Head not too bad?"

"I hardly notice it now," said Wainwright, but that could hardly be true. He was more like the youthful, eager assistant of the shop as he bowed to Lorna. "Good night, Mrs. Mannering. Good night, sir."

He inclined his head to Chief Inspector Fenn, and shot a last, lingering glance at Miranda. Then he went out.

Brash gave no sign that he had known anyone else was in the room.

"Now, Mr. Brash," said Mannering, quietly, "I think you owe us a little more explanation."

Brash didn't turn away from Miranda.

"Eh? Oh. What about?"

"Your visit here. Miss Smith and her affliction." That was the only word to use. It could have no effect on her, as she couldn't hear and could only lip-read if he spoke carefully while looking straight at her. "And if it comes to that——"

Brash stood up, slowly, his manner oddly deliberate. He turned round. In his pink, rosy-skinned way, he was quite nice-looking. Now that his eyes were calmer, his whole body relaxed; as if he had drawn some kind of assurance from Miranda Smith.

"I came to make sure she was all right. I don't trust Pendexter Smith, and he has no right to sell anything of hers. I understood he was going to offer some of her jewels for sale. That is why he came to you, isn't it? He won't defraud her while I'm alive to stop him. If there's any more trouble I shall complain to the police."

8

POLICE WORK

This was Fenn's cue to introduce himself, but he decided not to take it. His ability to fade into the background and become part of the furniture, as it were, was not the least of his craft. Bill Brash hardly knew that he was there, and no one took any notice of him.

And his silence was tantamount to a request : for Mannering to handle this.

"Do you know where I'm likely to find him?" Mannering asked Brash.

"Pendexter? At his hotel, I suppose. He always stays at The Glenn Hotel, Cromwell Road, when he's in London. Look here, why did you bring Miranda here?"

"Pendexter Smith went off and didn't come back."

"Didn't come *back*?"

"That's what I said."

"What did he go away for?"

"To get proof that Miss Miranda was the legal owner of the nest-egg he wanted me to buy."

"So that was his game," growled Brash. "I'd like to know what the old devil's up to. He's got Miranda where he wants her. She's absolutely dependent on him. Whatever he says, she does. But it's criminal!" He spat that word out. "She doesn't know what he's doing half the time, she trusts him completely. And——"

"You wouldn't?"

"Trust Pendexter Smith? I'd rather go to bed with a cobra! But I don't get this at all. You mean he went off to get proof that she owned the things, and didn't come back."

"That's right."

"Where's the nest of eggs?" Brash's eyes blazed with alarm, his cheeks turned bright red again. "Did he take that with him? He might have been attacked, might have been——"

"It's in good keeping."

"Oh, is it?" said Brash, relaxing. "Well, that's something, anyhow. And he was trying to sell it to you. I don't want to poke my nose into other people's affairs, Mr. Mannering, but you be careful. He's no right to sell it, and I wouldn't trust him with the money he'll get for it. What's it worth?"

"Somewhere between ten and a hundred thousand pounds."

"Somewhere between——" Brash broke off, looking puzzled; then he gave a quick grin which made him look more human and attractive. "You're pretty cagey, aren't you? The only thing that worries me is to make sure Smith doesn't have the handling of the money. Is there a way of making sure?"

"I don't know," said Mannering, reasonably. "That's a matter for the legal experts. If Miranda were found to be of unsound mind, then——"

"Don't be a ruddy fool," growled Brash. "She's as sane as you or me."

He paused for a moment, looking at her with distress in his eyes.

"She—she hasn't always been like this. Something happened, and——"

"What happened?" Fenn asked, very quietly.

"I don't know exactly. It was in France, I think. A car accident. She—she's always like this, she's forgotten everything, can't talk or hear or read or write."

"When did this happen?"

"Two years ago. She went off for a holiday with her father, and she came back like this. He said it was a car accident. They crashed, and there was an explosion and a fire. She's seen psychiatrist after psychiatrist, here, on the Continent, and in America, but they haven't been able to do a thing. Shock, they say—a nervous affliction, paralysis of certain nerve centres. There's no way of telling whether she can ever be cured." He spoke as if he were reciting something which he had learned off by heart; and it was easy to believe that he had repeated the phrases to himself time and time again, in a despairing effort to find some chink in the armour of failure. "She's been wonderful, but—well, *look* at her."

Miranda was looking at Brash.

The worst of the fear had gone from her eyes; she was almost as calm as when she had come into the shop. But she looked lost—lost, lonely, and so very lovely. Nothing that Brash said conveyed anything to her. Obviously she wasn't deeply interested in him as a young man.

"How long have you known her?" Mannering asked, fighting against the spell she cast.

"Oh, years! We once lived in the same street." he brushed that aside. "Mr. Mannering, can she stay here until Pendexter turns up? She'll be happier with a woman about. As a matter of fact someone ought to break the hold which Pendexter has on her, she wants to mix more, try . . ."

His voice trailed off.

"Yes," said Mannering, very quietly, "Miranda can stay here until Pendexter Smith turns up. Have you any idea where he would go to get the legal proof he wanted?"

"Oh, Lord, yes," said Bill Brash. "His solicitors—hers, too. Wilberry, May and Wilberry, Leadenhall Street. That's almost certain. Too late to telephone them now, though, isn't it? I wonder if he's gone back to his hotel."

. . . . .

Fenn took over, smoothly. He telephoned the Glenn Hotel; Pendexter Smith hadn't returned. He telephoned Smith's Sussex home, which had the intriguing name of Dragon's End, spoke to a man who said that Smith might be away for several days. Then after a word outside with his sergeant, Fenn telephoned the Yard, and set a sergeant on the job of getting in touch with Smith's solicitors at once.

That done, he turned to Brash.

"Can you name any of the psychiatrists who have seen Miss Smith?"

"Name 'em? No, I—wait a minute, though, there's a chap with a name that rhymes with mine. Nash—that's it, Nash."

"Lancelot Nash," Fenn said. "That's fine. Thanks. Where do you live, Mr. Brash?"

Bill Brash had a small flat in Victoria. He said that he was a travelling salesman covering South London and part of the South of England for a firm of paper merchants. Fenn didn't ask any more questions, and soon afterwards Brash left, obviously not easy in his mind.

Miranda showed no particular sign of regret; in a way she seemed to take him for granted.

"Now I'm going to get really busy," Fenn said. He followed Mannering out of the room and into the drawing-room, which overlooked Green Street. He didn't ask questions, but went with Mannering to the window, talking all the time. "Grimble's downstairs, I told him to follow Brash. We'll get after those solicitors and find that cabbie—he may be waiting at the Yard by now. Then I'll see Nash. It's time I had a talk with the prisoner, too." He said all this calmly, while looking out.

Brash appeared, and walked across the road to a two-seater M.G. which looked as if it had had better days.

A Detective Officer from the Yard got into a small car farther along the street, and started after him.

A taxi moved in the wake of these two, towards the Embankment, and, craning his neck, Mannering could just see who was in the taxi.

Fenn grinned.

"Likely lad, young Wainwright," he said, "qualifying for a job with us, apparently!"

"Not if I can stop him," Mannering murmured.

Fenn laughed; he was in surprising good humour.

"He could do worse, he could stay with you! I seem to remember seeing him before."

"Ominous reflection from a copper," Mannering said. "You haven't seen him, you've seen his father, Sir Jeremiah Wainwright. He died two years ago, and——"

Fenn snapped his fingers.

"I remember! Quite a collector of precious stones in his way, wasn't he, with a magnificent collection of rubies. Didn't he go bankrupt?"

"He was robbed, and hadn't insured fully," Mannering said. "He committed suicide."

Fenn looked more sober.

"Yes, I recall it now. You helped to jail the thieves. Bad business. And you're taking a benevolent interest in his son. You're an odd chap, you know."

Mannering's smile flashed.

"More odd than you know! But this isn't pure benevolence. Young Wainwright knows a lot about jewellery, and he's showing a lot more gump than I expected," Mannering added. "I thought his one desire in life was to brood over antiques and jewels. That crack over the head must have started something."

Wainwright's taxi turned the corner and disappeared.

"Nice-looking lad," Fenn remarked. "Looks pretty fit, too. I hope he doesn't make the mistake his boss is so fond of making."

"I'll buy it," said Mannering.

"Trying to do the job that the police ought to do," Fenn said mildly. "Mannering the Lone Wolf might get away with murder, but anyone trying to emulate him will land himself in trouble."

Mannering just grinned.

"Do you know anything about the history of these eggs?" Fenn asked.

"Yes," Mannering said at once. "I remembered the story when I really thought about the eggs. They come from a remote part of Indonesia. The story goes that the King of a country now absorbed and almost forgotten married the loveliest woman of his kingdom, but she did not bear him a son; and without a son, the dynasty would perish. So each year, at the Feast of Fertility, the King offered a gift to the gods of fertility—of a jewelled egg, a gift as splendid and as symbolic as he could conceive. And the nest was their resting place."

Mannering stopped.

"Did he get his son?" asked Fenn.

"The dynasty's dead, and the legend doesn't say."

"Where did you learn about it?"

"I vaguely recalled there was a story about them when I first set eyes on them," said Mannering, "and I looked it up before I left Quinns."

"Have you heard of these since the dynasty died?"

"If you mean, do I know of any modern owner, no. I don't think they've ever passed through the hands of the trade before."

Fenn went out soon afterwards, purposeful, and in a hurry.

•   •   •   •   •

Chief Inspector Nicholas Fenn sat at his desk, taking telephone calls, studying reports, listening to men who were reporting in person. It was a never-ending stream. For an hour after he returned to the Yard, he hardly had time to breathe. Gradually, an incomplete picture formed itself in his mind; and he put the relevant on paper, to make sure that the picture didn't fade.

Pendexter Smith had not been to the solicitor's office. He had left his taxi at one end of Leadenhall Street, given the cabbie a sixpenny tip, and been forgotten. The driver did not even remember which way Smith had walked. It would be the next day before porters, commissionaires, and passers-by could be questioned, but a call for information about the man was sent round to all London Divisions.

It could have been wilful disappearance.

The Midham police had been helpful, too.

Pendexter Smith and Miranda, also named Smith and his

POLICE WORK

only brother's daughter, had lived in or near Midham for many years. Pendexter had been a wanderer in his youth, his brother, Mortimer, had married, made money with the Midas touch, mostly on the Stock Exchange, and bought a big old house on the outskirts of the town.

"Proper museum, that place is now," the Midham superintendent had told Fenn. "He collects everything from Chinese dragons to snuff-boxes. Mortimer began it, and Pendexter kept it going. Couple of freaks, of course, everyone down here knew them well. Then Mortimer popped off——"

"When?"

"Two years ago."

"Natural causes?"

"Motor accident."

"H'm," Fenn had said, and rubbed his nose on the shiny black of the telephone. "And Pendexter took over."

"Yes," said the Midham man. "Miranda, poor kid, inherited the fortune. She——"

"How much?"

"Eh? Oh, the fortune? Well, the estate was finally valued at two hundred thousand, but I don't think it was the lot. No one could be sure of the value of some of the stuff at Dragon's End."

"Was that always the name of the house?"

"No. Mortimer's name for it. What was I saying? Oh, yes, Miranda inherited, and Pendexter managed the estate for her. All open and above board, and she always liked her uncle. Beauty and the beast, new version. And since her accident, he's been her ears and her mouth. Tragic business." The Superintendent's voice echoed real distress. "But to go back to the beginning, I've heard nothing about Pendexter or Dragon's End lately. Everything's been going on as usual, as far as I can find out. Can't imagine why she was in such need of big money, I'd say that Miranda was one of the wealthiest young women I know. But I'll see what I can find out."

"I'll be glad if you will," Fenn had said and then added: "Ever heard of a man named Mannering—John Mannering, of Quinns?"

"Who hasn't?" asked the Midham man. "Big dealer, isn't he, always showing Bill Bristow how to do his job!"

"That's the chap. He'll probably be down to see you. He isn't anybody's fool," Fenn went on. "I should let him have plenty of rope, if I were you."

"What's his interest?"

Fenn said, "Partly business, partly sentiment, if I'm seeing straight. I can't see that this is much of a job for us yet. If Mannering likes to probe, it might save us the bother. Has Miranda any friends down there?"

"Not really friends," the Midham man said. "They've always been a bit aloof, and she hadn't been back from finishing school in France more than six months when she had the accident. She's only twenty-one, now. And Pendexter's a freak. Miranda's only friend, as such, is a young chap named Brash, Bill Brash. The forlorn and faithful lover kind."

"Ever get the idea that he might be after her money?"

The superintendent hesitated.

"No," he said, slowly, "I can't say I did. Still, you never know. I'll keep my eyes open, and let you know if anything else turns up. Sure Mannering will be down here?"

"Pretty sure," said Nicholas Fenn, confidently.

He rang off.

He sat back, lighting a cigarette, looking at a photograph of a cricket XI on the wall. Superintendent Bill Bristow was in it. Bristow was now enjoying himself in South Africa, and deserved a break. Before leaving, he had gone over a lot of ground with Fenn, and something had brought Mannering into the conversation.

"Between you and me," Bristow had said, "Mannering's a lot better than most of us think he is. He just won't give up once he's started. He doesn't do much these days, often has to be persuaded to start looking round, but once he starts, that's it. He's an amazing chap. Can pick a lock with any cracksman we've ever put inside, and keeps up-to-date with safe and strong-room locks and mechanism. There isn't much he doesn't know about burglar-alarm systems, electric rays, and all the rest. Between you and me," Bristow had repeated in a sudden burst of confidence, "he was once a menace. A woman played fast and loose with him, and something snapped. Heard of the Baron?"

Fenn, thinking fast, could remember the shock which the name had given him; could remember, ten years or so ago, when he had been on the beat, hating the sound of the name Baron, dreaming a dream of catching the thief red-handed, yet forced into reluctant admiration for a thief whose exploits had set London by the ears, and given the police in Paris and Rome, Berlin and Budapest, too much to think about. The Baron had previously won a place in the heart of most people, for those he robbed had been not only wealthy but also of ill-repute; and the desperately poor had received great gifts from the man who was known as the Baron.

It was many years since he had worked as the Baron, and he had never been caught. As far as Fenn had then known, no one ever knew who he was. He had vanished off the pages of the newspapers, and the police had lost a thorn in the flesh.

"I've heard of the Baron all right," Fenn had said softly.

"Take it from me," Bristow had told him, "Mannering was the Baron. The Man in the Blue Mask, as we called him sometimes. He had the courage of the Devil, was as slippery as an eel, and—oh, but you know. Then he settled down, after marrying Lord Fauntley's daughter. But if you study the records, you'll see that as the Baron faded out, so Mannering came in as a private eye. Natural development—he turned a new leaf, but crime and jewels held him like a magnet. I'd trust him anywhere and with anyone now, but —well, he was lucky he didn't go inside."

Fenn hadn't spoken.

"If you get anything that looks like a Mannering job, let him in," Bristow had advised. "Especially if it's a sticky one. He'll take chances and risk his neck doing things we can't. And once he gets moving—phew!"

Just for ten minutes, Fenn had seen Mannering moving. He wanted to see more.

* * * * *

Fenn went down to see the prisoner, who was scared but refused to talk. He had no papers on him, and wouldn't give his name and address. Fenn worked on him for twenty minutes, then left him to stew. Back in his office, Fenn telephoned Lancelot Nash, a psychiatrist well known in London and the provinces.

Nash didn't need reminding about Miranda Smith.

"As a case, a complete failure," he said. "There's nothing organically wrong, but her nerve-centres just don't work. She can't articulate or hear, at times I wonder if she's really half-witted. Electric-shock treatment has failed, everything's failed.

"Still trying?" Fenn asked.

"She's with a Swiss chap now," Nash said. "Or she was two months ago. Why—what's her trouble with you?"

"I want to find out if she's under undue influence."

Nash said, "You mean Pendexter Smith? She'd be in a mess without him; he's almost the only person who's able to establish communication with her. Afraid I can't help you there."

Fenn said, "Well, thanks for trying," and rang off.

A picture of Miranda Smith hovered in front of his mind's eye.

9

NEWS FROM WAINWRIGHT

MANNERING'S flat was quiet.

Miranda was in the small spare room, Lorna with her. Richardson, a psychiatrist and family friend, had spent an hour with the girl, said little, promised to see Nash and left —giving the Mannerings the impression that he wasn't very hopeful. Soon after he had gone, Fenn telephoned to tell Mannering what Nash had said about Miranda, to say that there was still no news of Pendexter Smith; or news of any kind.

Miranda had behaved quite naturally, showing a little distress at times. Mannering seemed to have the trick of making her understand a little, and she was quicker to grasp what he tried to tell her.

Lorna showed signs of the strain—and of sharp distress for the girl. In the bad moments her beauty and her freshness made the tragedy more appalling.

Richardson had left some veronal tablets, to make sure that Miranda slept that night.

It was nearly ten o'clock.

Mannering felt a strange tension; as if he were being held on a leash. The unheralded appearance of Pendexter Smith, the girl, the gold nest, and the jewelled eggs had been enough for one day. This disappearance of Smith bordered on the fantastic. The attack on Lorna and the girl was easier to understand; but would the prisoner talk? And if he did, would Fenn pass on what the man said?

In retrospect, Bill Brash's interruption had its comical side. But that had also ended in a burst of action, a puzzle swiftly posed, and then—*swish*, and the scene changed, something else distracted his attention.

The telephone bell rang.

Mannering jumped, nearly upset a big bowl-glass of brandy that was by his side, and snatched up the receiver. That was an indication of the tautness of his nerves.

"There's a call from Midham for you," the operator said. "Hold on, please."

Midham, Sussex, where the girl and Pendexter Smith lived. Mannering knew it wasn't Fenn, and wondered if it were Smith. He waited, impatiently.

"Hallo," another man said, "is that Mr. Mannering?"

It was Wainwright!

"Speaking, Ned," Mannering said. "What's taken you into the country?"

"Well, sir, I don't mind admitting I was pretty mad," Wainwright said, earnestly. "About that crack over the head, I mean. And—well, that girl did something to me. I felt that I had to try to help."

That was how Miranda affected everyone.

"So what?" asked Mannering.

"Well, I followed this chap, Brash," explained Wainwright. "I had a chat with a sergeant from the Yard, nice young chap"—he did not know how that naïve remark made Mannering grin—"who told me the man's name is Brash. He came straight down here."

"By road?" Mannering asked sharply.

"Yes."

"And you followed in a taxi?"

"I know it's a bit expensive," said Wainwright, defensively, "but I felt it was worth it, sir, and of course I shall pay my own expenses. I wouldn't dream——"

"If I were you I'd dream about that plenty," said Mannering, dryly. "What happened when he got there?"

"He's staying at a hotel in Midham. He hasn't been out, and I'm rather puzzled about it. I thought you ought to know, especially——" Wainwright broke off.

NEWS FROM WAINWRIGHT

"Yes?"

"I've heard of you in action a great deal, sir," said Wainwright with some diffidence, "and I know you wouldn't take anything for granted, you'd always want proof, but—I *think* it was Brash who clouted me. I can't be sure, but it wouldn't surprise me. I didn't tell the police, I hardly thought that was justified, as I couldn't swear to it. I hope I did right."

"Perfectly right," approved Mannering softly. "What makes you think it was Bill Brash?"

"I caught a kind of glimpse of him. It was after the blow, when I was falling down and twisting round. I hadn't quite blacked out. I saw a face, just a blur—it was all pink and rosy, if you know what I mean." Wainwright hurried on: "Then I had a look inside his car just now. The Yard man said he thinks I was clouted with a cosh. Well, Brash has one —shiny leather thing, filled with lead shot. It was under the front seat. I left it there, of course."

"Have you told the police about that?" Mannering asked.

"Well, no. Do you think I should?"

"I do not. Ned, listen to me. I'm coming down as soon as I can. If you have to leave, make sure I can pick up a message. Where are you speaking from?"

"A call-box just opposite the Horsebox—that's the name of the pub where I'm staying," Wainwright explained. "Brash is at the Swan, a much bigger hotel down the road. I'm not very used to this kind of thing, Mr. Mannering, but if I can make a suggestion———"

Mannering was grinning. "Go ahead."

"I've discovered that Pendexter Smith lives in a big house down here. I had a chat with the barmaid. I think I ought to have a look at the place," Wainwright went on earnestly. "It's got an odd name—Dragon's End." He paused. "I haven't my car down here, but I've managed to borrow a bicycle. I ought to go at once, and watch to see if Brash arrives. Don't you think so?"

"Ned," said Mannering warmly, "you're doing fine. How far is the house from the village?"

"Oh, you can't miss it. Straight through on the Horsham Road, then up the hill, then along the drive through the white gate-posts. That's the place, I had a look round on the bike just before dark. I can expect you then, Mr. Mannering?"

"I'll see you at Dragon's End, or else at the Horsebox," Mannering said. "Take it easy."

"You know, Mr. Mannering," said Wainwright almost wonderingly, "I wouldn't have thought I'd be interested in this end of the business, but that girl——" He broke off, then added hurriedly, "Is she all right?"

"Sleeping sweetly."

"Thank the Lord for that!" breathed Wainwright.

Mannering rang off, and was very thoughtful. Wainwright might be naïve and over-earnest, but he was on the spot, and he'd shown both guts and initiative. He mustn't be left to fend for himself.

The door opened, and Lorna came in. She was frowning, for a moment she looked almost sullen. But Mannering knew better. She came across to him. They didn't speak at first, and he was glad of the respite, to let what Wainwright had said settle in his mind.

"Who was that?" Lorna asked at last.

"Ned Wainwright, turned detective."

"He's a nice-looking lad, isn't he?" Lorna said, although obviously she wasn't thinking much about Wainwright.

"Is he?"

"Don't you ever notice anything?" Lorna relaxed, actually smiled. "You'd know if it were a nice-looking girl! He'll be really handsome when he's a bit older and more solid. Miranda's asleep."

Mannering said, almost awkwardly, "That's fine."

Lorna eyed him speculatively.

"John, do you know any more than you've told me?"

"Not a thing."

"Are you going to leave it to the police, or try to sort it out for yourself?"

"What would you like me to do?"

She sat down slowly on the arm of his chair and looked at him, with her head a little on one side. It was a moment of true intimacy. Mannering knew what was in her mind; she was pretty sure what was in his.

"For once, go to it yourself," she said quietly. "I'm scared, for that girl."

"I know what you mean," said Mannering. "I'm going to have a shot. I don't think Fenn will go to Dragon's End tonight, but he's probably told the local lads to be on the look out."

"And you're going there?"

"I'd like to find out why Brash has gone," said Mannering, and told her what Wainwright had reported.

· · · · ·

The journey to Midham was an hour and a half's run through the deserted country roads. Mannering stopped for nothing, slowing down only when he saw a sign-post reading: Midham. The only sign of life was a solitary policeman trying the handles of doors in the wide High Street. The signs outside two hotels were illuminated, and Mannering could see the painted sign hanging from the wall of another pub—the Horsebox. This was in darkness. He pulled into the car park at one side, and walked round the little pub, with its low, tiled roof and its white walls and dark oak beams. There was a slight smell of beer, but all the windows on the ground floor were closed, and the three doors were shut and locked.

If Wainwright had come back here from Dragon's End, he would have been waiting.

Mannering drove off. In his driving-mirror he saw the flash of the constable's torch.

He drove straight through the town, a huddle of houses with a square-towered church at one end. Soon the headlights swung up a steep hill. Half-way up, he saw the white posts of a drive.

He slowed down, and turned off the road on to a grass verge. He fitted some thin adhesive tape to his fingers, to prevent finger-prints, then switched off all the lights, got out, and walked up to the gates. The stars were out, but there was no moon and he could see very little.

He walked briskly up the gravel drive.

He expected to hear a call from Wainwright, but none came. There were the rustling sounds of the night, that was all. At last the curving drive straightened out and, a black mass at the end of the drive, he saw the house, blotting out the stars.

Manning drew nearer.

There were no lights at the window, nothing to suggest that Wainwright or anyone else was here. But Wainwright wouldn't let him down, he would have been waiting if he were able to wait.

He had been attacked once. One man had used a gun. There might be others, also armed. Wainwright might have walked into trouble. Mannering, hand in his pocket about a small automatic, kept to the side of the drive, making little sound, and drew nearer to Dragon's End.

Then he saw something move, and heard the scrape of footsteps on gravel. He stopped abruptly, and strained his eyes to see who it was.

A man.

The man was coming nearer, but unless he switched on his torch Mannering wouldn't be able to see who it was. He stood in the blackness of the side of the tree-lined drive, and the other drew nearer, walking stealthily, a dark shape against the light of the stars.

Then he stopped.

"Mr. Mannering," he whispered. "It's me, Wainwright. Are you there?" His voice sounded husky, as it would be if he was scared out of his wits.

"All right, Ned," Mannering called, and stepped out of the cover. "Take it easy. Who——?"

He heard the movement behind him as he spoke. His heart leapt wildly when he realised that he'd been watched, followed, fooled. He spun round. He felt a heavy, glancing blow on his shoulder, then saw two men leap forward.

Wainwright threw himself bodily at one of them, while Mannering fought to keep his balance.

10

DRAGON'S END

WAINWRIGHT collided with the man he'd rushed at. The man who had attacked Mannering struck again, his weapon whistling through the air. Mannering swayed to one side, took out his gun, was half-prepared for shooting. None came. He heard the gasping and grunting from Wainwright and the other man, and saw his own assailant raise the weapon. He thrust out his foot. The man tripped over it and dropped the weapon, which clanged on the ground. Mannering went for him, but the man turned and fled. He didn't cry out, didn't wait to see what had happened to his accomplice, just fled down the drive.

The other two were still battling it out.

They parted, and Wainwright's face became visible. The other man turned and started to run, but almost fell into Mannering's arms. Mannering jabbed him beneath the chin.

"Catch, Ned," Mannering called mildly.

Wainwright grabbed the falling man.

Mannering chuckled, partly in relief. "We'll get along!

No need to be too gentle with him. Did you know they were about?"

"No, I——" Wainwright was gasping for breath. "No, I thought I saw a car's headlights, just now, and thought—thought it might be you. You all—right?"

"Fine."

"Brash——" began Wainwright, and then paused for breath again. "Brash is in—the house."

"Sure?" Mannering asked sharply.

"Yes, he—he *broke* in. Climbed through a window." Wainwright's voice was a hoarse, excited whisper. "It was only ten minutes ago. His car's on a cart-track near by. I couldn't make up my mind whether to follow or not, but decided I'd better not let myself get caught on enclosed premises. I thought if he stole anything we'd find it at his hotel."

"Or in his pockets," Mannering said softly. "Ten minutes ago?"

"Yes."

"Which window?"

"I'll show you," said Wainwright, "but——" He looked down at the man who was lying on the ground, a dark shape against the light gravel. "What about him? We can't let him get away, can we?"

"I'll break his neck if he does," Mannering said as if he meant it. "You didn't think to bring any cord with you, I suppose?"

He couldn't see Wainwright's face; but he could imagine what the youngster looked like, judging from the tone of his voice.

"Well, no, I didn't think——"

"You do his wrists," Mannering said, "I'll do his ankles." He took two small twists of cord from his pocket. "And we'll see if he's in a mood to talk."

He went down on one knee—and the prisoner darted up,

DRAGON'S END

struck at his face, tried to scramble to his feet. Mannering clipped him on the side of the jaw again, and he dropped back.

"Be careful, Mr. Mannering," Wainwright urged.

The prisoner exclaimed, "Mannering! It's not——" He broke off.

"Next time you try any tricks, you'll get hurt," Mannering said. "What were you after?"

"Listen, Mannering. If—if I squeal, will you let me go?"

"Squeal, and find out."

"To hell with that! Will you?"

Mannering hesitated. He didn't want a prisoner; taking the man to the police would mean admitting that he had come to Dragon's End, could lead to complications that certainly wouldn't help. Bill Brash was inside this house, and probably Bill Brash was much more significant than this prisoner.

He said, "I wouldn't be able to prove whether you told me the truth, would I?"

"Mr. Mannering, you can't——" began Wainwright, in what sounded like a shocked whisper.

"Give me a break," the prisoner whispered. "I've heard plenty about you, got a good name, you 'ave. Never thought I'd talk to Mr. *Mannering*. Listen, I'm working with Bill Brash, see. He's inside. Two of us were keeping cave. Thought—thought you were a copper."

It was very smooth. Too smooth?

"What does Brash want?" demanded Mannering.

"He's after anything he can get. Knows Smith's away, it's a good chance, never be a better."

"Brash and who else?" demanded Mannering.

He dropped his right hand to the prisoner's wrist, and twisted. The prisoner screamed. His whole body seemed to writhe as he reared up from the ground.

"Don't, you'll break my arm! Don't——"

"Brash and who else?"

"You're breaking my arm! I can't——"

"*Who sent you?*"

"Oh, gawd," gasped the little man, and then screeched as Mannering twisted that little more, not enough to break, but enough to bring sweat to the man's forehead, another groan from his lips. "Lemme go, lemme go, I'll tell you."

Mannering eased his grip, slowly, and let the man relax on to the ground. Wainwright was breathing hissingly through his nostrils, as if he had found that as much as he could bear.

"Let's have it, quickly," Mannering growled.

"It was Brash and Crummy Day," the little man muttered. "Crummy Day, you know, the pawn-broker, Aldgate High Street, that's who." He spoke hoarsely, fearfully. "Don't do any more, my arm's gone dead. I can't feel it, I just can't——"

"Get up."

"You—you won't——"

"Help him up, Ned," Mannering said.

Wainwright moved forward, but the prisoner got to his feet, without help. It was hard to tell who was breathing more wheezily, Wainwright or the prisoner.

"Hold his arms behind him," Mannering ordered. "This way." He demonstrated. Wainwright took the prisoner's arms and held them back, so that his chest was thrust forward, and he couldn't move. "Hold him tight."

The little man was moaning, but it wasn't all in pain. Mannering dipped into his pockets, and took out everything there; including a leather cosh. He slipped that into his own pocket.

"I ought to use it on you."

"My arm——"

"Just keep still." Mannering used the torch, shining it straight into the prisoner's face. It wasn't a sight for anyone to see, a small, pallid face, eyes closed tightly against the glare, mouth set too, a small button of a nose, ears which stuck out, low, wrinkled forehead. As he got used to the glare, his eyes opened a little and Mannering had a good look at him. "I'll recognise you again," he said ominously. "Keep him there, Ned."

"Okay."

Mannering knelt down, spread out the contents of the prisoner's pockets, and scanned them in the light of the torch. The only thing of real interest was a letter, addressed to:

> M. Dibben,
> 17 Penn Street,
> Whitechapel, E.

There were the usual oddments, a few pounds in cash, a railway ticket to Waterloo from Horsham, several keys, a comb that felt sticky with grease, two handkerchiefs, a couple of snapshots of "M. Dibben" disporting himself on the sea-front, probably at Southend.

Mannering kept the cosh and the keys, which might one day be useful. He stuffed the rest back into Dibben's pockets.

"All right," he said, "let him go."

"You—you're going to let him off?" gasped Wainwright.

"I think he told the truth, don't you?"

"Yes, but——"

"A bargain's a bargain," Mannering said, "so we'll let him go. He'll probably have to walk to Horsham, that'll teach him. I've got his name and address," Mannering went on, "and if he tries any monkey business with the car the police will be calling on him tomorrow morning and he'll be on the wanted list. Scram."

"He—he's still holding me," gasped the prisoner.

Wainwright let him go.

"Listen, Mannering," Dibben said, with a catch in his

voice, "I'll remember this, don't make any mistake, I'll remember."

He turned and started to run down the drive, but couldn't keep up the pace. He walked quickly. His right arm was limp by his side, he didn't seem to turn round, but disappeared into the darkness. It was some time before his footsteps faded.

Wainwright said as if amazed, "You can't rely on a *crook*. There's no honour——"

"It's worth the chance," Mannering said briskly, "and he certainly won't do any more harm tonight. Have you heard of Crummy Day?"

"Well, vaguely. Larraby seems to have mentioned him."

"We could use Larraby here, but it would be a pity to spoil his holiday." Mannering chuckled. "You aren't doing so badly! Game to try the house?"

"You mean—break *in*?"

"If we catch Brash red-handed it would do a lot of good. I think," went on Mannering, straight-faced, "that if we stated in court that we'd seen a man break in, and thought it our duty to follow, we would probably be forgiven if we were found on enclosed property."

Wainwright welcomed that point of view very seriously.

"I suppose you're right," he said, and squared his shoulders. "All right, *I'm* game."

They moved towards the house.

They walked on the grass verge, making little sound; most was from Wainwright. Mannering wished that he were on his own. Wainwright's breathing, loud and uneven, could be heard some distance away. It might be drowning sounds that Mannering wanted to hear: sounds of Dibben and Dibben's accomplice coming back, for instance.

He heard nothing.

They neared the house.

"It was a window on this side," whispered Wainwright.

"Let's make it."

They had to walk on gravel, here. Wainwright, obviously doing his damnedest to walk quietly, made twice as much noise as Mannering. He kept muttering imprecations against himself. They reached another grass patch, near the house. The stars seemed brighter. Mannering could see the tall windows on the ground floor, the window-ledges and the windows above, too.

Then he saw a light inside.

His hand closed round Wainwright's forearm, and Wainwright went as stiff as a board.

"Wha——?"

"*Quiet.*"

Mannering let the youngster go, and watched the light intently. It was visible through a window, and seemed to be moving. A man with a torch?

The light disappeared.

"Did you—did you see that?" breathed Wainwright.

"Brash, probably. Wait here. Don't climb in until I call you." Mannering went slowly towards the window, and found it open nearly two feet at the bottom; obviously Brash had left it open.

Mannering bent down, and climbed in. Once he was inside the room, the silence seemed more profound. He could not hear the soft noises of the night, or Wainwright's breathing; or any sound at all.

Then he heard soft footsteps.

A light appeared, very dim but getting gradually stronger.

The door of the room led into a passage, and someone was coming along the passage, making as much noise as a man wearing rubber soles might make.

Mannering moved slowly to one side, then towards the door. Behind the door he wouldn't be noticed.

If this were Brash——

Suddenly, a brighter light flashed on, the man in the passage exclaimed in swift alarm. Then came the roar of a shot, deafening, threatening, deadly.

11

THE "MUSEUM" BY NIGHT

THE door of the room crashed back. In the brighter light that flooded in, a man rushed from the passage. Mannering saw him clearly, and recognised Brash.

Brash made a rush for the open window, but turned round and looked over his shoulder. Another man appeared at the doorway. Mannering saw his dark shape, short and stunted, and felt sure that it was Pendexter Smith. He saw the gun in the man's hands, a rifle or a carbine; it might be a blunderbuss for all Mannering could tell.

"Stop there, you rogue!" roared the man with the gun.

Brash grabbed something from a table, and hurled it as he reached the window. His luck was as good as his aim. Whatever it was caught the barrel of the gun, and twisted it out of the little man's grasp. It clattered to the floor, but didn't go off. Brash hurled himself at the window, which rattled and boomed as he climbed through.

Wainwright could cope outside.

Mannering heard a shout out there, but the sound was drowned as the man in the room swore volubly, snatched up the gun and rushed at the window, feet clumping. Outside, the only sound was of thudding feet.

Wainwright wouldn't run, so Brash had got away.

The little man was in the grounds, now. The beam of a torch stabbed through the darkness. Mannering, near the window, saw Wainwright picking himself up, then saw the little man's legs moving like pistons as he ran after Brash. There was a moment's lull; and then a flash and the roar of another shot from the rifle.

Into the silence which followed, Mannering called softly, "All right, Ned?"

"I—yes, sure, I'm all right. Got a split lip, but I'm all right," Wainwright mumbled. He came up to the window, dabbing at a blood-stained lip with the back of his hand. "Wasn't—wasn't that the man who came to the shop this afternoon? The dwarf?"

"I think so. I'd like a chat with him, too."

"And—it's really his place," Wainwright muttered. "He's bound to send for the police, isn't he?"

"Probably. You nip down to the end of the drive, find my car and make sure no one slashes the tyres or lets the air out," Mannering said. "I won't be long here. If anyone questions you, just say you're waiting for me, but you don't know where I've gone."

"But——"

"Carry on, Ned." Mannering was brusque.

"If you think I'm going to let you see this thing out by yourself you're damned well mistaken!" snapped Wainwright angrily.

Mannering found himself grinning.

A car engine started a long way off: probably Brash's.

They went together into the house. There was no sound. A light was on in the hall, another in the passage outside, ceiling-lamps which hung on pendants, and had big, white shades which reflected the light downwards but didn't protect the eyes from dazzle.

Wainwright had started off with an attack of nerves which didn't last long. Mannering took one glance round the hall, and stood quite still; startled, almost stupefied.

Under the bright light, in that one spot, was the most astonishing collection of museum pieces he was ever likely to see together. It was so bizarre that it didn't seem true. By the front door, one on either side, was a suit of mediaeval armour, dull and tarnished, and a carved, life-size model of a Zulu warrior, complete with war-mask, painted body, leopard-skin shield, assegai, and all. Over the door, tied with pieces of rope, was the stuffed body of a wild-cat. Standing round the walls, every foot of space being crammed, were trophies of a hundred hunts from a dozen countries. Parrots, crocodiles, peacocks, native carvings, snakes—Indian ivory, Chinese lacquered vases, huge chests of beaten brass from the Middle East, a mummy lying in its coffin, a bust of an American Indian complete with colourful feathered head-dress, a totem pole—all these and a hundred other oddities were gathered together.

Everything looked freshly cleaned and dusted.

"Good gracious *me*!" exclaimed Wainwright, inanely.

That broke the spell, and did Mannering good. He grinned.

"I agree. But don't speak loudly."

Wainwright coloured furiously.

"Well, it *is* about the craziest conglomeration of old junk I've ever seen. Look at *that*." He pointed to the shrivelled head of a South American Indian. "And look, there are some Malayan blow-pipes, hill tribe stuff, and . . ." His whisper trailed off.

"Let's have a look round before Pendexter Smith comes back," said Mannering softly.

That seemed to jolt Wainwright out of his mood. He looked sharply at the closed front door. The windows were all curtained, the door tightly closed, so that no one could see in. He listened intently; but heard nothing.

"Where shall we go?"

"Downstairs first."

Mannering thrust open the double doors of a room opposite the side of the big, wide, shiny mahogany staircase, then stopped abruptly. For light from the hall shone into this room, and it looked empty.

A second glance showed a grand piano, several old-fashioned armchairs, a huge red-plush Victorian sofa, and two or three mahogany tables, all pushed in one corner, behind the door. The rest of the room was empty. The huge carpet was rolled up along one wall. Several floorboards were up, a screwdriver, claw hammer, and some nails were near the holes which this made in the floor.

Mannering went over and looked into the hole, saw nothing, knelt down, and explored. There were dusty joists, cobwebs, and plaster; nothing else.

"It's just a mad-house," Wainwright said, and then added in a different voice, his grown-up voice: "And to think she lives in this hole!"

"I wonder what they're looking for, or what they're hiding?" Mannering mused. "Come on."

The other rooms downstairs seemed to be in their normal condition—dining-room, morning-room and a small library. The furniture was old-fashioned, big, usually ugly, although there were a few nice pieces. Wherever there was a square foot of wall space, some kind of picture adorned it, often hideously bad, although here and there one looked interesting. In smaller spaces colourful stuffed birds, their glass eyes very bright, were stuck on to the wall. The four corners of the earth had been combed to bring something into nearly every room. A silver table from Italy looked incongruous against some huge Turkish poufs, a hookah, and a sedan chair which might well have been made in England two hundred and fifty years ago. Swords, mostly sheathed, filled the whole of one library wall—from the ugly Ghurka knife to Toledo swords of fine Spanish steel, Italian jewelled daggers, some African spears, a bayonet from the Second World War.

"What a collector's nightmare," Wainwright muttered.

"With here and there a dream," said Mannering. "We'll have the light off."

"Why, did you hear——?"

"I think so. Stand still."

He was by the door of the library when he switched off the light. That wasn't until he'd seen Wainwright's worried glance into the passage. It would have been ten times better if Wainwright had gone to watch the car.

Footsteps sounded clearly. A window closed with a bang. The footsteps sounded again, quick and light, those of a small, agile man. Obviously he was making a tour of the house.

Mannering and Wainwright stood in the shadows, but the man didn't come near them, just peered in their direction. Mannering didn't move. He had seen the figure of the near dwarf rushing after Brash, and it might have been Pendexter Smith—but could that old man have moved so briskly? Certainly he couldn't if he were as old and as stiff as he had seemed to be when he had been to Hart Row.

The movements were very brisk now.

Would the man go to the police?

Was there a telephone here?

Mannering remembered seeing one in the hall, close to a fist of tarnished mail. Would the man use it to call the police? Mannering listened for the *ting* of it being lifted, but heard nothing.

The footsteps now seemed to be farther away; they were on bare boards.

"He's gone into the big room," whispered Wainwright. "Shall we sneak out?"

"We'll make sure who he is," Mannering whispered back.

"All right with me," hissed Wainwright.

They heard the man walking about the boards of the huge, almost empty room. Then they heard him speak, as if to himself; next, he laughed. Then he began to hum.

"Take it easy," Mannering whispered.

He stepped into the hall. The light was still on, and the door of the big room was ajar. He beckoned to Wainwright, who drew nearer. The hall carpet muffled their footsteps.

"We'll go out the back way," Mannering whispered again.

"Okay."

Mannering kept close to the wall as he drew near the door. The man inside was humming under his breath. He hadn't telephoned the police, and he had no help—would one man be in this great barn of a house alone?

Mannering peered round the door.

A small man with a humped back, not Pendexter Smith, but someone much younger, was putting the floorboards back into position, and humming an air from Gilbert and Sullivan. By his side was the gun. He was side-on to the door, solitary and, apparently, quite unafraid.

Wainwright was breathing into Mannering's ear.

"That's not the chap Smith."

Mannering didn't answer. He couldn't stay and search the house while the man here was awake and alert. And he did not want Wainwright with him when he searched. It would be better to leave, and to come back alone.

Wainwright started violently.

Something whirred——

A clock struck a booming note from the other side of the hall. It was three o'clock. The little misshapen man in the big room was still humming and swaying, the notes of the clock were loud and slightly out of tune; their echo seemed to hum.

"All right," Mannering said. "Let's go."

They reached a passage which led to the kitchen. Using the light of the torch, they went through the kitchen window, closing it from the outside.

They hurried round the house. Heavy curtains hid most of the light from them, but they could see bright slivers at the sides and the tops of the windows. The stars seemed duller now. They reached the drive, and hurried down towards the car.

They got in.

"I don't mind admitting I'm glad we're out of that," said Wainwright. "Would you—er—would you mind if I had a cigarette?"

"Like a tot of whisky?"

"Wouldn't I just!"

Mannering produced a flask, and Wainwright took a generous swig, lit a cigarette, and soon afterwards became garrulous; nervous reaction, Mannering decided. He said all the obvious things. They ought to tell the police about Brash, and this Crummy Day—everything. And Pendexter Smith wasn't back, after all. Listening it seemed to Mannering that Wainwright was very young indeed. He was pleased with himself, too; he had booked two rooms at the Horsebox, one for Mr. Mannering, said he'd be in late, so had a key. He'd been right about Brash, too. The only thing that shadowed his pleasure was Brash's escape. He'd been a bit too close, and Brash had crashed a fist into his mouth.

"Probably as well you didn't stop him, we couldn't have had our look round otherwise," Mannering said soothingly.

. . . . .

Half an hour later, Mannering glanced into Wainwright's room, which was little more than a boxroom at the end of a narrow passage built three hundred years ago. The young man was fast asleep, lying on his back snoring faintly; yet it was easy to see what Lorna meant when she said that he was a nice-looking lad. "Lad" wasn't so right, now; asleep, he looked older.

Mannering closed the door quietly, went downstairs and outside to his car. After the first whine of the self-starter, it made little sound. He went quietly and slowly out of the parking-yard on to the main road, as quietly through the outskirts of Midham, and then with more speed up the steep hill towards Dragon's End.

There were two hours of darkness left.

He took the car right up the drive this time, parked it at one side, then sat in it for ten minutes, with all lights out. Nothing stirred, except the night creatures on their timid journeys.

He got out, and walked towards the house. The lights were out. The kitchen window had not been latched, he opened it easily and climbed in.

He was trying to recall Dibben's manner, the way he had squealed on Brash. It had come so smoothly and easily. Had he lied about Brash? Was Crummy Day his real employer? Or had he lied about both Day and Brash?

Brash had been here.

Yet Dibben's squeal had been too pat. Brash's name had been on the tip of his tongue.

Forget it; there were other things to do.

There was darkness everywhere, and the uncanny silence of a big house.

Mannering shone the thin pencil beam of a torch until he reached the big room. The door was closed. He pushed it open and stepped inside. His torch stabbed through the darkness—and fell upon the man who was nearly a dwarf, the happy, humming man.

He would never hum again.

One of the African spears had been hurled at his hunched back, and it pinned him to the floor.

12

SEARCH

MANNERING straightened up from the body of the little man, who had almost certainly died instantly. The spear had pierced his body to the heart, must have been thrown with tremendous force. There was very little outward bleeding; blood would come if the spear were taken out.

Mannering turned away.

Every moment he had been here, he had been intent on catching the slightest sound. He heard none.

He stepped towards the door, stood by it in the darkness and listened again. There was no noise anywhere. Yet someone had been here, waiting the chance, and struck savagely, murderously.

The floorboards were nearly all in position again; Mannering remembered that several had been out of place and that the man had replaced some before he and Wainwright had left. He had still been working when the silent killer had flung the spear, so that could not have been much more than half an hour after Mannering had gone.

Had the killer been in the house when Mannering had been here before?

Could he identify Mannering? And Wainwright?

Mannering moved slowly about the hall and passage, listening at the door of each room, letting thoughts jostle one another in his mind. He heard no one else, was quite sure that he would have heard breathing in this dark silence. Someone might be upstairs, but no one was down here.

He looked round, putting the light on in each room. Each was empty. He had come to search for any clue that might help to explain what had happened to Pendexter Smith.

The staircase, half-circular, was wide, massive, and carpeted from wall to banisters. He made hardly a sound going up. In the darkness it was eerie. The huge old house became full of little, creaking noises. He reached the landing, shining his torch round and then he took a chance and switched on the landing light. It was glaring and brilliant, like those downstairs, threw everything up into sharp relief; and it made black shadows.

The landing was crammed with museum pieces, too. The conglomeration was as farcical as that downstairs. Oddments from different corners of the world stood side by side. By one wall was a china figure of a praying Buddha, amazingly lifelike in its obese stillness. In spite of the tension, he went to look at it.

He turned away, and went into room after room. There was another library, kept surprisingly clean and tidy. In five minutes, he discovered that the items in the house had been catalogued in neat handwriting, a card-index system could hardly have been better. There was no safe.

Next door to this was a woman's room.

Going in, Mannering became immediately aware of a smell of perfume, not strong but very pleasant. He shone his torch to see himself across to the window, drew the curtains, then went back to the door and switched on the light.

The room was furnished as an expensive modern *salon* might be furnished by a firm of repute. The furniture was of polished walnut; the furnishings heavy and distinctive. If it were Miranda's, the girl had chosen a colour scheme of pale blue and gold; and there was no discordant note. The double bed had a mock canopy over the head panel. The large dressing-table, with its three tall mirrors, looked as if someone had sat at it, not long ago. There was a faint dusting of powder over the the exquisite *petit point* of the dressing-table set. One scent spray was very old; enamelled and very beautiful. The room gave the impression of being lived in by someone who knew how to live.

In the wardrobe were clothes that would suit Miranda.

On the dressing-table was a large photograph of Pendexter Smith which might have been taken yesterday. There was the old man to the life, with his glittering sunken eyes and his monkey-like mouth and chin, his wrinkled eyelids. It was hard to understand the girl's affection for a man who was so ugly.

Mannering found nothing that would help, switched off the light, and went to the next room. He opened the door with a stealth which was almost instinctive now; stealth which he had learned as the Baron, when a single false move would have made the difference between success and disaster; between freedom and jail.

He stopped and listened.

He heard breathing.

. . . . .

Someone was breathing in this room, quite noisily, but it wasn't quite a snore. Mannering stood with his fingers on the handle, making sure of the rhythm of the sound, that whoever lay there was asleep.

He went right in. The floor was carpeted thickly. The window was opposite the door, and he could see the stars through it.

The bed was behind the door.

Mannering shone his torch, and the pencil of light made a bright sword, pointing towards the head of the bed. It showed up the head and face of Pendexter Smith, stark, ugly, unmistakable.

Mannering let the torch shine fully into Pendexter's face. The old man did not stir. Mannering went nearer, keeping the light off the eyes. That slightly wheezy breathing was very steady. Something about this made Mannering study the old man very closely. Then he stretched out a hand and touched his shoulder.

Smith didn't stir.

Mannering gripped his shoulder tightly, and shook him. Smith still didn't stir.

A minute later, Mannering raised the lid and looked into one eye, which was held in the light of his torch. The pupil was so tiny that he could hardly see it. Pendexter Smith lay in a drugged sleep while another man, much younger but with the same kind of misshapen body, lay dead in the room below.

* * * * *

As Mannering left Dragon's End, dawn was breaking. The light was grey and weak, but the birds were waking and the trees and shrubs, the lawns and the flower-beds, began to take shape, were no longer an amorphous mass concealed by darkness. He could see the big oak and beech which lined the drive, antirrhinums, asters, and zinnias in huge beds, lawns and grounds which were beautifully kept.

Half-way down the drive, he turned to look at Dragon's End.

It faced south-east, and the first light shone upon its closed windows, reflecting faintly from the glass. The house, built of red brick, looked massive, with one turret topped by a steeple, odd pieces sticking out at the corners, the roof odd shaped, the chimneys massive and ugly. It was all ugly—but solid enough to stand there for centuries to come, a monument to the age when man almost forgot beauty of line.

He turned away.

Five minutes later, he was in his car.

Ten minutes later, he was in the call-box from which Wainwright had telephoned him.

* * * * *

Chief Inspector Nicholas Fenn, a bachelor, heard the telephone bell through the mists of sleep, cursed it, did nothing about it, but, when it persisted, eased himself up on one elbow and grabbed it from the bedside table.

"Hallo?" he growled.

He listened for a moment, then hitched himself up to a sitting position; sleep vanished.

Mannering spoke briskly and concisely. He gave Fenn the impression that he didn't think he would have to say any of this twice. He gave reasons for what he had done and what he was doing; good, cogent reasons. Then he said:

"It's up to you, now."

"All right, I'll get Midham moving, but leave everything else until you came to the Yard," promised Fenn.

When he rang off, he was thinking hard about what Bristow had told him.

. . . . .

The remarkable thing about Nicholas Fenn was that he didn't waste time saying that Mannering shouldn't have gone into Dragon's End. He kept to the point, and did not appear to be interested in the strict letter of the law.

It was a glorious summer's day.

The three windows of the office were open as far as they could come down. A few insects drifted in and almost as quickly drifted out. A smell of petrol fumes came in, too, but there was a slight breeze off the river, and the smell wasn't too unpleasant. The massive block of the London County Hall rose up so that Mannering, sitting opposite the window, could just see the roof. The noises of traffic, of people walking, of aeroplanes by the dozen, hardly seemed to penetrate the office.

Fenn sat listening intently.

Mannering finished.

"Some story," Fenn said, after a short pause, and went on smoothly: "Mind if I recap a few items?"

"Go ahead."

"Why didn't you tell your assistant, Wainwright, about finding the dead man?"

"I'd like to see how he reacts under a shock and strain,"

Mannering answered. "I think he's good, but I'm not sure."

"Where is he now?"

"I had a couple of hours sleep, then woke him, and we travelled up to London together."

"H'm, yes. Know where Brash is now?"

"No. My question," went on Mannering, and grinned. "Why didn't you keep after Brash last night? You sent Grimble after him, remember."

"He shook Grimble off."

"Or did Grimble lose him?" asked Mannering dryly.

"What's the matter?" asked Fenn in a flash. "Don't you like Grimble?"

"I'd like to be sure what happened."

"I had five minutes with Grimble myself," Fenn told him grimly, "and I think Brash slipped him deliberately. They got mixed up in the Oxford Street crowds. Brash dawdled for a bit and then nipped across the road. It may have been an accident, but I shouldn't think so. Wainwright was either good, unsuspected, or lucky. This man you caught——"

"Yes?"

"I ought to pick him up," Fenn said, and his brown eyes were devoid of expression.

"Do that, and we lose a spy who might pay big dividends," Mannering agreed. "If I were you, I'd leave him alone. I can always put the fear of death into him."

"I suppose you're right." Fenn looked at him steadily, as if he knew that Mannering had "forgotten" to tell him that Dibben had named a certain pawnbroker, one Crummy Day. "Another recap. The time of the murder?"

"Not before three-fifteen, not later than four o'clock, as far as I can tell you."

"Could Pendexter Smith have been the killer?"

"Have you ever tried to carry an African spear far, never mind throw it?"

"Well, no," confessed Fenn. "Pendexter too old?"

"Too decrepit, unless he's an expert. There's a job for you," Mannering added expansively, "find someone who's expert at hurling spears, and you have your man. I——"

"Brash," murmured Fenn.

Mannering said, very softly, "Are you sure?"

"I've been checking pretty closely," Fenn told him, "and Brash is one of these people with odd or unusual hobbies. Instead of playing games, he dotes on archery. I can't vouch for his spear throwing, but he can toss a pretty javelin. I'm pulling Brash in for questioning, and checking everything I can. Only one thing really worries me."

"What?"

"It seems too easy."

"Complaining?" asked Mannering.

"Just wondering," said Fenn. He gave his almost sly grin, and for a moment made Mannering feel almost uneasy. "Just wondering why you've told me all this, what you've kept back, and why you aren't handling this with your customary defiance of the law."

"You've got me all wrong," Mannering said earnestly. "Now it's my turn for questions, or are you putting the bar up?"

"Ask what you like, and if I can I'll answer," Fenn promised. "I'll tell you one more thing before we go any farther. The man caught at your flat yesterday hasn't said a word."

"Any record?"

"A three months for petty larceny and two years for housebreaking," Fenn said. "The housebreaking was four years ago, he seems to have been running straight since. Or that's what we thought. He's got the kind of nerve that a man gets when he knows someone powerful is backing him."

"Married?"

Fenn said mildly, "Yes, a pretty wife, I'm told. And yes, I'll watch her!"

"If they're as good as they seem to be you won't get any results from watching her," Mannering said. "What's his name?"

"Freddy Bell," Fenn told him. "And if you need to know, his wife's name is Dora Bell." The Yard man kept a straight face. "What are you going to do next?"

"Think."

Fenn jeered, "And where do you think that will get you?" He stood up. "Have you seen Miranda Smith this morning?"

"Yes," said Mannering, in a different tone. "Yes, I've seen her. Have you started checking that accident story?"

"We have."

"Any news from the medical front?"

"None at all," said Fenn.

"Richardson's coming to see her again this morning," Mannering said, "and if she doesn't show too much fear, he'll take her away for observation. He'll also check with Lancelot Nash, of course. Any objections?"

"No," said Fenn. "I only hope Richardson does what Nash couldn't."

"If you get any news from Midham——" Mannering began.

"I'll let you know," promised Fenn again. "Being co-operative, aren't I?"

"I can hardly believe you're a policeman," Mannering marvelled.

They chuckled, and Fenn saw his visitor to the door. As he left, Mannering felt that shadow of uneasiness again; was Fenn being almost too friendly?

Mannering drove straight back to Green Street.

Outside the front door was the little green M.G. which Brash owned.

13

CLASH WITH BRASH

Mannering hurried up the stairs, his heart beginning to thump. There couldn't be danger, his reason told him; but if Brash were a killer and had some reason to hate or to fear Miranda, anything might happen.

He heard shouting.

He thrust the key in the lock and pushed the door open—and Wainwright staggered back against it. In front of Wainwright, his face vermilion red and eyes flashing, was Bill Brash. He leapt forward, fists clenched and waving, with no more idea of fighting than a small child. He smashed a blow at Wainwright, who side-stepped it easily. Before Mannering could call out or stop the slaughter, Wainwright went forward and drove his fist into Brash's stomach. As Brash gasped and fell forward, chin open, Wainwright smashed an upper-cut.

Brash went scudding backwards, lost his balance, and fell at Miranda's feet.

She stared at the two young men with the fear which was so dreadfully wrong in her beautiful eyes. In that moment, when he was thinking only of Wainwright and Brash, Mannering looked twice at the girl. If a supreme artist had said, "Here is a model for all your beauties," no one could have been surprised.

Wainwright made as if to run forward.

Mannering grabbed his arm.

Then Lorna appeared from her bedroom, carrying a walking-stick, hurrying with the stick raised and the ferrule thrusting forward—as if at all costs she meant to separate the men. At sight of Mannering, she stopped abruptly.

"My lady roused and angry," murmured Mannering, his

eyes gleaming. "Sorry I'm late, darling! Ned, go and wait in the study, will you?" He moved across to Miranda, and looked straight into her face, and something of the fear died away. "I will not let them fight again," he said, shaking his head and pointing at the men. "Do you understand?"

She tried to say something, but no sound came. Her eyes flooded with tears, and she turned and hurried into the drawing-room. Lorna looked after her, then said quietly:

"That was over Miranda."

"Who started it?"

"Oh, Brash did."

"Why?"

Lorna was almost pensive. Mannering guessed what was going through her mind: a mixture of anxiety for Miranda, worry about what had taken place during the night, and amusement at the antics of the two young men.

"I think," she said carefully, "that it was because of the way Wainwright looked at Miranda."

Mannering grinned.

"And how did he look?"

"Oh, bother it all!" exclaimed Lorna, "it's so silly and yet so touching. If you want a word, it's adoring. He came in here with something very much on his mind, and when he saw Miranda again, he went to pieces. He dithered and fussed and blushed. Then Brash arrived and said something which annoyed Wainwright, something about Miranda not being safe here, and he wanted to take her away. And off it went."

"I can imagine that Wainwright wouldn't have much time for Brash this morning," Mannering said dryly. "Go and keep him occupied for a few minutes, will you?"

Lorna didn't ask why.

Brash was trying to get to his feet, looking dazed, and with a bruise beneath his chin which was already red and swelling. To win in that fracas, he had needed a knowledge of boxing, not archery. Mannering held him up. He stood swaying, feeling his chin and licking his lips; a little blood smeared one corner.

"Brash," said Mannering, very quietly, "the police are after you."

Brash's eyes, as clear a blue as Miranda's were a clear blue, wavered for a few seconds, tried to focus, and then succeeded. Alarm seemed to stiffen him.

"What—what's that? What do they want me for?"

"Don't you know?"

"I can't imagine——" Brash began, and then stopped; as if he knew only too well why the police wanted him. "How do you know?" he muttered.

"I've just come from Scotland Yard.

"What—what did they say?"

"They've put a call out for you—you're wanted for murder."

Brash was becoming much more composed; still scared, but not so badly frightened: nervous was the better word. At the sound of "murder" his expression changed. He was astounded and incredulous; and if he were acting, he was acting brilliantly.

"*Murder.*"

"That's right. The crime they hang you for."

"Hang?" echoed Brash. "Murder? I—Mannering, *I* haven't killed anyone. I'm sure I haven't!" He didn't seem to realise how ludicrous that "I'm sure I haven't" was. "Look here, you're trying to frighten me!" Anger pushed the incredulity out of his eyes, he became the pugnacious young man again. "I don't know what the hell you think you're playing at, but——"

"By now, there's a warrant out for your arrest," Mannering said. "Were you at Dragon's End last night?"

"Was I at . . .?" began Brash, and then his voice trailed off, the last sounds were only gibberish. He gulped. Then he grabbed Mannering's wrists and held them in a vice-like grip. "It isn't Pendexter? He isn't dead? Is he?"

"Someone at Dragon's End is dead. Were you there?"

Brash let his arms fall, and backed away.

"Oh, God, yes," he muttered. "Yes, I was, but I didn't kill——" He reared up, his eyes flashed. "Someone else was there, I saw them, someone came rushing after me. He must have done it, I didn't. I——"

He stopped abruptly.

"Mannering," he went on, in a different voice, as if he were trying very hard to keep himself from going to pieces, "look after Miranda. That's all that matters, looking after Miranda. I can't—I can't help her now. Not until I'm cleared of this. I didn't kill Pendexter, but——"

"Why did you go there?" Mannering demanded.

Brash said, "I was looking for——looking for some papers. I wanted to see if Miranda's been cheated or not, but I didn't kill—kill anyone."

He broke off again.

He backed to the door, hesitated, then opened it and went out. His little green car must have been beckoning him. Mannering let him go, and watched the street through the window.

Fenn couldn't have put the call out for Brash yet, because there was a Yard man in a doorway opposite, and he made no move to stop the youngster driving off. Brash showed up clearly in the open car, with the hood down; his face wasn't red, but very pale. The sun shone on his fair hair. He started off slowly, then trod on the accelerator. The car shot forward.

If he were the killer he'd put up a good show.

Mannering turned towards the study, and to Wainwright, but hadn't reached the room when footsteps sounded on the landing. He turned round, and opened the door before the caller touched the bell.

It was Richardson, stocky, broad-shouldered Roy Richardson, with a big reputation and a past which included a season or two as a Cambridge blue at cricket and Rugger, and whose wife was a close friend of Lorna. He had a brick-red face, dark-blue eyes, rather deep-set, piercing.

"Hallo, Roy," Mannering greeted. "You're prompt. Nice of you to come yourself."

"Don't want to scare the patient more than she's scared already," Richardson said. "Strangers frighten her at first. If she comes willingly, is Lorna coming with us?"

"Yes."

"Good. Both of you seem to have a calming effect on the girl," Richardson said. "Can't understand it!" He gave a broad, attractive grin. "All right, let's get moving."

Mannering went to the drawing-room.

Five minutes later, Richardson, Lorna, and Miranda went out together. Mannering didn't go with them, but stayed to study Wainwright's reaction. The young man had come out of the study in time to see Miranda. He had watched Miranda every moment, had not been able to look away from her; it was as if she held him under some spell, swiftly exerted, impossible to exorcise.

And he was good-looking, with a square chin, good mouth, a short, straight nose; a frank, open kind of face. He watched out of the window until the last minute, didn't move away until the car must have gone out of the street. Then he swallowed a lump in his throat and turned round, groping in his pocket for cigarettes. He met Mannering's eyes steadily, although there was a strange expression in his own; almost as if he were dazed.

"She's—so beautiful," he said.

Mannering said briskly, "There aren't many lovelier, but she isn't our worry at the moment. Why did you try to break Brash's neck?"

"Eh?"

CLASH WITH BRASH

"Pull yourself together!" Mannering was sharp.

"Er—sorry, Mr. Mannering," Wainwright said hurriedly. He lit his cigarette, and his fingers weren't quite steady. "He—er—he made me mad. Talked about taking Miranda away, and after what he did last night——"

Wainwright stopped abruptly, looked as if an electric shock had run through him. He stared at Mannering with something like horror leaping into his expression. He gulped, then choked, his eyes watered—and yet the look of horror remained.

"But you don't *know*, do you? We're in a hell of a spot!"

Mannering said coldly, "Don't talk out of the back of your neck."

"But we are! Chittering came round to Quinns to see you, you know Chittering, the *Record* chap. He told Sylvester he'd just heard that—that a murder was done at Dragon's End last night. Someone was killed with a spear, an assegai. Of course Brash did it, but we were there, too. We could have——"

He didn't finish, was almost incoherent.

"You sure about this?" Mannering swung towards the telephone.

"I'm certainly not making it up! Chittering was quite definite. He knew something about Pendexter Smith, knew he'd been to see you, that's why he came round to Quinns. He said he'd be in again later. We said you were out seeing clients, didn't want him to throw this in your face without you being forewarned. That's why I came round here. And to think that Brash had the nerve to say that Miranda wouldn't be safe here. I could break his ruddy neck!"

"You nearly did."

"Oh, to hell with Brash!" growled Wainwright. "What are we going to do?"

"What do you want to do?"

Wainwright stubbed out his cigarette, and then wiped his

forehead and his neck. It was warm, but not so warm as that. He didn't look away from Mannering.

"I'll be guided by you," he said carefully. "We didn't do it, so our consciences are clear. If the police start questioning us, it will stop us from doing anything much, won't it? I'd advise, keep mum. But I wouldn't like to say what would happen if the police started questioning *me*. I might make a fool of myself, and give everything away."

"You'll get yourself into trouble one of these days," Mannering said. "All right, Ned. Don't say anything to the Press, even if it's Chittering. Refer all inquiries to me. Who was killed, do you know?"

"It must have been that dwarf we saw. It's a man named Revell, anyway, a family servant, been there for years." Wainwright hadn't forgotten much of the newspaperman's story. "And Pendexter Smith was found there, Chittering said that he was drugged. But you can never really believe the Press, can you?"

"Not if they want to get information out of you," Mannering agreed. "Now, I've a new job for you." He paused. "That's if you want to carry on."

"I'm game," Wainwright said naïvely. "I'm not so good as Larraby, but I'm thirty years younger, that would be a help if it came to a scrap. What do you want me to do?"

"Go to the East End and find out what you can about Crummy Day the pawnbroker," Mannering said promptly. "Talk to the trade scouts, second-hand jewellers, other pawnbrokers, anyone who might give you the dope. Do they think he's trustworthy? That's the only thing you're trying to find out. If you're asked, say you're getting the dope for me. Crummy's offered me some stuff, and I won't touch it if it's hot. All clear?"

"You know," said Ned Wainwright, with a glow in his eyes, "I think I'm going to enjoy this side of the business! Er—any need to go armed?"

"I shouldn't think so, by day." Mannering kept a straight face.

"I'll be back as soon as I can," promised Wainwright. "Oh, I ought to telephone Sylvester, to let him know that I won't be back."

"I'll do that."

"Thanks," said Wainwright warmly, and hurried off. The door closed on him, and Mannering heard his footsteps on the stairs, then heard them stop; there was a pause and a puzzling silence.

Next moment, the bell rang softly.

Mannering opened the door, standing on one side, hardly knowing what to expect. It was Wainwright, back, looking eager, bright-faced.

"It's that chap Chittering," he whispered conspiratorially. "On his way up. Thought I'd warn you." He pushed past Mannering into the hall. "He won't know I've been here if I keep out of sight," he added, and made a bee-line for the kitchen.

Then the door-bell rang again, and the fair, curly head of Chittering of the *Record* appeared; he beamed, his face was plump and round, like a baby's, his cheeks were covered with down, and he looked much younger than he was.

"What's that clod-hopper Wainwright creeping about for?" he demanded.

14

MISSING MAN

WAINWRIGHT must have heard the newspaperman's comment, but he didn't appear from the kitchen. Mannering led the way to the study. Two minutes later, he heard the hall door close; Wainwright had gone.

All this time, Chittering had been watching him narrowly,

one eyebrow raised slightly above the level of the other, china-blue eyes suspicious.

"What is on?" he demanded. "*Were* you at Midham last night?"

"Don't make wild guesses."

"I verily believe you were," declared Chittering, and grinned a mighty grin. "Magnificent! Bold, bad Mannering at scene of savage crime. Ever done any spear-throwing, tossing the caber, or anything like that?" He took out cigarettes. "You are not yourself," he added; "you haven't denied it yet."

"Give me half a chance," Mannering said dryly. "No, no, no. Thanks." He took a cigarette. "What's on?"

"Don't tell me that Ned Wainwright didn't tell you that I've been grilling him and Sylvester," said Chittering. "I had Wainwright under the microscope for fully five minutes. Sylvester kept fluttering in the wings, trying to come to the rescue, but a photographer was with me, and he dealt with Sylvester. Sweetly, you understand. As a matter of fact," Chittering went on, "Wainwright isn't bad at all. I didn't get a thing out of him. Training him to be Larraby's successor?"

"In what capacity?"

"Legman and all the rest," said Chittering comfortably. "I wouldn't be surprised if he turns out very well. He was quite bland with me half the time, with a little more experience he'll almost be able to make a lie sound the truth."

"Why don't you take him in hand?" Mannering asked sweetly.

"Okay, John, I give up. What's blowing?"

"My chief worry is a girl who's deaf and dumb," Mannering said, in a tone which made it clear that he had stopped being flippant. "And yes, there is a job you can usefully do. Fenn——"

"I was going to ask about Fenn. How do you find him?"

"Unexpectedly co-operative."

"Be wary of Nicholas Fenn," warned Chittering, with obvious sincerity. "He of the smooth voice and the gentlemanly manners is cunning like a fox. And he's comparatively new; we don't know his methods yet. I suspect he's one of the 'come into my parlour pretty maiden' type, and that when he gets nasty he can be pretty foul. Still, you also have eyes and little grey cells. What," went on Chittering, sweetly, "is the dirty work you want this noble son of Fleet Street to do for you?"

Mannering rounded his eyes.

"You ask Wainwright how noble you are! Three things, Chitty. Find out all you can about Mortimer Smith and Pendexter Smith of Dragon's End. Discover all you can about their collection of head-hunters' pieces and museum left-overs—and see if you can get a line on a nest of jewelled eggs. The clue is Indonesia, Ba-Kona dynasty. Yes, I am quite serious." He described the nest of spun gold and the eggs that went with it, and something of his love of precious stones crept into his voice; and impressed Chittering.

"I'll do what I can," the newspaperman promised. "And report later, sir."

He gave a mock salute.

He hadn't been gone ten minutes before Fenn was on the line; and Fenn's voice was sharper than Mannering had heard it before—the voice of a man who wasn't going to stand any nonsense.

"Did you tell Brash that we wanted him?"

"I did," admitted Mannering.

"You damned fool. It's as bad as wilfully obstructing us." Fenn's voice could cut like a knife. "He's run for cover, his car's been stranded. If you'd kept your mouth shut, we could have picked him up in half an hour. Now it's a manhunt. I hope——"

"Fenn," said Mannering, in a voice so honey-sweet that it

stopped the Yard man in full flow, "I apologise, humbly and abjectly. A complete misunderstanding. If Bill Bristow had told me what you told me about Brash, I'd have taken it for granted that he wanted me to pass the news on—wanted to get Brash on the run. And it worked that way. But I repeat——"

"I'm not Bristow," Fenn said; and then gave himself and his game away. "What impression did you get when you told him he was wanted for murder?"

"He was surprised."

"Sure?"

"Yes. Surprised, shocked, shaken. Whether because he didn't kill or because he didn't think you'd get on to him so quickly, I don't know, but they were his emotions. Any idea where he is?"

"Not yet," said Fenn, "but we'll get him."

The receiver went up with a loud and deliberate snap.

Mannering smiled faintly as he looked at the ceiling and a solitary fly bumping against it in a series of futile assaults. He did a lot of thinking. He hadn't finished when he told Ethel that if anyone wanted him he would be at Quinns, and left the flat. He wasn't followed, although a man from the Yard was still on duty watching. He got into the Rolls-Bentley, and drove to Hart Row, left the car outside, and went in.

Sylvester and another assistant came forward from the shadows, but had no startling news to impart.

"I'm going to have a look at the nest-egg," Mannering said. "You haven't unlocked the strong-room this morning, have you?"

"No, sir, it hasn't been necessary to touch it," Sylvester said. "Would you like any help?"

"I'll manage," said Mannering.

He went into his office.

The strong-room was electrically locked and sealed with

rays which gave warning of anyone's approach; everything the Baron had learned about safes and strong-rooms and locks and burglar-proof systems had been used to make this as near impregnable as it could be. Once it had been raided; it was now three times as strong as it had been then.

He closed and locked the door, pressed control electric buttons and switched ray-control levers. Now he could begin to get into the strong-room. Next he shifted a filing-cabinet, and rolled back a corner of the carpet, revealing polished boards. These were so cleverly fitted that they looked quite solid and unbroken; but at the touch of another switch a trap-door opened. Beneath this was yet another steel trap-door; he needed two keys to open this.

He started down the short loft-ladder to the strong-room, which had once been a cellar. The walls had been strengthened with reinforced concrete, over a foot thick. The ceiling was the same. There were two small ventilation shafts, but neither led directly to the street or the tiny yard at the back of Quinns.

A dozen safes were almost as impregnable as the strong-room. Round the walls, some in crates and some unpacked, were treasures which connoisseurs would pay a fortune to possess; all lovely things, each a delight to any expert eye, something to brood over and to love. Men did love these things; the lustre of a Ming vase, the fire that seemed to be burning in the heart of a diamond, the perfection of a master's touch with a brush—this was a storeroom of treasures worth an incalculable sum; not all Mannering's, for much was held for sale on commission; but a great deal was his.

The nest-egg was in the middle safe of five along one wall.

Mannering opened this. The keys scratched against the metal. He pulled the great, heavy steel door open. His heart began to pound. There was much that he didn't understand about the case, in some ways it was almost uncanny; and suddenly he was afraid. It was impossible—but had someone broken in, had the nest-egg——

The case was there.

Mannering said, "Idiot," and wiped his forehead with the back of his hand, then took the leather travelling case out. He carried it to a small table, unlocked and opened it, and looked down at the superbly spun nest and the lovely jewelled eggs. When he switched on a powerful light, the jewels seemed to catch fire. He screwed a watch-maker's glass to his right eye, and examined each egg and each stone set round it, and he held his breath. All of these were perfect gems, the value was even greater than he had thought the night before. The nest might have been made by golden birds which could lay bejewelled eggs. It looked so soft to the touch, too, but in fact was hard and cool.

Mannering straightened up, and took the glass away from his eye. Studying jewels like this did something to him, touched a spark which had turned into a flame in the distant days of the Baron. He had a passion for precious stones which really amounted to mania. Rare and beautiful gems affected him physically. He felt cold and shivery, as if touched by fever. This was a battle which he had to fight and win over and over again. At one time the sight of such jewels as those would have broken down all his defences; he would have felt the longing for them so great, so fierce, that he would have stolen them rather than let them go to another man's possession.

Temptation, not these days to steal but to buy beyond his means, kept him almost daily company. In this strong-room he was filled with the tension, and knew that until he had gone upstairs, thrusting the jewels out of his mind, he would feel like this. He had made sure they were here, and nothing else really mattered. At heart, he knew that he had not needed to make sure, that the nest-egg was safe. The beauty of the gems had lured him down, to gloat as a miser would gloat over his hoard.

Once the doors of the safe were shut on them he would feel better, and when the trap-doors were in position, better still; and once he started looking through the morning's post, with Sylvester, he would be back to normal.

He went up the wooden steps towards the office, looked round at the safe once, gave a thin-lipped smile, climbed up the stairs, and for a split second had his eyes on a level with the floor.

Something moved.

It was beyond the desk; something bright and shiny which he saw through the opening of the desk, the spot where he usually sat. He stopped moving for a split second, then went on, but his heart pounded with a different kind of excitement.

He had seen a polished shoe. Someone was on his knees behind the far end of the desk, hidden from sight, waiting for him to turn round and lower the trap-doors.

Was the man armed?

15

SECOND MURDER

THERE were only seconds in which to decide what to do. Seconds, which were already ticking away. If the man crouching there were armed, then as soon as Mannering's back was turned he was likely to shoot. A shot would settle the account, there would be no need to worry about a struggle or a shout of alarm.

Mannering felt as if he were in the presence of death.

The seconds were flying.

He reached the floor. He couldn't see over the top of the

desk; the man was crouching in the one corner of the room where he wasn't likely to be seen, unless Mannering first went to the desk. If he did, it was inviting a bullet. He needed time, and time was against him.

He stopped.

He took out cigarettes, and flicked his lighter. He drew on the cigarette, coughed, and then muttered, "They're magnificent. Magnificent!" He drew on the cigarette again. His mind was empty, couldn't make up his mind which was the lesser danger. There was Sylvester and the other assistant, outside, probably hurt.

Mannering realised the one hope, and jumped from a standing start.

He reached the desk, saw the snout of a gun poking round the corner, thrust both hands against the desk and heaved. It tipped up on one end. The gun dropped lower. Flame spurted, a bullet roared out and shaved the carpet and smacked into a filing-cabinet. Mannering heaved desperately as he felt the end of the desk against the crouching man, who tried to brace himself to prevent the desk from turning over on to him. The gun still showed. Mannering saw the man's fingers. He heaved until the desk fell on to the man. The man squealed in agony and the gun fell free.

Mannering stooped down, clutched it, and snatched it up, then backed away. He was carried so fast by the momentum of his own movement that he fetched up heavily against the wall behind him and banged the back of his head on a bookshelf. His ears rang, tears started to his eyes, the picture of the crouching man and the desk, askew, was badly blurred. He thrust the gun forward, knew that he was holding it tightly.

"Keep still!" he shouted; but even his voice was betraying him, a thin sound came out. "Don't—move!"

The man was moving.

No, it was that blurred vision, he only seemed to be moving. Actually he was trapped, and staring up into Mannering's eyes. He had a scarf round his face, but it had slipped, and he didn't wear a hat. He had nut-brown, curly hair. His face looked deeply tanned, and he was good-looking in a boyish way. Now, he was terrified. His mouth was open, but he seemed to be breathing through distended nostrils.

Mannering's vision steadied.

The man was at his mercy; and the door was closed. The shot would have been heard in the shop, but no one came. The only sound was of his own and the other man's breathing. Mannering felt cold sweat on his forehead, and sweat at his back and his neck. He moved forward, and pushed the desk off.

"Get—up," Mannering said.

The man muttered, "I can't." The words were only just audible from behind the mask.

"Get up!"

"I—I can't. My back——" The man closed his eyes, and seemed to wince. "The desk must have squashed me."

Mannering said, "All right, crawl across the floor, go to the other side of the desk."

"I——"

"Get a move on!"

The man began to crawl, using only his arms and one leg. It was oddly, pathetically like a wounded crab. In two minutes, he hadn't moved more than a few inches, and sweat was gathering like raindrops on his forehead.

"All right, stop it," Mannering growled.

The man flopped down, arms by his side and head lowered. He made funny little groaning sounds. Mannering measured the distance between the outstretched man and the door, and moved slowly towards the door, but he was already convinced that there was nothing to fear from this man.

Was there another, outside?

If so, would the door have been closed?

Mannering shut the strong-room, set the electric and the ray controls, then went to the outer door. The man wasn't even looking up, there was no danger that he would attack. Mannering stood to one side, gun in hand, and opened the door a fraction. He saw no one outside; nothing but part of the dimly lit shop, old furniture, and close at hand, a lovely little Dutch panel of a river-side scene with magnificent colours.

He opened the door wider.

He caught his breath sharply.

Sylvester lay on the floor, half-way towards the front of the shop, but hidden from the street by an old settle. His head was towards Mannering, and the silvery hair bathed in ominous red.

There was a muttering sound.

A woman was saying, "Isn't it beautiful, dear."

That was the loud-speaker, which told the people inside the shop what was being said outside; and being planned. No shop in the world was better protected against such a raid as this, but a man had broken in, and Sylvester lay there like a corpse.

Mannering turned to look at the injured man.

He hadn't moved.

Mannering opened the door wider and stepped cautiously into the shop, but he saw no one else. He went to the door leading to the stairs, closed and locket it. Then he hurried to Sylvester; knelt by his side, and saw the bloody mess that had been made of Sylvester's head. He dared not move him. He saw blood pulsing out at one spot, found the artery and pressed with his thumb; the flow stopped.

Mannering looked up at the window. Two men and a young boy were looking at the single coronet on the purple velvet.

Mannering beckoned.

They didn't see him.

He shouted, and they did not hear him, but moved on. Mannering left Sylvester, grabbed the telephone and drew it near, dialled 999, then pressed the artery again.

The brisk voice of a man at Scotland Yard came quickly.

· · · · ·

A patrol car arrived first; then a Squad car; then an ambulance with a doctor. Mannering, sitting at Sylvester's desk, could see everything—in the office and in the shop. Police were walking about overhead, but had anyone else been hiding in the premises, they would have called out by now. Trevor, the junior assistant, had been out—sent on an errand by Sylvester. He came back, horrified when he learned what had happened.

Sylvester was taken out on a stretcher. A doctor was muttering gloomily. Mannering, pulling at a cigarette, was trying to get his mind off the sight of Sylvester's battered head. He did not think that the old man had much chance of survival.

A police sergeant said, "And what time was this, sir?"

"About twenty to one." Mannering stirred himself, then saw the door open and Fenn come striding in, with Grimble just behind him.

Fenn was in a hurry, and his lean body was so convex that he seemed to be leaning forward. He stopped by Mannering.

"You all right?"

"Yes—thanks."

"Suffering from a bit of shock," the doctor said. Mannering hadn't realised that he had come out of the office, away from the injured intruder. "He ought to be used to it by now."

"Sure you're not hurt?" Fenn insisted.

Mannering said, "I'm all right. Just feeling murderous." He stood up. It wasn't the forced entry; it wasn't the shock of seeing the man; it wasn't reaction after the swift burst of action: it was the sight of Sylvester's head, a sight he would remember all his life.

"I'm told you caught the man," Fenn said.

"In here," said the doctor, a chubby middle-aged man. "There's something badly wrong with his back. I've given him a shot of morphia. Sorry." He knew that Fenn would have liked to question the man first; but wouldn't have a chance now. "Mannering threw the desk at him."

"*What?*"

Mannering moved towards the office.

"I tipped it up," he said. "He was crouching behind it. After the eggs, I suppose." He moistened his lips, and then opened a corner cupboard and took out a bottle of whisky and two glasses. "Join me?"

"Let me pour that," Fenn said.

"I'm still on the active list."

"Please yourself, but not for me," Fenn said briskly. He brushed his sparse dark hair back from his forehead. "You understand I have to have a look round, Mannering?"

"Of course."

"Better close the shop, hadn't you?"

"Yes," agreed Mannering. "Yes." Wainwright was out on his eager business, and Larraby on holiday, so three men were not available. Available! "In your hands now," he said, "you're supposed to be watching it. I thought you had someone here."

"We had by night."

"Thieves walk by day."

Fenn said, "All right, I can guess how you feel. Like to go home? Or——"

"I'll stay."

"Thanks."

"You won't find stolen goods here," Mannering said, very carefully.

"I don't expect to."

"Kind of you. Found Brash?"

"No," said Fenn, and gave him a sharp, almost hostile look. "We have not found Brash. It's a good job for you that *he* isn't Brash."

The prisoner, who lay unconscious but with his lips twisted as if he were still in pain, was not at all like Brash. He was well dressed, and wore a gold signet ring on his right hand. His brown shoes were highly polished; that high polish had given him away. It looked certain that he had come here alone, that he had attacked Sylvester savagely, and would have attacked Mannering with the same brutal ruthlessness.

He looked young, wholesome, pathetic.

. . . . .

An hour later, Fenn said, "That's about everything we need worry about here, I think. I wish the doctor hadn't been so quick with his morphia." He looked broodingly at Mannering, who, feeling much more himself, was sitting at his desk. "You're a pretty powerful man," he said.

"Am I?"

Fenn said, "Look." He stood up, went to the desk, placed both hands on the edge, and tipped it up. He lifted it two or three inches off the floor, and obviously it was a great effort. He let it down slowly, and grunted; even then, it fell the last inch with a thump. "See what I mean?"

"You weren't expecting every minute to be your last."

"Strength of desperation?" Fenn said almost musingly, then added sharply, almost with that angry note of hostility: "You weren't feeling desperate last night at Dragon's End, were you?"

Mannering just looked at him.

Fenn was certainly reminding himself that only a person with great strength in his arms and shoulders could have thrown that spear; and Mannering must have great strength, or he could not have hoisted the desk up and let it fall on the back of the man who had broken in. He could understand Fenn's trend of thought, couldn't blame him, wouldn't blame him if he started looking for a motive.

"The second time you went to Dragon's End you were on your own, weren't you?" Fenn asked.

"Yes. No witnesses," Mannering said, dryly. "No motive, either. If you've got me as Suspect Number One, why not see what Bristow said in his little black book."

Fenn didn't smile.

"I'll reach my own conclusions," he said, aloofly. "Two of my men will be on duty in the street and one at the back, until further notice. Ever seen the assailant before?"

"No."

"All right," Fenn said, and seemed to relax. "If I were you, I'd go home and take it easy."

"Thanks," Mannering said. "What do you know?"

"About what?"

"Smith——"

"He's still unconscious," Fenn said. "I've been down to Midham, and had a look round. The nest-egg belongs to the girl all right—I've seen the receipted invoice. Her father bought it fifteen years ago, in Bangkok. It's fully insured, too."

"Something," Mannering said. "Found out where Pendexter went, yet?"

Fenn said, "No. We will."

He left soon afterwards, and the police went out, all their photographs and their measuring all their notes and all their searching done. The shop seemed empty; desolate. Mannering stood up from the desk, and moved into the shop itself. There was no silvery-haired man, and no eager yet punctilious youngsters ready to come and find whether he wanted them. He went upstairs. Here was the room where Miranda Smith had waited, where he had seen the terror which had come to her about the disappearance of Pendexter Smith. What had Smith done that day? Why had he not come back? How had he returned to Dragon's End, and how had he been drugged?

Mannering went downstairs.

He was at the door of the office when the telephone bell began to ring; and it went on, sharply persistent, with the note of imperiousness which was quite detached from anything else. Mannering didn't want to talk to anyone about business, but he lifted the instrument.

"Mannering, of Quinns."

There was no answer.

"Who's there?" Mannering asked sharply, and then a girl operator broke in:

"Just a moment, please. You're through, caller. Press Button A please."

Mannering heard the hollow note of the pennies dropping. He waited, less antagonistic to the caller; who would call Quinns from a call box?

"That Mr. Mann'ring?" a man demanded. His voice was rough, hoarse, and low-pitched, the words only just reached Mannering. "John Mann'ring?"

"Yes, who——"

"I'm Dibben, the chap you let orf last night," the man muttered urgently. "Listen, look aht for yourself, they're arter you. They mean to kill, see? Don't——"

"Who means to kill me?" Mannering asked, trying desperately not to shout. "Hold on, Dibben, I'll make it it worth your while if——"

But Dibben rang off.

His hoarse voice echoed in Mannering's ear.

"Look aht for yourself, they're arter you. They mean to kill, see?"

16

WHY MURDER MANNERING?

MANNERING went out in the heat of the afternoon. A middle-aged man limped past him, carrying his jacket, collar and tie loose, braces taut. A few people stood and looked across as if they expected further sensations. Two Yard men, including the comfortable-looking Grimble, now dressed in brown serge and almost hot enough to collapse, were in Hart Row. Grimble nodded. Mannering went along to his car, got in, lit a cigarette, and waited.

It was twenty minutes since Dibben had telephoned.

Mannering had just heard from the hospital; Sylvester was dead.

That was the harsh, cruel fact. The man who had served him loyally for years, gentle, patient, courteous, friendly to everyone, had been brutally attacked and murdered; and he had been protecting him, Mannering; protecting Quinns.

He hadn't even been able to sound the alarm.

Beneath Sylvester's desk had been a bell-push; once touched with the foot it would have sounded the alarm up and down Hart Row, upstairs in Quinns, down in the strong-room.

Mannering switched on the ignition, pressed the self-starter, and moved off towards Hart Row. Why should "they", why should anyone, want to kill him? Dibben had told what he believed to be the truth. Honour among thieves showed in expected guises and came from unlikely places; and he had used the right tactics with Dibben.

But why should anyone want to kill him?

He drove off, slowly until he was in the stream of traffic in Bond Street. He headed for Piccadilly and then New Scotland Yard. He watched the driving-mirror closely, but as far as he could judge wasn't followed. His mind wouldn't stop posing the question: Why did they want to kill him?

* * *

Fenn was in his office, just after five o'clock; in his shirt-sleeves, his tie loose, forehead and upper lip sticky with sweat. It was much hotter than it had been at midday, but the sun was behind a mass of almost black clouds. The cloud would open and the downpour come at any moment. Thunder rumbled some way off.

The telephone bell rang; it never seemed to stop.

"Fenn speaking."

"Grimble here, sir," came a deep voice. "Mannering left about an hour ago. No one has been to the shop, except a couple of customers who rang the bell once and then went off. I've their descriptions and all that, sir."

"Good. How'd Mannering look?"

"Like plain ruddy murder," Grimble said. "I wouldn't like to get in his way just now."

"Know him well?"

"Fairly well, sir."

"Trust him?"

"Trust Mr. Mannering?" Grimble sounded astonished. "Well, I would and I wouldn't. He's honest, sir, if that's what you mean, I'd trust him with my last penny or my young daughter, day *or* night, but he isn't above putting one across us. If he thought——"

"Go on," Fenn urged, when Grimble stopped.

"Don't know that I'm justified in saying that, really, sir," said Grimble cautiously, "but if he thought he could lay his hands on the brutes behind Sylvester's murder, I think he'd kill them himself. It's a funny thing with Mannering, once you're one of the family, so to speak, you're there for keeps. Anyone who works for Mannering is damned lucky, if you ask me."

"Except Sylvester."

Grimble paused, and then said slowly, "That's different, sir, isn't it? I don't mean that way."

"I know what you mean," Fenn said. "Thanks."

He rang off, and looked at the photograph of a Yard XI in white flannels, with absent Superintendent Bristow well to the fore. Bristow wouldn't have needed to ask Grimble that, but knowing Mannering too well had its disadvantages as well. The Mannering whom Fenn had seen at Quinns had been first dazed and then deadly; and Grimble confirmed that opinion.

Fenn studied reports which had come from Midham, and a dossier, already very thick, on Bill Brash. One thing had been discovered about Brash: he was a close associate of Crummy Day, a pawnbroker with an "iffish" reputation.

Brash's finger-prints were on the spear which had killed Revell. That was something that Mannering didn't know.

Fenn got up and hurried out and downstairs to the waiting-rooms. He thrust open the door of one, and Mannering looked up from an armchair in a corner.

"Sorry, Mannering," Fenn said, as if he really meant it. "The A.C. held me up, and then there were two or three jobs I couldn't avoid. Now I've all the time you want. Cigarette?"

Mannering took one. "Thanks."

"Care for a drink?"

"No, thanks," Mannering said. It was cooler in the waiting-room, which had one small window, but still too warm for comfort. Mannering looked grey about the cheeks; and still very bleak. "I'm taking a chance on you," he said, "and I hope you're going to justify it. The man I let go last night is named Dibben."

"Changed your mind, have you?" Fenn looked pleased.

"No. He telephoned me to say that I was on the spot—in line for murder. He didn't say why, just warned me, and hung up. There couldn't be any purpose in that, unless it were true."

Fenn looked his disagreement. "None?"

"What do you think?"

"If he'd wanted to put the wind up you——"

"That would make him an actor who could put himself over perfectly," Mannering said. "I've ruled that one out. I'd like to find out who he works for, what he's doing, and what contacts he has, and I can't do it myself. Will you—without pulling him in on the Dragon's End job?"

Fenn said, "Listen, Mannering, there was a murder down there. Remember."

Mannering looked at him levelly.

"I don't forget murder," he said. "I don't forget anyone's murder. All right, he could have done it. You'll know his name, directly you get any other evidence you can pull him in. I'm not asking you to do less than your duty." That was almost a sneer.

Fenn said, "I'll let him ride, Mannering. Dibben, eh?" He took out a pencil and a small note-book.

"M. Dibben, 17 Penn Street, Whitechapel," Mannering said.

"Thanks. Anything else?"

"Not yet," Mannering said.

Fenn closed his note-book, put his pencil away, and stood upright—ramrod straight, for once not looking convex. He smiled faintly, but his expression and his voice were serious.

"If I were you, John," he said, "I'd go home and take it easy. Talk this over with your wife. Sit back, and leave the rest of the job to us. You didn't get much sleep last night, you've had a strenuous day and bad shock. You might do something you'll regret if you don't give yourself a rest."

There was a pause; then Mannering gave a taut smile.

"Thanks," he said. "I appreciate that. If I don't do it, you can't blame yourself."

"Taken by and large, I'd rather see you alive than dead," Fenn said. "And I don't like this threat to you."

"Suspicion all over?" Mannering demanded. "I'm not any weaker physically, and still have a strong right arm."

Fenn just grinned.

On his way downstairs, into an early evening which was eerie because of a great dark cloud casting a pall over the centre of London, as if sulphurous smoke were pouring down from some turbulent volcano in the skies, Mannering thought of the way he'd started. "If I were you, John." A friendly gesture, and Fenn didn't make gestures, didn't do anything, without a purpose.

Mannering drove out into the Embankment, and was on the far side of Parliament Square, which was choked full with home-bound traffic, when the deluge came. A few huge spots of rain struck the cars, the huge red buses, the teeming pavements; and then suddenly the rain fell, as it does in the tropics, with a roar which scared a lot of people who had never heard its like before. It smashed upon London in a torrential stream. Cars, their drivers suddenly blinded, banged bumper to bumper. A dozen skidded. The pavements were suddenly emptied as everyone on foot rushed for cover. The thronged square and the long width of Victoria Street were as deserted as they would be at midnight; every shop doorway was tightly jammed with people; pale faces were turned up towards the lowering yellow sky, in awed amazement.

Mannering was jammed in.

The rain came down for ten minutes in one solid wall; and although traffic began to move again afterwards, it was only at a crawl. Cars were parked on either side of the road, with drivers who hadn't the nerve to go on. The hold-up gave Mannering time to think again, and he didn't want to think.

He had to tell Lorna about Sylvester.

WHY MURDER MANNERING? 127

She had known him for a long time, he was part of Quinns. She had been worried before, now——

She needn't know about Dibben's warning.

The rain was slackening, and the sun began to shine behind the clouds. The light was strange, almost yellow ochre in places, becoming a brighter yellow. It reflected off the glistening pavements, the streaming road, the roofs of the cars and the scarlet buses. Mannering got into a stream of traffic which was moving fairly fast.

Was Fenn right? Did they want to kill him for something which had happened at Dragon's End the night before? Something he had seen—or noticed—yet the significance of which he had not understood? Something in one of the grotesque carved figures, perhaps; or in one of the stuffed animals, perhaps even at the floorboards.

There was the other angle, the one at which Fenn had jumped immediately: that Dibben was simply working on his nerves. He didn't believe it. The man had been almost insolent at first, but it had been an insolence covering fear: he had begged for a chance, been given it, and—tried to make amends. One to Dibben.

Did his warning to Mannering put Dibben himself in danger?

Would Fenn keep his word?

The traffic thinned out, the rain stopped. Water was rushing down the guttering of houses and shops and pouring like miniature torrents down the kerbs. Great pools of water collected by the drains, twice Mannering had to drive through one. Children were already playing at the sides of the roads, dipping sticks in muddy puddles, trailing pieces of wood and paper boats, paddling.

He reached Green Street.

Only the Yard man was in sight, in a doorway opposite. Everything seemed normal. Lorna would be back by now, and Miranda with her; he could think of Miranda's glorious eyes and her pristine beauty, it could drive away the dark and ugly thoughts.

Lorna had to be told, remember.

He got out of the car, slammed the door, glanced up at the window. No one was in sight. Perhaps they weren't back yet.

He heard a sound, glass smashed, someone was shouting: the words became intelligible.

"John, John, John!"

That was Lorna, her voice strident with fear and with warning.

"John, John, John!" she screamed.

He ducked back from the doorway as he heard a vicious humming, then the thud of a bullet in the front door. He dropped to the wet ground and squirmed backwards into the cover of the car. Lorna had stopped shouting, but her cries and the roar of the shot were still in his ears.

He squinted through the window of the car, and from the crouching position saw the face of a man at the window of a house opposite; the first-floor window. He didn't recognise him, but saw the gun in the man's hand, levelled and waiting until he showed himself.

But the Yard man was on the move, his whistle shrilling out, and he came running into the road. Mannering didn't see but heard him, and shouted:

"Get back, get back!"

The Yard man came on, the gun barked, the man staggered. As Mannering caught sight of him, he did a funny little pirouette, and collapsed.

17

FLOOD

Mannering heard a splash which told him that the Yard man had fallen into the puddle near the car. Mannering edged towards the front of it. He heard the man grunting. There was no other shooting; apart from the Yard man's gasping breath and the traffic at the far end of the street, there was no sound at all.

Then footsteps clattered, the street door opened, Mannering glanced round and saw Lorna.

"Go back!" he cried, "go back!"

She ignored him and came running; but there was no more shooting. Breathless, she reached him, and he felt the tension of her body and the cold steel of a gun which she thrust into his hand.

"He's left the window," she gasped, and paused for breath. "He might go out the back way, but——"

Mannering was watching the door of the house where the man had been; where he was. It began to open. He rose, stealthily, his right hand holding the gun, his left on Lorna's arm, keeping her down. He looked over the rain-splashed bonnet, and saw the door opening wider; a hand appeared. Traffic swished by at the end of the street, but nothing turned into the street itself.

"Darling, be—careful." Lorna spoke jerkily.

"*Quiet.*"

The Yard man still lay in the pool of water, making no sound now. Was he dead? Unconscious? Mannering caught a glimpse of him lying on his side; at least he wasn't going to drown.

"Mind!" cried Lorna.

The door of the house opposite opened wide, a man leapt

into sight, short, stocky, dressed in light brown. His gun was pointed towards the car. Mannering took one shot, then ducked as the man emptied his gun at the Rolls-Bentley. A bullet smacked against the bonnet just above Mannering's head and richocheted off; Mannering felt it stir his hair.

"Oh, keep down!" Lorna cried, and held him tightly.

The man raced into the street, turned right towards the Embankment, and ran wildly. Mannering shook Lorna off, and stood up. The man was a moving target but within range; Mannering aimed for his legs.

Then he heard a scream.

He knew, in that instance, who it came from. It was strange, high-pitched, eerie, startling. The running man, traffic along the Embankment, everything else vanished from sight as he turned his head.

Miranda stood in the doorway of the house, mouth wide open, eyes filled with awful terror; *screaming*.

. . . . .

The moment passed. Mannering, teeth clamped tightly together, swung round towards the running gunman, who was close to the corner, nearly out of range.

"Look after her," Mannering rasped. "Phone 999, and see to that chap." The Yard man lay quite still, and Lorna didn't move, but turned and looked at Miranda as if the scream had paralysed her.

Miranda screamed again.

Half-prepared for it as he was, Mannering still felt its effect. It went through him like the screaming whine of a bandsaw scraping against metal. He clenched his teeth again as he pulled open the door of the car and slid into the driving-seat.

The gunman had turned the corner.

Mannering started the engine, swung the wheel, swished through water a yard from the feet of the unconscious Yard man. In his driving-mirror he saw a taxi turn into Green

Street from the King's Road end; possible help for Lorna. He put his foot down, and the car leapt forward. Then almost in front of him the surface of the road broke, a gush of seething, muddy yellow water leapt two yards into the air. He jammed on the brakes, then gradually swung the wheel. The force of the water caught the side of the car, and the wheel was almost wrenched out of his hands. He held on, tyres squealing against the kerb. The car quivered, and slithered to a standstill. Just behind him, the water gushed like a huge, tumultuous fountain; it was already running axle-deep beneath the car, flooding the kerb and the pavement, and coming half-way up the car's wheels.

As it gushed and rushed past, Mannering knew that he no longer had a chance to catch up with the man. Trying would be a waste of time. He turned and looked back. The gush was coming out of a burst main more slowly now, just a tumbling hillock of turbulence, but water several inches deep stretched right across the road.

The taxi had stopped, with water up to its running board.

The driver and young Wainwright were lifting the Yard man from the water. Lorna stood in the doorway, an arm round Miranda, but Mannering couldn't see Miranda properly. For the first time, he felt a spasm of irritation with her; but for that scream he would have brought the gunman down.

He got out and hurried across the road, wading ankle deep.

"You managing?"

"Okay," said the cabbie, a short middle-aged man wearing a brand-new trilby hat, startling on top of a head of untidy grey hair and above a face badly in need of a shave. "We'll take him in."

Mannering turned towards the house. Lorna couldn't do anything because Miranda was clinging to her, the tension of her slim young body was evident, and Lorna just couldn't get free. Miranda was crying, her shoulders quaking, odd little whining sounds were coming from her lips.

She had *screamed*.

It was the first sound Mannering had heard her utter, yet his first swift reaction had been resentment, not far removed from anger. He didn't think much of himself for that. He squeezed Lorna's arm as he went past. No one was in at the ground-floor flat, and he ran up the stairs, finding Ethel and a neighbour at the open door of the flat on the first floor.

"Is—is everything all right, sir?" She was trembling.

"Not too bad, Ethel. Mrs. Harington"—the neighbour was a friendly fifty or so—"a man has been hurt, and they may want to bring him into your flat."

"Oh, *dear*," Mrs. Harington exclaimed. "I'd better turn down a bed. May Ethel lend me a hand?"

"Of course." Mannering was already half-way up the stairs to his flat.

He dialled 999, reported briskly, and then called Fenn; Fenn wasn't in. Mannering moved away from the telephone. The sun was shining a long way off, but immediately overhead was a dark cloud which looked as if it were going to drench the district again. A few big drops of rain fell. There was a strange yellow tinge in the sky, on the surface of the Thames, on the moving traffic, the roofs, the roads; everything. The centre of the storm was moving sluggishly northwards.

He felt a little easier, without knowing why.

He hoped that policeman wouldn't die.

He kept seeing a mind picture of the assassin.

· · · · ·

Mannering went into the bedroom, and closed the door. Lorna was sitting at the dressing-table; when he had come in she had been looking at herself intently, and without any satisfaction. Now, she turned sharply to face him. The swiftness of her movement betrayed her tension; even though she relaxed into a smile, evidence of nervous strain was still there.

It was nearly half-past eight; and the first time they had been alone since the shooting in Green Street.

The police had come, an ambulance had followed, but the Yard man hadn't been badly hurt. That was his good luck; a bullet had grazed his temple, and the wound had bled freely. He had been taken to hospital but not detained.

There had been the usual stream of questions, the routine, the deliberate hand-written notes in thick note-books, all this at an exasperatingly slow tempo.

Then Grimble had arrived and quickened things a little. But there hadn't been much that Mannering could tell him, except to describe the man who had fired the shot.

Miranda had been the big problem.

The shooting seemed to have done something to her which nothing else had succeeded in doing. Except for the screams, she had uttered no intelligible sound, but—she *had* screamed; some release of terror had made her find her voice.

Richardson, whom Lorna told by telephone, was non-committal, said that he was going to discuss the case with Lancelot Nash, and promised to report as soon as he could.

·   ·   ·   ·   ·

Wainwright had helped the police, then reported to Mannering; and although it was obvious that his mind was really on Miranda, he hadn't skimped the reports of his inquiries. It was quite simple; seven different contacts, most of them friends and trusties of the absent Larraby, had warned him not to have anything at all to do with Crummy Day, of Aldgate High Street.

"Of course, I couldn't tie any of them down to a specific reason, sir," Wainwright had said, "but they just didn't trust him. Two or three just laughed at the thought of you having anything to do with him. Simply *laughed*."

"Then we won't have any truck with him," Mannering had said, with outward solemnity.

Wainwright had grinned.

"And while I was in the East End I made a few inquiries about that man Dibben," he went on. "He has a shocking reputation. He's a—ah—mobsman, of course, and has quite a reputation for forcing locks. It's common rumour that he works for Crummy Day. And Day uses a lot of young chaps to lift—steal, sorry, sir—for him. He buys the stuff. I'm told Day's reputation is bad even among crooks," went on Wainwright, with great precision. "No one trusts him."

"Did you see Dibben?"

"No, but I met his wife."

"What's she like?"

"As a matter of fact," said Wainwright, with great candour, "she is quite a nice little thing, pretty and really quite smart. She wouldn't say anything about Dibben, but obviously she was worried about him. He's been away for several days. It's common talk among his friends that he's 'working'."

"You managed to get around," Mannering had remarked.

"As a matter of fact, I met a friend of Josh Larraby's, right at the beginning," Wainwright had said. "He has a little trinket shop in Chenn Street. He recognised me, and—well, I had a kind of open sesame to all Larraby's friends. He has an astonishing number, all knowledgeable," Wainwright had gone on, "in his way he's quite a genius."

Larraby was now the manager of Quinns; had at one time been Mannering's contact man in the East End and, before that, been in prison for four years for jewel robbery. Wainwright didn't know that, and Mannering didn't enlighten him.

But Larraby was getting old, Wainwright apparently saw his chance of getting well in the line of succession. And now that Sylvester had gone . . .

   .   .   .   .   .   .

Mannering went across to Lorna, put his hands on her shoulders, and looked at her and his own reflection in the dressing-table mirror. She hadn't been satisfied, but he saw no reason to complain. They looked at each other steadily, Mannering quiet and sombre, Lorna pale and still tense.

He told her about Sylvester.

He could see the little colour she had left ebbing from her cheeks. She didn't speak. In a lot of ways he wished she would.

He didn't tell her about Dibben's message, but that was poor consolation, because she knew that a man had been lying in wait for him.

He said, "It won't last much longer. If Miranda could tell all she knows, she might be able to put an end to it in a matter of hours." He squeezed Lorna's shoulders, then moved away, sitting on a window-seat, lighting a cigarette. "No, don't move." He could see her profile in the mirror while her face was turned towards him. He didn't smile.

"There was one thing Richardson said that I didn't tell you," Lorna said. "Miranda's trouble was caused by a shock, and another shock might cure her. Also——" Lorna paused.

"Yes," said Mannering, softly.

"A shock big enough to cure her might also kill her, or else turn her mind for the rest of her life," said Lorna with great precision.

Mannering said, "I see." He moved restlessly, frowning. "What actually made Miranda scream?"

"I think it was your gun."

Mannering didn't speak.

"She'd screamed before, upstairs," Lorna said. "It was the scream that made me go to the window. She was looking out, and I heard this sound, it was—well, uncanny's hardly the word. It really scared me. Then I ran to the window. She was looking at the man across the road, and he had a gun, pointing it at you. I think——"

She broke off, jumped up, spun round.

Mannering was off his seat and streaking towards the door in a split second.

For Miranda screamed again.

18

A CAUSE OF FEAR

As Mannering reached the hall, the awful screaming stopped. The door of the drawing-room was ajar, and Mannering saw Wainwright, who had been in there with Miranda, with his back to the door. Mannering ran in. Miranda was sitting in an easy-chair, her face buried in her hands, sobs wracking her body, but hardly a sound coming from her lips.

Wainwright turned a pale face towards Mannering.

"What happened?"

"I——"

"What on earth *happened*?" Lorna came hurrying in, turned on Wainwright, and was flushed and angry. "What did you do to her?"

"But—but I didn't do a thing," Wainwright protested. "On my word I didn't, Mrs. Mannering. She looked much better. I'd tried to keep up a kind of conversation with her, and fact—in fact I think I made her smile. Then I needed to use a handkerchief, and I pulled it out of my pocket. Thi—*this* fell out."

"This" was on the floor; an old-fashioned automatic pistol, nearly black, a relic of the First World War.

"And that scared her?" asked Mannering softly.

"Well, I can't think of anything else. Until that moment I thought everything was going along so nicely. She was much more relaxed."

Mannering picked the gun up. The girl wasn't looking.

"Where did you get it?"

Wainwright coloured almost as furiously as ever Brash could do.

"Well, one of the fellows I saw this afternoon sold it to me. He said that if I were going after Crummy Day I'd probably need it. I knew that Larraby sometimes carries a gun, and there was that armed man last night. The whole ruddy business is violent, anyhow!" he snapped, suddenly defiant in his determination, "I thought it would be wise to have some kind of protection. If you don't agree——"

"I think I do agree," said Mannering, mildly.

Wainwright said weakly, "Oh."

Mannering looked at Miranda's bowed head. She was much quieter, and Lorna had moved away from her.

"But you'll need a licence," Mannering went on. "I don't think there'll be much trouble about that." He looked straight into Wainwright's eyes. "Quinns was raided this afternoon. Sylvester was killed."

Wainwright didn't seem to understand. He just stared bleakly. Then his expression began to change, he actually backed away until he touched the arm of a chair; and he looked as if his legs would fold beneath him.

"The old boy—*killed*?"

"Yes."

There was a long pause.

"So that's the way they work," Wainwright said slowly. "Kill an old man. What about Trevor? You always insist that at least two should be at the shop. Don't say that Trev——"

"Sylvester had sent him out, as I was downstairs in the strong-room."

"Oh, God," groaned Wainwright. He clenched his fists, and then burst out, "Look here, Mr. Mannering, when are we going to get at them? I'll work night and day if only we can see them hanged for that!"

"We'll get at them soon," Mannering promised sombrely. "But you're not working tonight, Ned. You had only a couple of hours' sleep last night, you'll be a wreck and easy meat if you don't catch up on rest. If I need anything urgently, I'll call you."

"Promise?" Wainwright was so like a boy.

"Yes."

"Well, all right," Wainwright conceded. He looked at Miranda's bowed head, as if there were something she did not want to see; or was afraid to open her eyes for fear of what might be close to her. "Good night, Mrs. Mannering. We—we'll get through."

He went out.

His last glance was at Miranda.

His last words brought the first smile to Lorna's lips since Mannering had come home. That smile brought a sudden peace to the Mannerings, for no good reason they felt better.

Men were in Green Street and at the back of the house now, and there was little risk of another attack here; so little, that Mannering did not even allow himself to think about it.

"If only you knew why they wanted to kill you," Lorna said.

"That's only one of the questions I'd like answered," agreed Mannering. "Why does the sight of a gun scare Miranda like that?"

Before Lorna could speak, Ethel tapped.

"Yes, Ethel?" Lorna called.

"Dinner's ready, ma'am, I don't know whether you know."

Again Lorna smiled in spite of herself.

"Bless you, Ethel! Yes, we're coming." She stood up slowly, turned to Mannering, took his hands and gripped them tightly. "Get it over, John, don't let it drag on," she begged. "I hate every minute of it."

"It won't be long now," said Mannering.

But a question haunted him.

What had he seen or what did he know that made the killers want him dead?

. . . . .

Fenn said to Mannering, "No, I haven't much else. If it makes you happy, Brash's prints were on the assegai which killed Revell." His gaze was cold. "Pendexter Smith has come round, and says that he didn't remember anything at all after leaving your shop. That might be the truth. The evidence is that he was under the morphia when Revell was murdered last night. These psychiatrists are virtually beaten by Miranda Smith, but Richardson says it's almost certainly a case of the collapse of certain nerve-centres, which a shock might correct. And a shock might also kill her." Fenn paused to let that sink in. "The man who attacked you at Quinns is conscious, but the doctors won't let me question him. You broke his back."

Mannering didn't speak.

"Freddy Bell, the man you captured here at the flat, still won't talk," went on Fenn. "If it's news—he's been inside twice. He's known to be pretty close with Crummy Day, and we had an eye on him for a murder job a few months ago. We couldn't fix it on him, but we're still trying."

"What do you know about Crummy?"

Fenn gave a quick, unexpected smile.

"Crummy Day is a pawnbroker, and probably the most successful fence in London today—and as you're so ill-informed about things like this, perhaps I ought to add that a fence is a receiver of stolen goods," Fenn said, heavily sarcastic. "Also, he is the particular pawnbroker who apparently interests a young man named Wainwright. Wainwright, of course, did all his investigating this afternoon off his own bat; he didn't tell you anything about it!"

Mannering said, "I give up."

"Who named Crummy Day?" asked Fenn. "Dibben?"

"Yes."

"I thought so. And that's one of the reasons why I came round to see you myself," Fenn said. "I don't have to take action on what you tell me, but if Grimble heard a thing like that I'd be forced to do something. What did Dibben say about Crummy?"

"That he had sent Brash to Dragon's End."

"That all?"

"That's all he admitted."

"Well, I've been after Crummy Day for a very long time," Fenn said softly, "but I've never got very close to him. He's been raided twice, when hot stuff's known to have been on the premises—he's a three-storey place at Aldgate, with the shop on the ground floor—and he got away with it. We'll find out how, one of these days." Fenn's discursiveness gave Mannering the impression that he hadn't yet got to the main point. "He's as sly as they come, too. I'm told that he'll buy from new people in the game, and pay pretty well, but once they're known to the police, he drops them."

"He didn't drop Dibben."

"Oh, Dibben's on his payroll," Fenn answered. "These other people—Freddy Bell and Middleton, the man whose back you broke, seem to be strangers. Middleton hasn't a record. I can't find a line from them to Crummy Day, and don't think it would be any use raiding Crummy's place yet. He's got this hidey-hole, always has time to get the hot stuff into it."

Quite suddenly, Mannering realised why Fenn had come and what he was getting at.

Fenn was almost bland.

"If you won't object to me making a suggestion, Mrs. Mannering, I'd like your husband to have a word with Dora Dibben."

Lorna said mildly, "Wainwright reports that she is surprisingly neat and quite pretty."

"Your young man gets around," said Fenn, as if he were surprised. "She's known to be scared of the police, but she might talk to Mr. Mannering. It's worth trying. If Crummy Day is the man behind all this——"

"You could hold him on suspicion?" suggested Lorna.

"I haven't a case that would stand up," said Fenn. He glanced at his watch. "It's getting late! I must fly." He jumped up. "No, I won't have another, thanks. Good night, Mrs. Mannering."

He was gone two minutes later.

. . . . .

In the study Lorna said, "John, how much do you think Fenn knows?"

"About what?" asked Mannering absently. Then: "He thinks it would be a good idea if I were to have a look at Crummy Day's place—break in when Crummy isn't expecting visitors. For a Scotland Yard cop——" He broke off, and chuckled. "Especially for Nicholas Fenn!"

"That's what I mean," Lorna said. "What do you think he knows? If Bristow had suggested that, you'd know it was because he was remembering the Baron. Can Fenn know about the past?"

"I don't care what Fenn knows," Mannering said thoughtfully. "I'll go and see Dora Dibben, and I think I'm going to have a look at Crummy Day's place soon, too."

Lorna said, "I don't think you should. No," she protested when Mannering was about to interrupt, "I don't simply mean what I always do. I know you've got to fight this time, but think—Fenn practically invited you to go to Crummy Day's. Supposing he wants to catch you there." She leaned forward and gripped Mannering's hands. "We could trust Bristow, but can we trust Fenn? Bristow would know you had nothing to do with the crimes, but Fenn might believe that you're involved with Day. Quinns *is* a wonderful centre for holding stolen goods. I don't think ——" She paused again, and Mannering didn't interrupt but gave her a chance to finish her case: "I don't think I trust Fenn," she went on slowly. "I think he wants you at Crummy Day's."

"So do I," said Mannering mildly. "I needn't let him catch me, though." He moved his hands until he was holding her wrists. "Don't worry so much, my sweet. If Day's the man employing the killers, we want Day. Fenn may be positive that it's Day but have nothing to use against him. The certain thing is that these swine killed Sylvester, and if they have long enough they'll get me. It isn't a job to sit on."

"Listen to me," Lorna urged. "Don't go tonight. Wait until you've had a chance to talk to Dibben's wife, and to Pendexter Smith. Especially Pendexter. If you get nothing out of them——"

She didn't finish.

. . .

It was nearly twelve o'clock next morning when Mannering passed the Horsebox, at Midham, and drove through the High Street towards Dragon's End.

He had already seen Dora Dibben. She measured up to the reports of her, but he didn't think she knew anything— except that Dibben had told her on the telephone that a man had had him where he wanted him; and let him go.

"No one's ever given him a break before," Dora had said, with a kind of defiance. "If only the police would—oh, what the hell! He's right for me, and I'm not going to let him down, see."

"That's fine," said Mannering. "Stick to it, Mrs. Dibben."

Having Dora meant that Dibben's luck wasn't all bad.

The sun was shining, the great mass of Dragon's End showed red and ugly against the pale sky. An elderly woman opened the door, grumbled, went upstairs, and then returned and took him up to Pendexter Smith's bedroom. The old man was in bed; he looked like a mummy surrounded by white sheets and huge pillow-cases.

"Mr. Mannering, I've just seen that London policeman, Chief Inspector Fenn," Pendexter greeted, "and I can't tell you another thing, not another thing." He licked his lips, as if nervously. "I'm truly grateful for the way you're looking after Miranda, that—that was the first thing I asked about. She has plenty of money, she can afford any fees. While— while I'm like this, will you continue to help her?"

There was something oddly pathetic about Pendexter Smith; but possibly he traded on his age, his cracked voice, his pathos.

"Can't you help her more?" Mannering asked sharply.

"Oh, no. A poor, frail old man like me——"

"What happened after you left my shop?" Mannering demanded abruptly.

Pendexter Smith said slowly, deliberately, "I have told the police about it, three or four times. I was walking towards the solicitor's office. It is approached through a narrow lane. I felt everything going black, and must have fainted. I don't remember *any*thing."

That was his story, and he was going to stick to it.

Mannering said, "All right, Smith, but let's have some of the truth. Why were you so anxious to sell the nest-egg?"

"I wanted to turn it into money for Miranda so that she could invest it and have an income," said Pendexter Smith promptly, "and I wanted to make sure I could trust the dealer. You've a wonderful reputation, but I preferred to rely on my own judgment of men, and I wanted to see how you would behave. Admirably," he added, hoarsely, "admirably! And for your kindness to Miranda——"

"Why don't *you* try being kind to Miranda. Just tell the truth. Why did you talk about giving her hope? What was frightening you? Something was—what was it?"

Pendexter closed his eyes, and stretched out a frail, claw-like hand for a bottle of pills on a bedside table. Fumbling he unscrewed the cap, shook a tablet out on his hand, and swallowed it.

"I must rest," he said chokily. "Must rest. I've told you everything I can."

. . . .

When he was back in Chelsea Mannering looked across at Lorna, smiled, and said lightly, "I think you get younger every day."

"Living with you makes me twice my age," Lorna said, but she was unusually relaxed for a time of strain. "Well, I can't argue any more, I know you'll have to try to raid Crummy Day's. But don't forget that Fenn may have sown the idea to make you risk your neck."

"Could be," Mannering conceded, "but I don't think so. He's well disposed to us. I telephoned him after getting back from Midham, and he told me what Pendexter had said, didn't seem to hold anything back. I think he has a peculiar idea that Bristow and the Assistant Commissioner wouldn't approve at all."

Lorna said dryly, "That you can find out things that the police can't?"

"Spare my blushes!" Mannering grinned, and added almost casually. "I'll look in on Crummy Day tonight. Dibben may have been lying, but——" He shrugged. "We'll see. Lone Wolf Mannering, the bold bad Baron——"

"Quite alone?"

"Yes."

"Wainwright would give his right hand to go."

"He can keep his right hand. I'll have no guards, no look out men, no accomplices except my wife, and her only in spirit," said Mannering, and kissed her, hugged her, felt her tension. "The last time that I went out with help I nearly came a cropper. I'll be happier making my own mistakes."

A CAUSE OF FEAR 145

Half an hour later he left the Green Street flat. He was not followed. Whatever Fenn had in mind, he certainly wasn't watching Mannering all the time. Mannering went by bus to Victoria, then by taxi to a side street not far from the station, next on foot to a little cul-de-sac where there were several lock-up garages. He kept a car there, registered under a false name, always ready for emergency use.

He kept a make-up case there, too.

He unlocked the door and stepped in, made sure that he wasn't watched, closed and locked the door and then looked about him. The garage was clean, but smelt faintly of petrol.

He seemed to change as he moved into the garage. He wasn't John Mannering any more. He had moved back over the years, into that other guise—the guise of the Baron. He was going to work alone. He was going to break into the premises of a man who was certainly bad, and might be a killer or a man who hired killers. It did not occur to him, as it did to Lorna, that he had hardly given a second thought to the risks of the raid, once he had decided to go. He took risks like this as other men gambled with money; and whenever he gambled the odds were against him.

The change in his mood, in his very character, wasn't the only change. He sat in the back of the car, with a bright light on in the roof, a mirror fastened to the back of the front seat, a make-up case on the seat by his side. He used make-up—grease-paint, eye black, cheek pads, a wig—as an expert would use them, and he was absorbed in the task of making himself up.

The last thing he did was to slip a loose plastic covering over his fine white teeth, so that they looked yellowed and ugly. Then he sat back, and examined himself in the mirror. He looked at a man ten years older, harder-faced, flabby, without a trace of good looks.

Next he changed into an old suit, padded round the waist and at the shoulders, which he kept in the back of the car.

He wound a tool-kit round his waist, too, and stuck thin adhesive tape, almost a second skin, to his fingers.

At last he was ready.

An hour after he had entered the garage he drove out at the wheel of an inconspicuous, medium-sized Austin with a specially tuned engine. It purred sweetly through the almost empty streets, crossed Parliament Square and Westminster Bridge, then headed towards the City and the East End.

It was a little before midnight when the Baron reached Aldgate station. He turned towards the right and, in a square near Aldgate Pump, parked the car with several others, then walked briskly towards the High Street. Few people were about, although it was busier than the City or the West End at this late hour.

Mannering walked past a pawnbroker's shop, which bore the legend:

C. R. Day
Jewels Bought and Sold
Securities Taken

The shop itself was in darkness, but there was a light in a window on the floor above.

Mannering passed the shop again on the other side of the road. No one seemed to be watching. He felt sure that he would have been able to tell if any police were there; but the only policeman was one in uniform, up by the station, talking to a man in plain clothes.

Mannering turned down a narrow side street, and found the approach to the back of Crummy Day's premises.

No one was in sight.

Mannering still had a chance to back out; there was no compulsion, but there was a powerful driving force which he couldn't resist.

Unless Crummy Day's place was different from most

others, getting in would be simple; getting out would be the trouble.

Did the answer to the vital question—why was he being attacked?—lay inside, with the answer to Pendexter Smith's reason for bringing the nest-egg and Miranda? Would he find the answer to Miranda's deafness and her pathetic agony of mind?

Fenn thought so.

Well, Fenn had pretended to think so.

Mannering moved out of the narrow side street towards the little area at the back of Crummy Day's. By now he felt excitement burning through him like an electric current. The excitement came fiercely and almost uncontrollably; it had fed the Baron in the past, it was the force that drove him now.

19

AT CRUMMY DAY'S

THE Baron stepped into the kitchen at the back of the pawnbroker's shop.

The only sound came from the High Street—faint, echoing noises of traffic, footsteps, and passing cars and buses. An aeroplane, its lights showing, droned overhead when he turned to close the window. The only light came from the stars and from a house, a few doors away; and that made a dim glow.

There was no blind; no curtains.

He moved to the back door, and examined it carefully in the light of his torch. There was a burgler-alarm cable, delicately adjusted, as there had been at the window. He had moved that carefully, nerves on edge, until he had been able to climb in without jolting it. He still listened, trying to make sure that it hadn't been touched, that no one was lying in wait.

He studied the alarm-cable fastenings carefully, then prised the staples out with a claw tool, laid the cable down gently and double-folded it alongside the wall. Next he went to the door. The bottom of the door cleared the insulated wire by a fraction of an inch.

He unlocked the door, then drew the bolts.

The pawnbroker obviously relied on his burglar-alarm system, the lock and the bolts were old-fashioned, had probably been there when the premises had been built, eighty-odd years ago.

Mannering closed the door, but could open it at a touch; a means of escape was ready. He didn't leave the kitchen at first, but waited in a corner, looking intently through the window. No one approached. If anyone had seen him and had waited to lull him into a false sense of security, they would have come by now.

If the police had been watching——

Surely this was the one time when he need not worry about the police.

There was doubt about Fenn; he felt it, Lorna felt it. He wished he hadn't thought of Lorna then. Lorna came between him as the Baron and as Mannering, made him too human, weakened his resolve. His nerve had been steady until that moment; now it began to quiver.

He moved; and movement helped.

The kitchen led into a passage; on the right was a room with a window overlooking a narrow alley and the yard he'd come through. A storeroom; a junk room, if it came to that. He could smell the fusty junk, could make out the shapes of cardboard cartons, show-cases, pictures. This was part of the stock-in-trade that Crummy Day used to make it look as if he ran just a genuine business.

Next to this was the shop.

The door leading to it from the passage was heavily bolted; Mannering didn't think that was to stop anyone from getting into the shop, but to prevent them from getting out if they broke into the shop from the street. He went to the front door, at the side of the shop, shone his torch on it, and whistled softly.

The burglar alarm here was cleverly fitted, and the lock was intricate and strong; few men would be able to force it.

The Baron turned to the staircase—and had his first shock.

The staircase had been walled off at landing level, and at the head of the stairs was another door, as strongly protected as the street door. This explained why the back entrance had been easy to force; and told its own story. Crummy Day kept his valuables behind that locked door at the head of the first flight of stairs.

The Baron shone the torch on the lock.

It was the latest Landon; he'd seen several like it, knew that many of them were electrically controlled; this might be electrified. He tested this out by tossing a tiny piece of fuse wire; there was no flash, nothing to suggest that the metal was alive.

Inside the house there was a strange quiet; outside, the traffic noises and people laughing and a drunk breaking the calm by singing raucously.

The Baron bent down and looked at the stairs themselves. They seemed solid, and were covered with linoleum that had been down for ages.

If he went out again and tried to get into the first floor by a window, he would probably run up against strong defences. And he would increase the risk of being seen. He didn't want to go back. He squatted, studying the stairs, as patient as if he had a day and a night to spare.

He murmured softly, "I think this is it."

He unwound his tool-kit from his waist, laid it on the

floor, put the torch into position so that it gave him some light, and selected a knife. He cut the linoleum off two stair treads, then the upright piece between them. He put these aside carefully, making sure that they didn't lie so that they could trip him up if he were in a hurry.

He fitted a bit in to a brace, fingers moving quickly and dexterously; just a craftsman who seemed intent on what he was doing. He began to drill. The wood was deal, soft and yielding; and the oiled bit went in almost as smoothly as a knife into cheese; the only sound was the softly whirring drill.

After drilling each hole, the Baron paused.

The drunken singer's voice was farther away at each pause. Traffic was getting quieter. There were no sounds in the house.

When he had drilled four holes, close together, he put the drill away. He didn't leave it ready for further use; he might have to up and off in sudden alarm. Long practice and the thorough self-training of bygone years were a great stand-by.

Even listening for sounds came automatically; so long to listen, so long to work. When actually using the tools he could thing over anything that seemed different—any changes in the atmosphere, any hint of sounds.

He screwed a cup-hook into the upright piece between the treads, then fitted a blade into a small saw-handle, and used this instead of the brace and bit. It made little more noise. He didn't stop so often, but sawed through the supporting piece between the two threads, and the saw bit swiftly into the soft wood.

At last, he was able to move a large piece, pulling it away with the cup-hook.

He laid it aside.

Getting at the treads above and below was easy, then. He had room to squeeze through here, and he looked down into a cupboard built beneath the stairs; at coats and hats, a set of golf-clubs, walking-sticks, all the oddments one might expect to find.

He wasn't interested in the cupboard.

The joists supporting the weight of the floorboards above the cupboard were thick, but also of deal. It wasn't so easy to saw through these, he had to keep his hands at a tension; but he got through.

He listened for longer stretches now, for the noise he was making was nearer the living-quarters above the shop, and more likely to be heard. That light had been on in a front room; he wasn't sure that it was out.

Next came the landing floorboards, and with these he had his first real luck. They had been cut two or three times, for gas pipes; he was able to push two or three up with little trouble. That meant the floor covering was loose. He held his breath as he pushed one or two boards aside.

Dim light came from the landing.

He kept very still.

The light was steady, and he heard no sound. He shifted a board. It scraped a little, and the noise seemed worse to him than it did in the landing. He paused, then moved another.

Soon there was room for him to climb up into the living-quarters.

He hauled himself from the staircase cupboard.

He had his tool-kit round his waist again, everything else in his pockets, he was ready to run; but there was no hint of alarm. The boards creaked, but he didn't slow down. First his head and shoulders, then his chest, were above the level of the landing floor. He got a leg up and over, a moment later was standing up, breathing softly, heart racing.

The light came from a bulb fitted against the wall just above a door; it was a low-powered, very small bulb. He didn't doubt that it was a kind of night-light.

High on the wall was a square wooden box, like the kind

used for electric fuses. He opened this carefully, standing on a chair. Inside was a powerful burglar-alarm bell. He smiled with satisfaction as he disconnected the hammer, climbed off the chair, and felt much happier.

He put the floorboards back loosely, opened the flat door from the inside, and left it ajar. Now there was no need to fear an alarm; and a way out was ready.

He looked about the landing.

It was spacious, the boards were polished, there were three skin rugs and several old oak pieces of furniture; this was like the entrance to the flat of a wealthy man who had good taste.

A passage led to the right; and three doors led off the landing itself.

The Baron studied the layout, and found another, narrow staircase, at the end of the passage. He went up this, keeping close to the wall by force of habit and so lessening the danger of creaking boards.

The top landing was much smaller, and didn't seem so well furnished. Here were three doors. One led to a big room, obviously used as a stock-room—and here the Baron's torch moved slowly round, the beam shining on lovely things, treasures which would not have been out of place at Quinns. There were ordinary run-of-the-mill antiques, too, it wasn't exactly a treasure house, but it was more a dealer's stock-room than the storeroom of a pawnbroker.

In another room there were empty show-cases. He hadn't found the safe.

He went into the third room on this floor, and as he opened the door, his senses whispered a warning. He stopped instantly. In that moment he was tense but very calm; he could hear anything.

What he did hear was breathing.

His heart began to pound, from the reaction. He heard no other sound at all. When he was steadier, he pushed the door wider open. The window of the room was not curtained, no blind was drawn, and lights from the High Street filled it with a soft glow. He didn't need to use his torch. He went towards the bed, where a man lay sleeping.

He recognised Bill Brash.

20

DISCOVERY

MANNERING closed the door of the room behind him, very softly. He hadn't stayed long. He had taken the key out of the inside of the lock, and now he inserted it from the outside, and turned it; it clicked sharply. He stood waiting tensely, hardly breathing until he was sure that Brash hadn't been disturbed. Then came the old, familiar thumping of his heart.

He turned away.

He didn't want to think about Brash, yet; the meaning of this might be obvious; it was even possible that Fenn suspected that Brash was here, but if that were so, wouldn't he have made a search?

He moved to the landing, and noticed a draught of cool air sweeping over his face. Alarm flared; for a door might have opened, someone might be coming upstairs. He saw and heard nothing.

He moved again, and felt the current of cool air, went to one side and saw an open window. It was too narrow to climb through. He looked out, awkwardly. It would tax the agility of a tiny monkey to climb up here, for the window was set in a blank wall which overlooked an alley and the wall of a house behind the High Street.

Mannering shone his torch, carefully.

This window wasn't the usual kind; was more like a small

glass door. It could be fastened like a door, too. Then he saw that part of the wall was different here. In fact, a section of the inside wall had been taken out, but could be put back to cover and to conceal the window.

He moved both the window and the piece of wall; each was fitted on hinges which moved smoothly and without the slightest sound. Opposite, in the other house, was a large window. He didn't think there was much doubt about the purpose of the windows. If the police raided Crummy Day's, and Crummy carried "hot" jewels on the premises, they could be thrown out of this window to the house opposite—and when the inside was closed and covered, no one would know that there was anything but the blank wall. If it were ever found by the police, the stuff would have been sent to safety first.

Mannering moved away, listened at Brash's door, heard nothing, and went downstairs. He hadn't yet found the safe, but need he look? If the police came and found Brash——

He reached the landing, and went to each of the doors. Two were locked, two unlocked. He looked into a bedroom and a bathroom. The bedroom overlooked the High Street, there was some traffic and light from street-lamps; and a low-pitched, rhythmic snoring. Mannering moved cautiously towards a large double-bed. A bearded man and a heavy-looking woman lay there, face to face. The man's beard showed up grey even in this poor light; it was he who snored. The woman's hand was close to his almost bald head.

Mannering remembered the story of Crummy Day's soubriquet; he always had crumbs on his beard.

Mannering took the key out of the lock, and locked the couple in. Search first, tackle Crummy afterwards.

Would anyone else be at the house?

There were only the locked rooms to search, now; and he had plenty of time. He hadn't been much more than an hour from the time he had started working on the window of the

DISCOVERY 155

kitchen. Nothing suggested that Crummy Day thought there was the slightest need for alarm.

Then, out of the brooding quiet, came a crash of sound, the clattering roar of a burglar alarm. He'd found one, and not searched for another; but there was one.

   .   .   .   .   .   .

Mannering stood still for a breathtaking moment of time; and then he moved. He heard the bell as if it were a distant but menacing thing. He turned the key in the lock of Crummy Day's door, then turned and ran towards the landing and the second staircase. He went up, not down. He heard a man bellow, then heard a woman's voice. He reached Brash's door, unlocked it, and stepped swiftly into one of the stock-rooms. No one could sleep through that din.

He heard Brash shout, "What's that, what's the matter?" in the kind of voice a man might have in a nightmare. There were creaking sounds, followed by footsteps. Downstairs, the woman cried out. Then Brash's door opened and he rushed to the stairs, calling, "What's the matter, what is it?"

Mannering crept out.

Brash reached the foot of the stairs and disappeared. Mannering went after him. . . .

"*Charlie, Charlie!*" a woman screamed.

"Crummy!" cried Brash. "No, don't—*no!*" His voice screeched upwards.

Two shots roared.

Mannering heard the woman scream again, heard Brash shouting, heard the barking of the gun. Next came a thud, as if someone had fallen. He could see Brash staggering back in the hall. Suddenly Brash lurched forward, still shouting, but the woman was sobbing in a strange voice:

"Charlie, Charlie, Charlie!"

Mannering moved swiftly along the passage towards the landing. He saw the woman from the double bed on her knees, holding Crummy Day's head in her lap. She was staring into the old man's face, at the red mark in the middle of his forehead. Such despair and grief showed in the woman's eyes that she reminded Mannering of Miranda.

He went swiftly past.

She didn't look up, was oblivious of everything but the body of her husband.

The door which Mannering had left ajar was wide open.

Brash was rushing down the stairs, making the loose boards rattle, following a man who was just a shadowy figure against the poor light of the High Street.

Brash moved to one side, and flattened himself against the wall. A bullet thudded into one of the stairs.

Mannering waited, safe from bullets. Brash appeared against the light, a dark silhouette.

"He's dead!" wailed the woman. "He's dead, they've killed my Charlie."

"Oh, no!" cried Brash. "No!"

He turned back desperately.

Mannering was now at the foot of the stairs; to Brash, he would be a stranger, even if Brash could see his face. Brash's face showed in the light from the landing—terror filled it, he looked as if he didn't know which way to turn.

Mannering slipped round the foot of the stairs, hurried into the kitchen, and went out the back way.

As he reached the back-yard, he heard a police whistle shrill out.

He hurried towards the High Street, reached it, and saw light streaming out of the doorway at Crummy Day's, and two uniformed policemen—and Bill Brash.

Brash was trying to run, kicked out, and dodged to one side. A policeman grabbed him, the other pinioned his arms. Other police came running, and a patrol car screamed towards the spot.

Mannering hid in a doorway.

The sound of voices floated back; he didn't hear the

DISCOVERY 157

words, but could guess the gist of them. Brash, awakened from sleep, had run into murder—and into arrest.

But he hadn't killed Crummy Day.

Did anyone but Mannering know that?

. . . . . .

Brash, under arrest. Crummy, dead. Brash on the burgled premises—of course he would deny that he had killed Crummy Day, but who would believe him? Who would give the slightest credence to the story of another intruder? Unless there was clear, unmistakable evidence, Bill Brash was heading for the nine-o'clock walk. Crude; but brutally true.

Mannering was cleaning off the grease-paint in the garage at Victoria.

He could tell the truth, and admit that he had been at the shop. No, that wasn't so. He *couldn't* tell the truth. If Brash were on the point of being hanged, if there were no other hope in the world of saving him, then—yes. But not yet. If Fenn discovered how Mannering had got in, if the law could prove what he had done, there would be an end to Quinns; to reputation; to life as he knew it; to all the things that were precious to him and to Lorna.

Mannering couldn't think of anything else.

There might be some other way to save Brash; the killer had taken his gun away. Hadn't he? *Hadn't he?*

The killer must have followed Mannering into the house, crept up, come to kill—who? Crummy Day? Brash? That was just guesswork.

There was a lot of guesswork.

Chittering had telephoned Mannering from Fleet Street, telling him about the murder. The police and the Press knew that there had been a second alarm system, which Crummy Day had set up in the bedroom. Mannering had probably disturbed him, and started the wild sequence of events.

Who had killed Crummy? Did the police suspect that

anyone else had been present? The gun had been found, Mannering knew; deliberately left behind by the killer.

There was bright sunlight on a cool morning. Outside, the scene on the Embankment at Westminster hadn't changed, except that there was no sultry, sulphurous yellow pall over the sky and the city. The sun glinted on the windows of London County Hall and, if Mannering cared to go to the window of Fenn's office, on to the broad bosom of the Thames. Pleasure craft were moored in midstream, two launches moved downstream towards the Pool, all pennants flying.

Mannering was waiting for Fenn.

Fenn had sent for him. Not curtly or peremptorily, but through Sergeant Grimble, who had never seemed more reassuring; but he would probably look like that to a man he was going to arrest on a charge of murder.

It was eleven o'clock.

The morning papers had carried streamer headlines about the murder of Crummy Day and the arrest of Brash.

Now Fenn, as if with intent to fray his nerves, kept Mannering waiting.

Mannering smoked two cigarettes, then got up and looked out of the window. He had hardly reached it when footsteps came thudding along the passage, the door opened quickly and Fenn came in; alone.

"You won't believe it," Fenn said, "but I'm sorry. I was called out while you were on the way up."

Mannering grinned; as might be expected of him.

"The Assistant Commissioner, I presume."

"No," said Fenn. "No." He didn't sit down, but moved so that he could see Mannering more clearly. With the light on his face, Mannering looked youthful and powerful; and if his eyes seemed a little tired, slightly red-rimmed, as much could be said of a lot of other people at Scotland Yard.

For all Mannering could tell, Fenn might know, or think

DISCOVERY 159

that he knew, that Mannering had been at Crummy Day's the night before.

"No," Fenn repeated, while Mannering felt the strain of trying to look mildly expectant. "It wasn't the Assistant Commissioner. It was that poor devil, Brash."

Mannering said softly, "Police sympathy for a killer?"

"In a way," agreed Fenn. "Yes, I feel sorry for him, although that's not for publication." He moved to his desk and the tension seemed to ease. "He said he wanted to make a statement. I had to be there. He's being held at Cannon Row until the first hearing, and will be up before the beak in half an hour."

Fenn stopped.

"Did he make a statement?" Mannering hoped that he sounded just as interested as he should be, and no more.

"Oh, yes," said Fenn. "He admits that he was at Dragon's End the night before last, but denies murdering Revell. He says he handled an assegai which he tripped over. It was lying on the floor. He admits that he was at Crummy Day's last night—he had to—but swears that he didn't shoot Crummy. It's almost pathetic and very nearly convincing. But—well, we found the gun in a corner, wiped clean of prints. He'd naturally do that. Day's wife accused Brash, too. We'll ask for an eight-day remand in custody, and get it. And in a week from now he'll be committed for trial—unless we get fresh evidence."

He stopped again.

Questioningly?

21

REMAND

". . . UNLESS we get fresh evidence," Fenn had said. His brown eyes were turned intently towards Mannering, his pause seemed deliberate; as if he were inviting comment.

The door opened unexpectedly, and Fenn looked away; Mannering had a moment's respite. It wasn't one that he enjoyed. The case against Brash must be overwhelming, or Fenn wouldn't talk like this.

The newcomer was a tall, melancholy faced Superintendent, Fisher.

"Sorry, Nick, didn't know you had distinguished company." He grinned dolefully at Mannering. "Had anything more from Midham?"

"No."

"Thought I'd tell you, only prints at Crummy's place, apart from those we'd expect, are Brash's and Pendexter Smith's." He put two sheets of paper, foolscap size, down in front of Fenn. "The finger-prints of these bad men always turn up sooner of later, don't they, Mr. Mannering?"

Mannering kept a straight face.

"Invariably," he said.

Fisher chuckled, and went out.

Mannering lit a cigarette.

"On the evidence we have, Brash will hang all right, but I've an uneasy feeling that we don't know everything," Fenn said. "Crummy Day's wife is venomous against Brash. I think she could gladly have killed him when we let them meet, early this morning. If we can take what she says as gospel, Crummy helped Brash out of the goodness of his heart, and for some unknown reason, Brash killed him. She's quite sure that the killer was Brash, but there was plenty to suggest that it was an outside job."

Mannering kept a poker face.

"Was there?"

Fenn said, "A hole in the stairs, back door forced—nice job of burglary. But Brash could have fixed all that."

"Why should he?" Mannering asked.

He was thinking of Bristow, who was in South Africa. Bristow would have been after him by now, suspicious, menacing, knowing that the evidence of burglary at Crummy Day's shop had the hall-mark of the Baron. Fenn didn't know. Fenn wasn't high-pressuring him. Fenn had a ready-made suspect in Brash, and was vaguely uneasy, that was all.

New evidence was needed to save Brash.

Was Mannering the only man who could give it?

"If Crummy Day knew that Brash killed Revell, he could have been deadly to Brash," Fenn said. "Can you see why I'm worried?"

"Pendexter Smith's prints?"

"That's it. He was at the Aldgate shop. We found a handkerchief of his, and several letters——I was pretty sure before we got the prints. You know that he swears he doesn't know what happened, but went dizzy, was helped by a stranger, and woke up at Dragon's End. No doubt he was at Day's, but whether he knew it or not, I don't know."

"Does Brash mention him?"

"Brash hates the sight of him," Fenn said. "He says that Pendexter Smith is afraid that he, Brash, can get Miranda Smith free from his influence, and that Pendexter Smith would kill in order to keep his hold on her. That's anyone's guess. We knew that Pendexter was held at Crummy Day's and that Brash was on the scene of both murders. I'd like to make Pendexter Smith tell all he knows," Fenn added, with rare feeling.

Mannering said evenly, "Did Brash say why he went to Dragon's End?"

"He tells a story—that he thought that Pendexter was trying to get legal control of all Miranda's fortune, and wanted to find out. He'd an idea that Smith was seeking power of attorney."

"Was he?"

"I've no evidence."

"How long had Brash and Crummy been working together?" asked Mannering.

"I don't know. Mrs. Day says that Crummy was fond of Brash, that they didn't work together—were more like father and son. I can't find a motive to explain why Brash should do all this, unless——"

Mannering said for him, "Unless he's after Miranda's fortune, blackening Pendexter Smith's reputation as he goes. If he thought Smith was going to get power of attorney, then he'd want to act fast."

"That's it," said Fenn. "Brash hates Smith, Smith hates Brash, either could be after Miranda's money. And Brash might have killed Revell because Revell caught him at Dragon's End and because Crummy knew about that. We now know that the two prisoners and Dibben have been on Crummy Day's pay-roll, but Brash could have hired them for a special job——"

Mannering said, "There's an angle I don't think you've seen."

"What's that?" Fenn almost barked.

"Brash went to Dragon's End. Crummy could have sent him there and planned to frame him. That would give Brash a motive against Crummy Day."

"Where does Smith come in?"

"He was at Crummy's. Did he work *with* Crummy? Were they conspiring together, and did Brash find out? Is that it?"

"Could be," Fenn conceded. "But why did Pendexter

Smith come to you to sell the nest-egg? He just says they wanted it turned into cash—but he was in a big hurry, according to you."

"He was in a hurry," Mannering asserted dryly.

"I know, I know, we haven't got the truth out of him yet," Fenn said. "But if he's a crook, why did he come to you? There's the big flaw in your theory."

Mannering said, "Don't I know it."

"I've a theory, too," grunted Fenn. He rubbed his nose. "You'll hoot." He rubbed his nose again. "Have you considered the possibility that Miranda Smith is putting on an act?"

Mannering positively gaped.

"I have *not*."

"No physical or psychiatric explanation of her affliction," Fenn said gruffly. "Oh, I know I'm crazy. But could she be playing one man off against another?"

"For Pete's sake, *why*?"

Fenn said, "There's a catch in her father's will. She inherits, but until she's twenty-five, she can only touch capital with Pendexter Smith's approval. It just makes me wonder if she's all she seems. Supposing she and Brash——"

"Forget it," Mannering said brusquely.

But it wasn't so easy.

Nor was it easy to forget that Brash was being held on a capital charge and that he, Mannering, could clear him only by damning himself.

Only?

. . . . .

Now the hope was Pendexter Smith.

Mannering had to see him soon.

. . . . .

Chittering of the *Record* stood at the door, smiling cherubically, looking angelic. His fair hair was turning slightly grey, but that showed very little. He wore an old raincoat and a battered trilby on the back of his head, for he liked to ape the casual reporter of the screen.

"Hi, Maestro," he greeted, as Mannering got up from a chair in the office of Quinns, a little after two o'clock that afternoon. "Busy?"

"Clearing up a few odds and ends," Mannering said.

"So Ned Wainwright gave me to understand," said Chittering, squatting on a corner of the desk. That meant that his face was just a little too close to Mannering's for comfort, and Mannering couldn't move away without bumping the back of his head against the wall. "John, how's the silent beauty?"

"Miranda? About the same."

"I have been doing considerable research," declared Chittering, "and I don't know how much Fenn's told you, but so has he. Researched, I mean. Into the past of our Miranda. Or your Miranda. Or just Miranda. Even before the accident, she used to visit Crummy Day quite often. And I think there's a lot of evidence that Crummy Day used to sell a lot of hot stuff to Mortimer Smith, down at Dragon's End. It wouldn't surprise me to know that Miranda was a go-between. Have you had another shot at Pendexter Smith?"

"I'm going this afternoon."

"Taking Miranda?"

"Yes."

"John on the target," said Chittering mildly. "I've a feeling that if Pen Smith told you the real reason why he came here in the first place, you'd have the answer to a lot of puzzling questions. Set one or two innocent traps for Miranda," urged Chittering. "Just make sure that she is as deaf as she makes out."

Mannering said flatly, "She's deaf."

"I hope she isn't fooling us," said Chittering, as if he meant it. "By the way, heard what happened to Brash?"

"An eight-day remand."

"And a hangman's rope already dangling over his head. It's an odd business. I can't find anything else against Brash. He lives within his modest income, has a good record, seems just to be another young man in love with a girl who won't have anything to do with him. Taken by and large, I like the bashful, blushing Billy Brash. I'd like to find another villain. Mind if I come down to Dragon's End with you?"

"Why don't you follow?" Mannering asked.

Chittering chuckled, but Mannering found it difficult to be flippant. The fate of young Bill Brash was heavy on his mind. This was much more than a vengeful search for Sylvester's killer; for the murderer of the others; or for explanation of Miranda Smith's affliction.

He had told Lorna everything, but they hadn't talked much about it. She also knew that there was only one answer: find the truth, and pray that it would clear Brash of Crummy Day's murder. That—or full confession.

Pendexter Smith must be made to talk.

Miranda?

Fenn was a realist, Chittering was also down to earth. Neither had any reason for wanting to damn Miranda; no personal motive, anyway. Both were seekers after the truth, both had a soft spot for Bill Brash.

Mannering rang the bell, and Wainwright came to the office at the double.

"Yes, sir?"

"Ned, I'm going down to Dragon's End, with Miranda Smith. I want you to follow. You do drive, don't you?"

"Oh, lord, yes!"

"Hire something nippy and fast from Bladdon's, the garage near me at Bell Street. Follow us, at a distance. Chittering may follow too, but don't worry about him. I don't know what else to expect, I'm not even sure that I expect anything, but keep your eyes open."

"Think they'll have another crack at you?" Wainwright asked.

"They might."

"I'll tell you one thing," Wainwright said, "I spoke to that Sergeant Grimble about a licence for a gun. He said Fenn said I could carry one, provided I'd applied for the licence. I have."

Mannering found himself smiling; and more cheerful.

"All right," he said. "It's half-past three now. I'll be leaving Chelsea at five, and should reach Dragon's End about half-past six. I'll drive straight up to the house. You stay at the entrance to the drive unless I send for you."

"Right ho," Wainwright said, then gulped and spoke more quickly; almost nervously. "I suppose you're right about letting Miranda go back there."

"I hope I'm right."

"If anything happens to her," said Wainwright, very softly, "I'll murder the man who does it."

Here was more evidence of the effect of Miranda on young men. Brash would follow her anywhere, make any sacrifice for her. Wainwright was in a very similar frame of mind. There might be others, several others.

What had he, Mannering, seen at Dragon's End to justify the attack on him?

Or had it been at Dragon's End? Could it have been something Miranda had made clear to him?

He telephoned Fenn, told him where he was going, and added, "I hope you won't have me followed, but you could keep track of me *en route,* and warn your Midham people to stand by. Pendexter Smith might talk more freely if he doesn't expect the police are at his ear, but I'd be happier to have them fairly handy."

"Bristow wouldn't recognise you," Fenn said, dryly.

22

DRAGON'S END AGAIN

MIRANDA looked straight ahead of her.

Mannering drove through the wide High Street of Midham about half-past six, and glanced at the girl, but she took no notice of the people walking up and down, the buses parked in the big market-square with queues waiting for others; the red-roofed buildings or the white-faced, oak-beamed houses and the ancient gables.

Since he had told her that she was coming back here, to see her uncle, she had seemed calmer, almost happy.

They reached the outskirts of the town, and slowed down. Wainwright, in a little Triumph, had been held up by traffic-lights. His car came into sight in Mannering's driving mirror, and Mannering moved off again.

He reached the gates of Dragon's End.

Miranda was staring straight ahead of her. Hopefully?

He said abruptly, "Miranda, don't look like that!"

Not even by the flicker of an eyelid did Miranda show that she had heard.

Twice they had passed a car backfiring so loudly that it had made Mannering jump. She hadn't stirred. He did not think there was any chance that she had heard a thing; was quite sure that she was deaf.

Nothing had happened on the road.

While Brash had been free, Mannering had been attacked, there had been acute danger. The same was true while Crummy Day had been alive.

Mannering drove slowly up the winding drive. The grass verge was newly cut, there was a smell of new-mown hay. Flowers, shrubs, and bushes, farther back from the drive, were kept in perfect symmetry. Tall trees sheltered them from the warm evening sun.

They came within sight of the house.

Mannering was thinking, "If Brash killed Revell, does it matter if he hangs for Crummy Day's murder?" and it was some time before he managed to drive the thought out of his mind.

The house stood huge and ugly against the clear-blue sky, but the beauty of the trim lawns and the flower-beds took away something of the ugliness of the building itself. The drive turned into a circular carriage-way in front of the house, and the other obviously led to garages or stables at the back.

No one was in sight.

Mannering stopped the car and got out. He helped Miranda. The only sign of emotion that she gave was in her eyes; of satisfaction? Mannering thought so.

They stepped on to the wide porch. Mannering pressed a bell, then waited, glancing back down the drive. Some way off he could see the main Midham Road, and could make out the spire of a church; elsewhere there were meadows and wooded land, and two gently sloping hills topped by copses. There was no sign of Wainwright or of the watching Midham police; but Mannering was quite sure that Fenn would not miss this chance.

Footsteps sounded. He turned to the door, and Miranda moved, clutching his arm.

An elderly woman whom Mannering hadn't seen before, wearing a faded blue smock and big black shoes, opened the door. She started, at sight of Miranda. Mannering glanced at Miranda, and saw recognition in her eyes, but no particular pleasure.

"I—I didn't expect anyone," the woman said busily, and now her gaze searched Mannering's face. "Does Mr. Smith know you're coming, sir?"

"I don't think so," Mannering said.

The woman stood to one side.

"Well, sir, you'd better come in," she said. "He's up and in the study today, with his nose in a book. Burglary and murder don't make any difference to *that*." It was hard to say whether she was being critical or whether she was showing admiration for Pendexter Smith's strong nerve.

"May we go up alone?" asked Mannering.

"I'll be glad if you do, sir, how anyone can expect one pair of hands to see to everything in *this* house——" She broke off. "It isn't *so* bad," she amended unexpectedly, "there's daily help, and when Mr. Revell was alive it wasn't too bad at all."

"Do you sleep in?" asked Mannering.

She didn't seem to find the question surprising.

"Oh, no, sir, I come from Midham, nine till six, usually, but *some*one has to cook Mr. Smith's dinner for him. He always eats at seven sharp," she added. "Will you be staying tonight?"

"Don't worry about dinner for me," smiled Mannering.

He led Miranda up the stairs. She held his arm lightly, as if determined to make sure that he didn't forget how helpless she was. He remembered every turn in the passages, and every door. The library door was closed. He went towards it briskly, and had a feeling that Miranda was as eager.

Mannering didn't tap; just thrust open the door.

Pendexter Smith was sitting at a small desk in the far corner, writing. It was gloomy in the room. Miranda, by Mannering's side, stared at Smith—*smilingly*. He looked up obviously lost in what he was doing, and expecting to see the woman in the blue smock.

He saw the visitors.

His mouth fell open slowly, his eyes seemed to thrust themselves out of those deep sockets. Here was ugliness itself —beast to Miranda's Beauty.

"Ma-Ma-Mannering," he croaked. "What——?" He didn't finish, but the pen dropped from his fingers, as if they had suddenly become nerveless. "Miranda," he gasped, as if with a great effort. "Miranda!"

He started to get up.

"Sit still, Pendexter," Mannering said, and the little old man stopped where he was, crouching above the desk, leaning against it. "Just one or two questions, and this time let's have the truth," Mannering went on. "Why did you bring Miranda and the nest-egg to me?"

"But—but you know!"

"Why leave her with me?"

"You *know*," breathed Pendexter Smith. "I was going to see the solicitors, I got a taxi, I was walking along the narrow lane in the City when I blacked out. Mr. Mannering, that's everything I know. I just blacked out. The very next thing I remember, I was back here, and the police were talking to me. I don't remember a single thing of what happened after I'd left that taxi."

"You don't lie well," Mannering said.

"It is not a lie!"

"Pendexter Smith," said Mannering, very softly, "you lied to the police and to me yesterday, and now you're lying again. Why did you bring Miranda to Quinns?"

"I told you," said Pendexter Smith shrilly. He had got over the shock of surprise, but didn't lower himself to the desk. He moved round towards Miranda, and stretched out his old, claw-like hands, with their liver-brown spots and the sharp sinews. "She needed to sell the nest-egg, she——"

"Why?"

"She needed the money to invest——"

"She's a wealthy young woman."

"I tell you she needed the money!" insisted Pendexter Smith. He reached the girl, and took both her hands. He stood on tip-toe, and she lowered her head, so that he could kiss her. It was strangely touching. "Hallo, my dear," he said, very slowly and clearly as if she could hear and understand. "So you've come back. It's early, but I think it will be all right, now."

Mannering said sharply, "Why? What's changed?"

"I believe that a lot of things have changed," said Pendexter Smith. "Mr. Mannering, I'm sorry, but there isn't anything more I can say to help you." His voice was soothing and pleasant, still a startling contrast to his hideous looks. "I just can't say any more than I have. Except—that on reflection I think Miranda has reason to be very thankful to you and your wife, for giving her shelter when she needed it so much. I hoped that she would be with you for a little longer, although I can understand that it wasn't possible. But I think she'll be all right now. The danger is past."

Mannering moved slowly, and deliberately gripped Smith's thin, bony wrist. The man was nothing but a bag of bones.

"Why should she be all right now, and not when she came to see me?" Mannering asked softly.

"People have died, Mr. Mannering, and things have changed. Just for a moment, when you appeared without warning, I was reminded of all the fearful things that have happened. Earlier, I'd told myself that Miranda was safe and happy with you, and I was disappointed at seeing her back. But it doesn't really matter. Not now. I only wish there was some way in which I could help her to hear and to speak again."

He looked as if that mattered more than anything else to him.

Mannering said, "Do you know what caused the shock?"

"But surely you know, too. An accident——"

"It was more than an accident."

Pendexter Smith said, "Was it, Mr. Mannering? I can't stop you from guessing, but I am sure that it will not do any good at all to reconstruct the accident, to go over all the old ground. Poor, poor Miranda."

He was holding her hands, but looking at Mannering. It was all oddly impressive; and as he stood there, Mannering found himself believing good, not bad, of Pendexter Smith. But the old man knew much more than he had said, and his knowledge might save the life of young Bill Brash; and Mannering from disaster.

Studying him, Mannering began to realise that there might be one way, only one way, to make this old man talk.

If anything were certain, it was that Pendexter Smith loved the girl; his love, clear and bright, showed in his buried eyes, in the way he held her hands.

"Smith," Mannering said gently.

"I hope you will stay to dinner, Mr Mannering. Meg downstairs is a bit rough, but she is an excellent cook, and I am sure——"

"I'm not thinking of dinner," Mannering said. "I don't think you know what you are doing."

"I know very well," Pendexter Smith assured him quietly. "I can only repeat that I think it is for the best. Don't waste your time trying to make me change my mind."

"You still don't know what you're doing," Mannering looked at Miranda's profile.

Something seemed to tell the girl that he was staring at her, for she turned towards him. Her eyes were still shadowed, there was no gaiety in her manner, and yet she smiled. That more than anything else convinced him that she was truly deaf.

"You're making a new kind of hell for Miranda," Mannering finished, very quietly; for he knew that this was his last hope.

Pendexter didn't speak; but he let the girl go and moved back so that he could look more squarely at Mannering.

"What do you mean?"

DRAGON'S END AGAIN

"Miranda is in more trouble than she's ever been."

"No," said Pendexter Smith, sharply. "That is impossible." But he was shaken. "If you think you can frighten me——"

"Listen to me, Pendexter Smith," said Mannering harshly. "I don't care whether I terrify you, frighten you, or haunt your dreams. You don't matter. But Miranda matters, and I mean to help her."

"You have done, more than you know. Indirectly perhaps, but——"

"Do you *want* to see her hanged?" demanded Mannering.

. . . . .

Pendexter Smith did not speak at once; just stood there with his hands raised in front of his pigeon breast, his little eyes suddenly afire. The word "hanged" seemed to echo about the room. Miranda moved towards the window, and stood looking out; Pendexter Smith did not look at her.

"Because she could be," Mannering went on. "It's a greater danger than you know."

The old man's voice seemed to break. "What—what do you mean? What *can* you mean?"

"Exactly what I say. The police have reason to believe that Miranda is working with the murderer of Revell and Crummy Day." He had left Day's name out of the conversation until then; now he flung it at Pendexter Smith. The old man flinched. "They think she works with Brash, that Brash carried out her orders. If you know she didn't, if you know what the killings are all about, now's your time to talk. You can save Miranda from arrest, charge, misery, trial—you might save her from hanging. What's the truth of it? Come on."

After a pause, Smith said hoarsely, "I don't believe it."

"All right, let her hang."

"They wouldn't be such fools."

If he recovered from the shock, and began to think clearly, he would know that this was bluff. The one chance of making him talk was to keep up the pressure, work on his frayed nerves.

"They think they've plenty of evidence," Mannering rasped. "Come on, let's have the truth. Why did Miranda go to Crummy Day so often? What went on between a notorious London fence and pretty Miranda? The Press knows about that, the police know too. They think that Revell and Day could have betrayed Miranda, and were ready to—that she worked with Day, that she had them both killed to stop them from talking; that she made Brash kill them. If it isn't true, what is the truth?"

Pendexter Smith said, "Oh, no, no! It's a travesty of the truth, Miranda is goodness itself, she always has been." He was in despair. "Mannering, you can't mean this!"

It was working; turn the screw a little harder, and Smith would talk yet.

"I brought her away from London because I thought the police would detain her if I didn't," Mannering flung at him. "I hoped I'd have a chance to save her, if you'd see sense. Let's have it, Smith. If you care anything at all for her——"

He looked deliberately at Miranda.

She was staring out of the window, quite calmly, as if she found some kind of balm for her troubled spirit in this house. She did not look towards Mannering, but her lips were curved gently, as if what she gazed upon was good.

Pendexter Smith looked at her, too; fearfully.

"Miranda," he breathed, "my darling Miranda. It is wicked, evil, and all they want is to rob and cheat her."

"Who?" demanded Mannering.

"There was Day, and there's Brash and that other man. I get so confused," Pendexter said, and pressed the heels of his thumbs against his forehead. "Mannering, don't let them do this awful thing to her. I'll tell you all I can, everything. Her father began it, my brother Mortimer—oh, he wasn't bad, not bad like Day, but they were partners. No one knew, no one suspected—but my brother Mortimer was a thief, and all his stolen goods were sold through Crummy Day. Then years ago, he reformed, broke the partnership, and made much money legally. He began to collect many beautiful things. But Crummy Day hated him, wanted him back, and then planned to get control of his treasures. He sent one of his murdering beasts after him. That was—that was when poor Miranda had the terrible accident."

Miranda was looking out of the window, with that strange calmness.

Pendexter Smith went on hoarsely, "It was in France. Mortimer was driving. A man with a gun sprang out on them. He fired, shattered the windscreen and made Mortimer lose control, and the car crashed down a steep embankment. You know what happened. You know——"

"How do you know this?" Mannering asked, softly.

"How do I *know*? Day boasted of it. Boasted, gloated! But I was still left to look after Miranda, and I controlled all the treasures that she inherited. I fought—how I fought. I knew Brash was a friend of Day's, that Day wanted him to marry Miranda, just to get his hands on those lovely things. But it became too much for me, Mannering, I had an illness, I became so frail. I couldn't go on. They were just waiting for me to die, just sitting and waiting and gloating. And if I died and Miranda was left alone, then Brash or that other man who worked for Day, together they would —they would pretend to help her. But they'd rob her, Mannering, I knew they would, and I couldn't tell the police. There was no physical threat to us, they were just waiting for me to die.

"But if Miranda had stocks and shares, documents and certificates which they couldn't cash, that would be very different, that would give her a chance. So I decided to sell. The nest-egg was the biggest single treasure she had. It was the one which Crummy Day desired above all others. The day before I brought it to you, there had been an attempt to steal it. That decided me——"

Mannering broke in, "Did you tell the police?"

"No," Pendexter Smith answered, and went on steadily: "Some of the treasures at Dragon's End were not legally ours—were stolen years ago. I was afraid to go to the police. I wanted, God forgive me, I wanted to spend my last days in freedom. So—I had to find a man whom I could trust. Knowing your reputation, I came to you, needing action quickly—oh, so quickly. Every single moment seemed vital. I was going to ask you to visit Dragon's End, once I was satisfied that you were honest, but—I was followed from your shop. I didn't realise it until I was in the narrow lane near the solicitors' office. A man overtook me, pressed a gun in my ribs, terrified me. He made me go with him to Crummy Day's. Day wanted to know what I was doing at Quinns, and what I'd said to you. Then he drugged me. I was astounded, astounded, when I came round, when I realised that I was alive."

Mannering said, "I can believe it. Go on."

The girl turned and looked at Pendexter Smith, then moved towards him, as if she were troubled by his expression. He turned and smiled at her.

"There isn't much more," he said, "but I know they want her treasures. Day wanted the nest-egg, desperately. Oh, not for the money, he gloated over rare and beautiful things, he had a storehouse filled with treasures. He was a miser for beauty, the craving almost drove him insane. That's why he and Mortimer parted. Mortimer wanted to run a legal business, they'd done well and had the capital, but Day craved more and more and more precious things. I tell you, Mannering, he laughed himself sick when I said I'd gone to you! He said he'd got his eye on Quinns, that he had——"

Suddenly, awfully, Miranda screamed.

. . . . .

The scream cut across the old man's words, made Mannering swing round, made Pendexter Smith jump up from his chair.

Miranda screamed again, as she stared towards the door.

Mannering saw a man with a scarf over his face, cap low over his eyes, standing in the open doorway with a gun in his right hand.

. . . . .

Mannering leapt towards Miranda, pushed her behind the desk, and almost fell on top of her. The gun roared three times. Next moment, a man shouted, somewhere outside. Mannering heard the gunman turn, actually caught a glimpse of him rushing towards the door.

The attack had come as swift as lightning, the danger was gone almost as swiftly.

Mannering scrambled to his feet.

Pendexter Smith was lying back in his chair, and the hole in his forehead was as neat and tidy as the hole that had been in Crummy Day's.

It hadn't yet started to bleed.

Mannering knew that it wasn't worth losing a second to try to help Pendexter Smith. He reached the door, grabbed the handle, and pulled—then heard something he had never heard before, an unbelievable thing, strange and devastating.

"Uncle Pen, Uncle Pen!" cried Miranda in a strange, painful voice. "What have they done to you, what have they done?"

23

THE REAL DIBBEN

MIRANDA was on her knees beside the little old man, one hand clutching his, one holding the hair back from her forehead. She must know what had happened; she must know the full significance of the hole in his forehead.

It was beginning to bleed.

"Oh, no, no!" she cried, "Pen, Pen, don't die, don't leave me, don't die."

She flung herself upon the frail, lifeless body.

Outside, there was shouting; another shot; more shouting, then a thudding of footsteps on stairs and in the hall.

A scream.

"Pen, Pen, don't die, don't leave me," sobbed Miranda. "I can't stand it, I'll kill myself, I'll *kill* myself!"

Then she stopped speaking.

She straightened up and looked about the room, at the desk and the books and at two daggers, on the wall. She didn't look towards the door and Mannering. She brushed her hair back again, in a strangely calm gesture, and moved towards the daggers. So great was the spell that Mannering let her go within a yard of them before he moved.

"Miranda!" he cried.

She paused and glanced round in sudden, startled fear. She could speak, she could hear; and the shock which could do this might cause her death. There was despair in her heart and a dagger within reach of her hand.

She jumped to get it.

Mannering leapt across the room. She touched the handle of a dagger, but couldn't lift it off the hook. Mannering reached her, gripped her waist, and pulled her round. She kicked and struggled and fought to try to free herself, but he held her fast, without speaking or trying to soothe her. He could feel the wild beating of her heart, was still afraid lest this paroxysm of rage should bring about a fatal seizure.

Gradually, she quietened.

Suddenly, she went quite limp, and collapsed in his arms.

And outside there had been another burst of shooting.

In the room Mannering felt a gripping fear, lest Miranda was dead.

. . . . .

"He says he'll be here in two shakes of a lamb's tail," said the woman in the faded blue smock. "He's a good doctor, I will say that for him. But whether he can help her——"

She looked at Miranda with great compassion.

Mannering had carried Miranda into her room, just across the landing. The woman had come hurrying up, had loosened Miranda's clothes and kept her head remarkably well, much more concerned with Miranda than with anything else that had happened; she didn't know, then, that Pendexter Smith had died. Now, she had telephoned for a doctor.

Miranda's face was the colour of white wax. She was breathing, but so softly that there were moments when she seemed to have stopped completely, when death hovered about her.

"What happened to cause it all?" the woman demanded.

"Did you see anything?" Mannering asked.

"I saw a man running out of the front door," she said, "and I heard the shooting. Is Pendexter Smith——?"

She broke off, shot a startled glance at Miranda, and seemed to realise what had caused the girl's collapse. She moved away from the door and dropped heavily into an easy-chair, lowering her head into her hands.

. . . . .

Some police were already in the grounds, searching for the killer. Others came to the house, and with them a breathless Wainwright. Chittering was also in the grounds, searching.

.   .   .   .   .

"I'll never forgive myself," Wainwright said, gaspingly. "I saw him, I actually saw him within a few yards and fired and—and *missed*." He looked as if he couldn't believe such a thing possible. "At a dozen yards, I *missed*. I'd followed him up the stairs, but he started shooting too soon for me."

Mannering had heard Wainwright's footsteps on the landing.

"Did you recognise him?" demanded a heavily built Midham sergeant, who was in uniform.

"Well, I did and I didn't," said Wainwright, breathing a little more steadily. "I think it was a—ah—a fellow I've seen before." He went red; almost as red as Brash. "A man named Dibben."

"Where've you seen him before?" demanded the sergeant.

"He was a runner for Crummy Day, we've come across him in business several times." Mannering came smoothly to Wainwright's rescue. In fact Wainwright could only have seen Dibben here, but didn't want the police to know that. "Which way did he go?"

"I *think* he doubled back," Wainwright said.

"Well, he won't get away," said the constable, with heavy confidence. "We've got all roads blocked and all lanes covered. Never had such a cordon, Mr. Mannering. Only mistake we made was not having anyone close enough to the house itself, and that wasn't exactly a mistake—we had one chap, who got caught napping and banged over the head. Well, I'd better be off, want everyone we can get outside."

"May I come?" Wainwright was eager.

"If you want to."

"We'll both go, Ned," Mannering said. "Mind if we find our own way, Sergeant?"

"Just as you like, sir."

THE REAL DIBBEN 181

He went out of the big room, a room no longer nearly empty and with the carpet rolled back, but crammed with the fantastic assortment of museum rejects. Mannering hadn't given these much thought. There was Miranda, upstairs with the doctor and a nurse already in attendance, and Richardson on the way from London. The woman in the faded smock had sent to the village for emergency help. Local police were busy in the room where Pendexter Smith had been killed; his body, getting cold now, was lying on a big double bed in one of the old-fashioned bedrooms overlooking these lovely grounds.

Mannering led the way to the front door.

Wainwright said, "I could kill myself! To let him get away——"

"Forget it, Ned."

"Not if I live to be a thousand," Wainwright growled. "The swine's after you, isn't he? And—and if that weren't enough, even if he hadn't killed old Sylvester, look what he's done to Miranda." Wainwright gulped, and looked almost pleadingly, into Mannering's eyes. "She will be all right, won't she?"

"We all hope so."

"*Did* she actually speak?"

"Oh, yes."

"It would be wonderful if she recovered fully," Wainwright said, in a husky voice. "Good would come out of evil after all." He gave an embarrassed quirk of a smile, then scowled at nothing at all. "As for me—I'm going to take a course of lessons in pistol shooting. Fancy missing! He'd come up through the grounds, must've followed us, I should think. In an M.G. So I got behind him, but he knew a short cut and beat me by a couple of hundred yards. I just caught a glimpse of him climbing through a window. Recognised him right away. I suppose I ought to have shouted to warn you, but I was so anxious not to let him know he'd been seen.

The truth is," he added, with another flush, "I was trying to cover myself with glory. If I'd done the sensible thing——"

"I told you to forget it."

"Listen, Mr. Mannering," Wainwright said savagely, "I wouldn't expect you to be anything but decent about it, but I ought to be hung, drawn, and quartered. If anything should happen to you I'd always blame myself. The only thing is, now——"

He paused.

"Yes?"

"Well, now Dibben knows I recognised him too, you might not be in such danger," said Wainwright. "He'll guess that I've told the police. Obviously the reason why he wanted to kill you was because you recognised him and talked to him in the grounds the other night. That warning 'phone call you told me about was just to take suspicion off him."

"Could be," said Mannering briskly. "We'll find out. Which way would you say he went?"

"Oh, over in that copse." Wainwright pointed. "Not much doubt about that, sir. It's the thickest wood for many a mile. The police are gathering there, too—ready to beat the copse and flush him out. I'd like to be there when they do, I'd teach——"

"We want him alive," Mannering said sharply.

"Oh, I know," Wainwright muttered. "I won't do anything crazy. You mean—so that he'll talk."

"Unless I've made a big mistake over Dibben," said Mannering, "he isn't the mind behind all this. He hasn't that kind of ability."

"He could be a pretty cunning swine," argued Wainwright.

Mannering didn't comment.

They walked across the fields towards the copse. The

evening sun shone on beech- and oak-trees, on the thickets and the undergrowth. On the far side Mannering saw the police converging; and there were police at a stile near him, police at every thin point in the hedges where a man might scramble through; at all the five-barred gates, too. There were road blocks everywhere; the sergeant hadn't boasted idly, even though he may have boasted in vain.

"Mind if I hurry on?" Wainwright said, abruptly. "We're dragging a bit, sir."

"My old age," Mannering said.

He quickened his step, and Wainwright didn't complain again. They reached the field with the big copse. Against the darkening skyline several policemen showed up. The ground rose sharply here, the going was heavier.

Mannering began to breathe hard.

Wainwright wasn't finding it such easy going as it had been.

Nearer the copse, they could hear the noises of the field and the whisper of wind through the trees. In places the undergrowth in front of them was so thick that it seemed impenetrable; if Dibben were hiding in one of these, he would take some finding.

Mannering heard the braying of a dog.

Wainwright snapped, "They've got bloodhounds out!"

"It sounds like it."

Wainwright said, "So we're going to get him." The satisfaction in his voice had to be heard to be believed. "You don't think he'll be alone, do you?"

"I'm not sure. I'm simply sure he doesn't work alone. There could be someone else here with him," Mannering went on, and put a hand to his pocket about the handle of his automatic pistol. It was gloomy in the copse; the sun was hidden by the crest of a hill not far away. It was difficult to see ahead clearly.

There were the creaking, rustling noises, the baying of

the dog, the murmur of police voices, an occasional sharp command. Police were at all the vantage points behind Mannering and Wainwright. If Dibben were flushed and ran across the meadows he would come into their arms. In two hours' time or so, when darkness began to fall everywhere, they would have to bring up cars and searchlights; but the beat was on, and Dibben would probably be driven out before true dusk.

A lull came in the gentle noises.

There was a clearing straight ahead of Mannering, where it seemed brighter; and around the clearing, undergrowth much thicker than anywhere else.

They came to a fork in the path they were following.

"Which way, sir?" asked Wainwright. "Right or left?"

"Any preference?"

"No, I can't say——" began Wainwright. "Supposing we split up."

"No," said Mannering, "we'd better keep together." He didn't want to say in so many words that he didn't trust Wainwright simply to stop Dibben, or try to catch him alive; he didn't trust the youth to leave vengeance to the law. Wainwright had his own failure to wipe off the slate, too.

"Right," said Wainwright, obediently.

They went on, slowly, stealthily now. The police weren't far away, on the other side of the copse. If Dibben had run here for cover, he hadn't much hope now; it wouldn't be long before he was forced to run.

Then a man out of sight shouted, *"There he is!"*

A whistle shrilled out.

Wainwright gasped, "Careful, sir!"

"He's going right," shouted a policeman out of sight, "over towards those copper beeches."

"*Here!*" gasped Wainwright, pointing to the great beeches. "We'd better——"

Then a man broke through the thicket.

It was Dibben, and he had a gun.

Mannering saw him, and jumped for the cover of a tree. But Wainwright didn't seem to think of taking cover, just ran towards Dibben, shouting:

"Look out, Mannering, look out!"

Dibben turned towards him, face twisted, rage easy to see, even in that gloom. Wainwright dodged to one side, then fired twice. Dibben's bullet went close to his head. Wainwright's first bit into Dibben's chest, the second into his forehead.

A small round hole, a familiar-looking hole, seemed to leap into the forehead. Dibben fell, his eyes rolling, and died as Crummy Day and Pendexter Smith had.

Police came crashing through the undergrowth, but were still out of sight.

And Wainwright bent down, grabbed Dibben's gun, and turned it towards Mannering.

Only then did Mannering understand the truth.

24

HORNET'S NEST

THE truth was in Wainwright's expression, in the speed of his movement, in the way he turned with the gun and covered Mannering. It ought to have been easy, but two things saved Mannering; a flash of insight and a flash of memory. He fired first. His bullet struck Wainwright's wrist, and the man looked baffled, horrified.

His gun dropped.

"Over *there*!" a policeman was shouting, and the crashing through the undergrowth came louder, drew nearer.

Wainwright's breathing was louder, too.

"Keep still, Ned," Mannering said, in a voice he hardly recognised as his own. "Keep quite still."

"To hell with you, I'll get you yet!" Wainwright slid his uninjured left hand into his pocket, and turned towards the thicket.

Mannering shot him again.

Then the armed police burst into sight, and Wainwright, face distorted with pain, blood dripping from his right hand and down from his left shoulder, made an ineffectual effort to get away.

The police caught him.

Mannering didn't move.

Three minutes later, a policeman came out of the undergrowth at the spot where Dibben had appeared, and reported that he'd found a hollow tree; obviously it had been used as a hiding-place and a rendezvous.

Wainwright heard this, but didn't speak.

Dead Dibben didn't hear.

A Midham Inspector came hurrying up, looked at Mannering intently, began to speak, but stopped. That was because of the way Mannering was looking at Wainwright, with a strange pain in his eyes.

Wainwright just glared.

Mannering turned away.

. . . . .

It seemed a very long and lonely drive back, later that evening.

. . . . .

Mannering turned into Green Street, and wasn't surprised to see Fenn's car pulled up outside the house. Fenn wasn't in it. A sergeant, walking up to him, said that the Chief Inspector had been upstairs for half an hour.

What had he been saying to Lorna?

Did it matter?

Lorna had heard or seen Mannering's car from the window, and was at the flat door to greet him. He forced a smile for her, and was glad of the firm, understanding grip of her hands. She didn't speak.

"All over," Mannering said. "Fenn amiable?"

"Very. So he should be."

"Yes," said Mannering. "I suppose so. You'll sit in with us, darling." He didn't want to talk to Fenn alone, although he would have found it difficult to give a reason. They went into the drawing-room, where Fenn was standing by the screened fire-place, a whisky-and-soda in his hand. His smile was full and free, his body quite convex as he moved forward, hand outstretched.

"Good to see you," he said. "Thanks for everything."

"Thanks? I ought to see a psychiatrist," Mannering growled. "Once I knew, everything told me the truth. And the time it became so obvious that I should be kicked for missing it, was after Wainwright shot Pendexter Smith. He told me he'd recognised Dibben when we saw him in the grounds at Dragon's End. He couldn't have; it was dark, he didn't see the man's face, he actually held him with his hands behind him. I was the only one who saw Dibben. So, it was a lie."

Mannering dropped into a chair.

Lorna mixed him a whisky-and-soda.

Fenn said, "I'm not so sure it was that obvious."

"It was. I should have seen it much earlier, too. Or suspected it, at least. Sylvester——" Mannering clenched his hands, and Lorna about to hand him the glass, held it back. "He killed Sylvester, of course. Sylvester saw him come in, didn't give him a second thought, hadn't the slightest doubt that all was well. And as he turned his back, Wainwright must have smashed at his head."

"Yes," said Fenn. "Wainwright was reported as being seen near Quinns that day. Why not? He was the one man I passed right over. But you'd have tumbled to it eventually.

That's almost certainly why he decided to kill you. You had a blind spot, but it would be bound to go." Fenn paused. "Dibben left a letter, in which he says as much. When you let Dibben go, you really made a friend."

Mannering took his drink, and forced a smile at Lorna. "Thanks, sweet." He sipped. "Oh, I can see plenty now. Almost from the beginning, when he told me he found a cosh in Brash's car. He was never attacked by Brash of course. When we were first at grips with the case, and Wainwright followed Lorna here to make sure that she wasn't threatened he knew all about the man who was waiting for her. Freddy Bell. Talked to Bell?"

"Yes. He's cracked, now that he knows Wainwright is under charge. No room left for doubt," Fenn said. "Wainwright was the evil genius. Incidentally, he's not as young as he makes out; thirty-one. He'd pass for the early twenties with that nice, ingenuous manner of his. Wainwright had one of the gang hit him over the head, to produce that convincing-looking lump he showed us."

"Gang," echoed Lorna, as if the word hurt.

"I think I've most of the story clear," said Fenn. "There may be odds and ends to fill in, but not many. There are really two sides to it. Wainwright's and Crummy Day's."

The story was pieced together in the days which followed, and Mannering studied it until he almost knew it off by heart. Months before he had even heard of Pendexter Smith, he had been unknowingly involved, for Crummy Day and Wainwright, between them, had been planning a big raid on Quinns.

Wainwright, who had an unblemished reputation, was of good social standing and well liked, was bad; just bad. Several years before, he had stolen jewels from the home of a friend, and had been introduced to Crummy Day as a fence; that began their partnership.

Both men had believed that when Pendexter Smith died

Miranda would be easy prey. And, to help make sure, Crummy Day had used Bill Brash, who was as innocent of crime as Miranda herself. He had come to know Day when selling him paper and envelopes for Day's extensive business; Day had befriended him, encouraged him to renew his acquaintance with Miranda, been sure that on Pendexter Smith's death, Miranda would be guided by Brash—who would be advised by Day himself.

To threaten Pendexter, wear him down, and bring his death nearer, Day had used Wainwright.

Wainwright was planning a big raid on Quinns, to look like an outside job. Then Pendexter Smith took the nest-egg there, and above everything else, Crummy Day wanted to possess the nest and the jewelled eggs. Both crooks knew that there was reason to fear Mannering; actually feared that Smith had told him the story, implicating Crummy Day. So Pendexter had been waylaid and made to talk; then drugged and taken home.

Crummy wanted action.

Wainwright needed a stooge.

Suspicion was thrown on Brash, who was ready made. Brash, hating Smith, told Crummy Day that he was going to see if Miranda's uncle had started to take over her fortune— and Day had sent Dibben and other men to watch, and to act as needed. The main purpose, by then, was to distract Mannering's attention—get him to Dragon's End and after Brash, while Wainwright broke into Quinns for the nest-egg and other treasures.

But Wainwright could not break in.

He had got Mannering out of the way, but was beaten by the strong-room doors. So he had to wait, and work by day. Knowing Mannering and Sylvester were at Quinns, and that Trevor was out, he and two accomplices had broken into Quinns.

Once Sylvester had been killed and entry forced, Wainwright had gone out by the back way. But the men left behind to deal with Mannering had failed, one had not reckoned on murder, got cold feet, and run. The other had fallen to Mannering.

From that moment Wainwright knew that sooner or later Mannering would realise that Sylvester had been killed by someone he knew and trusted. Wainwright had made this clear to Crummy Day, in Dibben's hearing, and set out to kill. Day had opposed this.

Wainwright was tired of taking Day's orders, and tired of feeding Day's insatiable lust for treasures. Brash, already suspected of Revell's murder—and Revell had been killed so as to trap Brash—was at Day's and Wainwright saw his chance to kill Day, have Brash framed, and be his own master from then on.

He knew where Day kept his treasures, had meant to take them all. The police had found these now, a treasure trove of priceless things, enough to bewilder and bedazzle even Mannering.

Wainwright had known that for his own safety, Mannering and Pendexter Smith—who had seen him at Day's and would name him if he saw him at Quinns—must both die. He had planned the murders at Dragon's End, and relied on Dibben to help. Dibben had refused to kill Mannering. He had hidden in the hollow tree in the grounds, awaited his chance, and warned Mannering.

Of all his deep regrets, Mannering's deepest was that Dibben had died. He had broken the news to Dora Dibben himself, had tried to ease the blow, and left, distressed by her obvious grief. He would wait a while, then find some way to help.

One thing crowded out thought even of Dora Dibben, and the story itself.

Would Miranda recover?

At the hospital where she had been taken, Brash was waitng and praying. A simple, eager, ardent Brash, who had been sure that Pendexter Smith was planning to turn Miranda's treasures into securities, but not dreamed why; and who, being a dupe of Day's, had been taken for a rogue by Pendexter Smith, and seen as a menace to Miranda.

* * * * *

Three days later, Richardson telephoned Mannering.

"Miranda Smith will pull through," he said, "I thought you'd like to be the first to know. . . . Yes, quite certain. . . 'Bye."

* * * * *

Lorna and Mannering stood by the window of the drawing-room, watching the end of Green Street. Neither needed to tell the other of the strange tension gripping them. Whenever a car appeared, Lorna flinched; and when eventually Bill Brash's green M.G. turned, snorting, into the street, Lorna bit her lip.

But when she looked at Mannering, she was smiling.

"Idiot, aren't I?"

"Crazy," agreed Mannering, and kissed her nose. "May you get worse and worse! It's a pity it's the middle of the afternoon, I could do with a drink."

"Richardson says——"

"Fenn said——"

They stopped, half-laughingly.

"The reports appear to say that she is really normal again," Mannering said with great care. "Are people being kind? Is that your worry?"

Lorna nodded.

"There's one thing," she said, "if Miranda needs someone to help her through, she couldn't do better than Bill Brash. I hope——"

Mannering finished for her. "She marries him."

The car had drawn up beneath their window, out of sight. Soon the front-door bell rang, and Ethel, almost as worked up as the Mannerings, crossed the hall. The Mannerings had the drawing-room door open, ready to greet Bill Brash and Miranda.

What would she say?

How would she feel?

The door opened. Bill Brash stood back a little, as if he wanted all the spotlighting to be on Miranda. She smiled at Ethel, who mumbled something and stood aside. She looked into Mannering's eyes; then into Lorna's. She hadn't changed at all. She was fresh and lovely, with those clear blue eyes, and perfect figure; and she had the same familiar grace.

Lorna went forward, hands outstretched.

"It's good to see you, Miranda. And you, Bill."

"It is lovely to be here again," Miranda said, in a quiet husky voice; almost a tired voice, but natural and clear and without a suggestion of an impediment. "You have both been so very good."

"And listen!" Bill Brash burst out, turning the colour of a turkey cock. "It's all settled, ding-dong, wedding-bells, she *is* going to marry me! And you'd never believe, she used to think I might be mixed up in that crooked business. She says that's why she wouldn't say 'yes' before. Do you think——"

"Darling," said Miranda Smith, very gently, and with a gleam in her eyes, "don't you think it is time you let me speak for myself?"

THE END